My Sister's
Voice

Books by Mary Carter

SHE'LL TAKE IT

ACCIDENTALLY ENGAGED

SUNNYSIDE BLUES

MY SISTER'S VOICE

THE PUB ACROSS THE POND

THE THINGS I DO FOR YOU

Published by Kensington Publishing Corporation

My Sister's
Voice

Mary Carter

KENSINGTON BOOKS
www.kensingtonbooks.com

KENSINGTON BOOKS are published by

Kensington Publishing Corp.
119 West 40th Street
New York, NY 10018

All Kensington titles, imprints, and distributed lines are available at special quantity discounts for bulk purchases for sales promotion, premiums, fund-raising, educational, or institutional use.

Special book excerpts or customized printings can also be created to fit specific needs. For details, write or phone the office of the Kensington Special Sales Manager: Kensington Publishing Corp., 119 West 40th Street, New York, NY 10018. Attn. Special Sales Department. Phone: 1-800-221-2647.

ISBN-13: 978-0-7582-8550-8
ISBN-10: 0-7582-8550-7

First Kensington Trade Paperback Printing: June 2010
10 9 8 7 6 5

Printed in the United States of America

*To my friends, colleagues, and teachers
in the Deaf Community. This book is for you.*

*The characters in this book are a work of fiction
and are not intended to represent the views of any
individual, organization, or community.*

Acknowledgments

I'd like to thank Lynne for encouraging me to do a book about interpreting, Arnine for giving me tips, and Terri for allowing me to use one of her stories.

I'd like to thank Evan Marshall for reading a draft and sharing his thoughts, and I'd like to thank my editor, John Scognamiglio, for his endless support, encouragement, advice, feedback, and conversation.

Lastly, I'd like to thank all the Deaf people, interpreters, teachers, students, and agencies I've worked with over the years. This book is fiction; their real-life stories could fill entire libraries shelved with Kindles. Here's to you.

Chapter 1

It was here, in the City of Brotherly Love, at twenty-eight years of age, that Lacey Gears first discovered she had a sister. An identical twin. Of course it wasn't true. A joke, a hoax, a prank. *As if.* It was completely ridiculous, and although she of all people appreciated a good Gotcha! she didn't have time for games today. She had to buy an anniversary gift for her boyfriend, Alan, then race off to paint a chubby Chihuahua and its anorexic owner. An identical twin. Funny, ha-ha.

The hoax came by way of her red mailbox. She wasn't going to open the mail; she usually waited until the end of the day to sift through it, preferably with a glass of wine, for a single bill could depress her all day long. But as she jogged down her front steps, she caught sight of the mailman wheeling his pregnant bag down the sidewalk. He had just passed her house when he caught her eye. He made a dramatic stop, and waved his arms at her as if she were an airbus coming in for a landing instead of a 5'6" slip of a girl. He jabbed his finger at her mailbox, then patted his large stomach, and then once again jabbed his finger at her mailbox with an exaggerated wag of his head and a silly smile. Lacey had to laugh. She gave him a slight shrug, held her hands out like Can-I-help-it-if-I'm-so-popular?

He winked, blew her a kiss, and then pointed at her mailbox again. She caught his kiss, pretended to swoon, and blew him a kiss of his own. By now they had an unappreciative audience. The woman who lived next door was standing in the middle of her walkway, hands on hips, glaring at the mailman. She was a large white woman in a small red bathrobe. He gave Lacey one last wave, one last jab at the mailbox. Oh, why not. If it would make him happy, she could spare a few seconds to open it. Lacey waved good-bye to him and hello to the woman in the red bathrobe. Only one wave was returned. She turned her attention to the mailbox.

He wasn't kidding. It was stuffed. She had to use both hands to get a grip on it, and exert considerable effort. She managed to yank out the entire pile, but she moved too fast, causing the precarious mound to shift and slide through her hands. As the mail swan-dived to the steps, she bent at the knees and lowered herself, as if she'd rather let it take her down than give up. She finally got a rein on the loose bits and, nervous she was wasting time, she began to flip through the day's offerings.

Bills: AT&T, Time Warner. Catalogues: Macy's, Target, Gallaudet University. Advertisements: Chow Chow's Chinese Restaurant, 20 percent off carpet cleaning, Jiffy Lube. Waste of time. Lacey stuffed the mail back in the box, and was about to close the lid when she spotted a white envelope sticking out of one of the catalogues. She'd almost missed it. She pulled it out and stared at it.

No address, no stamp, no postmark. Just her name typed across the front, looking as if it had been pecked out on a typewriter from the Jurassic period. An anonymous letter with its mouth taped shut, a ransom note. For a split second she was worried someone had kidnapped her dog. She glanced up at her bedroom window, and to her relief spotted her puggle, Rookie. His nose was smashed up against the windowpane she'd spent hours cleaning, drool running down and forming Spittle Lake, brown eyes pleading: *How can you leave me?* She air-kissed her dog an obscene number of times, then once again turned her attention back to the envelope.

Lacey Gears

Mysterious letter in hand, she jogged down the steps to the curb where her Harley Sportster 883 was parked, slung her leg over her motorcycle, and perched comfortably in the custom-made leather seat. She soothed herself in her fun-house reflection elongated in the bike's polished chrome, detailed in Red Hot Sunglo and Smokey Gold. A feeling of peace settled over her. When she was on her bike she felt sexy and confident, something every woman deserved to feel. Some days she wished she could figure out how to stay on it 24/7.

She'd bought the bike after selling her first piece of abstract art, a kaleidoscope of hands coming together in slow motion, bought by PSD, the Pennsylvania School for the Deaf, where as a little girl Lacey had longed to go. At least a piece of her was there now, hanging on the walls as a reminder to Deaf children that they could be anything, achieve anything, do everything but hear. It sold for a decent amount of money, leaving her feeling giddy and slightly guilty as if she had gotten away with something. She bought the Harley as quick as she could, in case they turned around and asked for the money back. Alan said it was proof she could stop painting pet-and-owner portraits and focus solely on what she wanted to paint. But despite her luck with the one sale, the only paintings she was doing besides the portraits were ones she didn't want to share with the world. Not just yet. And for the most part, she liked her job. She had to admit, she usually liked the pets a little more than the people, but even most of them weren't so bad. She turned her attention back to the envelope, peeled the edge up, and slid her finger across the inside top. The envelope sliced into her finger, cutting a thin line across her delicate skin. A drop of blood sprouted and seeped onto the envelope. She jerked her hand back as a slip of white paper slid out of the envelope like an escaped prisoner and fluttered to the ground.

Lacey hopped off the bike and chased the paper down the sidewalk. It stayed just enough ahead of her to make her look like an idiot chasing it. A slight breeze picked it up and lifted it into the air. It hovered midstream, like a mini magic carpet. *Make a wish,* Lacey thought. She reached out and caught it before it sank to the ground. After all this fuss, it had better be good.

> You have a twin sister. Her name is
> Monica. Go to Benjamin Books. Look at
> the poster in the window.

Lacey looked up the street, convinced the mailman was standing by with another wink and a laugh. He wasn't. He was way up the street, his cart parked in the middle of the sidewalk, his bag now slung over his shoulder, thwapping into the side of his leg with each long stride he made. Bathrobe woman was nowhere in sight either. For all Lacey knew, she only came out once a day to wither away civil servicemen with a single look.

> You have a twin sister. . . .

Robert, it had to be her best friend, Robert, the terminal jokester. Or maybe it was Alan. He probably knew she was off to buy him an anniversary gift and he was offering a not-so-subtle hint that he wanted a book. Benjamin Books was in Old City, where she happened to mention she was going shopping. But Alan knew she usually brought in the mail in the evenings, making it too late to get his "hint." No, it had to be Robert. He was the actor, the comedian. She should text him. *Evil twin, ha, ha, ha!* She'd do it later, she had to get going. She shoved the letter in her jacket and secured her helmet. Her first client would kill her if she was late again, giving her less than two hours to find Alan's gift.

When would she learn not to put things off until the last minute? She'd tried to get up early to shop, really she'd tried, but Alan had pulled her back into bed, wrapped his body around her like a cocoon, and said: "You're my gift." They'd made love, and before she knew it, it was early afternoon, and she still had to get him a gift. Six years was worth celebrating, and she knew he would definitely have a gift for her; he'd probably bought his ages ago. At the least, judging from the strange letter, if nothing else, she'd be able to give Alan quite a story.

When Lacey finally reached Old City, she parked her motor-cycle in the shadiest spot she could find. It was going to be a scorcher. It was only June, and early yet, but the temperature was rising with each passing second. The brick buildings in Old City were holding their heat like hot water bottles, soothing to those who liked to touch. Lacey liked to touch. She stopped and pressed her cheek against the nearest wall, behind which Benjamin Franklin had once burned the midnight oil. The bricks were slightly scratchy, but the warmth was a reassuring friend. Lacey had an urge to strip naked and plaster herself against the wall like a slug on a stick. Instead, she kept walking.

She loved the city. She loved the Italian market where she spent numerous Saturday mornings lifting her face to the sun and wandering the streets in search of spices and sales. She loved cheese steaks loaded with slippery, fried onions, she loved painting in the dog park next to the world's oldest Methodist church, she loved the Liberty Bell (some crowded day she was going to ring it, make Alan yell "Dinner!" and run away); she loved Elfreth's Alley populated with original town houses, where each time she visited she picked a different one she pretended to own, and imagined coming home to it every day.

She loved Reading Terminal Market and Boathouse Row; she loved Third Street, where artists such as herself peddled their wares and drank wine on Tuesdays; and although the city's violence was not something to overlook, like the oil paint that often caked underneath her fingernails, she wouldn't want to scrub the city of all its grit; she loved its imperfect, almost Bohemian feel. This was her city: big enough to lose yourself in, but small enough to eventually be found. Today was the exception. Today, everything felt slightly off, as if she were a train chugging off track.

It was too hot, she was too hurried, she had no idea what to buy Alan, and the last person she wanted to stare at for four hours was Sheila Sherman and her Chihuahua, Frank. The poor thing was chubby, yes, and it was disconcerting, like seeing a chubby Asian person, but that didn't excuse Sheila's reaction. She had the poor thing on a vegan diet. As usual, Lacey had a little Baggie of bacon with her, which was the secret behind Frank's sitting still for four hours. The meat went straight to Frank's belly, and to Sheila's befuddlement, the dog would often curl up and stare dreamily at Lacey the entire time she painted. She wished she could say the same thing for Sheila. Oh, she just wasn't in the mood for her today. And she certainly didn't have time to play into a prank, but Alan loved books, so it wasn't a bad idea for a gift, and she couldn't let go of a good joke, she just couldn't, which is the only reason why she was headed in the direction of Benjamin Books.

Up ahead, Lacey stopped to admire the posies and chrysanthemums that were being planted in a sidewalk plot next to a pair of newborn trees. Two women knelt in the dirt, wielding small spades, stabbing at the ground in unison. It looked cathartic; Lacey wanted to ask if she could have a stab too, but thought better of it. They tossed their spades aside, then picked up the next flower grouping from their trays, and efficiently lowered the square pods of dirt into the ground. They were positioning the flowers in a circle around the baby trees, as if the petals were about to join hands and play ring-around-the-rosy. Lacey thought the women themselves looked like flowers: their blond and brunette ponytails the petals, their colorful head wraps the ovaries, the curve of their backs the stems. Kneeling across from each other, they looked like mirror images, they looked like twins—

Lacey moved on. Her pace grew faster, her breath became slightly labored, her heart picked up the pace. She felt like going for a run, or racing her Sportster down the highway. She needed something physical to release all this energy. A twin. She was never going to give Robert the pleasure of knowing he'd made her think twice. A twin. What had given him that idea? Was he doing a new play about twins? That was probably it. He was using her as a guinea pig, studying how she would react, most likely in revenge for the time she made him stand for a portrait when she was doing that series on Deaf artists. He said she painted his nose too big, his eyes too far apart. They'd been friends since the first Deaf Professional Happy Hour that Lacey had attended, six years ago. *He* was the evil twin. Lacey laughed and shook her head. Okay, he got her. She still wasn't going to text him right away; she would draw it out, let him think she had really fallen for it.

She'd certainly pranked him enough over the years. Once she introduced him to a Deaf friend of hers he'd never met, Greg. Only before bringing them together, she'd told Robert that her friend was hearing, and didn't know any sign. She told Greg the same thing. She immediately left them alone and ran around the corner to watch them. It was hilarious! Two Deaf men speaking, and gesturing, trying to read each other's lips. Finally they gave up and spent the next ten minutes writing notes back and forth to each other. Brilliant! She'd never laughed so hard in her life. They eventually saw the humor in it too. And that was just one of many pranks she'd played on Robert over the years, so yes, she'd let Robert have this one.

The antique stores on Pine Street had their doors thrown wide open, propped with various items designed to keep them ajar. Lacey took in the objects with an artist's eye. A tan rock the size of a child's head, a rusty iron with flaking green paint along the sides, and under the last open door, a section of the *Philadelphia Inquirer,* rolled up and stuffed underneath.

The people passing by were just as interesting to Lacey. Despite the heat, Philadelphians and tourists were out and about. Mothers pushed baby carriages, lovers strolled hand in hand, senior citizens grouped on benches, and young girls who bared their limbs in summer dresses that left little to the imagination were trailed by boys in long baggy shorts. Summer was here. It wasn't even noon and the ice cream soda shop on the corner already had a line out the door.

And just beyond that was Benjamin Books. Lacey glanced at her watch. In less than forty minutes she was due at Sheila Sherman's. She would have to stare at that woman's I've-just-sucked-on-a-lemon face for four hours straight. Sheila had been making

that face ever since Lacey came out and asked her why in the
world she named her Chihuahua Frank. It always baffled her
why people were so thrown by direct questions. She meant no
harm in asking, she truly wanted to know (and still wanted to
know) why she named the pooch Frank. Maybe that's why the
poor thing overate; she was gender-confused. Because the dog
was a female that Sheila loved to dress up (drown) in pink bows
and rhinestones.

Lacey stood at the entrance of Benjamin Books and was
about to pull the door open and step inside when she caught
sight of a large poster taped to the window. Every single thought
in Lacey's head evaporated. She felt nothing but a slight buzzing
in her ears. She took a step forward. The poster was an advertise-
ment for a book reading. She frowned and read the title.

THE ARCHITECT OF YOUR SOUL. Alan was an architect.
Sort of. He was actually working as a general contractor, but he
majored in architecture in college. Of course Lacey knew the
book probably wasn't about architects. Hearing people liked to
play with words just like Deaf people played with signs. Not a
book she would ever think to pick up. Lacey wasn't a big reader
to begin with. When she did read, she liked to devour auto-
biographies. Admittedly, she loved reading firsthand other people's dirty secrets; they made her own a little more palatable.
Gossip made the world go round. This book sounded like self-
help mumbo jumbo. But none of that mattered. What mattered, what was rooting Lacey to the spot, was the woman on
the poster, the author of the book. She had Lacey's face.

There were slight differences. The hair on the poster was cut
in choppy waves, framing the face, and the impostor was wearing glasses. Green and trendy, with diamonds flashing on the
stem. Her smile mocked Lacey with slightly straighter, whiter
teeth, and from what Lacey could see of her blouse and jewelry,
she wasn't a thrift store shopper like Lacey. But there was no
doubt about it; it was her face. Somebody had stolen her face.

Lacey pressed her hands against the glass and peered in to
read the name on the book. Monica Bowman. The name
meant nothing to her. Lacey tried to remember if she had ever
cut her hair like that, owned glasses like that. No. Did someone

(Robert?!) steal Lacey's picture off her Web site, Photoshop her face? Or was Monica Bowman so ugly she couldn't put her own mug on the cover of her book?

She was going to get to the bottom of it, that was for sure. And once she caught the little cranial thief, there might even be a modest amount of green in it for her. Not that she was greedy, but if this Monica Bowman wanted to flaunt her face, it was going to cost her. She wasn't going to be a jerk about it, though, and who wouldn't be slightly flattered?

Lacey was often told she was beautiful. She was as thin as she was in her teens, and in addition to her thick black hair, her mysterious gene pool had blessed her with blue eyes so pale she'd earned the nickname Ice. Deaf people used name signs to identify themselves, and Lacey's name sign was the letter *L* making the motion of the wind. That name sign was given to her by Margaret Harris, her house mother at Hillcrest Children's Center.

You're like the wind, Margaret used to say. *Your moods sweep in and blow everything around.* As a child, Lacey wanted her name sign to be something cute, like the letter *L* on her dimples, but once Margaret introduced the wind sign, it stuck. It was the first thing Lacey did as an adult, change her name sign, but this time instead of the *L* on her dimples, it was the *L* and the sign for "paint." Many Deaf friends still called her Ice. Deep down, it didn't feel like her name, it felt stolen—like she now felt about her face.

She stared at the poster again, willing it to disappear. It did not. There had to be an explanation. Was this a local look-alike contest? Not that Lacey even came close to being a local celebrity, but her picture had been in the paper last week announcing her upcoming art show. Someone must have seen the article, Googled her, and cut and pasted her face from her Web site.

That was it. The author had seen Lacey's picture in the paper, and then had the nerve to steal her face. Maybe Robert hadn't orchestrated this prank, maybe he was just alerting her to the fraud.

Because there was no doubt about it, this was her face. There were probably plenty of women who looked a little bit like Lacey, resembled her in some ways, but not down to the exact icy irises, slope of her nose, height of her cheekbones, curve of her chin, depth of her dimples. Except for a tiny freckle to the left of her chin, which Lacey found herself touching; poster girl didn't have the freckle.

It was almost laughable, that someone would try to get away with this. This wasn't a doppelganger, someone who looked eerily like her; this was her face with different hair and glasses. She should text Alan.

She slipped her BlackBerry out of her purse and stared at the screen. What would she say?

Alan. Benjamin Books. My face in window.

Alan, I wrote a best seller!!

Alan, I'm famous.

Alan. I look good in glasses and feathered hair.

Alan, I have a twin—

The word slammed into her like a wall of jagged ice, and a shudder that started in her solar plexus spiked out like a starfish, electrifying her limbs. For the first time, it didn't feel like a joke. A hand landed on her shoulder, and Lacey jumped as if she'd been attacked. People should never, ever, sneak up on a person like that. If they weren't a mugger, they were going to get it. She whipped around to find herself only inches away from a mustached mouth moving a mile a minute.

The guessing game began. He either said:

"You have a small bass."

Or:

"You have a nice ass."

Or:

"You've stained the glass."

She soon had her answer. He gestured with nicotine-stained fingers to the spot on the glass where Lacey had planted her hands. Lacey turned and saw the aftermath of her fingers splayed out on either side of the poster. Ghost hands framing her stolen face. That's when the mustached-lips stopped moving. He leaned in and looked at the poster. He looked at Lacey. A smile spread across his face, and this time, when the lips started up again, they were moving slow enough for Lacey to catch "love your book" and "I'm so sorry." Before she could say a word, he linked arms with her and marched her into the bookstore.

Once inside, he propelled her to a table in the center of the store, where copies of *The Architect of Your Soul* were propped up to form the frame of a house. Next to the table was another poster. Bottled water and three Sharpie markers were lined up on the table, and the man glanced from them to her as if to gauge whether or not she was pleased with his offerings. Then he started talking again, pointing to the sign announcing the book reading. He frowned and looked at his watch. She thought she caught the word "squirrelly," but from the context she gathered he said "early." Lacey smiled and shook her head while pointing at the author's name.

I'm not her, she's not me. Did he understand? He swiped up a marker along with a book, and thrust them at her. He did not. Lacey didn't move even though she was sorely tempted to sign the book. If Ms. Bowman was going to steal her face, she could steal her signature. She'd use grotesque penmanship, she'd massacre the name, she'd write *MY BOOK SUCKS!!!! Love, Monica Bowman!!*

Instead, Lacey shook her head one more time and pointed at her face on the book. *Don't you see I'm a victim of face theft?* No, he didn't. He parried the book again, and set his jaw in a hard line. Knowing she would have to pay for it, Lacey grabbed the marker and the book, and scribbled on the front of it. When she handed it back to the clerk, her smile beat his by a mile. Besides the feathered hair and trendy glasses, there were now other distinct differences between the real-life her and impostor-book-girl her. Whereas real-life her had a smooth upper lip and an invisible halo, impostor-book-girl her was the proud owner of a thick handlebar mustache and big, fat devil horns.

Chapter 2

A fter calling her:
   a: a cyclone
   b: a silo
   or
   c: a psycho
the manager fled, but Lacey didn't budge. She couldn't. Her legs were tree trunks, her roots burrowed into the floor. She wished her hands tentacles instead of ungainly branches; she wanted to lash out and strangle all of the impostor's books, strangle and squeeze, squeeze and strangle. She wanted to watch every last one of them crash to the floor. Every nerve ending in her body was pulsing. She was electrified. It was Morton's Horse Farm all over again.

   Lacey was ten. The orphans were on an outing. They stood in an excited clump, surrounded by saddled horses. Both children and horses were swishing their tails, lifting their hooves, ready to ride. Every child's eyes were glued to the beautiful beasts except Lacey's. Hers were feasting on the tempting silver wire running the length of the fence surrounding them, strung taut and gleaming in the midafternoon sun.

One of the staff members must have followed her gaze, for he stepped in close to her, too close, always too close, so that all she saw was a giant pair of gyrating lips. His breath reeked of coffee and menthol cigarettes. He lifted his hands and moved them along with his mouth, pointing at the magic wire. He jabbed a thick, calloused finger too close to her collarbone.

Kids, touch, don't. Touch, horse, ride won't. Understand? Lacey, look at me. Eye contact, Lacey. Touch, don't. Understand? Do you hear me?

But of course, she didn't.

Lacey, look at me. Put your hands down. No. Not even with the tip of your pinky finger. No. Not even a tiny tap.

A tiny, tentative, exploratory tap . . .

Because it will zap you, that's why. It's electric. Understand. Touch, zap. Ouch! Who said die? Nobody said die. Hurt. Ouch. Hurt. Forbidden. You know our toaster? Home. Toaster. Kitchen. Would you stick your hand in the toaster? Oh. Well, you shouldn't do that. Don't do that again. Lacey, focus. It was just an example. Lacey, finish. If the bread is stuck, you call one of the staff over to get it out, you don't stick your hand in it. No. No fork. Fork bad bad bad idea. No, I don't need to see the scar. Yes, I see it. You want another one? Lacey, finish. Touch, horse, ride, won't. Understand?

Three bales of hay were parked along the fence nearest to where Lacey stood, hands flexing, her entire world distilled into a magic, vibrating wire. If she climbed on the bales and got on her tippy-toes, she'd be able to reach it. They were lifting children onto the horses now; she was invisible. When you have only one shot, you'd better aim. So Lacey didn't just place the tip of her pinky on the wire as she might have if they'd only let her indulge her curiosity; instead she grabbed it with both hands and squeezed.

Zzzzzzzzzzzzzzzzzzz snap! Zzzzzzzzzzzzzzzzzzzzzz.

Her brain screamed at her to let go, but her hands remained stubbornly clenched. Despite the shock, and yes, pain, she was exhilarated. *Zzzzzzzzzzzzzz.* Who knew she could take such a shock, a jolt, a *Zzzzzzzzzzz,* and live?! She could still feel a stinging sensation spiking through her limbs and tummy long after a staff member pried her off. Needless to say, she didn't get to ride a freakin' horse that day. Even Kelly Thayler, who had only one leg, got to ride.

And here she was, eighteen years later, standing in Benjamin Books next to a book she didn't write, feeling the *Zzzzzzzzzz* back in her body. It took her an eternity to realize her Black-Berry was buzzing. She pulled it out and looked at the message.

I can't wait until tonight. I love you. XOXOXO. P.S. How's the Sour Puss?

Sour Puss. Alan's nickname for Sheila Sherman. Oh God. How long had she been standing there? What time was it? She was supposed to be there in ten minutes. It was at least twenty minutes away, forty if she paid attention to things like traffic lights and speed limits. Last week she was five minutes late, five minutes, and Sheila lectured her for at least fifteen, picking up every clock in the house, of which there were bizarrely many, and pointing out the hands of the clock as if Lacey were a child. Lacey stared at the poster again.

The book reading was scheduled for six P.M. Her dinner with Alan was at seven. At this rate, she'd be lucky to finish the portrait sitting by five, which meant she'd have to run home, shower and change, and get back to Benjamin Books in time for the reading. Dinner was just going to have to be a little late, just a little late. Lacey picked up the book again and turned to the back jacket. There was her face again. It gave little else to go on except that Monica Bowman lived in Boston with her boyfriend, Joe, and her puggle, Snookie.

Outrageous. Now Lacey knew she was being played. She was stealing her dog too, only slightly distorting his name. Did she mention Rookie on her Web site? Of course she did, when the interviewer asked her if she had any pets of her own. She lifted her head and scanned the bookstore, half convinced she would spot Alan or Robert hiding in the shelves, watching their prank unfold live.

There was another option altogether, that this wasn't a prank at all. If that was the case, then the woman was a lunatic. And the lunatic was going to be in for a big surprise when Lacey showed up at the reading. Maybe she'd bring Rookie. She'd bring Rookie, sit in the front row, and—

She was going to need an interpreter. She couldn't count on the bookstore accommodating her, not after she'd defaced one of the books. And even if they were willing to pay for an interpreter, it would be difficult at best at such late notice. She didn't have time to figure it all out now; she had to get to Sheila's.

There was a parking ticket on her Sportster. Very unsportsmanlike. The meter couldn't have run out more than five minutes ago. Seventy-five bucks. Lacey crumpled it up and tossed it over her shoulder. She threw one leg over the bike. She looked at the ticket mangled on the ground. Alan would kill her. She stuck her leg out and tried to nudge the ticket toward her with her foot. An inch too short. What if she'd never received the ticket? What if someone else, jealous of her Harley detailed in Red Hot Sunglo and Smokey Gold, had taken the ticket, crumpled it up, and tossed it down the sewer before Lacey ever laid eyes on it?

Lacey started the bike and pulled into traffic. It was then that the word "twin" came back to taunt her. It faded in and out of her vision, torturing her along with an ancient Doublemint gum commercial. Identical, smiling blond girls, jaws gnashing up and down, as they chewed in unison.

Twin. The infuriating part was—it wasn't out of the realm of possibility. The idea was so jarring, Lacey had to force it out of her head so she could weave in and out of the cars at her usual speed. Hopefully, if she went fast enough, she would calm down. She headed out of the city, flying past Boathouse Row, feeling the wind in her face, the vibration of the engine in her thighs, the handles beneath her strong grip.

After a few minutes she forced herself to slow down. The last thing she needed today was a speeding ticket.

Twin, twinship, twins. No. It just wasn't possible. Someone had Photoshopped her face and stolen her puggle's identity. But the newspaper article on Lacey came out only last week, and her Web site didn't have a close-up face picture like the one on the poster, so how could someone have stolen her face? Lacey reached the exit to Sheila's before she could dive any further into her conspiracy theory.

As Lacey dismounted the motorcycle, she thought she caught

Ms. Sour Puss peeking out the window. Were those binoculars? The conspiracy theory reared its ugly head again. Maybe Sheila was behind some strange plot to turn Lacey's life upside down, maybe all of this was her punishment for being five minutes late. Suddenly, Sheila dropped out of sight, only to reappear a few seconds later, sans binoculars, at the front door. She was uncharacteristically smiling. Frank was tucked in the crook of her arm. Sheila raised her paw and waved at Lacey. Lacey didn't wave back; it wasn't a waving kind of day. Instead, Lacey studied Sheila and Frank up close.

As a pet-and-owner portrait artist, Lacey knew it was common for owners and their pets to start to look alike. Sheila Sherman, however, was definitely cultivating the look, if not out-and-out manipulating it. With the exception of Frank's unfortunate weight gain, both dog and owner were sporting feathered brown hair, hot pink fingernails, and matching rhinestone collars. Lacey had been using Desert Tan for both Sheila's skin and Frank's fur, and Neon Pink for their necklace and collar. The colors would stay wedged underneath Lacey's fingernails all day no matter how much she scrubbed.

Sheila, who didn't know a lick of sign language, kept up the business of raising Frank's paw and shaking it at her, as if she were an interpreter. Lacey was secretly hoping the dog would have enough of it and give her a good bite, but so far the little Chihuahua was completely docile, and appeared to almost enjoy the humiliation. Lacey tried to push negative thoughts out of her mind as she painted; she found when she didn't like her subjects, it showed in her work. Luckily, Sheila Sherman didn't seem to notice. In fact, she was talking up a storm, and Lacey felt sorry for the dog for having to listen to it.

Lacey tried several times to indicate she wanted her to stop talking, but it was useless. As a result, she painted her openmouthed, having already decided she would eat the cost if the woman threw a fit. Four hours didn't exactly fly by, but eventually Lacey got into the zone and found herself disappointed when the sitting was over. This round of paint would have to dry, and with a little luck the portrait would be completed in the next round.

Lacey put down her brush and gave Sheila the signal that she was done. Sheila looked at her watch and tapped it, trying to signal something about next week. Lacey held up her hand and shook her head. The art show was in two weeks, which meant Lacey would be busy all next week preparing for it. She'd told Sheila this a million times. Lacey sliced her hand across her throat—"Cut!" She didn't have the energy to write out a full explanation, so instead she reached in her bag and handed Sheila the flyer for the art show once again.

Sheila glanced at the flyer, then tucked her head to the side and mimicked rubbing her eyes with both fists balled up. Then she threw her head back and laughed. Frank, seemingly startled by the noise, hurled herself at Lacey and sniffed her heels. For the first time ever, Lacey picked up the dog and gave it a kiss on the nose. That's when she noticed the name on the collar: Fran.

Whoops. Well, that made a lot more sense than Frank. It happened with lipreading, little misunderstandings. In fact, only eighty percent of the English language was usually lip-read correctly, and that was one-on-one in perfect lighting conditions. Fran. Lacey gave the dog a pat before putting her down. Fran looked up at her with pleading eyes. *Take me home.*

"Sorry," Lacey signed to the dog. "You're stuck with her." Sheila smiled, revealing blotches of red lipstick on her teeth. Lacey pointed at Sheila's mouth and then mimicked wiping the lipstick off. Sheila's smile faded. The sour look was back. Lacey picked up her bag and her motorcycle helmet. She reached for her keys on the small table next to the easel. They were gone. She looked under the table, and not finding them, scanned the rest of the pristine wood floors. She looked up at Sheila, who, mouth still open, lipstick still on teeth, was dangling Lacey's keys. In her other hand she held some kind of brochure. Lacey reached for her keys, but instead of handing them to her, Sheila thrust the brochure at her.

It was a bus schedule. "I ydie kdhwe youe drive, dkehd. Ije sidn safe." Lacey caught the word "drive" and "safe." Normally she could lip-read better than that, but Sheila's tiny mouth al-

ways moved in weird ways, so she normally tuned her out.
Sheila was shaking her head no at the same time.

Lacey took a deep breath and held it in until the urge to hurl
the table lamp at her subsided. Then she flipped open her wallet and showed Sheila her driver's license. It never ceased to
amaze Lacey how ignorant people were about deafness. Forget
understanding Deaf Culture. Forget hearing people respecting
them as a linguistic community with a shared history, language,
and pride. That was way beyond most hearing people's understanding. Their perspective was that of pity, impairment, and
fixing. Lacey was proud to be a Deaf woman, wouldn't want to
become hearing for anything in the world.

When she got into arguments with hearing people about
this, they either thought she was delusional or a bigot. She wasn't
either. She didn't think she was better than hearing people, simply equal. She didn't want more rights than they had, she wanted
the same. She didn't want to change the way they led their lives,
she just wanted to be left alone to live hers. It was draining to
constantly be looked at as deficient, handicapped, in need of
fixing. Other people's opinions—that was the handicap she faced,
not her hearing loss!

The view that she was "less than" because she used a different language to communicate. The view that she could only do
certain things, be certain things, have certain things. The biggest
barriers she faced were man-made, not physical. The ceiling
was not only glass, it was soundproof as well. Assumptions were
the root of all evil. Limitations slapped on her by people who
"meant well." Immediately her intelligence and abilities "capped"
because of someone else's ignorance. Hearing people just
couldn't seem to grasp it. And maybe she couldn't expect them
to understand the nuances and beauty of a culture they'd never
experienced, see that she was just as passionate about watching
a skilled ASL-user paint a story before her eyes as hearing people were about listening to a symphony, but couldn't they at
least comprehend that Driving While Deaf was not against the
law? Couldn't she just get through one day without someone
saying something incredibly condescending? Apparently not, if
Sheila Sherman was around. Next week she was going to have

to paint whiskers and claws on her, and she didn't mean Fran. She watched Sheila take in the driver's license.

"Oh," Sheila said. "Oh no." Sheila ran to the window and opened the shade. Lacey followed. A tow truck was backed up in front of her Sportster. The driver was lowering his cab. Sheila just stood there. Lacey yanked the window open, pushed Sheila out of the way, and screamed bloody murder.

Chapter 3

Lacey pushed the Harley past eighty, as if trying to outrun the tow truck. He was nowhere to be seen, probably still reeling from the Tasmanian devil who threw herself out the window, mounted her bike, and sped away before the ramp from his evil little truck even grazed the ground. Next item on the agenda: Snag an interpreter for the book reading. Alan was a possibility, but she wasn't ready to tell him about this, not yet; there wasn't anything to tell. A good story needed an ending, and this one was still dangling over the volcano. Besides, Alan wasn't prone to temper like Lacey, and there was a slight chance he wouldn't approve of her plans to ambush the impostor at her own book reading.

Professional interpreters were supposed to be neutral; they couldn't interject their own opinions or talk about the assignment to anyone else. If Monica Bowman was the lying face thief she appeared to be, Lacey didn't want Alan witnessing the scene Lacey was going to make. Was there any way she could get through it without an interpreter?

Not in a large crowd with a person speaking from a podium.

When Lacey talked with a hearing person one-on-one, there were a gazillion tools she could employ to communicate. She was always willing to write back and forth with hearing people as well as use gestures. And although Lacey could use her voice and be understood, she preferred not to. It brought back too many memories of excruciating speech lessons, staring into a mirror or clutching a balloon to feel the vibrations of her words. *Feel my throat, bah, bah, bah, mah, mah, mah, dah, dah, dah, ha, ha, ha. Don't squeeze the balloon. You're squeezing. Gentle hands. Gentle hands. Feel my throat. Gentle hands on my throat. Pah, pah, pah. Good girl. Good speech. Back to the balloon. No! That hurts my ears. If you pop one more—*

Sometimes, Lacey would leave the lessons in tears; other times she'd float out feeling like the Queen of the Hearing World. She would believe the speech therapist. What a wonderful voice she had. How clearly she spoke. It was magic. Sounds reverberating in her chest and throat, lips moving to push out the words, the key to the hearing empire at the tip of her tongue. But when Lacey tried out her "good girl" speech with strangers, and waitresses at restaurants, they didn't understand her. Instead of a "good girl" pat on the back or a yellow smiley-face sticker, she got blank stares, scrunched-up faces of incomprehension, and disgusting sticky white rice instead of the French fries she'd tried to order.

Funny, she could understand what they said to each other after she tried to speak. What did she say? I didn't understand her, did you? She's deaf and dumb. And when they did understand her, it was even worse. They would make a humiliating fuss as if she should be awarded the Nobel Peace Prize for enunciating "I want milk." Lacey had an urge to bark like a dog whenever anyone told her she "spoke well." Well, guess what. She signed well too, she had absolutely beautiful ASL, her classifiers were flawless. American Sign Language was her language, her birthright, not some subpar substitute for English.

But tonight wasn't about her identity as a Deaf woman, it was about identity period. This wasn't about expelling myths about Deaf people, this was confronting a face thief. And for that, she was going to need an interpreter. Unfortunately, she knew just who she was going to have to ask.

Kelly Thayler came to Hillcrest when she was thirteen, after a car accident that took her parents and her left leg. Her parents were killed on impact but her left leg lingered until the doctors had no choice but to amputate. Kelly had been at Hillcrest only three years when an aunt who was a tango dancer in Argentina swooped back to the States and took Kelly to California with her. But until then, Kelly stuck to Lacey like glue. All it took was Lacey teaching her the signs for "bitch," "cookie," and "lesbian" (all used to talk about Margaret Harris, their house mother, behind her back) for Kelly to be hooked on the secret finger talk.

In addition to her wheelchair, Kelly had a metal prosthetic leg that had a funny way of disappearing in the middle of the night and showing up in the oddest places, like in the center of the dining room table on Thanksgiving with dandelions and wish flowers from the backyard sticking out the top like a Frankenstein vase. Lacey told her she should blow out the wish flower and wish her leg would stop disappearing.

But no matter what Lacey did to Kelly, Kelly loved her. And apparently, it was the kind of love that never wore off. A few years ago, Kelly looked Lacey up and e-mailed her. When Lacey didn't respond, Kelly started an all-out campaign. She sent Lacey recipes, pictures, jokes, chain letters, e-cards, and umpteen album links with pictures of a smiling Kelly in different settings with the same purple turtleneck, until Lacey finally relented and e-mailed her back.

Kelly had Googled and Facebooked everything she could on Lacey, and was quick to congratulate her on all the parts of her life she had missed out on: graduating with a Master's in fine arts, learning to ride a motorcycle, skydiving, and establishing herself as a Deaf artist. Kelly raved about how beautiful Lacey still was, and how lucky they were to live in an era where technology could help disabled people like them. Kelly proudly announced she had a cutting-edge prosthetic leg that allowed her to run her first 5k and chase after her children. Then Kelly dropped one final bomb, the one she'd probably been waiting to drop all along, that she'd grown up to become a certified sign language interpreter and that she too was living just outside Philly. If Lacey wanted an interpreter at this late notice, and didn't want to pay, it looked like she was going to have to pay a visit to her stalker.

"Can you interpret for me tonight? Book signing." They were sitting in Kelly's crowded living room on a flowered couch. Lacey and a Tickle Me Elmo were sitting at one end, Kelly on the other, and sandwiched in between them was a four-year-old Korean girl who giggled every time either of them signed.

"I'd love to," Kelly said. "But I won't be able to get a sitter this late, so I'll just have to bring the kids." Becoming an interpreter and getting a fancy new leg weren't the only things Kelly Thayler had been up to since she escaped Hillcrest; she'd also been busy adopting children. She had six, all plucked from orphanages. The other five were playing in the backyard, just behind the living room. From her vantage point on the couch, Kelly could watch them while she conversed with Lacey.

"You're so lucky you're deaf," she said. "They're loud." The little girl nodded in agreement and covered her ears with her hands. Lacey glanced at the living room floor, littered with toys. Kelly seemed completely comfortable with chaos.

"Can your husband watch the kids?" Lacey asked. A smile appeared on Kelly's face, along with the look of someone who had a juicy secret.

"My wife is out of town," she said, still smiling. "She's in New York until the weekend." Lacey nodded, determined not to show the shock Kelly had clearly been anticipating, even relishing.

"Thanks anyway," Lacey said. Kelly looked crestfallen; she obviously wanted Lacey to grill her about her wife.

"They'll be fine," Kelly said. "They love books."

"No," Lacey said. "This isn't a kid's book."

"Benjamin Books has a great play area. They'll love it." Six children bouncing off walls while Lacey tried to confront Monica Bowman? No way.

"Sorry. It's not going to work."

"Why not?"

"I have to go." Lacey was about to stand when Kelly thrust her index finger forward and shook it at Lacey.

"You're hiding something," she said.

"I am not," Lacey said.

"You are too. You did the thing."

"What thing?"

"You touched your nose." The little girl on the couch saw Kelly touching her nose, giggled, and touched her own nose. She looked at Lacey. Lacey didn't comply.

"So what?" Lacey said.

"You did that as a kid too. Every time you pulled one of your stunts and Margaret was grilling you, you'd touch your nose."

"I did not."

"How do you think she always knew when you were lying?" A dozen punishments flashed through Lacey's mind. There was a time Lacey believed Margaret when she said she had eyes in the back of her head. She'd lie awake nights imagining those eyeballs burrowed underneath Margaret's mass of tangled salt-and-pepper hair. Truly terrifying.

"Why didn't you ever tell me?"

"I had to have some power, didn't I? The way you used me."

"Used you?"

"The things you used to make me do!"

"You could've said no."

"You always said you wouldn't be my friend if I didn't."

"Are you crying? That was a million years ago."

"Nothing's changed," Kelly said. "You're still trying to rope me into doing things without telling me what you're doing."

"I asked you to interpret. Not rob a bank."

"I became an interpreter because of you."

"Then you should be thanking me. It's a nice-paying job."

"It's not about the money." Kelly crossed her good leg over the bad and took a deep breath. "I wrote you so many letters," she said. Little pink and blue envelopes with postmarks from California floated through Lacey's memory. The little girl on the couch, whose name Lacey was ashamed she couldn't remember, snuck a tiny hand over to her mother and patted her knee. She didn't know what her mother and Lacey were saying, but she knew her mother was on the verge of tears. Lacey felt like the biggest loser on the planet.

"I know," Lacey said. "I'm sorry."

"Why didn't you write me back?"

"I didn't even open them," Lacey said.

"What?" Kelly asked. Lacey sprang off the couch and maneuvered around the toys until she reached the window. She sat on the sill.

"You got to leave," Lacey said. "You moved to a sunny place with a beach. You had a family. A cool aunt who traveled, and danced, and didn't hide liquor bottles under the couch cushions and put salt in the cookies." Kelly stood up. Lacey wanted to tell her she was happy she had a new leg. In the past, standing up would have required a ton of effort and clunky movements. With this new leg, Kelly could stand gracefully. Lacey wished she had it in her to be nicer. But just seeing Kelly was bringing back memories of Hillcrest, and Margaret; it was almost as if just thinking about those days would bring them back. As if Lacey could blink, and she'd be a child again, back in her room, her bunk, making puppet shadows on the wall and plotting an escape that didn't come quick enough.

"I missed you," Kelly said. "I hated California. I only wanted you. You were like a sister to me."

—You have a twin sister. Her name is
Monica—

"I have to go," Lacey said.

"Didn't you miss me?" Kelly pleaded. She looked like a child herself, lost and needy. Lacey didn't want to hurt Kelly's feelings, but she also had to be honest.

"No," she said. It was true, and it wasn't. She had missed

Kelly at first. But she also hated her for having a beach, and a cool aunt. Lacey knew deep down there was something wrong with her; she didn't have whatever it took inside to attach to other people. Whenever she got too close, she'd go on lock-down. Probably a childish reaction on her part as well, but one she didn't know how to undo. The only reason she and Alan had been together for six years was that he didn't put any demands on her. Had he wanted a traditional life, a traditional wife instead of a live-in girl who wanted to take things a day at a time, she knew they never would have made it this far.

"I never forgot you," Kelly said.

"I'm sorry," Lacey said. "But I had to forget you. You weren't coming back. I went on with my life."

"So you didn't think of me as a sister?" Lacey didn't know what to say. The answer was no.

"That's a great leg," Lacey said instead. Kelly just looked at Lacey and for a second all movement in the room ceased. Even the shadows on the wall sat still. "No," Lacey said. "I didn't think of you like a sister."

"I see," Kelly said. She started tidying up, plucking toys off the floor and tossing them into a large tub in the corner of the room. "Blunt as usual, aren't you?" Kelly added. She continued to swipe at the toys with the proficiency of one who did it twelve times a day. The child scurried over to the tub of toys and picked up each one that was tossed in, examining it as if she'd never seen it before in her life, before throwing it back herself. The child, Lacey noticed, didn't gently toss the toy like her mother; instead she slammed it into the tub, then peered in after it to see if it had survived, before waiting for the next one to maul.

"I didn't think of anyone as family," Lacey said. "Not you. Not Margaret, not one of the other dozens of kids I lived with. We were just animals in a zoo."

"My God," Kelly said. Just then the screen door opened and five other children piled in, three boys and two girls. Leaving the door wide open behind them, they ran through the room to the adjacent kitchen, opened the door to the basement, and disappeared down the steps. Lacey wanted to laugh—it was like a herd of bulls had just stampeded through—but Kelly didn't look as if she could take a joke. Kelly walked over and shut the sliding glass doors.

"They're my life," she said, staring at the basement door.

"Better you than me," Lacey said.

"Lacey the lone wolf," Kelly said.

"I have to go," Lacey said.

"What about Alan?" Kelly asked. "Do you consider him family?"

"He's my boyfriend."

"That doesn't answer my question."

"I have to go."

"I'll see you at seven." Kelly said as she walked Lacey to the front door.

"No," Lacey said. "I'll find another interpreter."

"Why don't you just tell me what's going on? Why don't you let me in?" Lacey hated the look on Kelly's face. She was letting her down, disappointing her. But she couldn't give her what she wanted. Kelly did get to leave. She did get a beach and a cool aunt. She didn't have to smell Margaret's morning breath or get used to new kids every year, or put up with a dozen new staff members who wanted to be "friends" only to skip out the first chance they got. The truth was, Lacey cried for a week straight after Kelly left. Not because she missed her, but because she was left behind. Lacey would've given up one of her good legs to go to California with Kelly. Then maybe she would've loved her like a sister. There was no use going into old history now.

"I know you're up to something," Kelly said. "And you know I'll find out, so you might as well just tell me."

"Interpreters are supposed to be neutral," Lacey said. "Not stick their nose in where it doesn't belong." The little girl ran over to Kelly, wrapped her arms around Kelly's leg—Lacey couldn't remember if it was the good or the bad—and smothered it in kisses. Kelly ruffled her hair.

"You don't know what you're missing," Kelly said. "Family is everything. Without them I'd be nothing."

*   *   *

Without them, I'd be nothing. Who was Kelly kidding? She'd be a one-legged pain in the ass, just like she was now. So much for being a professional interpreter. Lacey hadn't meant to hurt her feelings, but it had to be done. There was no way Lacey would be able to keep this sister-impostor secret if Kelly got wind of it. Now she had only three hours until her anniversary dinner, and she still didn't even have a present for Alan. Maybe she would paint him something. That was it. She could whip something out in an hour, something abstract. She should have thought of it before; Alan loved everything she painted. It was one of the things she loved about him.

She would go home, grab clothes to change into for dinner, go to the studio, paint like a madwoman, then change into dinner clothes, go straight to Benjamin Books, then race to dinner. She was working up a sweat just thinking about it.

Lacey arrived home and walked through their tiny backyard and around to an enclosed porch. When she opened the door and stepped in, she found Alan, stretched out on the His and Her Adirondack chairs they bought at a festival last summer. She was hoping he wouldn't be home yet. He had a bottle of beer for himself and a glass of wine waiting for her. A jar of fresh daisies sat on the little table in between the chairs. Lacey could have sworn they weren't there this morning.

"Welcome home, beautiful," Alan said. He rose to greet her. She gave him a brief kiss. He took her helmet from her and hung it on a hook by the door.

"You're home early," she said. She covered her annoyance with a smile. It wasn't his fault she had a woman to stalk. He returned her smile, but his beat hers by a million men marching.

"It's a special day," Alan said. He wrapped his arms around her and pulled her into him. Lacey couldn't believe how attractive she still found him, how fast the six years had flown by, the last three of which they'd lived together, still going strong despite her constant fear of being swallowed whole. He was tall, a little on the skinny side, and blessed with a mop of curly brown hair. She loved his chest and biceps best; they were strong and lean, and always there for her. He had a tattoo on his left shoulder, his parents' initials in sign language. She loved him. She loved touching his tattoo. She loved kneading her fingers through his soft curls. She loved that his hair smelled like pears and occasionally sawdust. She loved how he would get a little flush of red along the side of his neck when he was nervous. It was there now, a faint line rising from his collarbone. She had to resist the urge to kiss his neck, lick away the red. It would lead to other things, things she didn't have time for. Why was he so nervous? Who would have thought she would end up with a hearing man?

What she loved most about the relationship was the freedom to just be. Sure, they fantasized about their future, but instead of dreaming about a wedding and names for their children, they talked about the house Alan would build and—as he liked to tease—Lacey would paint.

She wanted a lighthouse in Maine; he wanted a big house in Boston. He proposed a compromise. Their big house in Boston could have a turret, and maybe they could build a summerhouse in Maine. He didn't pressure her about marriage or kids. If she wanted to be a part of an institution, she'd pick one that came with free Jell-O and bingo night.

Boston, Lacey thought. *Monica Bowman lives in Boston. With her fiancé, Joe, and her puggle, Snookie.*

Alan pulled her toward him and kissed her long and hard. *I have a face thief,* Lacey thought as she tasted his lips on hers. *Or a twin. Why aren't I telling him?*

Because she didn't know anything. She wouldn't know anything until she saw the woman for herself. Rookie ran onto the porch. Lacey picked up his wiggling body and kissed him. He too smelled like fresh shampoo.

"Did you give him a bath?" Lacey asked. Alan smiled at her. His neck was flaring.

"It's a special night," he said. It was the second time he'd said that.

"I might be late," Lacey said. "Can we do dinner at eight?"

"Eight?" Alan looked alarmed. Lacey mentally flashed through the evening. Book reading at six, then who knew what was going to happen? They would talk settlement terms most likely. How much was her face worth? If only she didn't have to go in disguise; she might be able to kick the price up a bit if she was dolled up. But it had to be a slow attack, she wanted to draw the moment out, then show her face to the audience. *Look, I'm her. She's not!*

"Eight," Lacey said. She put Rookie down and headed for the bedroom. Alan followed at a close clip and before she could climb the stairs he tapped her on the shoulder.

"What's going on?" he asked. Astute as ever, on full alert.

"I'm running late," Lacey said. "I have errands."

"What errands?"

"I can't tell you." Lacey ran up the stairs and headed into the bedroom. She stood in front of the closet. Alan tapped her on the shoulder again, even though she already knew he was there.

"What?"

"What errands?"

"I can't tell you."

"You're kidding, right?" Alan said. "I thought we were over this."

Translation in English:

By *we* he meant *her.*

By *this* he meant *secrets.*

By *over* he meant: *Tell me!*

In ASL:

Secrets. Me. You. Finish!

Translation: *Tell me!*

Okay, so maybe she and Alan weren't as close as they could possibly be, maybe she used to keep everything to herself, maybe she still did. But wasn't it enough she came home to him? She wasn't lying to him, or cheating on him, or stealing from him. Although he would argue shutting herself off to him was stealing from their relationship. But tonight was different. Tonight she could feed him a fish.

"It's our anniversary," she said. "You can't make me tell se-crets." It worked. The worry lines across Alan's forehead disappeared. He smiled again. Why didn't she just tell him the truth. *I got a letter. It says I have a sister. A twin. Her name is Monica.*

Maybe it would be a joyous reunion. Maybe it would be the beginning of a friendship, a kinship, a twinship. Alan was still staring at her. She should tell him. Or she could get her jacket, pull the letter out, and hand it to him. Together they could go to the computer and Google Monica Bowman, *The Architect of Your Soul.* She lifted her hands. It would take little effort to produce the signs. But it was back. Her internal "lockdown," the sensation of closing in on herself, a selfish clamping of information, the inability to share, and the self-pity it produced. Was it a power trip, or self-punishment? If thoughts and experiences were dancers, meant to leap across the stage and give of themselves, Lacey's were lame, crippled, knocked and locked at the knees.

"I can't wait," Alan said.

"What?" Lacey said.

"Dinner. Big fat spaghetti. Big glass wine." He mimed sucking a strand of spaghetti into his mouth, making her laugh. She put her hand out and touched his face. *This is home base,* she thought, stroking his cheek. *Never lose sight of home base.* She pulled her hand back. Alan reached out and held it again. The worry line visited his forehead again, looking like it was here for a long stay this time.

"What?" she asked.

"You're shaking like a leaf," he said. He pointed out the window to the large oak that graced their backyard. He gyrated his hand in a shaking motion. English idioms weren't part of Deaf Culture just like Deaf idioms were lost on a hearing person who didn't sign. Alan said he used to act them out for his mother, in their kitchen after school. He carried on the same tradition with Lacey, and she didn't have the heart to tell him she already knew most of them. It was amusing to watch him exaggerate the whole bit, act them out like mini plays. The tree, the leaf, the wind, how the leaf fluttered. He looked like an idiot, but he was her idiot. But this time it didn't look like he was joking. Lacey stared at her hand. He was right: She was shaking.

Twin twin twin twin twin twin twin twin twin twin twin twin
twin twin twin twin twin sister sister sister sister sister sister sister
sister sister

"Too much coffee," Lacey said. She didn't tell him about the
parking ticket either. Or Sheila Sherman calling a tow truck.
Or visiting Kelly. *At dinner,* she convinced herself. *I'll tell him at
dinner.*

"Deaf coffee," Alan said. Deaf coffee was a Deaf idiom. It
meant decaf.

"Deaf coffee next time," she assured him. Rookie raced into
the room, wedged himself between them, and began to spin in
circles.

"Genius," Alan said, looking at him. "Our dog is a pure genius."

"When good pogo sticks go bad," Lacey added, quoting Alan.
Then she looked at Rookie and signed, "Outside." Rookie stopped
spinning and started jumping. He knew a half dozen signs:
walk, sit, work, bathroom, outside, and cookie. In other words,
the important stuff, and the good stuff.

"You're taking Rookie?" Alan asked. "Why?"

"He loves to ride in the jeep," Lacey said. She made eye contact with Rookie. *You have a twin,* she conveyed telepathically.
Her name is Snookie. Rookie sneezed, shook his head violently,
and lowered the front half of his body so that his butt was sticking in the air. Then, he bared his teeth and growled. *Exactly,*
Lacey thought. *That's exactly how I feel.*

Chapter 4

Lacey stood in front of the closet in the guest bedroom with the simple black dress she planned on wearing slung in the crook of her arm. Technically, it was Alan's closet. She had the reign of the big one in the master bedroom, but a couple of months ago she'd snuck a few pairs of high heels into his closet, and she was going to need a pair of them tonight to go along with her dress. She slid Alan's suits over to get a better look at the floor where her heels were hiding. But just as she moved the last suit out of the way, her hand brushed a pocket, and her fingertips danced across a hard surface. Before she could talk herself out of it, she reached into the pocket and pulled out a blue velvet box.

Don't open it, she told herself. She opened it. It was a diamond ring. One carat. Princess cut. Platinum band. Lacey shut the box and put it back in the suit pocket. She took it out again and opened it. Shut it. Put it back. Took it out. Put it back. Took it out. Opened it. Shut it. Put it back in the opposite pocket. Took it out. Tried to shove it in her pocket. Her jeans were too tight. Put it back. Shut the closet door and leaned against it.

Oh God. Didn't he know her at all? Hadn't he been listening? Didn't she make her views on holy matrimony oh so perfectly clear? Didn't she drop enough hints, enough digs for him to get the picture? Didn't she always point out couples they knew who were either miserably married or getting a divorce? Didn't she place bets on how long celebrity marriages would last? Didn't she draw little skulls and crossbones over the engagement section of the Sunday *Times*? If nothing else, dressing up as the Bride of Frankenstein last Halloween and telling Alan it was the only time he'd ever see her in a wedding dress should have been a clue.

That's why his neck had been red. She didn't need this right now, she couldn't handle this right now. She grabbed her pumps and threw them in a backpack along with her little black dress. She didn't care anymore if it got wrinkled. Maybe if she showed up looking like the Bride of Frankenstein, he wouldn't propose.

She turned off her thoughts, moving about the house on autopilot. She would figure it out later. She still needed to get to the art studio and whip up a painting for Alan, one that now said I-love-you-but-let's-not-ruin-a-good-thing-by-getting-married. Then bookstore, cat fight, dinner. She looked at her watch. It was too late. She had to get to Benjamin Books now. Then she would go to the studio. She could text Alan and push dinner back to nine. Or ten.

Lacey tucked her hair into one of Alan's ProBuild baseball caps and concealed her blue eyes behind mountainous sunglasses. Given that it was way too hot to hide anything else, she threw on a pair of shorts, a T-shirt, and her flip-flops. Rookie's little paws were sensitive to the hot summer sidewalks, so Lacey nestled him in the crook of her right arm. As she neared the bookstore, she wondered if bringing him had been a huge mistake. This Monica was also pretending to have a puggle, so instead of fading into the background, she would notice Lacey right away. Maybe that was the way to go. Maybe she shouldn't have disguised herself at all. Should she hurry back to the jeep and change into her little black dress? After all, she had already received the shock of a lifetime; why shouldn't Ms. Monica? Lacey realized the flutter in the pit of her stomach wasn't just fear, it was excitement. She was actually looking forward to shocking this woman.

She stopped at the entrance of the bookstore to take a deep breath and look at the poster. She managed only one out of the two. The poster was gone. The windows were wiped clean, there were no prints, no dust outlines of the poster, no vestiges of Scotch tape. Lacey looked at her watch. It was 5:50. Lacey wanted to stake out the perfect seat. Not too close, not too far. Who had stolen the poster of her stolen face?

She hurried into the bookstore and made a beeline for the table laden with Sharpie markers and the copies of *The Architect of Your Soul* propped up like the frame of a house—

Gone, gone, gone. Table gone. Sharpies gone. Folding metal chairs set up facing the table, gone. Books gone. Somebody was playing a trick on her.

Alan. The proposal. Oh my God, she was such a dimwit! *The Architect of Your Soul.* Snookie instead of Rookie. Access to her picture and Photoshop. Oh, he got her good! He was going to propose, here, tonight. A twin. She had actually started to believe she had a twin. She took her BlackBerry out and texted Alan.

You got me! Ha-ha. Where are you? She wandered the bookstore as she waited for his reply. Was he hiding in Science Fiction? Horror? With the way she felt about marriage, he should be. She hoped the store didn't throw away the poster or the fake book. She wanted to keep copies. That didn't mean she was going to say yes. But she had to give him credit for originality. She always figured Alan would be more traditional. Candles, champagne, on his knees.

What???? Where are you?

Science Fiction. Where r u?

Lacey. This is Alan. What is going on?

I'm sorry. I'm early. Surprise is ruined. Come out.

What???????????

This was a little much. He was busted, he should just fess up.

She glanced up to find herself in front of the information desk, where a young girl listlessly shuffled books from one side of the desk to the other. She lit up when she saw Rookie. She reached her hands out and made a cooing face.

Lacey. What's going on????

It wasn't like Alan to keep up a joke this long. Lacey slipped a notepad out of her purse.

The Architect of Your Soul. 7:00???

She slid the note over to Rookie's new slobber toy. The girl wiped her hand on her pants and took the note. Passing notes back and forth was a technique Lacey applied everywhere but banks. Tellers tended to overreact when you silently slipped them notes. But this was a bookstore and writing was welcomed. The woman scribbled something and slid the note back. Lacey asked another question. When they were finished, the piece of paper looked like this:

The Architect of Your Soul. 7:00?
Canceled.
Why?
Rude!
Me?
No. Author. Rude!!! What's your dog's name?
Rookie.
Cute!!!
Thank you.

Lacey paused and held Rookie out as bait. The girl took Rookie in her arms. Lacey started writing again.

What did she do?

Refused to sign Benjamin's book and drew a mustache and horns on her own face!!!

Benjamin?

The owner.

That little nerd MANAGER was the owner? The day, Lacey realized, was an exclamation mark day.

We don't take that!!!

The words *I won* rose in Lacey's mind and kept resurfacing even though she tried to shove them down. Still, Lacey wasn't convinced.

You're sure this isn't a joke? A marriage proposal?
The girl handed Rookie back. Clearly confused. She stared at Lacey's question. Then she stared at Lacey.
I want to see the book.
The girl shrugged and reached over to a pile of books behind her. She handed Lacey the book. Lacey flipped through it. It was a real book, all right. She flipped through the pages.

> You can't build a house alone. Learn to work in
> large groups—

Lacey shut the book. Monica Bowman was a real person. A real face thief. How did she take the news of the cancellation? Did she demand an explanation? Deny it? Did Benjamin even tell her why he was canceling? Did she pursue a line of questioning, demand to see the security tapes from the store? Would she go to any lengths to find Lacey? Get a glimpse of this woman with her face and a concealed Sharpie?

Lacey had blown her chance at a sneak attack. Even if she confessed right now that she was the rude one, the evil scribbler, it was probably too late to get Monica to come back. There was a chance that Monica didn't know why the reading was canceled, and didn't care because she was happy to have the evening off. If she followed her own self-help crap, she was at this moment—Lacey opened the book again and flipped to a random section—

Constructing a New Framework

> Drawings are constantly revised. Plans change.
> Change with them or your life projects will
> stall! Think of small changes as decoration. A
> new coworker is like new window shades, or
> new pillows for the couch. Who doesn't like to
> freshen up a tired old space? Major changes
> can be difficult to deal with and the reason is
> obvious. Major changes require a complete re-
> build, a new set of drawings. Major changes are

time consuming and expensive. But don't fight
it! Use it to improve yourself. As long as you're
tearing down walls, why not add that bay window you've always wanted, or that walk-in
closet—

Total crap. Lacey slammed the book shut.
Lacey???????????
Sorry, Alan. See you at Mario's.
What was that about?
Just a joke. See you at 8:00. Maybe 8:30.
I don't need a present. Just you.
Then: *Xoxoxoxoxoxxoxxoxox* and on and on until they ran off
the screen.

Lacey disconnected from Alan but kept her BlackBerry out.
She brought up her "contact" screen and tried to ignore the
faint throbbing of guilt as she texted him. She had no choice;
she had to turn to another man.

Chapter 5

Lacey's art studio was located in a warehouse in downtown Philadelphia, relatively free from the hustle and bustle of the nine-to-fivers. She and a hearing artist, Mike, shared the top floor. Three thousand square feet of creative reign. It had thick wood-beam floors, concrete walls, and exposed pipes. Lacey painted the pipes maroon, and the walls a shade of gray that looked almost black at night but turned silver in the sun. Mike, who was a sculptor, had two large pieces displayed in the entrance, ten feet of twisting design. They were mirror images of each other except for the materials: One was made of steel, the other driftwood.

The pair kept vastly different schedules, but even when they were there together, they had enough space not to get in each other's way. Mike had the warehouse first, and although tons of artists were dying to share the space with him, Lacey was chosen because she was deaf. And not because Mike pitied her— Lacey would have never put up with that—but because his constant noise didn't bother her. He soldered, he hammered, he chiseled, he drilled, he sawed. She worked peacefully throughout all of it. Sometimes she felt the vibrations, but she welcomed them. It was like painting on one of those vibrating motel beds you fed with quarters. And it was totally worth it for the space. Lacey's fifteen-hundred-square-foot section was all the way at the back of the warehouse near two windows facing I-95 and the Ben Franklin Bridge. In the middle of the room they had a communal sink and refrigerator, along with a couple of leather sofas and chairs.

The loft was messier than usual since the two of them had been too busy preparing for the gallery show to clean. Lacey stood in the middle of the floor, knowing she should start on Alan's painting, but her thwarted sneak attack on the sister impostor and the engagement ring fiasco were consuming her. Mike was out; they would have the place to themselves.

She put on a pot of coffee. Robert would be there any minute. His current play with PDA, Philadelphia Deaf Actors, was rehearsing just down the street from the warehouse.

The overhead lights in the studio flashed, pulsing out news that someone was at the door. Lacey greeted Robert, who bounded into the room still in his costume: a purple-and-green body suit, striped tights, curly shoes, and a floppy hat adorned with bells. It was an outfit any grown man would look ridiculous in, but his height of six-foot-five elevated it to ludicrous. His play, *Deaf Jest!*, opened next week. Robert had the nervous energy of an actor waiting in the wings, and immediately began bouncing about the place, touching everything in sight. He flipped through sketch pads. He winged an eraser off her worktable. He picked up paintbrushes and charcoal sticks, and rubbed them between his thick fingers. When he ambled over to a large green tarp covering a group of paintings propped against the back wall, and bent down as if to remove the cover, Lacey snuck up behind him and whipped off his hat.

"Nosy," she said when he turned around. She steered him away from the green tarp and pointed. Across the way, several of Lacey's pet-and-owner portraits were openly displayed: on easels, against the wall, on top of her table. Robert got as close to each one as he could and studied them.

There was a chubby man and his bulldog, both with equally drooping jowls. An old lady and her poodle, sporting identical tight, white curls. An Irish setter and a beautiful redhead. Robert waved his hand to get Lacey's attention and when she finally looked his way, he signed, "What kind of dog for me?" He thrust out his chest and lifted his chin. Lacey studied him for several seconds.

"No dog," she said. "Gorilla." Robert bent over with his large hands scooping the ground and did his best gorilla impression.

"Funny," Lacey said.

"Where's Mike?" Robert asked.

"He's out somewhere," Lacey said. Mike was a hunk and Lacey always suspected Robert had a little crush on him. Even Alan seemed jealous of Mike.

"Where's Rookie?" Robert asked. Lacey clapped her hands. Rookie raced past Robert. Robert laughed and chased him until he caught him. Then, with the dog cradled in his arms, he wandered into the middle of the warehouse and flopped on the couch. Lacey followed. He spread his arms open.

"Big problem, what?" he asked. Lacey hesitated. She really wanted to talk about her sister impostor first, but that would usurp the proposal. She described finding the diamond ring. Robert jumped up and enveloped her in a hug. She pulled away.

"Congratulations," he said. "But I thought you didn't want to get married."

"I'd rather slit my throat," Lacey said. "He's going to ruin everything."

"I think you should say yes," Robert said. Lacey perched herself on the arm of the couch.

"Join us for dinner tonight?" she asked.

"Ha-ha," Robert said.

"You, me, Alan, dinner," Lacey repeated.

"No," Robert said. "Yourself."

Lacey stared at her ring finger. "Please? Please?"

"You love Alan."

"I know."

"What's the problem?"

"I don't want to get married."

"You should marry a Deaf man."

"I don't want to marry a Deaf man. I don't want to marry any man."

"How about a man dressed like this?" Robert winked at her suggestively, but he was kidding. He was very happy with his current boyfriend.

"I don't want to get married at all."

"You're lucky," Robert said. She didn't know he was still carrying her paintbrush until he flipped it in the air and tried to catch it behind his back. He missed. When he bent over to pick it up, it was with considerable grunting.

"Lucky?"

"You can marry in any state you want, in any church you want, by any preacher you want."

"Don't want, don't want, don't want."

"Not normal," Robert said.

"Exactly," Lacey said when he was upright and looking at her. "I'm not normal." She moved over to the coffeepot and filled a mug. She raised her eyebrows at him and tilted her head to the coffeepot. He shook his head no.

"Is it a nice rock?" he asked. He held his hands out as if clutching a giant diamond. Lacey shrugged.

"I'd rather have a new motorcycle," she said. Then she walked over to a sketch pad she had mounted on an easel facing the couch and wrote *Engagement Ring* on one side and *New Motorcycle* on the other.

"What are you doing?" Robert asked.

"Thinking." *Divorce,* she wrote under *Engagement Ring. Sex,* she wrote under *Motorcycle.*

Fat, she wrote under *Divorce. Lean and Mean,* she wrote under *Sex.* Robert looked down at his protruding belly. He and his partner, Eric, had been joined in a commitment ceremony last year.

"That happens to single people too," he said. Lacey wrote *Paranoid* under *Fat. Relaxed,* she wrote under *Lean and Mean.*

"Paranoid?" Robert asked. "You're talking about marriage or marijuana?"

"Every married woman I know is paranoid," Lacey said. *In love,* she wrote under *Relaxed. The End of Love,* she wrote under *Paranoid.* She tossed the marker across the floor. They stepped back and studied the list.

Engagement Ring	New Motorcycle
Divorce	Sex
Fat	Lean and Mean
Paranoid	Relaxed
The End of Love	In love

"When's your dinner?" he asked.

"Eight."

"What are you going to do?"

"Make him change his mind."

"Men don't like rejection," Robert said.

"I'll borrow your outfit," Lacey said. "He couldn't propose to me if I looked like you." Robert bowed and then did a little tap dance and wiggled his curly toe. Lacey laughed. *I have a twin,* she thought. *A face thief. Just tell him. Show him the note. Tell him! Show him the book!*

Robert jumped off the couch and began swatting dog hair off his pants.

"Gotta go," he said. "I'm almost on."

"Thanks for coming," Lacey said.

"DPHH is tomorrow," he said. "You should come." DPHH was Deaf Professional Happy Hour. The group met once a month at a different bar.

"We'll see," Lacey said. Robert pointed at Lacey and then made the sign for "hearing," but instead of making it at his mouth, he made it at his forehead. It was a sign given to Deaf people who acted like hearing people. It wasn't a compliment.

"I'm busy," Lacey said.

"You have to socialize," Robert said.

"Fine. I'll be there. Maybe."

"Wow," Robert said. "It's not just marriage."

"What?"

"You don't like to commit to anything. Not even drinks with other Deafies."

"I said I'll be there."

"It's because you were an orphan. Because you didn't go to a Deaf school." She didn't belong to either world, that's what he meant. Lacey just shrugged. It wasn't her fault. She had wanted to go to PSD, Pennsylvania School for the Deaf. Oh, the arguments she'd had with Margaret, ones she'd lost every time.

"Text me what happens," Robert said. He slipped his Sidekick out of his pocket.

"I'll get her," Lacey said.

"Her?" Robert asked. "Who?" Lacey stared at Robert, unable to answer.

"Nothing," Lacey said. "You're due on stage." Robert tilted his head, then nodded. He glanced at his Sidekick, as if it could help explain things. "I didn't know court jesters had Sidekicks," Lacey said.

"It's a modern version," Robert said. "The King has a plasma TV too." He grinned and was gone.

Lacey stood across the street from Mario's, the cozy Italian restaurant where she and Alan had their first date. Lacey was a freshman at Penn State when she met Alan. He was a senior who sat next to her in poetry class. Most of the students in class were enthralled with the sign language interpreters, but Alan couldn't take his eyes off Lacey. Especially after he watched her sign "The Road Not Taken" by Robert Frost. After that, he started an all-out campaign to get her to go out with him. Lacey had dated only Deaf men, and every time he asked her out, she turned him down flat.

It took three months, but he finally wore her down. She promised if he stopped harassing her she would have dinner with him. Once. She held up her index finger and repeated herself. Once. He said he wanted to take her to Mario's.

He'd eagerly offered to pick her up, but Lacey insisted they meet at the restaurant, even though they both had to travel into the city from campus. He was already at Mario's when she arrived. He looked a little surprised when she showed up with a sign language interpreter, but he added another seat to the table without complaint.

At first, Lacey was worried she'd made a huge mistake, bringing an interpreter, but once they started to converse she was proud of herself for hiring her. Now there were no limits to their conversation. She answered all his questions about Deaf Culture. She corrected his conception that sign language was universal, telling him that every country had its own sign language. She told him she was Deaf with a capital *D*, which signified a specific group of Deaf individuals, those who used American Sign Language, and were proud of their identity as Deaf persons. Given the choice, she assured him, she wouldn't want to be hearing.

"My group uses American Sign Language, ASL, as their primary communication," she told him through the interpreter. "We do not consider ourselves handicapped, we do not want to be 'fixed.' We have 'Deaf Pride'—we are happy being deaf. Deaf people share a history, a language, and a shared fight for our rights. We have Deaf poetry, Deaf art, Deaf slang, Deaf jokes. When we sit and converse at a dining table, we take the flowers or other large obtrusions out of the center so we can see each other." Alan held up his finger at this point and removed the single rose out of the center of the table and set it in front of the interpreter, effectively blocking out her face. Lacey laughed. The interpreter did not.

Lacey shattered the myth that Deaf people were "quiet." "Until I was about six," she said, "I thought my name was Shhh. Hearing people are freakishly sensitive when it comes to sound. I was shushed for everything from humming, to tapping my foot, to chewing my food, to breathing, for that matter. Shh, shh, shh, shh, shhhhhhh. And we play our music really loud at parties. Believe me, the police might be called.

"We don't want to be called Hearing Impaired (don't want to be fixed!), Deaf and Dumb (duh), or Deaf Mute. Whether or not we choose to use our voice and/or can lip-read varies from individual to individual, but that has no real bearing on our identity. Just don't assume we're all the same."

She summed it up by telling him Deaf people could do everything but hear. Alan soaked up every word. Later, the interpreter told Lacey that when she excused herself to go to the ladies' room, Alan turned to the interpreter and said, "Do you think it's too soon to ask her to marry me?"

When Lacey came back from the bathroom, Alan leaned back in his chair and looked at both women.

"This is the best evening I've ever had," he said. The interpreter just stared. Lacey's fork fell to her plate and onto the floor. Alan hadn't spoken the sentence, he'd signed it. Fluently. Lacey turned to the interpreter.

"Thank you," she said. The interpreter nodded and said her good-byes. Lacey continued to stare at Alan, hoping he'd shrink under her gaze. He didn't.

"What's going on?" Lacey demanded.

"I'm sorry," Alan signed. "I'm a CODA." Lacey folded her arms across her chest. CODA meant Children of Deaf Adults.

"Your parents are Deaf," Lacey said.

"Guilty," Alan said.

Lacey pounded the table. "Why didn't you tell me? In class. The very first day!" There was an unwritten rule that hearing people who knew sign should identify themselves whenever they were around Deaf people. Otherwise the Deaf people might be carrying on an extremely private conversation, assuming no one around them could understand them. To not identify yourself was a betrayal of trust.

"I didn't want to get into it," Alan said. "Not in class."

"You should have said something."

"Don't be mad. Even though you're beautiful when you're angry."

"This isn't *Children of a Lesser God*," Lacey said. "You can knock off the beautiful-angry deaf girl thing."

"Fine."

"Tell me about your parents." And so, he did. They were kind, and funny, they were bright, and stable parents.

Standing across the street, watching their first date all over again, Lacey felt tears coming to her eyes. She never got to meet Alan's parents; they died Alan's first year in college. His mother died of breast cancer, and his father shortly afterward of a heart attack, but Alan was convinced it was a broken heart. Either way, it left Alan an orphan, just like her. He said his parents were lucky; they'd found true love, just like him. He assured her they would have been thrilled he was dating a Deaf girl. Lacey wiped her eyes and took a deep breath. She was pretty sure they wouldn't be thrilled with her now. Given that she was possibly about to break his heart and all.

I really love him, Lacey thought as she walked into the restaurant. *I have to tell him what's going on. I have to convince him we don't want to get married.*

He was seated at a table in the back; he stood when he saw her coming. He was wearing the suit Lacey had found the ring in. She tried not to stare at the pocket. They kissed.

"You look nice," she said.

"You look beautiful," he said. He pulled out her chair, and Lacey wanted to run. Instead she sat down and dived into the breadsticks. He couldn't ask her to marry him if she was chewing like a cow, so her immediate plan was to never stop eating.

"So?" he said. "What were all those texts about?"

"I thought you were hiding in Benjamin Books," Lacey said.

"What?"

"I was in Benjamin Books and—I thought you were playing a joke on me."

"I'm lost."

"I know. It's been a really strange day. And I'll tell you everything—but can I just relax first?"

"Of course." Alan flagged a nearby waiter. He ordered a bottle of wine and asked them to turn the lights up a little. It was hard to have any kind of signed conversation in a really dark restaurant. Alan watched the waiter leave. Then he turned back to Lacey.

"I remember every second of our first date," he said. Lacey held his gaze.

"Me too," she said. "You were such a jerk."

"A jerk?!"

"You should've told me," she said. Alan laughed.

"I know," he said. "But I learned so much about you that night. Things I might not have learned if you knew I was a CODA."

"Still," she said.

"You're the one who brought the sign language interpreter," Alan pointed out. Lacey laughed. "At first I thought you hated me and were bringing a friend, then I thought you wanted a threesome," he added with a wink. Lacey ripped off a tiny piece of bread and threw it at Alan. He tried to catch it in his mouth. He missed, but his charm was infectious. Lacey had better watch herself or he was going to seduce her into saying yes. "It's been awhile," he said, "since we've talked about our future. "

"Sometimes," Lacey said, breaking off another piece of bread, "you're like the woman in this relationship." Alan didn't laugh at her joke. He frowned and shook his head. Lacey gave him a big smile. "Kidding," she said. He looked at her as if he didn't believe she was. The waiter returned to see if the lighting was adequate. Alan nodded and thanked him. The waiter remained by their table.

"Would you like a menu in Braille?" he asked. Alan looked at Lacey.

"Ask him if I can bring in our seeing-eye puggle," she said.

"She's deaf, not blind," Alan said. "And she can read just fine." The waiter turned red and shuffled away.

"Sheila Sherman called a tow truck today," Lacey said. "Because it's dangerous for deaf people to drive."

"Oh my God," Alan said. "You must have flipped."

"I didn't kill her," Lacey said. "But I wanted to." The waiter came back with the wine. He poured and presented the glass to Lacey, as if wanting to make up for his earlier faux pas. Lacey took the glass and brought it up to her eyes, then crossed them. The waiter took a step back. She didn't dare catch Alan's eye or she wasn't going to be able to keep a straight face. Next she tipped her ear to the cup as if she could hear something inside.

The waiter was starting to sweat, and he was continuously glancing at Alan, who kept his eyes glued to Lacey as if her behavior was perfectly normal. Finally, Lacey put the glass of wine in her cleavage and wiggled her chest. Alan burst out laughing. The waiter set the bottle of wine down on the table and left without pouring their glasses. Alan poured it instead, his laughter causing the bottle to jiggle as he poured.

"Happy anniversary," Lacey said.

"Happy anniversary." They clicked glasses. *I love you,* Alan mouthed. *I love you too,* Lacey mouthed back. Alan started to reach for his suit pocket. Lacey threw her hands out. Alan stopped.

"What?" Alan said.

"I have something to show you," Lacey said.

"Me first," Alan said.

"No." Lacey reached for her purse and pulled out *The Architect of Your Soul.* It was missing the cover. She handed the book to Alan. She saw him repeat the title. He gave her a quizzical smile. He started to flip through the book.

"Is this my anniversary present?" he asked. "You think I need help?"

"What do you think?"

"Is it new?"

"Yes."

"Where's the cover?"

"The girl was so hot-looking, I took it off. Didn't want you drooling all over her during our anniversary dinner."

"I'm sure she's nowhere near as hot as you," Alan said.

"You'd be surprised." Alan continued to flip through the book. Lacey watched him intently, praying that any minute he'd tell her he thought the book was a load of crap. He stopped.

"Look," he said turning the page toward her. "This is a good one." Lacey glanced at the title. "Building Your Future." Why had she shown him the book? What if he really liked it? What if he thought she was smarter than Lacey? He definitely couldn't pretend he didn't think Monica was hot. Lacey snatched the book away and shoved it back in her purse.

"What's wrong?" Alan asked. "What did I say?"

"It's not your present," Lacey said. "It was a joke."

"I don't get it."

"Deaf joke," Lacey said.

"Explain."

"The book is total crap," Lacey said. "Couldn't you see the book was total crap?"

"Why are you getting so upset?"

"How's your brother?"

"Why are you changing the subject?"

"How is he?"

"Fine."

"Is he still getting divorced?"

"Yes."

"Then how can he be fine?"

"What is going on here?"

"Must be really hard on the kids."

"Yes. We'll have to visit." Lacey reached over and took Alan's hand.

"Let's never get married."

"What?"

"Then we'll never get divorced."

"Because Tom is getting a divorce? He's a workaholic. He's been ignoring her for years. That's not me."

"Most marriages end in divorce."

"I would die before I would divorce you."

"Another good reason not to get married. No marriage, no death." Alan signaled the waiter. They ordered. There were no jokes this time, no laughter. How quickly things changed. Life was unpredictable. After a moment, Alan reached across the table and took Lacey's hand. He didn't speak, he simply held it. He knew something was wrong, and without prodding, he was waiting for her to tell him. The touch of his hand softened Lacey, breaking down the tightness she'd felt in her stomach all day. Letting go of it was like sliding down a rope; it started to unravel, and the farther she slipped, the more it burned.

She didn't want to cry, she didn't even know why she was crying. She should be angry, angry someone would leave a letter like that in her mailbox. Who left that letter in her mailbox? Who? Who in the hell was Monica Bowman and how was any of it even possible? Lacey didn't want to face what she'd been thinking all day, what she'd been avoiding thinking, throwing up roadblocks about face thieves and Photoshop. It wasn't her. That was the terrifying thought occupying Lacey's stomach. The picture wasn't stolen from Lacey, the picture was of Monica Bowman, and Monica Bowman was her twin. Lacey let go of the rope, and tears flooded her face. Alan took her other hand as well; he was there for her. He was always there for her.

"Tell me," he said. He handed her a napkin and gave her back her hands. She wiped her face, took a deep breath, started for her water, but took a drink of wine instead.

"I could have brothers and sisters," she said.

"Yes," Alan said. "You could."

"I want to find out."

"Why?"

"Why not? I have a right to know where I came from."

"You've never shown any interest before." It was true. She was abandoned at Hillcrest Children's Center as an infant. Baby in a basket. Or was it a car seat? It didn't matter. "There's something you're not telling me," Alan said.

"I'm going to pay Margaret Harris a visit," Lacey said.

"Your house mother from Hillcrest?"

"Yes."

"You said you'd rather eat live toads than ever see her again."

There's a woman out there with my face. She's writing books and getting famous and stealing bits of my life right out from underneath me. She's using my image on her book jacket and her Web site. Monica Bowman. What if you were meant to be with her? What if you would love her more than you love me? What if she's my twin? What if what if what if?

"I'm sorry," Alan said. "Of course you should visit Margaret. Do you think she can help?"

"She must know something."

"Do you want me to go with you?"

"I'm going with Kelly Thayler." Alan kept his mouth shut, but Lacey knew what he was thinking. She'd made it clear what she thought of Kelly Thayler as well.

"I think it's great," Alan said. "I fully support you."

"You do?"

"Yes. Wanting to know where you came from, who your family is—it's a very good sign. I just don't want you to get hurt. You may not find out anything."

"Of course."

"Just promise me one thing."

"What?"

"When you're done looking into your past, you'll start thinking about our future." Lacey smiled at Alan, the man who'd been there the past six years, the man who was pretending he didn't have a ring in his pocket because he could feel her fear. She'd never loved him more. And she still wasn't telling him the truth.

"I promise," she said. She crossed her heart and squeezed Alan's hand. It was because she had an itch, she told herself, that she was touching her nose.

Chapter 6

"I can't believe you want to visit Margaret," Kelly said. "She's going to be so excited to see you." They were in Kelly's car, driving the hour and a half to the Pittsburgh suburb where Margaret lived. Lacey was pleasantly surprised that Kelly jumped at the opportunity to visit Margaret and didn't even mention bringing any of her brood. The car smelled slightly like sour milk and crayons. Like Kelly's living room, toys littered the back-seat of her car. *Margaret excited to see me,* Lacey thought. *That's not going to last long.*

"She's disappointed you haven't kept in touch with her," Kelly said. Lacey gave her a look. It wasn't anybody's business. Little Miss Only At Hillcrest Three Years And Everyone Is Family.

Life with Margaret hadn't been all bad, but it hadn't been all good either. In rare nurturing moments, Margaret would wrap you in an enormous hug, make you disappear into her per-fumed folds. She was a good cook too, and when she was feel-ing generous would step in to spice up the meals or sweeten the desserts. She lived on the grounds in a little caretaker's cabin in the back, a mere brisk walk from whatever trouble the kids were getting themselves into.

But Margaret had mood swings. She would be smiling one minute and screaming the next with hardly a breath in between. She was strict too. It was lights out at nine P.M. whether you were six or sixteen. Sometimes she put salt in the cookies instead of sugar. And at night, once the kids' lights went out, Margaret's liquor bottles came out.

Lacey also knew, despite all this, Margaret thought of herself as a mother, whereas Lacey had always thought of her as a care-taker, and she felt no compulsion to stay in touch with Margaret after she left. If she could see anyone again, it would be her art teacher, Miss Lee. She came every Wednesday for at least five years, and she always made Lacey feel special, loved even, and signaled out for praise and instruction. She was so pretty too, wavy black hair and kind green eyes. She was the most exotic woman Lacey had ever seen. Tall and thin, always in a long flowing black skirt, white lace blouse, topped off with a turquoise necklace. Lacey probably became an artist because of her. Miss Lee didn't treat Lacey like she was any different because she was deaf, and she even knew a few signs. Lacey loved her; she didn't even remember her name; she was just Miss Lee. But she disappeared eventually; they all disappeared eventually.

And even if Lacey wanted to keep in touch with Margaret or anyone else, it would have been difficult. Hillcrest Children's Center lost funding shortly after Lacey left, and the school closed down a short while later. Public schools were now main-streaming handicapped children with the "able-bodied" popu-lation. It was all so long ago. According to Kelly, Margaret now owned a bakery. "I still think we should have told her you were coming with me," Kelly said. Lacey once again wished she hadn't let Kelly drive; they would have been there by now if Lacey had been behind the wheel.

"I told you," Lacey said. "I want to surprise her." By surprise, she meant ambush.

"I see," Kelly said. "This wouldn't have anything to do with your twin, now would it?"

Lacey was glad she wasn't driving; she would have crashed into something. She wanted to slap the look of self-satisfaction right off Kelly's face. She hated that Kelly liked to snoop, and even worse, that she was extremely adept at it. "You followed me?" Lacey asked. "To Benjamin Books?"

"No. I just called the bookstore, asked who was giving a book reading. Then Googled the name Monica Bowman. Saw her Web site and nearly fell off my chair!" Lacey stared out the window. This wasn't happening. She was supposed to be in control. She didn't want anyone knowing about Monica. She couldn't even explain why. This was her battle. She couldn't take anyone else galloping into her fight.

"At first I thought you were playing some kind of trick on me," Kelly continued. "Using a pen name. I was like—she even gave her dog a pen name! And Alan. Then I was like—wait a minute—why would Lacey ask me to interpret for this woman if it was her—and I was like—"

It was amazing how Kelly could sign and blather at the same time; someone should really stick a sock in her mouth and tape it shut. Of course, in ASL, she wasn't signing the "I was like" portions of the conversation, but Lacey could catch it on her lips. And whereas most Deaf people could drive and sign at the same time with the same ease as hearing people talking and driving at the same time, Kelly didn't have the skill mastered. Several times, Lacey had to grab on to the dash and remind Kelly to watch the road.

Maybe it wasn't such a bad thing somebody knew about her evil twin. At least now she could get someone else's opinion. Lacey told Kelly about discovering the poster, and then reached into her purse and showed her what she did to the book cover. She joined in as Kelly howled with laughter.

"Oh my God," Kelly said. "You're the reason the book signing was canceled."

"Yes."

"Have you looked at her Web site?"

"Yes. More of the same. The same picture—the same quotes from her book. Total crap."

"You think? I was kind of inspired. I was thinking, after you become friends, I'll take one of her workshops and get a signed copy—"

"After we become friends? The lunatic stole my face."

"Or she's your twin."

"No—" Admitting the possibility to herself was one thing. Saying it out loud was charged with a voltage Lacey wasn't wired to handle.

"You'll be famous," Kelly said, oblivious to Lacey's pounding fears. "You'll be all over the news. You're going to meet Matt Lauer. Can you get his autograph for me? I've always had a little crush on Matt. I was never so happy as when Katie left. She was always touching him. Why do short women think they're so much better than us? It's like the opposite of the Napoleon complex for women—"

"Stop."

"Sorry. This is so exciting!"

"Nightmare."

"Have you e-mailed her?"

"No."

"Why not? Do it now. Where's your BlackBerry?" The car swerved as Kelly wrenched around to gawk at the backseat. Lacey braced herself and pointed straight ahead. "Watch the road!"

"I'm going to pray for you," Kelly said. "I'm going to pray she's really your twin."

"Just pray we don't crash," Lacey said.

"Lone Wolf Lacey."

"Shut up."

"You never let anyone get close to you. Even me. Unless you want something." Lacey curled her right hand into a fist but kept it hidden from Kelly. She wanted to yell "One-legged freak!" as loud as she could, but she didn't. She wanted to tell her she loved Miss Lee, but she didn't do that either. In the first place, she couldn't remember if Miss Lee showed up before or after Kelly left. In the second, she wanted to keep her memories of her art teacher all to herself; if Kelly were to tell her how Miss Lee doted on her too, told her she was special, beautiful, could do anything—Lacey wouldn't think twice about kicking Kelly out of the moving car. Miss Lee belonged to her.

"I lost my parents too," Kelly said. "But I knew who they were. I knew where I came from."

"Just drive," Lacey said.

"Why do you think we called you Ice?" Kelly continued. "There was always a cold, hard part of you, and you messed over anyone who ran into you. Like an iceberg." Lacey watched the yellow line on the road flash by like bouts of lightning. *You used to call me Princess Prank too,* Lacey thought. *Because I was fun. Because I was brave. The only one not afraid to cause a ruckus in the evening and face up to Margaret in the morning. I was cool. Lone Wolf. Ice. Fuck off!*

This part of the highway ran along a dense stretch of nameless woods. Lacey could easily rip Kelly's fake leg off, beat her over the head with it, and bury her body in the woods. Nobody would ever know.

Did you hear? everyone would ask her. *Did you hear what happened to Kelly Thayler?* Lacey would point to her ears, shake her head no.

No, I didn't hear; how could I have heard?

"I'm sorry," Kelly said. "I just want this for you. A family. A sister." *If it can't be me* hung silently from the end of Kelly's fingertips. Kelly loved Lacey. Why did love work this way? How could one person feel so strongly, and the other not care? Despite her recent fantasy to murder her and bury the body in the woods, Lacey didn't have bad feelings toward Kelly. But she didn't love her. She didn't think of her as a sister. She didn't think of anyone as a sister. Maybe she just wasn't capable of that kind of love. Maybe if you didn't get it early enough, you were screwed. Lacey put her head back and closed her eyes. She didn't care if Kelly jabbered to herself the rest of the way there; as long as she closed her eyes, her world would be filled with nothing but the vibrations of the road, and a long, blissful silence.

A little over an hour later, Kelly took the next exit. Lacey opened her eyes and took in the sights. The place had a cozy, small-town feel. The houses were so close together, the neighbors could pass dinner back and forth through their windows, but they were all freshly painted, and flowers adorned almost every single porch. Then they passed a post office the size of a postage stamp, and a street sign warning: SLOW. DEAF CHILDREN. Kelly glanced at Lacey.

"I'm an adult," Lacey said. "Go fast." Kelly laughed but maintained her slow speed.

"What?" Lacey continued. "Because they're deaf they're not going to look both ways before crossing the street?"

"You know," Kelly said, "I used to be afraid of you. Now you amuse me."

"Great." Soon they entered a section of town littered with shops and restaurants. Kelly spotted a parking place and pulled in alongside a bakery. Lacey looked at the sign. HEAVENLY TREATS. "Is this it?" Lacey said. "Or are you hungry?"

"I'm always hungry," Kelly said. "But that's not why I'm stopping." She looked at the sign, and a little smile played across her face. "Do you think she still puts salt in the desserts?" Kelly said.

"There's only one way to find out," Lacey said. A warm, sweet smell wafted toward them as they approached the bakery.

"I want a chocolate éclair," Kelly said. "Or a cinnamon bun." Lacey wanted a glazed donut and answers.

Dogs, Lacey thought as she entered the bakery. *Margaret's life has gone to the dogs.* Man's best friend was everywhere. In line for biscuits, sitting by the door, barking at something crawling up the wall, and licking the shoes of humans in line with them.

"It's a bakery for dogs," Kelly exclaimed. "You turned her against children." She and Lacey shared a laugh.

"She wouldn't even let us get a dog back then," Lacey said.

"That's right," Kelly said. "You led a hunger strike over it."

"I made it twenty-four hours. Nobody else made it past snack time." Kelly made a face; Lacey knew she didn't like to be reminded of how weak she was back then.

"Now you paint dogs and she feeds them," Kelly said. Lacey was more than just a pet and portrait artist, and Kelly, who'd scoured the Internet for everything pertaining to Lacey, knew this very well. Lacey's Web site showcased her abstract paintings, her landscapes, her still lifes. Kelly was just getting back at her for the jab about the hunger strike. It was true, Kelly wasn't afraid of her anymore. Bummer. "They smell so good I could actually eat one," Kelly said.

"A dog or a biscuit?" Lacey asked.

"Funny."

"Go ahead," Lacey said. "I won't tell."

"You touched your nose," Kelly yelled. "You touched your nose!"

"I did not," Lacey said. Kelly signed "lie" and shook her finger at Lacey. Enough of the good old days. Lacey looked down the line of canines and owners and tried to spot Margaret behind the counter. She saw a young girl with a round face and mousy brown hair pulled into a ponytail, and a skinny boy with thick sideburns and a receding hairline despite his baby face.

"I'll go ask them about Margaret," Kelly said. Lacey hung back, and soon the round-faced girl pointed out a narrow staircase to their right. The girl was easy to lip-read.

"She lives up there." Kelly hurried over to Lacey and started to interpret, but Lacey was already headed for the stairs.

"Wait in the car," she told Kelly.

"No," Kelly said. "Why?"

"This isn't exactly a friendly visit," Lacey said.

"I know," Kelly said. "I'm in."

Lacey went first, taking the steps two at a time. At the top of the stairs were a small vestibule and a closed door. It was plastered with Polaroid photos of various animals. On closer look, they were all pictures of a fluffy black cat. There had to be at least fifty of him. In most his fur was sticking straight out of his massive body, as if he'd just stuck his little paw in the nearest outlet. The name *BLACKIE* was displayed underneath each picture. Blackie curled up on the bed, Blackie sitting on the arm of the couch, Blackie stretched tall, as if someone had just yelled, "Sit up straight," Blackie wearing a tux, Blackie next to a giant cutout mouse, Blackie sitting on the kitchen counter with an apron and a chef hat, and finally, in the bottom corner, Blackie at what looked suspiciously like Disney World.

"She never took us to Disney World!" Kelly said. "Wait. Did

she take you guys to Disney World after I left?" Lacey stared at Kelly's protruding lower lip and debated messing with her. In the end, she told the truth. She needed Kelly on her side.

"Never," she said.

"Bitch," Kelly said. She made a fist and knocked on the door. They waited. She knocked again. "Do you hear anything?" Lacey asked. Kelly stuck her ear up to the door, then shook her head. She knocked a third time.

"Margaret?" she called. "It's Kelly and Lacey."

"You didn't tell her I was coming, right?" Lacey said. Kelly looked away. "I told you not to tell her!"

"I'm sorry. I thought she'd be thrilled."

Lacey pushed Kelly aside and pounded on the door. "Margaret," she yelled. "Open the door." Lacey didn't know exactly what her deaf voice sounded like, but later Kelly would tell her that, down below, dogs began to howl. Lacey tried the door. It was locked. She stepped back.

"What are you doing?" Kelly asked. Lacey pulled her right leg up, pre-kick. "Margaret!" Kelly yelled. "She's going to break your door." Lacey geared up to give it everything she had. A split second before her foot made impact, the door swung open. Lacey kicked at the air, then lurched forward. She knocked into Kelly, and the two of them stumbled into the apartment, tottering like they did on the night they stole a bottle of Margaret's vodka and drank themselves sick by the drainpipe in the backyard.

"Hello, girls," Margaret said. Kelly hugged Margaret. Lacey quickly stepped aside and scanned the room. It was a studio apartment, with a small open kitchen on the right, the living room area straight ahead of them, and a Murphy bed against the far wall, open and unmade. Red faux velvet curtains hung over the lone window on the left wall, as if barricading all outside light. Lacey remembered how dark Margaret kept the group home at Hillcrest too, and it suddenly made her angry. No wonder she always felt so pent up.

Was that why Lacey hated curtains, why she would rather let the light shine in, no matter what time of day? Margaret's place was cluttered and smelled like stale cigarettes and kitty litter. Lacey had a sudden image of Blackie with a lit cigarette hanging out of his mouth, and it made her laugh. Had Margaret always been such a pack rat? The kitchen counter was buried in cereal, boxes of canned cat food, and jars filled with congealed jellies. More pictures of Blackie wallpapered the fridge. The furniture looked heavy and drawn. Margaret was the exception to the rule "People look like their pets"; Margaret resembled her furnishings.

Although she'd always been heavy, she'd put on even more weight. Her face was heavily lined; her hair, once black, now completely gray. Lacey didn't know why, but tears came to her eyes. Before she could stop her, Margaret ambushed her with a hug. Lacey kept her body stiff at first, then relaxed into it, as if driving across an icy bridge. *Turn into the slide, not against it.* Terribly difficult when all you wanted to do was slam on your brakes and swerve. When Margaret finally let go, she led them to the stained green couch floating in the middle of the living room. She picked up a box of cookies sitting on the edge of the coffee table, and held them out. Lacey and Kelly simultaneously refused. Margaret gestured for them to sit on the couch, then lowered herself onto an orange recliner. The chair rocked back from the weight of her behind, then forward from the counterweight of her massive bosom. Kelly and Lacey lowered themselves onto the sofa, and then sank, despite both women being thin. Lacey could feel a metal coil poking her in the ass.

"I'm so glad to see you," Margaret said. She rocked back, clasped her hands below her breasts, and watched Kelly interpret. "Look at you," Margaret said, shaking her finger at Kelly. "You're good at that finger talk now." Margaret held up her own hands, bulging with ropey veins and age spots, and examined them. "I never got the hang of it," she said to Lacey.

"Bitch, cookie, lesbian," Lacey signed. Margaret smiled.

"Oh, it's such a beautiful language," she said. "Like a dance in the air." She threw her own hands up, as if dancing.

"Bitch, cookie, lesbian," Lacey signed again.

"Just beautiful." She turned to Kelly. "What did she say?"

"She said you haven't changed a bit," Kelly said and signed at the same time. Lacey laughed out loud, and Margaret beamed.

"We're horrible people," Lacey signed to Kelly.

"How do you like my bakery?" Margaret asked. From out of nowhere, Blackie materialized and jumped into Lacey's lap without an invitation. Kelly engaged Margaret in small talk while Lacey petted the cat. Lacey knew she should be paying attention; after all, Kelly was signing and talking at the same time so she could follow the conversation, but she just couldn't feign interest. She still hadn't gotten the hang of hearing culture, the polite bullshitting you were required to do before you could come to the point.

Some said Deaf people were too blunt, but Lacey knew they were just straightforward. When you experienced most of the world through your eyes, you said what you saw. It was as simple as that. If you saw a Deaf friend you hadn't seen in years and he used to be skinny and have a head full of hair, and was now bald and fat—

Hearing culture: "You look great." (Pained, fake smile).

Deaf culture: "What happened?! You're fat and bald!" (Eyebrows arched questioningly, genuinely interested smile).

But she was in the hearing world, so she let Kelly go through their phony little ritual. Lacey didn't want the cat on her lap either. She was wearing white Capris and now they were covered in long, black hairs. When she couldn't stand it any longer, she pushed the cat off her lap and waved her hands until Margaret and Kelly stopped talking.

"I need to know where I came from," Lacey said. Kelly interpreted.

"Don't tell me you want the stork story again," Margaret said. "If I recall, you were the one who took it upon yourself to educate the rest of the children on how babies were made." It was true. Lacey was only nine years old when she found the book *Your Body, Yourself* wedged in the bottom of a box in the attic, and acted out every aspect (as she understood them) of menstruating, mating, and childbirth to the other kids, enthralling and sickening them with a slew of biological horrors.

"Please," Lacey said. Margaret looked around, adjusted her glasses, shifted her massive thighs.

"A basket," she said, gesturing as if holding the basket in her hands. "On the porch." A baby in a basket. It was the same old story. How was it possible Lacey once swallowed this fish whole?

"How old was I?" Lacey asked.

"I'm not sure," Margaret said. "A few months?" Kelly leaned forward to listen, for Margaret's voice had dropped to a whisper.

"How did you know I was deaf?"

"What?"

"I was just a baby. You just happened to be running a home for disabled children. But if I was only a few months old, how did you or anyone else know I was deaf?"

"I don't know. Maybe they left a letter."

"They? Why do you say 'they'?"

"Or she. Or he. Or whoever. You were left on the porch in a basket, possibly with a note that might have said you were deaf."

"Do you still have this note?"

"For goodness' sake, Lacey Ann, that was a long time ago," Margaret said.

Lacey looked around the living room. "You haven't thrown out a magazine since 1953, but you threw away the letter that may or may not have come with me?" Margaret looked at the stack of magazines against the wall. She folded her arms and frowned. Lacey rose from the couch. "They didn't check newborn babies for deafness back then," she told Margaret. "They do now, but they didn't back then." Margaret didn't reply; she simply stared and rocked, rocked and stared. "What about the basket?" Lacey asked. "Did you keep the basket?" She spotted a basket underneath the metal TV stand, filled with yarn and knitting needles. She walked over, removed the basket, and parted balls of yarn as if looking for a baby. Blackie pranced over and sat at her feet. Lacey tossed him one of the balls. He put one paw on it, then looked up at Lacey as if he had been seriously gypped.

"Is this it?" she asked. "Is this the basket?" Margaret looked at Kelly and shook her head, as if Kelly were to blame for Lacey's outburst. Lacey walked over to Margaret, tossed the box of cookies off the coffee table, and sat so they were face-to-face.

"You're lying," she said, using her voice. Margaret's double chin wiggled. She wrung her hands together and smacked her lips. She looked away. Lacey nodded at Kelly to interpret again. "I won't be mad," Lacey said, inching forward. "I just need to know."

"You're telling me you had a horrible childhood, is that it?" Margaret said. It took considerable effort, but she dislodged herself from the chair, grabbed the basket Lacey left on the floor and the ball of yarn from Blackie's uninterested paw. "I did the best I could. These days you have one teacher to every three students in homes like those. I was all by myself with ten of you. I did the best I could."

"You were wonderful," Kelly said. "You really were." She gave Lacey a look.

"I appreciate how difficult it must have been for you," Lacey said. "I wasn't an easy child. I know that. I'm not here to punish you. I just want to know who I am. Where I came from."

"You girls should eat." Margaret shuffled into the kitchen and yanked open a drawer. When she turned around she was holding a wad of cash and a coupon. "I don't cook anymore," she said. "But I have a coupon for Friendly's."

"Are you coming with us?" Kelly asked.

"No, no. I'm sorry. I have biscuits to make."

"I don't want ice cream," Lacey said. "I want answers."

"They don't just sell ice cream," Margaret said. Her face was flushed and animated, her breath labored. "They have burgers, and sandwiches, and—what day is this? Because they make a really good meat loaf, but I think it's only on Tuesday."

"Lacey just wants to know about her family," Kelly said.

"Don't speak for me," Lacey said.

"Remember when we were kids?" Kelly signed to Lacey without speaking. "How Margaret used to say no to everything at first? If we stopped bugging her and left her alone, then she'd finally give us what we wanted?" Lacey thought about it. She couldn't remember things as clearly as Kelly, which was ironic given Kelly was there for only three years and Lacey had a life sentence. Then again, she was pretty self-involved back then. "Trust me," Kelly said.

"Fine," Lacey said. "We'll go to lunch."

"We came a long way to see you," Lacey said, snatching the Friendly's coupon out of Margaret's hand.

"But it took you ten years," Margaret said. Her chin quivered, and she turned away and began moving jars around the counter. Guilt hit Lacey like a fastball to the gut. Margaret opened a drawer in the kitchen. It was stuffed with papers. She pulled out a newspaper article. Leaving the drawer hanging open like an unanswered question, she handed the article to Lacey. It was the interview the *Philadelphia Inquirer* did with Lacey about her artwork and the upcoming show. "I've kept up with you," Margaret said. "And you've never even sent me a Christmas card." A series of quick movements distracted Lacey. She turned toward the disruption. It was Kelly. She was crying and furiously digging through her purse. Margaret pulled something else out of the drawer, a tissue she handed to Kelly.

Lacey felt a yearning for Margaret, coated with a restless guilt that was pushing her to do what Margaret wanted. Apologize. Claim her as her long-lost mother. Tell her that from now on she would write, she would visit, she would call. And then what? Before she knew it, Margaret would have her set up with an easel in the bakery so she could paint every dog that came in the door.

"Come to lunch with us," Lacey said. "No more questions. Just lunch." Margaret sniffed and shook her head, but her body shifted, became straighter, her chin lifted up.

"I guess we all need a little something in our bellies," she said. She went to the coffee table, bent down and tried to peer underneath.

"My purse," she said, pointing. Lacey went to get the purse. It was on the floor under the table, all the way toward the couch. Lacey got on her hands and knees and pulled it out. The combination of cat hair and dust made her sneeze. The coffee table had one lame leg, propped up with a book, and Lacey couldn't help but think of Kelly (a thought she was smart enough not to share, no matter how blunt Deaf Culture was), when she noticed the title of the book propping up the table. Lacey dropped the purse, and yanked it out. She backed out of the coffee table as fast as she could. She came up too soon and banged her head on the table's edge. Pain and dizziness hit her as she stood, but it didn't stop her from turning on Margaret. She held the book up to her face, forcing Margaret to stare at Monica Bowman, with her feathered hair, green-stemmed glasses, and slightly whiter teeth.

"Oh my God," Kelly said. "You liar." "Bitch, cookie, lesbian," she signed to Lacey. Margaret stared at the book, then slowly, her entire being transformed. The quivering look was gone. Her shoulders, in a downward curve since they'd arrived, thrust back. Her face took on a hard, weathered look; suddenly, the years were gone. The woman Lacey remembered most often from childhood was back.

"Get out," Margaret said. She grabbed the book and tucked it under her armpit. "You're still so beautiful," Margaret said. "But so angry."

"I'm angry too," Kelly said. She pointed to the book. "That's her sister. Her twin sister."

"I said get out."

"No," Kelly said. "What aren't you telling her?"

"I want no part of this," Margaret said.

"Part of what?" Lacey said. "Part of what?"

"I'll see you out," Margaret said. She stood by her door and pointed the way out. Blackie followed Margaret at a trot, then rubbed up against her, weaving in and out of Margaret's legs like a shark circling a cage. Kelly started in on Margaret again.

"Let's go," Lacey signed to Kelly. "I have an idea." Kelly looked at Lacey as if she were crazy, as if she were leaving a boxing match before they'd reached the knockout. "Trust me," Lacey said. Kelly looked unconvinced but followed Lacey out the door and down the staircase. Margaret trailed at a safe distance. Lacey let Kelly get to the bottom. Then she stopped and turned to Margaret.

"Bathroom," she said. It was the one sign she knew Margaret remembered. Margaret's mother died of bladder cancer, in part, Margaret always said, because her mother was too busy looking after her children to stop and pee the minute she knew she had to go. At the group home, Margaret was constantly making the children go to the bathroom. It was a sacred command, one she always adhered to, no matter what else her mood.

"It's by the kitchen," Margaret said, moving out of Lacey's way and pointing up the stairs. Lacey nodded and signed to Kelly.

"Car keys," Lacey said.

"What?" Lacey signed the request again. Kelly dug in her pocket and threw her the keys.

"Make her give you a tour of the bakery," Lacey said. "Now, do it now." Lacey raced back up the stairs.

The minute Kelly got into the car, Lacey pulled out. "I didn't say you could drive," Kelly said. Her sentence was cut off as the car lurched forward. "Jesus," she said. She fumbled for her seat belt and snapped it in place. They were speeding on the highway when Kelly glanced in the backseat and noticed a large, black bag.

"Whose bag is that?" she asked. Lacey switched lanes so she could pass the car in front of her. It was going seventy miles an hour.

"Oh my God," Kelly said. "It's moving. The bag is moving." Lacey passed the car and pulled in front of it.

"Blackie," Kelly said. "You stole Blackie." Lacey slowed down.

"How did you know?" she asked.

"Because I'm hearing," Kelly said. Lacey frowned. *Meow, meow, meow,* Kelly mouthed.

"Oh." Lacey turned around. She looked in the rearview mirror. "Shhh," she said.

"Real effective," Kelly said. "Can the poor thing breathe?"

"Of course. It's a cat bag." Kelly leaned over the seat and turned the bag around. Green eyes glowed behind a netted window in the side.

"We're cat-nappers," Kelly said. "We can't do this."

"Calm down," Lacey said. "We're not going to waterboard him."

"This isn't right," Kelly said. "This isn't right."

"And lying to me my entire life is? Keeping my twin a secret?"

"You have a point." Kelly looked back at the cat again, and shook her head. *Meow, meow, meow,* she mouthed again. "You're lucky you're deaf." Then a little smile played across her face.

"What?" Lacey said.

"I wish the other kids were here to see this," Kelly said. "She's going to freak." Her smile turned into an all-out grin. "She's going to fucking freak." They smiled at each other, and just like that, they were mischievous little girls again, creeping and giggling in forbidden shadows, clasping their hands in fright, not at the funny shapes things took on in the night, but in the sheer awe of what they might do, the taste of the trouble they could cause. It was then and there, in that car, racing down the road with a kidnapped cat (meow, meow, meow) and a one-legged mother of six who was laughing so hard she had to lean forward and clutch the dash to catch her breath, that Lacey decided she loved Kelly a little bit after all. Just not like a sister. Not even close to the way she thinks she could have, would have, should have loved a sister.

Chapter 7

Lacey sat at her kitchen table, scissors in hand, scouring a magazine. Blackie and Rookie sat atop the table, inches from her face, engaged in a mano a mano, feline-to-canine stare-down. The old teak table where Lacey sat could handle their claws; every etch gave it character. Over the years the table had been used for eating, writing, painting, and on a couple of wild nights when Alan and Lacey were first dating, lovemaking. From where she sat, Lacey had a view of the kitchen counter, so clean Lacey would lick it from one end to the other without the slightest hesitation. After returning from Margaret's cluttered apartment, Lacey turned into a cleaning Tasmanian devil, leaving nothing on the blue-tiled countertop but the coffeemaker, two clay mugs, and a triple-slotted stainless steel toaster.

From where she sat, she could see out the screen door to their enclosed porch; the daisies from a few days ago were just starting to droop their petal heads. Was it just a few days ago Lacey had discovered a bomb in her mailbox and dodged a marriage proposal? The kitchen wall to her left, which Lacey and Alan painted three times before she found the perfect shade of sage, held a large Ikea clock and the first painting she'd ever given Alan: the ubiquitous bowl of fruit, except instead of boring bananas and pitiful pears, Lacey used mangos, kiwis, and plums, experimenting with shades of greens and reds and purples against a black, white, and gray background, as if the ripe fruit had been left on a forgotten countertop in an abandoned building. And although she'd greatly improved her technique over the years, it was still one of her favorite paintings, embedded with the kind of protective nostalgia parents felt for their first child—

Twins, twins, twins, twins, twins. Who popped out first? Who were their parents? Who adopted Monica, what kind of—

She didn't realize Alan was in the room until he tapped her on the shoulder. Startled, she looked up. He pointed to the animals.

"On the table?" he signed. "Where we eat?"

"I've thrown them down a hundred times," Lacey said.

"I wish you could hear them. One growling, one hissing. I can't tell which is which." Lacey looked again. Sure enough, both animals were slightly baring their teeth.

"How long are you cat sitting?" Alan asked.

She shrugged.

"A few more days."

"Why are you cutting letters out of a magazine?"

"Work project. I thought you had a meeting."

"I do." He bent down and kissed her cheek. The kitchen lights flashed; someone was at the front door. Lacey also had flashing lights for the phone and the fire alarm. Her alarm clock, which was a device she put under her pillow, vibrated. Rookie flew off the table, startling even Blackie, who jumped about a foot in the air. Lacey tried to pat it down, but most of Blackie's fur remained standing on end. Alan headed for the door; Lacey calmly straightened her magazine.

"Mommy's here," she signed to Blackie. Blackie's large green eyes blinked at her. Lacey patted the cat and then made her way to the door. Margaret stood in the entryway, flushed and in tears. When she spotted Lacey, she began out-and-out wailing. Alan caught Lacey's eye and signed, "Cat sitting? Cat sitting?"

"Hello, Margaret," Lacey said. Blackie jumped off the table and landed with a thud. Margaret rushed past Lacey and picked up the massive fur ball. She planted kisses all over his furry face. "Lock the door," Lacey told Alan.

"What is going on?" Alan said.

"Meet Margaret," Lacey said. "My house mother. Is she just like you pictured her?" Lacey and Alan glanced at Margaret, who had bent over to set Blackie down. Her large ass was covered in flour and animal fur. Alan looked away.

"She said you stole the cat," he said. "Did you?"

"Don't you have a meeting?"

"Tell me you didn't steal her cat."

"Where's his carrying case?" Margaret said. She was shouting, as if Lacey were merely hard of hearing and not profoundly deaf.

"Right here," Alan said, opening the closet where Lacey had stashed it.

"Thank you," Margaret said. Blackie willingly jumped into the case. Rookie ran over to as if to zip it up himself. Margaret picked up her prize and headed for the door. Lacey stood in front of it. The two stared at each other.

"Your man," Margaret said, glancing back at Alan. "Does he know?"

"Know what?" Alan asked. Lacey didn't answer.

"You haven't really changed, have you?" Margaret said.

"Excuse me," Alan said, joining them at the door. "What is going on here?" Margaret removed an envelope from her jacket and thrust it at Lacey.

"You weren't supposed to get this information until I was dead," Margaret said. Lacey took the letter.

"You're kidding," Lacey said, using every ounce of self-restraint not to add *and when will that be?*

"I tried to protect you," Margaret said. "Like I would my own daughter."

You were never my mother, Lacey thought. It was a sign of maturity that she didn't say it.

"Be careful what you wish for, dear," Margaret said. Alan interpreted, although Lacey had been reading Margaret's lips all along. This time she didn't smell booze on Margaret's breath, and strangely she missed it. "It's all I know," Margaret continued. "So please don't contact me again—unless it's really to see me." She reached for the doorknob, and Lacey let her go.

Alan stood staring at Lacey. Lacey stared at the envelope.

"What?" Lacey asked. Alan threw up his hands in frustration. Then he looked over at the dining room table.

"Were you writing a ransom note?" he asked. Lacey couldn't help but smile.

"This isn't funny," Alan said. "You're shutting me out. What is going on?"

"Unresolved childhood issues," Lacey said, staring at the envelope. Did Margaret trick her, or did this envelope hold the key to who she was?

"More secrets?" Alan said. "Did she know something about your past or not?" Lacey held up the envelope. "Are you going to open it?"

"Of course."

"Just not in front of me."

"I have to go," Lacey said. "So do you." She moved past him.

"Is this because of that book?" Alan asked. Lacey felt as if she were suspended from the ceiling.

"What do you mean?"

"Some kind of ill-advised self-help bullshit?" Lacey didn't reply. She tried to move past him. "Don't shut me out." He moved in front of her and blocked her.

"You have to give me some time," Lacey said. "Some space."

"I'm late," Alan said. He brushed past her and grabbed his keys from a hook by the door.

"I'll be at the studio," Lacey said. Alan didn't turn around. For the first time in six years, he left without kissing her good-bye.

The minute Lacey pulled up to the warehouse, a feeling of calm settled over her. She couldn't say the same thing for Rookie, who was vibrating as if he'd lapped up twenty bowls of

Red Bull. For a moment Lacey was jealous of her dog. Had she ever been that excited over anything? Rookie jumped on her and licked her face. *Must be nice,* she thought as she planted a kiss on his nose. Then again, a dog's life probably wasn't the one for her. She'd never been one for sitting, shaking, or kissing butt.

She hated upsetting Alan, she hated that he left without kissing her good-bye, she hated that she was keeping secrets. But she just wasn't ready to talk about this. She had to read Margaret's letter alone. Only when she knew exactly what she was dealing with could she open up to Alan. *It doesn't matter what the letter says,* she told herself as she and Rookie made their way to the studio. *I have a good life. A job I like. A man I love. And of course a hyperactive puggle. The letter can't change that. It can't change anything.*

Once inside, Rookie took off, zooming across the floor until he was nothing but a gyrating wheel of fur in the distance. Lacey knew he would run himself into oblivion and eventually tucker out on the La-Z-Boy chair. Lacey headed straight for the leather couch. She sat down and removed the letter from her purse. Her heart was pounding. She placed her hand over it. *I should have bought a bottle of Johnny Walker, Margaret. If I don't feel like toasting you after reading this, I could at least get smashed.* She took a deep breath and opened the letter.

> *My Dearest Lacey,*
> *It was so good to see you after all these years. And yes, as you already know, you have a twin. She's identical to you except that she is not hearing impaired.*

Deaf. All this time and Margaret still didn't get that Lacey wanted to be called Deaf—

> *She was kept in the car when you were dropped off, but I could see her in the backseat. Both of you were carrying on something awful. You were three years*

*old but you were fighting like a tiger, biting and claw-
ing everyone in sight.*

Three years old? So much for the baby in the basket. So that
was the truth behind her "lost" baby pictures. Margaret said
they'd been ruined in a flood.

> *I know you were led to believe that your biological
> parents had passed away. I'm so sorry, Lacey. I don't
> know where they are now, or if they're still alive, but
> they were the ones who dropped you off.*

Her biological parents? Her biological parents? Lacey put
the letter down. "Rookie," she screamed, not bothering to clap.
"Rookie!" He came racing over so fast he tripped on her feet
and landed belly up on the floor in front of her. She picked
him up and held on to him, burying her face in his fur. He
smelled like corn chips. He licked her face. *My biological parents
kept my twin sister and dropped me off at Hillcrest? My biological parents?*
   She'd wondered about them over the years, of course; every
orphan played the Who Are My Parents game.
   They were Russian spies. It tore out their hearts to give her
away, but the CIA was closing in on them, they had to go home,
and they didn't want to subject their delicate, newborn infant
to harsh Russian winters and lukewarm Stroganoff. Although
they could have hidden all their secret gadgets in her diaper
bag—
   They were young and in love and died tragically right after
she was born. Her handsome father wheeled her mother out of
the hospital and opened the back door of their Volvo. He gin-
gerly took Lacey out of her mother's hands and called to a
nurse walking past, just beginning her shift. "Here," he said
handing Lacey over. "Hold this for just a sec." Then he lifted
her mother out of the wheelchair—she was perfectly capable of
walking, but he was a romantic and was overcompensating for
missing the birth because of twenty crucial seconds left in the

Giants game. He was about to place her in the car when a rogue ambulance jumped the curb, killing both of them instantly—

Her mother was a princess who fell in love with a pauper—

Her father was a respected Harvard professor who wanted nothing more to do with her mother when he found out she was with child—

A pilot and a stewardess—

A priest and a nun—

Fat and retarded—

Midgets who couldn't handle tall children—

Clowns on the run—

They were desperate—

They were addicts—strewn out on city steps with needles hanging out of their arms—incapable of raising a child, sacrificing their life with her so that she could have a better one—

Lacey had imagined every possibility under the sun. Except this one.

Her biological parents were "normal" and alive. They dropped her off at the group home. Where did they drop Monica off?

She should stop reading the letter, that's what she should do. Forget all about it. It never happened. They didn't exist. It didn't work. The letter pulled her back.

> *And as far as I know, Monica, your twin, was*
> *raised by them.*

Lacey would have thought she was immune to shock. Wasn't there a limit to the amount a person could take, a point at which your system simply shut off and couldn't feel anymore? But this one pitted and cored her. And not just because Margaret anticipated her question. They kept Monica? Raised her? They kept Monica and dumped Lacey off to be raised by Margaret Harris? There were no words, only a sudden free fall into a chasm of grief. Why should she even care? Why should she even give a fuck? Thank God they weren't here to see tears dripping down her face. Screw them. Screw Monica too.

Monica. Lacey finger-spelled her name. M-O-N-I-C-A. She

said it out loud. "Monica." Did it feel familiar? No, she was a stranger. Rookie cocked his head and licked her again, but this time even a dog's selfless tongue couldn't stop the sharp pain still searing across her heart. Was she that bad? That damaged? That unloved? Was there some part of her that remembered? She wanted to throw something, if nothing else, herself, to the ground, pound her feet and fists like a child throwing a tantrum.

Keeping the letter clutched in her hand, Lacey began to pace. She wondered if there was any wine left in the kitchen. The small counter space next to the refrigerator revealed only half a bottle of red that had been there forever. Mike kept a special bottle of scotch in the cupboard. Single malt something or other. He was saving it, it was rare and expensive, that was all she knew. Whenever he was having a bad day, he would come to the cupboard and just hold the bottle to his chest. She really shouldn't be doing this. She was just going to hold the bottle, that's all. She didn't even know if she'd know the difference between cheap and expensive scotch, just like she didn't know if she preferred the music of Meat Loaf or Mozart.

Besides, she was only a two-glasses-of-anything-alcoholic girl, always had been.

The bottle was still there, unopened in the back of the cupboard. She brought it to the couch and continued with the letter.

> *At the time, I thought it was best you didn't know any of this, my darling Lacey. I can't imagine parents giving up one of their children, separating her from her twin no less. And I couldn't imagine burdening you with this kind of pain. I'm sorry you're hearing this now, and I hope you understand I only did what I thought was best. Legally, I wasn't allowed to tell you the circumstances surrounding your situation, and I'm breaking the law even now, but you've seen the book, they can't blame me for that. Just please try and keep my name out of this. Your biological father is a man of considerable influence. I don't want, nor deserve, to face his wrath.*

My father. My biological father. The head sperm donor. Face his wrath? Leave it to Margaret to be dramatic.

>   *You and your sister are still young; maybe you'll be
>   the best of friends. You can look her up. Like you,
>   your sister has a Web page. See? Something in com-
>   mon already. And in the bottom of the envelope, I've
>   included the little toy you were clutching when you
>   arrived. It appears to be broken. I believe your sister
>   had the other half.*

Toy? What did she do with the envelope? She dove her hand into her purse and yanked it out. A handful of items burst out with it, briefly arching into the air before hitting the floor, scattering in different directions. A tampon, lipstick, blush, her keys. She left them where they lay. She picked up the envelope and, on second thought, stomped on the lipstick. Desert Red oozed out like congealed blood. Lacey felt a strange sense of satisfaction, looking at the mangled tube. So she stomped on the blush. The plastic case cracked and a Kiss of Summer shot straight out, then caked the floor with shimmering, beauty-promising dust. Lacey was sweating. Her heart was pounding. She felt clammy. All the classic symptoms of a panic attack. She should be doing something, texting someone. She should text Alan. She should not open this rare bottle of scotch that does not belong to her.

>   *You didn't speak for six months after you arrived.
>   Apparently, you and your sister had a language all
>   your own, and it made you furious when the teachers
>   of the hearing impaired wanted you to learn Ameri-
>   can Sign Language.*
>   *If it's any consolation, I've never seen a woman
>   looking so destroyed as your mother did on that day.*

Lacey threw the letter down and escaped into the bathroom. Rookie followed, cautious and watchful. She flipped on the light and met her blue eyes in the mirror. Did her mother look more destroyed than Lacey did right now? Did she look like her mother or her father? Correction. Did "they" look like their mother or their father? She was a "they." She always thought she'd never have access to her family tree; it would remain stripped and barren, ghostly branches stretching out to nowhere. She preferred it that way.

Now she had a living mother. A father. Or she did. Who knew if they were still alive? There were so many questions. Too many. Even some kind of sick game show, some sensational reality flick, wouldn't force her to face so many questions at once. Take it one step at a time. She had a sister. Who looked just like her.

Someone else saw Lacey's exact face in the mirror every day. So much for "we are all unique," so much for snowflakes. Someone who was out there right now. Someone who shared her exact DNA. And she didn't even know she existed. Or did she?

Lacey was not an original. It felt so wrong. Draconian. Identity theft! Lacey saw pain in her face, and fear. She saw beads of sweat along her jawline and underneath her lip. Rookie nuzzled her ankle, as if apologizing for something. Lacey did not bend down and pet him. *You have no idea who you are,* she told her reflection. *Your entire life has been a lie. Your family threw you away like a piece of trash.*

Because she was deaf? That wasn't possible. This was the United States of America. *Whoops, we accidentally got two, would you like one? Here, take this one. She's slightly damaged.* According to the hearing world, the one she had no choice but to live in, the one whose labels she'd been trying to dodge her whole life—that's who considered her damaged—she was "as is." No refunds, no returns.

Lacey didn't hold this view of herself, or her culture. She'd jokingly wished she could live on a completely Deaf planet, live a life free of the limitations hearing people tried to rope her with, communicate only through American Sign Language, never have to explain, or tutor, or teach, or "Speak, Lacey, speak!" or play the system. She'd never wanted to be on that planet more than she did right now.

Right now, breaking into someone else's bottle of rare scotch didn't seem like such a big deal. Sussing out everything she could on those monstrous people who deserted her was the only thing that mattered. And drinking was the only way she could finish the letter. With renewed purpose, Lacey marched back to the coffee table and snatched up the letter.

> *Your father stayed in the car, so I didn't see him, but like I said, your mother was a wreck. She kept saying, "It's for the best. They insist it's for the best."*
>
> *I can't imagine any reason good enough for abandoning your own child, and even though you were the one who gave me the most gray hairs, you'll always be one of my favorites. I wish you the best in your search for your twin.*
>
> *Much love,*
>
> *Margaret*
>
> *P.S. If you ever come within ten feet of Blackie again, I will call the police and TAKE OUT A RESTRAINING ORDER!!!!!!!*

Lacey was halfway to drunk when she finally dug into the envelope and pulled out the toy. It was a small, blue plastic horse. Well, half of one anyway. The back half. It looked as if it had been sawed down the middle. It was littered with tooth marks. Just holding the sawed-off horse was making her hands shake, or maybe it was the alcohol. She would have to tell Mike he was right, this was the good stuff. She took another swig. At first it burned, then it was silk sliding down her throat. The room was spinning. Rookie curled up on the La-Z-Boy, with one eye tucked into his paw, the other staring up at her reproachfully.

Taking the horse and the bottle of scotch with her, Lacey got up and wobbled across the expanse to her section. She needed the comfort of her easels. She needed to smell and touch her paints, see her brushes tipped upside down in their assigned cups, a yellow plastic one for acrylics, an old jam jar for her oil brushes, and a regular drinking glass for her watercolor brushes.

But it was really the stack of paintings against the back wall she was after. She banged her hip on her table and sloshed a bit of the scotch. The containers wiggled, the brushes shimmied. She slammed the bottle of scotch down on the table and giggled. She headed for her paintings, the ones she'd never shown anyone, not even Alan. She put the toy horse in her mouth, dropped to her knees and yanked off the tarp that hid them.

There were at least a hundred of them in different poses and sizes. In some he filled the whole canvas; in others, his face was as tiny as the toy she held in her mouth. The colors in the background varied, but he was always painted with a tinge of blue, be it eyes, hooves, even blue nostrils on one. And it was always just his head, and the front half of his body—did she ever realize that? A hundred painted horses and not one with hind legs, a rear end, or a tail? She'd been painting him ever since she picked up a brush at the age of five. She'd always thought painting the front half of the horse was an artistic choice. She'd been wrong. All this time. She wasn't just expressing herself as an artist. She'd been trying to tell herself something. All these years, she'd been painting a message to herself. All these years, she'd been painting her other half.

Chapter 8

It would be easy enough to blame the bottle of rare scotch. But who was responsible for taking it out of the cupboard, unscrewing the cap, and taking the first of many sips? She wasn't used to drinking alcohol. Already having a problem with balance, she never liked the feeling of being tipsy; it was akin to vertigo, and even though she could usually handle a glass of wine with dinner, or one or two beers with Alan on the deck, anything stronger would send her body spinning in the most unpleasant way. She didn't want a carousel in her head.

She could blame dumb luck. After all, she'd never, ever, seen Mike come into the studio on a Sunday, and they'd been sharing the space for five years. In one way, she was grateful he appeared; at least he took the rest of the bottle of scotch away from her. In her state she might have finished it off. She was sitting in the middle of her horse paintings and quite drunk when he came in. She had the paintings spread out on the floor, as if waiting for them to speak to her, tell her the story of her missing half. In some, the horse looked sad. In most, he looked angry, his head tossed back, his nostrils flaring. In many his two front legs were reared up, and with his lower body hacked off, looked like a ghostly equestrian specter rising out of the heavens. From the shocking white of blank canvases to the blues and grays and blacks of backless horses flailing their hooves through swirling clouds, their neighs and whinnies fell on deaf ears. Why couldn't she remember her sister? Nine months in the womb. Did they hold hands? Kiss? Kick each other in the groin? Wrestle with the umbilical cord, try and pull it apart like a wishbone? Three years together as toddlers, a whole life, a secret language. She never questioned that most of her memories started at the age of four.

From somewhere behind her, Mike entered the studio and flashed the lights. This was the protocol they had set up in the beginning. Lacey didn't like people sneaking up on her. But this time she didn't even notice the lights blinking on and off. She was too taken with her thoughts, her inner carousel of sawed-off horses spinning. She didn't even feel his footsteps or see his shadow stretch along the wall beside her. A hand touched her shoulder and she jumped. Mike's expensive scotch sloshed out of the bottle, coating both of them in sticky sweet. They stared at each other, equally surprised. Lacey watched Mike's face register disbelief and then horror as he realized that the near-empty bottle in her hand was none other than his prized bottle.

"I'm sorry," Lacey said, using her voice. Being drunk and deaf, it wasn't a pretty sound. Mike opened his mouth, but there was nothing for Lacey to lip-read, for nothing came out. She started crying. She didn't want pity, she just couldn't take any more of this day. "I'll pay for it," she said, holding up the bottle, sloshing some more. Mike took it out of her hands and turned away from her. Oh no. How angry was he? She couldn't tell. His face was blurry, and he was turning away from her.

She liked Mike. Sometimes when they were alone in the space, she found herself watching him, totally absorbed in his work: sawing, soldering, hammering. Then came the part she liked best. He'd take his safety goggles off and stand back, contemplating his creation. It was "eye-dropping" on these private moments that made Lacey feel as if she could understand his thoughts, live inside his creative dream.

He was tall with dark curly hair and green eyes. He had muscles from carving through steel and wood. His nose was perhaps a little too big for his face, maybe his eyebrows a little too bushy, but his imperfections made him appear friendlier, more accessible. Lacey could tell he had a nice laugh, even though she could only see it. Mostly he kept to himself. Sometimes they'd chat by writing back and forth, sometimes they shared magazine articles or books. He knew a few signs, but more often than not they conversed in writing. He never tried to hit on Lacey, nor had she ever dreamed of seducing him.

"I'll pay for it," Lacey said, stumbling after Mike. He didn't even turn around. She felt like she was throwing her voice down an endless well. He disappeared into the kitchen. Lacey followed, wondering how she could make this right. He must really hate her. But when he turned toward her, he was holding a glass of water and a towel. He brought the towel up to her face and began to dab away the scotch and tears. His kindness ignited a flame of longing in Lacey, and the wall of denial she'd spent all morning assembling, brick by brick, collapsed. In an instant she was sobbing against his chest.

"Shh," he said, even though she couldn't hear him. "It's okay." He stroked her hair. She laced her hands behind his neck. She pulled him closer. She just needed to be held. She knew it should have been Alan. She knew it *would* have been Alan if only she had told him what happened at the bookstore. *I have a twin sister* was all she had to say. *I have a twin sister.*

Mike felt different from Alan, he smelled different from Alan. Not good, not bad, just different. One second she was wondering what it would be like to kiss him, the next she was leaning in to find out. She channeled all the day's frustrations into his lips. It was a gentle attack, an act of release. She pressed him against the kitchen counter so she could lean all the way into him. She reached down, put her hands over the outside of his jeans. She should stop. It was not too late. So far they'd just shared a little kiss, a one-way grope. They would part, awkward, yes, but it would soon be forgotten. She was drunk. Drunk men pawed at sober women all the time; surely she'd be forgiven. She could stop now and confess everything to Alan:

My biological parents didn't die tragically at a young age, they threw me away like a piece of trash and kept the perfect one. Oh, and I stole a bottle of Mike's scotch and apologized by sticking my tongue in his mouth and my hand down his pants. Are we good?

No, it was too late, and even if it wasn't, she wasn't stopping. She unbuttoned his snap, pulled down the zipper. Did it make a ripping noise? Was it silent? He pulled away. He tried to get her to look at him. She wouldn't. She started undressing as she backed up toward the couch. She pulled her T-shirt off in one go. The bra was next. She didn't stop even though he was zipping up. When she felt her backside touch the couch, she reached down and unzipped her jeans. She locked eyes with Mike. He looked stunned and hesitant, but made no move to stop her. This made it easy on Lacey to keep going, having someone else to blame. She slipped out of her jeans and lay down on the couch. Then she slowly pulled her panties off and pulled her knees up as Mike watched. In a second, deliberate movement, she spread them. Mike didn't need a sky writer. Message "Sent" and "Received."

In her imagination:

He climbed on top of her, smothering her with the weight of his body, crushing his lips to hers, exploring her with his fingers. The first time he tried to enter her, he missed. *Whoops, a little too far to the left, try again—no, that's too low—he doesn't think I want it THERE, does he? No, he just slipped. Is he drunk too? Should I help guide him in? The Deaf leading the blind? AAAAAAA. Bingo! You're in—oh God, yes. Yes, yes, yes. I'm not really doing this, am I? Shut up, it feels good. I'm sorry, Alan, but it does. Don't say his name, don't see his face, stop, stop, stop. Oh God, don't stop. Don't stop. I just want to forget. I want a few fucking seconds to forget.*

In reality:

He stood there, staring at her. Then he jerked his head toward the front door. Lacey saw the look on his face, and then of course she knew.

She offered Alan no explanation as to why she was drunk, crying, and spread-eagle in front of another man on the used leather couch. In their six years together, she had never cheated on Alan, not even close. The ceiling was really spinning now; it was just too much of an effort to sit up. That all changed when she saw Alan taking a swing at Mike. She rolled off the couch in a hopeless effort to stop him.

She didn't bang her head on purpose, but in the end it saved Mike another punch. Alan had just landed one on Mike's nose; blood gushed from his left nostril. Mike put his hands up to his face, trying to shield himself as he backed away. He didn't attempt to hit Alan back; he was an artist, not a fighter.

Lacey fell face forward onto the edge of the coffee table, which ironically was made by Mike. He got to hit back after all, except it was Lacey who took the blow. The table was solid wood framed in steel. A beautiful piece of functional art, but not when you're smashing into it face-first. Her left eye took the brunt of it as her hands slipped on the side, impaling her palms with little splinters. Pain seared through her frontal lobe, and blood trickled down her cheek.

Lacey wondered if Alan believed in a just God at that moment or, at least, Good Old Karma. She certainly did. Luckily, it turned out to be just her eyebrow that was slashed; her eye was still intact. She knew she was an almost-cheater and all, but she didn't think she deserved to be struck blind. Just because Helen Keller lived an amazing life, didn't mean it was the lifestyle for her. Alan must have yelled at Mike to get out, for he was promptly heading for the exit. Lacey stared at the back of his head as he left and couldn't help wondering—had he been turned on at all?

Alan brought her ice in a towel, held it while she dressed, handed it to her when she was clothed. It was the second time a man had handed her a towel today. What were the odds of that? What were the odds of having an identical twin sister you never knew existed? The absurdity almost made her laugh, and she had to use every ounce of energy not to. Alan wouldn't have understood. She sat on the floor with her back against the couch and held the ice-filled towel up to her wound, leaving only her right eye free to meet Alan's equally cold stare. He sat in the La-Z-Boy chair, leaning forward, elbows on knees, chin on fists, indignant, righteous, and pained.

"Nothing happened," Lacey signed. Her signs were jerky, slurred.

"Are you kidding me?" Alan said.

"He didn't do anything," Lacey said. "He just stood there."

"What did you do, Lacey? What the hell were you doing?"

I have a sister, she thought. Followed by *you're never going to forgive me.* Then something caught Alan's eye and he flew off the chair and stood next to one of Lacey's easels. He was looking at the large sketch pad where Lacey had written the cons of getting married for Robert. Lacey watched Alan's shoulders tense.

"You knew?" he said, turning around and pointing to *Engagement Ring.* Lacey looked away. "Divorce. Fat. Paranoid. The End of Love." Alan paced with each utterance, walking back and forth on a four-foot path he cut out for himself in front of Lacey. Then he slumped back into the chair and alternated between staring at the list and staring at her. She knew he was about to cry and she couldn't watch. She just couldn't take it.

"Where's Rookie?" Lacey said. At first, Alan glared at her as if it were the worst possible thing she could've said. But after a minute, he too looked around. Then, a strange feeling invaded Lacey's legs. It felt as if someone were *chewing* on them. She shook them out, but the feeling remained. "Shit," she said, not bothering to sign. She was still drunk, but this time she made every effort to haul herself up. Once she was on her feet, she stumbled in the direction of her work space.

She saw Rookie just ahead, splayed out on one of her horse paintings, jaw gnashing up and down. She dropped the towel and attempted a run. She wasn't even thinking about Alan or what he'd just caught her doing; she felt as if she were going to die. She fell to her knees in front of Rookie and pried his jaws open with her hands. He fought her with his paws, but she was stronger and more determined. She reached into his hot, pink mouth and pulled out the drool-smeared, severed toy horse. Alan must have thought she was trying to save Rookie from choking, for he picked up Rookie and said, "He's all right, he's all right." But Lacey was still examining her horse. Something about her expression must have finally clued him in, for Alan set Rookie on the floor, knelt in front of Lacey, and signed, "What the fuck is going on?"

Lacey looked at Alan. "Me nothing," she signed back. "Damaged. Parents throw. Trash. Hearing twin keep. Hearing twin keep. Sister. Sister sister sister sister sister sister."

Chapter 9

Monica Bowman closed her eyes and listened to the murmur of the crowd. This was the part she loved best. A few stolen moments before she went on, listening from the wings, or in this case, partitioned cubicle walls, allowing the overlapping voices from the audience to rush over her, empower her. She was here to give them hope, yet they gave her strength. She was happy to hear male voices in the mix; when she started out, it had been all females. But the messages were powerful enough to transcend gender, and although part of her hated to admit it, having males take her seriously had tremendously boosted her career. Not only was *The Architect of Your Soul* rising in the ranks on Amazon, but ever since the men started coming, her workshop attendance had doubled.

You are a unique individual. There is no one and never will be anyone like you ever again. Harness your individuality! Change your blueprints, change your life. You are the Architect of Your Soul.

She could give the workshop in her sleep. Joe, her fiancé and silent partner in crime, had seen to it. She wanted to give him the credit, if not all of it, then at least share it, but Joe wouldn't hear of it. He didn't want his colleagues making fun of him for one—they weren't the "new age type," and besides, he said, the idea would sell better coming from a gorgeous young woman.

He loved her, he was helping her launch a career, supporting her creative endeavors. And some of the ideas had been all hers, hadn't they? Although not everything was orchestrated the way she wanted it. The book belonged to her, but the enterprise, Help Yourself Inc.!, a series of motivational workshops, belonged to Josh Paris. Which explained the disco lights, confetti, and "Celebrate Good Times" that blasted at every interval. Not to mention the required sales pitches of all the other motivational books in the series. "Enterprise" was right; sometimes it all felt alien to Monica, and she prayed in the middle of some workshops that someone would just beam her up and she could be done with this workshop, and this life, altogether.

Every job had its downside; she was lucky, she reminded herself. *I'm helping people. I am helping people.*

"Ladies and gentlemen, I give you Monica Bowman." At her assistant Tina's introduction, the audience broke into applause. Monica touched the small plastic bottle in her blazer pocket just before she walked through the swirling flakes of colored paper falling from the ceiling. She stood center stage and lifted her arms.

"Hello, Boston." She waited for the response. They shouted hello back, but it was not quite the level of hysteria she'd contractually promised to generate. "I said, 'Hello, Boston.' " This time they erupted into cheers; the cynics clapped only slightly louder, and the people pleasers leapt to their feet. They'd have sore throats tomorrow. "This is my hometown," Monica shouted before they had completely died down. "It's good to be home." More shouts, a few whistles. "As you know, I am Monica Bowman, and I am the Architect of My Soul." The loudest response yet. Monica allowed this one to completely die down before continuing. "But I am not the only one. You are all the architects of your souls. So why, some of you may ask, does life seem so unfair? Why are some of you living in broken-down RVs in the middle of nowhere, while the person next to you is luxuriating in a castle in the sky?" Monica had this down to a science: the split second it would take for the audience to glance at the person next to them, the laughter the room would generate when they caught on to the joke, the way they'd eventually settle in to listen, even the cynics. She was always attuned to their energy and would monitor her movements, her voice, and her cadence to match.

"It's not fate, or luck of the draw, that determines your life's abode, my friends. It's you. It's the choices you've made up until now. And if you love that RV, then by all means, stay and enjoy, but if you want the castle in the sky, then stick with me this weekend, because I'm going to let you in on a powerful secret. You can have it. You can build it. You are not stuck with the blueprint you've been given. It's as simple as ripping it up and starting a new one. That's it. That's the message. Sound simple? It is. Sound powerful? It can change your life. And I'll spend the rest of the weekend showing you how."

Tina joined her in passing out booklets and breaking the crowd into small groups for the first series of exercises and discussions. Once Monica got through the embarrassing bits, and the small groups began sharing the "Fatal Flaws in their Foundations," time flew. Monica truly wanted to send these people home with renewed hope, and once that desire kicked in, she felt truly alive. And the more Monica did the workshop, the more she realized people were basically all the same. They varied in dress, and background, and culture, but their inner cries were all the same:

I work too much.
I hate my job, husband, kids, house.
I'm broke.
I'm fat.
I don't have the time.
I'm tired all the time.
I'm too old. (A twenty-five-year-old girl said this once, sobbing as she lamented her recent birthday.)
I'm not smart enough, pretty enough, thin enough, young enough, lucky enough—

Enough, Monica wanted to shout sometimes. *Just—enough.* These are the moments she forgot she was here to help them, she had a job to do. She'd give another pep talk after the small-group activity, just to stop them from piercing themselves with their forks during lunch, and promised when they got back she'd teach them to "Build a Better Base." Confetti would fly again, and disco music and lights would assure them that good times were coming. Sometimes she fully expected people to walk out, tell her she was full of crap, never return.

They hardly ever did. It's the only thing that kept her going. By the end of the day, participants seemed to really be getting the hang of it, and those brave enough came up to the front of the room to demonstrate how they could go about "Redecorating their Rooms." Monica would assign them a little homework before dismissing them, a visualization exercise they should be ready to share the next morning. Tina gave her a thumbs-up at the back of the room, and the lights and music played, indicating their day was done.

Monica left Tina to staff the book sales at the back of the room, and slipped out a side door. She was longing to get back to the privacy of her room. But just as the elevator doors were about to close, hands shot in and pried them back open. Tina, a five-foot-two bundle of sparks, smiled from the other side. Her short blond hair, cut like a pixie, was always slightly more spiked at the end of the day, as if the excitement they'd generated during the afternoon had actually lifted her roots. Green confetti clung to her left cheek.

"Don't forget your interview," she said. "Seven o'clock by the pool."

"Oh, right," Monica said. "I forgot all about it."

"He's dreamy," Tina said.

"He's here?" Monica asked.

Tina nodded. "I'll stand in for you if you want," she said with a smile and a raise of her dainty eyebrows. Monica was sorely tempted to take her up on the offer; all she wanted was a hot bath and a glass of wine.

"Join us if you'd like," Monica said. "But I think I should be there."

"No prob," Tina said. "Just—you know—do something about that hair, will you?" Monica touched her hair. Tina laughed. "And that body, and those eyes, and no matter what you do, don't throw your head back and laugh. This guy is mine, do you hear me? I've already blueprinted him." Monica laughed. Tina pointed at her. "That's what I'm talking about," she said. "Don't do that." Monica waved her away.

"See you at seven," she said.

"Feel free to make it eight," Tina said as the elevator doors closed.

Monica's new hotel room was better than the first one they gave her. All it took was a polite but firm phone call. She didn't want a view of the parking lot, did they have anything facing the pool? She was proud of herself as she stood before the open window, staring down at the Olympic-sized outdoor pool, where any minute the lights surrounding it would start to glow and the table and chairs beyond it would fill with guests drinking wine and laughing into the night. Soon she would be one of the guests sitting down there, answering questions about her workshop for yet another newspaper reporter. A dreamy reporter, apparently.

Monica kicked off her pumps and removed her gray blazer. Her feet were killing her. She sat on the edge of the bed and rubbed them. She flung herself back on the bed and took deep, cleansing breaths. There was always a slight letdown at the end of the day, a natural consequence of expending so much energy, she supposed. She would get the interview over with, get a good night's sleep, and be raring to go tomorrow. Tomorrow was a new day. She would even think about leaving the pills up in the room.

Maybe she'd have a glass of wine with the dreamy reporter. But just one; she was a lightweight when it came to alcohol. *You've heard of load-bearing walls, right?* she could hear Joe say. *Well, let's put something in the book about the load your soul can bear. It's important to know the exact weight you can handle. Too little and you're not carrying your full potential; too much and you'll collapse!*

Your book is total crap. Monica froze. The voice, her internal critic, was back. So much for cleansing breaths.

She sat up, turned, and caught sight of her reflection in the window, a ghostly version of herself. She was surprised by what she saw. *You look sad,* she thought. *Why doesn't anyone ever notice?* She peeled off her hose and then closed the curtains before taking off the rest of her clothes. She stood in front of the closed curtains in her bra and panties, and entertained a strange urge to rip them open, stand there, and see if anyone would notice her. She'd never been an exhibitionist, and she'd no intention of starting now, but she was amazed that the thought had even crossed her mind, like a person discovering a hidden talent.

Don't dress sexy, she heard Tina tease. She should probably try and call Joe before the interview. Let him know how the day went. She walked over to the dresser where she'd tossed her purse and was about to go for her phone when she remembered. He was working on plans for a huge bid this weekend. Should she call anyway? *Guess what I'm wearing?*

Joe wouldn't be amused. *Maybe the dreamy reporter will.* What was wrong with her? Childish, that's what she was this evening. She should call her parents. But then she remembered they were going to the cabin this weekend, getting ready for Aunt Grace's big party. Forty-something, Aunt Grace would never tell. Monica and Joe and Tina would be headed to the cabin after the weekend. Monica was actually looking forward to it for once.

At least it would take her mind off herself for a while. Off the bottle of pills in her pocket. Off the feeling that she was being watched, even though she knew better, she knew no one was there. It didn't stop her from turning and looking, sometimes several times a day. Was she going crazy? Did she inherit the Bowmans' "delicate states of mind," as her mother described the family she'd married into? She was definitely having a glass of wine with Mr. Dreamy. It was too bad the hotel didn't allow dogs; it would be nice to have Snookie to cuddle with tonight. She wondered, as she put on a rose sundress and slipped on her gold flip-flops, if it was a bad sign that it was Snookie, and not Joe, that she wanted to cuddle with.

* * *

Tina was already at the poolside table, cornering the market on the head-thrown-back-in-laughter. In fact, Monica heard her before she spotted her. Oh, how she envied Tina's frivolity. Some days Monica thought Tina should be the one giving the workshops; she certainly had the gusto. Despite her pixielike nature and light blond hair, she wasn't exactly a beauty. Her nose was just a little too long, her eyes a tad too close together, but when it came to her personality, she outshone everyone; males and females alike were attracted to her endless enthusiasm. Monica knew within ten minutes of interviewing her that she would be her assistant. They'd been together two years now, and Monica knew she wouldn't have come this far without her. Tina's only downfall was men. Although she tried to brush it off with her usual carefree approach, Tina wanted to fall in love, get married, and have babies. Monica tried to tell her the book taught you how to change things you could control in life, not the randomness of love, but Tina was adamant she could use it to "hook a husband." And from the sounds of her, she was in the middle of trying to bait one as they spoke.

Maybe Monica should turn around and go back to the room, let Tina have the hunk all to herself. But it wasn't Tina's book, so Monica kept walking to the table. She'd make it short, answer the questions, then leave the potential lovebirds alone. Just as she rounded the corner, she saw him. He looked up, and their eyes locked. He was staring at her so intently she had to tell herself to keep moving. She smiled, although she felt slightly sick. He was very good-looking, all right; dreamy was an apt description. He had thick waves of dark hair, a strong face, and green eyes that surely drew as many compliments as her ice blue ones. He stood as she approached, and held out his hand. Monica didn't dare look at Tina, whose laughter had abruptly stopped.

"Hi, I'm Monica," she said as their hands touched. He smiled as he gripped her hand in his, but shook his head slightly, as if he couldn't quite believe he was meeting her. Monica felt her face flush; she wasn't that famous.

"I'm Mike," he said.

"Sit down," Tina said, pulling out a chair. It was only then that Monica realized they hadn't let go of each other's hands. Monica pulled away first, and he waited for her to take her seat before taking his own.

"This is so weird," he said, gazing at her. Monica laughed, and glanced at Tina. Tina laughed too, but whereas Monica's was nervous, hers was hollow.

"I take it you're a fan?" Monica asked.

"A fan?" He sounded genuinely confused.

"Of the book," Monica said quickly. "I didn't mean me."

"Oh yes, the book," Mike said. "That's totally why this is so weird." He continued to smile, but no more words fell from his lips.

"Who wants a drink?" Tina said.

"A glass of Chardonnay would be great," Monica said. Mike reached for his wallet.

"I'll get it," Tina said. "You two can start the interview—get it over with—while I get the drinks, then we can just—relax and enjoy." *Don't be desperate,* Monica wanted to say. But who was she to judge? A motivational speaker who carried around a bottle of sleeping pills because just having them on hand calmed her down, that's who she was.

"What would you like, Mike?" Tina said. She gave a little hoot at the rhyme as she waited.

"Uh—Chardonnay for me too," he said.

"Really," Tina said. "I pegged you as a Pilsner Urquell guy." She winked. "I'm a martini girl." Mike smiled and held out his hands.

"I'm open," he said. "Surprise me." Tina laughed and rocked up on her toes.

"I like the sound of that," she said. "Be right back." Monica gazed out at the pool. The sun was just starting to set, the lights barely glowing but visible. Potted plants and shrubs completed the outdoor Eden. It was romantic, and he was gorgeous—she had to face it, he was gorgeous. That's why her heart was tripping, why the thought of being alone with him made her giddy.

"Where are you from?" she asked.

"Philadelphia," he said. She frowned. "Is something wrong?"

"No—I just—assumed you were from a Boston paper."

"Oh. Right. That makes sense."

"What paper are you from?"

"Um. It's more of a local artists' co-op," he said.

"Oh. Cool."

"Yeah. We have some of Philly's most talented people in the co-op, if I do say so myself."

"Are you a writer too?"

"I'm a sculptor, actually."

"Really?" Monica said. Dreamy and artistic. She'd better not have more than one glass of wine. "What's your medium?"

"I've worked with everything over the years, but right now I'm dabbling in steel." Dabbling in steel. Very sexy. Luckily, she didn't say this.

"I'm impressed," she said instead. "Maybe I should be interviewing you."

"Believe me," he said. "I'd much rather hear about you." He reached into his back pocket and pulled out a piece of paper. He laid it on the table and smoothed it out. Most reporters had little notebooks with them, or even tape recorders. He was different. Monica felt herself relax.

"I don't understand," she said. "Why are you interviewing me? I'm not from Philadelphia."

"I know, I know," he said. "But—um—your work has caught the eye of several members of our co-op—and, uh—well, to tell you the truth, we needed a little filler in our next newsletter."

"Oh," Monica said. "I see." This would be much better than a stuffy interview with a real newspaper. A co-op of artists wanting to interview her. How cool.

"Do you have a pen?" Mike asked. Tina came back with the drinks, and Monica admonished herself for being disappointed as she handed Mike a pen.

"You have a beautiful voice," Mike said suddenly. Tina's head jerked in Monica's direction.

"Were you singing while I was gone?" she asked.

"No," Monica said.

"No," Mike said. "It's just—great to hear you talk."

"Huh," Tina said. She looked at Monica and said, "It *is* nice to hear you talk. I mean, it's not like I have to listen to you yak all day long." She moved her hand in a talking-puppet position, opening and closing her fingers to signify the "yak, yak, yak" portion of her statement. Then she gave a laugh as if trying to underscore it was a joke. Finally, Tina picked up her martini and took a long sip. Monica picked up her wine and did the same.

"So," Mike said. "Let's just go through these questions, shall we?" Monica nodded. "Okay. First question. Where are you from?"

"Boston," Monica said.

"Right," Mike said. He wrote something on the piece of paper.

"Do you have a big family?"

"No. Just me and my parents as far as immediate family goes." Mike started to write, then hesitated. He looked at Monica. She felt her heart constrict. He looked—pained.

"No brothers," he said. He cleared his throat. "Or—a sister?"

"Nope," Monica said. "Just me."

"I have three sisters," Tina said. "My poor father."

"Do you have brothers or sisters?" Monica asked Mike.

"Me? Yeah. I have two brothers. One older, one younger."

"Stuck in the middle with you," Tina sang. When no one commented or joined in, she stopped. Then her tongue darted out and slowly licked the rim of her glass.

"Okay. Two parents. No sister." Mike looked at Monica before reading the next question. He cleared his throat again.

"I saw on your Web site that you have a dog," he said.

"Snookie," Monica said. "My puggle." The pained look was back on Mike's face.

"Do you have—uh—proof?" he said.

"Excuse me?"

"I mean—uh—do you have pictures of Snookie?"

"I'm sorry," Monica said. "Did you say 'proof'?"

"I might have," Mike said. "I'm not a writer. I just—thought maybe you could show me a picture of your dog"—he glanced at the paper again—"or, uh, maybe call someone that has the dog—so I can—uh—hear him bark."

"You're kidding, right?" Monica looked around. "I'm being pranked, right?" She threw her head back and laughed. Tina kicked her under the table. Monica tried to get it together. "Call Snookie so you can hear him bark. That's funny." Mike laughed too. He held up the paper with a shrug.

"You're right," he said. "That's ridiculous. Never mind. Um—are your parents both alive?"

"Yes," Monica said.

"Are they, um—you know—healthy and—in their right minds?"

"Tina," Monica said. "You're setting me up." Tina shook her head no. Monica slowly turned back to Mike and stared at him. "Are my parents in their right mind?" she said as if she were pondering the question. "I'm not sure. Should I call them up? Would you like to hear them bark?"

"Ha!" Tina said. "Ha-ha."

"How do you feel about bats?" Mike said. His ears were turning red as he started reading the questions rapid-fire. "How old were you when you—oh God, I can't ask that one—um—are you any good at Photoshop, have you ever stolen someone's identity—"

"Enough," Monica said, holding her hand up. "Just stop." The laughter rolled out of her, he was keeping such a straight face. If Tina wasn't behind this, then who was? Joe? No, Joe would never be that spontaneous.

"Do you have a birthmark on your, uh—well, it's the hip area—uh—a half-moon—just a little to the left—" Monica's laughter slammed shut. She flew out of her chair. It took everything she had not to touch the little birthmark, a half-moon, just above her pelvic bone. How did he know?

"Who are you?" she asked.

"I'm so sorry," he said, throwing the questions down and standing. "These aren't my questions."

"Have you been watching me?"

"Watching you? No. God no."

"I should call the police."

"Monica," Tina said. "Calm down."

"It's not like that," Mike said. "I swear to God it's nothing like that. I would never. I'm not—these questions aren't mine."

"Whose are they?" He didn't answer. "Answer me," Monica said. "Were they written by a pervert or a fourth grader?"

"Neither. But believe me. If it were me, I'd be asking you about your writing process and—your visions as an artist—and I'd sure as hell want to know if it was your idea to play 'Celebrate Good Times'—"

"You were there?" Monica asked. "You were at the workshop?"

"Just the tail end of it. And—I'd ask you if you had a boyfriend. I'd definitely ask you that." Tina slunk in her chair, finished off her martini in one gulp.

"What did you think of it?" Monica demanded.

"What?" Mike said.

"My workshop."

"Oh. Like I said—I just caught the tail end—"

"So what did you think of that?"

"I think you—you are very engaging—I just didn't get all the disco stuff."

"That's not mine. The disco stuff is not mine."

"I didn't think so. See? It didn't fit. You seem so genuine, even when you're spouting—" Mike stopped himself.

"Spouting? Now I'm spouting?"

"Not—all the time—sometimes you were right on the mark—incredibly genuine, you know. You had me on the edge of my seat. Really." Monica couldn't believe this guy. He was backpedaling. Spouting. He said she was spouting. He saw through her! He knew she was full of shit, he saw right through her. Even worse, he was trying to spare her feelings. She hated that. She suddenly hated him. A lot. She hated him a lot. *Go,* she wanted to shout at Tina, *leave us alone.* Tina didn't budge.

"How did you know about my birthmark?" Monica said.

"It's not my question. You must have mentioned it—on your Web site, in another article, in the book—I don't know."

"How did you get that black eye?" Monica asked. It was faint, but he definitely had a black eye; there was enough of a hint of it.

"Monica," Tina said.

"Did you startle someone else with your invasive questions and someone clocked you?" Monica asked.

"Actually," Mike said, "it was a total misunderstanding. Unprovoked."

"I doubt that," Monica said.

"I don't care," Mike said. "Still the truth. Don't you talk a lot about truth?" They stared at each other. God, he was gorgeous. Who hit him? She wanted to touch it, kiss it, lick it. She wanted to make him feel better. She wanted him to make her feel better. She wanted to push him in the pool, jump in after him, and plaster her wet body to his. What was she doing? What was she thinking? Oh God, could he tell what she was thinking? He was looking at her like he could tell what she was thinking. Was he smiling? He wasn't smiling, was he?

"I'm sorry," Monica said. "I have to go." She glanced at Tina. "I'm sure my assistant would be happy to answer any more of your questions." Tina sat up straight.

"Love to," Tina said.

"Monica," Mike said. "I'm so sorry." There it was again, the squeezing of her heart. Who was this guy? Why did part of her want to kick Tina to the curb and stay up all night drinking wine and answering his bizarre questions? Then again, what if he was a sick pervert and she was siccing him on Tina?

"Don't be too late," Monica said. "We have an early start tomorrow."

"No problem, boss," Tina said.

"Don't forget," Monica said, pointing behind her. "I'm right up there." Now, why did she say that? If he was a sick pervert, he now knew where she was staying.

"I wish you wouldn't go," Mike said. "I wish I could start over."

"It's fine," Monica said. "I'm just tired."

"Off to bed, then, boss," Tina said. "I've got it from here."

Back in her hotel room, Monica slipped into a tub of hot water and submerged herself until her lips were barely above the water. Oh, if they could see her now, great advisor, architect of her soul, wishing she could slip under the bubbles and drown. They would definitely want their money back. Baths were supposed to be calming. She was supposed to feel better. Instead, her fists were clenched, her heart was racing, and she was using every ounce of energy she had not to run to the curtains and see if Mike and Tina were still out there. Her hand trailed down to the tiny birthmark. Had she mentioned it in an interview?

Definitely not. And it wasn't on her Web site or in the book, she was sure of it. Did he actually say he wanted her to call someone so he could hear Snookie bark? He was off his head. Totally off his head. He was probably Ted Bundy. A charming sculptor / serial killer. He probably encased his corpses in steel. And she'd left Tina alone with him! She had to call her, warn her. Yet Tina had been there to hear the whole thing, and she was still hanging on. Desperate, the woman was so desperate—

Monica slumped farther down into the tub. He wasn't a serial killer. And he wasn't comfortable lying. Which is why he got all squirmy when she asked what he thought of her workshop. He hated it. She could tell.

She was so absorbed with her thoughts, it took her a while to realize the phone was ringing. She climbed out of the tub, swiped a towel from the rack, and wrapped it around her wet body. She padded out of the bathroom and headed for the bedside phone, leaving wet footprints in her wake. She stubbed her toe on the bed and fell forward. She grasped for the handle and banged her knee into the end table. Her hands slipped again on the receiver, and she whacked her chin with the phone before she finally brought it up to her mouth. She was laughing when she said, "Hello." She wouldn't have to take pills or drown herself after all; at this rate, her own clumsiness would do her in.

There was no answer. "Hello?" she said again. Suddenly, she wanted someone to be there, someone to talk to. No one spoke, but they were still on the line, she could hear them. She lay down on the bed, holding the phone, oddly comforted by the strange silence. "Talk to me," she said. "Are you there?" Was it him? What was she doing? There was another moment of breath-filled silence, then a distinct click, followed by the hollow rejection of a dial tone. Disappointment engulfed Monica. She felt like a child playing a game of telephone with cans connected by a string. The other can had been dropped in the dirt, abandoning Monica as she held up her end, straining to hear something, anything, in the silence.

Chapter 10

"I can't believe her," Monica said. "I just can't believe her." Joe didn't answer right away. He was pushing eighty miles an hour in an attempt to get them there. Monica clutched the door handle, something she did that Joe absolutely hated, and prayed he wouldn't retaliate by kicking the Toyota up to ninety.

"He seems nice," Joe said. "Tina seems crazy about him."

"She just met him," Monica said. "She's desperate." Monica tried the radio again, but the closer they got to Moosehead Lake, the worse the reception. She clicked it off in disgust.

"They can go to the cabin without us," Monica said. "Let's go somewhere else. Anywhere else."

"I don't get you," Joe said without slowing down. "It's paradise. The woods, the shooting range, a fully stocked kitchen— how many fireplaces?" Monica took a deep breath. She didn't want to be a bad sport but she certainly didn't want to listen to Joe wax poetic about the hunting cabin. There were three fireplaces, but she didn't offer this.

"And you love hiking," Joe said. "What is it with you and that cabin?"

Monica looked out the window, tried to lose herself in the trees hugging the highway, the oblivious blur of green. What was it about the hunting cabin that filled her with dread? She had good memories of target shooting with the Colonel, or berry picking with her mother, even a few family Scrabble games around the fireplace, yet she still dreaded going there. And as Joe implied, "cabin" was a misnomer; it was indeed a fully equipped hunting lodge, twice the size of the Victorian home where Monica grew up. There were woods to lose yourself in, vines lying in wait across creeks, fields of grass to play hide-and-seek, and furtive deer (those lucky enough not to be shot, stuffed, and mounted in the Colonel's study) skirting through tall pines.

"I don't know," Monica said. "I guess it makes me feel like a little kid again, under my mother's shadow and my father's thumb." And then there were the nightmares. As far back as Monica could remember, every bad dream she ever had revolved around the cabin. She'd be lost in the woods, staggering through overgrown bushes, screaming for help. Often she was barefoot and bloody, dressed in torn and dirty rags, as if she'd been plucked out of "Hansel and Gretel," having just escaped the witch's oven, wandering, searching for someone to save her.

"I love it there," Joe said. "Maybe it's a guy thing."

"You just like the moose head in the guest room," Monica teased, trying to lighten the mood. Joe put his hand up to his heart.

"His big, glassy eyes follow me wherever I go." Monica laughed. Joe gave her a quick glance and boyish smile before adjusting his glasses and focusing on the road. He was a good guy. Hard worker, very intelligent, he had the whole sexy-professor look going on. Sandy hair, wire-rim glasses, navy blue eyes. Tall and trim. Predictable. He liked golf, hunting, and planning. Oh, how he liked planning. Without Joe, there never would have been a book. And he truly liked people, went out of his way to be friendly. He absolutely adored her dad, and treated her mom like gold. Even Aunt Grace—

"Oh shit," Monica said. She slapped her hand on her knee.

"What?"

"I left Aunt Grace's present at home."

"That's it? You shouldn't startle me like that."

"We're only what? Forty minutes?"

"No."

"Joe."

"Honey, I'm not going back now. You can mail it."

"It's not the same."

"We have copies of the book in the back; you can give her one of those." Monica glanced in the backseat, where umpteen copies of *The Architect of Your Soul* were stacked up. Next to them, Snookie snored in his crate. Monica was dying to wake Snookie and cuddle him, but it would start a fight with Joe. He said taking Snookie out of the crate was like plucking a kid from its car seat. At least he was sleeping peacefully; he'd whined the first twenty minutes. *Here's your proof, Mike,* Monica thought. *Maybe I should wave Snookie out the window like a courtroom exhibit. Why is he here?*

To see you, to see you, to see you—

"Aunt Grace doesn't need the book," Monica snapped. She immediately felt guilty; it wasn't Joe's fault Mike was following them. But did he ever think about anything other than the book? Did he ever think it just might be total crap anyway? And why did Aunt Grace let the Colonel talk her into having her party at the hunting cabin anyway? They could have rented the Dew Drop Inn in Portland. Monica knew her aunt loved the quaint inn with views of the ocean, and the restaurant down the way with the best lobster and champagne for miles. This was all her father's idea. Grace always let the Colonel bully her. What a pair. Where the Colonel was hard, Aunt Grace was soft. She was like a hummingbird: precious, nervous, and fragile. Aunt Grace you loved, whereas the Colonel you feared. She had a smile line etched into her face, whereas he had a permanent crease across his forehead, deep as a trench behind enemy lines on the battlefield of his face. Maybe it was the age gap; Grace was fifteen years younger than her father. She was obviously a "whoops" baby. Maybe her grandparents had been easier on her.

"What's wrong?" Joe asked. "Did the workshop not go well this weekend?"

"Since you ask," Monica said, "several participants say they thought the disco lights and music were totally cheesy—not at all in line with my style."

"Talk to Josh Paris," Joe said. That was Joe. Practical. She'd only met Mike and he'd been completely passionate about her—well, maybe not her—but the stupid music and confetti— it was as if he were invested in her and her vision, cared about her as an artist. What the hell was she doing? She just met this guy. He didn't know her, he didn't care about her. Joe knew her. Joe cared about her. Thank God he couldn't read her mind. Monica put her hand on Joe's thigh.

"Let's pull over and have sex," she said. Joe swerved. The tires squealed and when they lurched back into their lane, Tina beeped at them. Joe tapped the horn and waved back.

"Jesus, Monica," he said. "Don't do that." Monica didn't dare look back. What was Mike thinking? What on earth were they finding to talk about? Was he grilling Tina about her? How did he know about her birthmark? It was still bugging her. His explanation was total BS. If there was one good thing about his coming, it was that she was going to force him to tell her how he knew. "Are you going to tell me what that was all about?" Joe asked.

"I was trying to be spontaneous," Monica said. "It's in my blueprint. Remember blueprints, Joe? Your idea, right out of 'our' book."

Make a map or blueprint of the life you want to live.

Goals became "rooms" with specific measurements; the book even included several drafts of architectural drawings so the reader could sketch in various blueprints. Later they'd be allowed to decorate it, and even switch out the decorations, showing that goals were permanent, but the routes by which you get there could be switched around, like adding a new throw pillow to a couch—

That had been Monica's contribution. There were a lot of fun and practical things in the book. She shouldn't be so cynical. But if it really worked, why wasn't Joe ravishing her by the roadside right now?

Because you can't blueprint other people. Exactly what Monica tried to tell Tina about Mike—

"Making love under a dead moose is spontaneous," Joe said, gently removing her hand. "Dying in a fiery crash is not."

Yes, you couldn't blueprint other people. So why should that stop her? Why couldn't she follow her plan anyway, without Joe? Monica was going to do just that. She unbuttoned her jeans and stuck her hands down her pants. It took Joe a lifetime to notice, and when he did he was anything but turned on.

"What are you doing?"

"Trying to arouse you."

"On the interstate? Really?"

"I'm in the mood."

"Tina and her boyfriend are behind us." Monica yanked her hands out of her pants.

"He's hardly her boyfriend," she said. "She just met the guy."

"What is with you today?"

"I want sex, okay?" Monica said. There, she'd said it. "I want passionate, exciting sex." Joe shook his head.

"We're going to your aunt's birthday party where your father—the Colonel—keeps a hundred and twenty-two polished rifles."

"Air rifles," Monica said.

"Honey, you can play with yourself all you want, but it's not happening." Joe was right. Between the moose, the rifles, and the endless target activities, there wouldn't be any spontaneous sex this weekend. They'd be lucky if they got through the weekend without the Colonel making Aunt Grace cry. That was the fragile part about her; she'd be smiling up to a point, but Richard eventually got under her skin, and family functions often dissolved into fights, which for Aunt Grace meant lots of tears. There wouldn't be any spontaneous sex this weekend— unless it was Tina and Mike.

Over her dead body—

What was wrong with her? She needed sex, that's what. It was a myth that men were the only ones who went crazy without it. Because Joe wasn't spontaneous anytime, anywhere. He'd never do it anywhere but a closed bedroom. Never in a million years would he take her in the woods, on the beach, against an abandoned building. And she knew, no matter what he said, or how many blueprints she drew up, he was never going to make love to her under that freaking moose.

The long, winding driveway leading up to the cabin was littered with cars. There would be a spot for Monica and Joe saved at the front of the line. Tina and Mike, who'd stopped at a shopping center just before the turnoff, would have to fend for themselves. Monica told Tina they didn't need to bring anything; she was annoyed they obviously didn't listen to her. Was Tina going to have a quickie with Mike in the car behind the Stop & Shop? And if she was, what business was it of hers?

The Colonel was holding court on the wraparound porch. He was holding his latest Thermal Pneumatic Double Pump Air Rifle in his arms, showing it off to an appreciative crowd. A box filled with cartons of eggs lay at his feet. He saw Monica, grinned, and pumped the rifle in acknowledgement. Joe waved his hand in a huge greeting, and his grin nearly swallowed his entire face. Poor Joe, her father was never going to love him like he wanted. Nobody would ever be good enough for his little girl, didn't Joe get that? It was heartbreaking to watch. The Colonel picked up an egg and hurled it at Joe.

"Duck," Monica said. But Joe stuck up his hand to catch it. It cracked on impact; yolk dripped out of his palm and onto the ground. "Dad," Monica said.

"Last one here's a rotten egg!" her father yelled.

"You should have saved it for Tina, then," Monica said. She reached into her purse and handed Joe a Kleenex. He was still grinning.

"Is that it?" he asked the Colonel, gesturing to the rifle in his hand. "Is that the new one?"

"Hot off the press," the Colonel said. "What do you think, offspring?" It didn't matter how many times Monica asked him to stop calling her that, at the very least in public, her father never wavered.

"It looks good," Monica said.

"Are you going out to the range?" Joe asked, eyeing the bucket of eggs. The range was a large fenced-off parcel of land in the back, set up for target practice.

"What else?" the Colonel said. "You think I'm making an omelet?" The crowd laughed.

"Dad," Monica said. He was always putting Joe down. And Joe, who loved the Colonel like his own father, never seemed to notice.

"Did you bring a rifle?" the Colonel asked.

"No, sir," Joe said. Monica pinched Joe's small love handles. How many times had she asked him not to call him "sir"?

"Well, I don't know what you're going to shoot with, then," the Colonel said. "Mine have been claimed."

"This is why I was driving so fast to get here," Joe whispered to Monica.

"Did I just hear you say you were speeding with my precious offspring in the car?" Richard belted out. Joe looked like a deer in one of her father's crosshairs.

"No. No, sir."

"Maybe Monica will let you borrow her rifle," the Colonel said loudly. Monica gave her father a look and shook her head. He grinned back. He really enjoyed giving Joe a hard time.

"Would you, Monica?" Joe asked.

"I don't have the slightest idea where it is," Monica said.

"Just saw it this morning," her father answered. "George," he called to the man behind him. "Would you bring us Monica's rifle? Joe wants to use it." Monica reached over to squeeze a warning into Joe's arm, but he'd already moved away from her, toward the Colonel. She should go inside instead of staying to witness the upcoming accident. Damage control, she told herself when she didn't make a move, although a teeny tiny, demented part of her wanted to see the look on Joe's face when George handed him her rifle. When it came to her father, would Joe ever learn?

Monica heard the laughter before she saw the rifle. George made his way through the crowd, then thrust it at Joe. It was Monica's tenth birthday gift: The Pink Pumpmaster. It was, as its name implied, completely pink. Joe turned red as laughter exploded from the crowd. Nobody laughed louder than the Colonel. To Joe's credit, he laughed too, although his face remained as bright as a Maine lobster.

"Very funny, Dad," Monica said. "It was my tenth birthday present," she told Joe. "Can you believe that?"

"You loved it," the Colonel said.

"I wanted a Madonna poster," Monica said.

"We gave you a poster," the Colonel said.

"Of a woodchuck with a target on its heart!" Monica said. Her father chuckled and picked up the bucket of eggs.

"Let's go," he said. "I like mine scrambled; how about you, Joe?"

Monica entered the cabin, grateful her father ended on a nicer note with Joe. The main entrance to the house opened directly into a large living room. The logs that made up the house had also been flattened, sanded, stained, and put down on the floors. Directly across from the front door stood the center-piece of the living room, a huge stone fireplace that rose all the way up to the ceiling, ending just underneath the overhang of the second floor. A large buck was mounted on the fireplace, and as usual, Monica tried not to look into his enormous glassy eyes.

How many people had they invited? It seemed more like a wedding than a birthday. She didn't even know half the people. Her mother was no doubt in the kitchen; Monica could smell the sweet aroma of a stove that had been in use all day, and guests were already nibbling appetizers off little china plates. On every single surface, Monica could see her mother had put down lace coasters. She picked one up as she moved through the room. She'd forgotten her mother's obsession with lace. It had been a while since she'd seen the whole collection: table-cloths, coasters, shams. What a pair, her parents. Rifles and lace.

To the left of the living room was the dining room, and just beyond that the kitchen. Monica made her way to the swinging door. Her mother came out just as she'd crossed the threshold of the dining room, wearing an apron and wielding an oven mitt. Monica waved and smiled. Relief flooded her mother's face as she swooped in and wrapped her in a hug.

"I was so worried," she said.

"Hello, hello, hello," Monica said. "The food smells delicious." Monica pulled back and kissed her mother on the cheek. Katherine Bowman brought her wrist closer to her eyes and squinted at the tiny watch adorning it. *She's so delicate,* Monica thought. *I could snap her in two.*

"Did you run into traffic?" her mother asked.

We certainly didn't stop for a quickie.

"Just the usual," Monica said. "But I forgot Aunt Grace's gift."

"Did you get my e-mail?" her mother said, ignoring her present-less plight. Monica followed her mother into the kitchen, hoping to busy herself for the lecture that was about to come. She rued the day her mother learned how to use the Internet. Her mother, the worrywart, sent her daily barrages: jokes, chain letters, and horror stories. The latest was how to stop a raging kitchen fire with nothing but a bag of flour and a sporty sock. The truth was, Monica had been deleting her mother's e-mails lately; she was swamped, and getting rid of them gave her little stabs of joy.

Monica said hello to the women helping out in the kitchen, kissing the ones she knew, politely shaking hands with the ones she didn't, and praying her mother would have enough food to stir, and poke, without doing it to her.

"I want to say hello to Aunt Grace," she said when her mother insisted she didn't need any help.

"She's in the back den," her mother said. Monica started to head out when she felt her mother grab her arm, squeezing her to the point of pain. "Wait," she said. "There's something I have to tell you." Her voice dropped to a low whisper.

"What?" Monica said.

"She's having one of her spells."

"A migraine?"

"It's more than that. She seems very confused. She's mixing things up in her mind."

"She's only in her forties, Mom—"

"I think she might be off her medication." Monica didn't know exactly what medication Aunt Grace was on; anytime she tried to figure it out, the conversation was always slammed shut. Bipolar, schizophrenic, simply depressed? Monica was dying to know, but her father's family prided itself on keeping secrets. Katherine leaned even closer to her daughter.

"Your father is thinking about finding her a home."

"What?"

"I don't want to get into all of this right now. I just wanted you to know—in case—she doesn't seem herself."

"My God," Monica said. "She's so young."

"She's spoiled, if you ask me," her mother said.

"Mom."

"I'm sorry. I know it's her birthday and all, but here she is making a scene again."

"She's not feeling well. You said it yourself."

"I know, I know. And maybe she's not. I can't help but think it's a cry for attention."

"I'm sure it wasn't easy growing up in Dad's shadow," Monica said.

"Stop blaming everything on your father."

"Mom." How was it she was only in the house a few minutes and they were already on each other's nerves? Were all families like this?

"Ask her if she'd like a cup of tea, or lemonade," her mother said, turning back to the stove. "God knows she's not going to ask for it herself."

Chapter 11

The back den, with windows overlooking the backyard and woods beyond, had always been Aunt Grace's favorite spot. Monica found her there, dozing alone on the love seat. Monica sat on one of the chairs next to her and watched Aunt Grace sleep. She looked peaceful, so young. She was tall, like the Colonel, and a woman Monica always thought of as handsome. She had a strong face, high cheekbones, and unruly, dark curly hair that used to trail down her back, but the past few years she'd taken it to a bob just below her chin. She'd never been married or had kids. Was it because of her depression? Was she a lesbian? Or was it because her older brother never let anybody near her?

Put her in a home? That was ridiculous. If she was depressed, it was because she was off her medication, and she would just have to go back on. As far back as she could remember, whenever Monica had a fight with her father, Aunt Grace had always taken her side. Now she was going to take hers. As if sensing her presence, Aunt Grace opened her eyes and lit up with a smile.

"Monica," she said, holding out her arms. Monica wrapped Aunt Grace in a hug.

"I hope I didn't wake you," Monica said.

"Not at all," Aunt Grace said.

"Happy birthday," Monica said.

"Don't remind me," Aunt Grace said. She patted the spot on the sofa beside her. Monica sat next to her. They held hands.

"You were smart to sneak away," Monica said, jerking her thumb toward the living room. "It's overpowering when we're all in the same room."

"Yes," Aunt Grace said.

"How are you feeling?" Monica asked softly. Aunt Grace laughed.

"Who told you? Your mother?"

"What do you mean?"

"Did she tell you he's threatening to put me in a home?"

"Did you two have a fight or something?" Monica asked. She wasn't going to come out and ask Aunt Grace if she was taking her medicine. Aunt Grace was a private woman, and it certainly wasn't Monica's place to bring it up.

"I'm reading your book," Aunt Grace said.

"Oh," Monica said. "I was going to give you a copy." She felt guilty she hadn't done it sooner. She didn't think Aunt Grace needed the advice in the book, but of course she should have known she would buy it anyway.

"I particularly identified with the chapter on cleaning out the clutter."

"Oh?" Monica said. She didn't want to talk about the book. It was getting harder and harder to drown out the thought that it was really Joe's book. Although Joe had suggested "Cleaning House" as the title for that section, and Monica changed it to "Cleaning Out the Clutter."

"There's a lot of clutter in this family," Aunt Grace said. "We should have cleaned it up years ago."

"Well, it's never too late," Monica said. Although if Aunt Grace was talking about her relationship with the Colonel, the book wasn't going to be of any help at all. Monica knew her father: He wasn't the type to willingly engage in emotional discussions; he definitely wouldn't be up for healing any sibling rifts.

"Monica," Aunt Grace said, grabbing her hands and looking her in the eye. "I want you to know I'm terribly ashamed of myself."

"Aunt Grace," Monica said. "What a thing to say."

"Listen to me. I'm sorry. I am so, so sorry."

"Sorry for what?" Aunt Grace pulled her hands away. She seemed to age ten years.

"For everything," she said, looking out the window. "Absolutely everything."

"Don't talk like this," Monica said. "It's your birthday."

"I don't care if he does put me in an insane asylum. You have to know the truth. You deserve to know the truth."

"What truth?"

"Your sister should be here," Aunt Grace said.

"What?" Monica said. Aunt Grace was definitely off her game. Was she talking about her mother's sister? Aunt Betty? "Betty died five years ago," Monica said softly.

"I'm sorry," Aunt Grace said. "They're all going to hate me. Dicky is never going to forgive me now, is he?" Aunt Grace was almost in tears. She was the only one of them who called Monica's father Dicky, for obvious reasons.

"The Colonel isn't mad at you," Monica said. "In fact, we're all here today because of how much we love you." Monica put her hand around her aunt's shoulder.

"Do you remember her at all?" Aunt Grace said.

"Remember who? Aunt Betty?"

"Monica." The door opened and Katherine stepped into the den. "There you are," she said as if she hadn't just left her daughter. Monica smiled at her mother, although she really wanted to scream. Why did her mother have to be so nervous? Was she ever going to stop hovering? "What are you two young ladies talking about?" Katherine asked. *She's using her fake voice,* Monica thought. *Who is she putting on the big act for? Aunt Grace?*

"Aunt Grace was talking about Aunt Betty," Monica said.

Then she felt immediately guilty, bringing up her mother's older sister. She'd died five years ago, and her mother rarely talked about it.

"I wasn't talking about your aunt Betty," Aunt Grace said. She looked Katherine in the eye. "I'm tired of lying," she told her. "You and Dicky have burdened all of us with your lies. We're going to clear out the clutter! Right, Monica dear?"

"Right, Aunt Grace," Monica said.

"Monica," Katherine said. "Why don't you get Aunt Grace a glass of water?" Monica stood. Aunt Grace grabbed Monica's hand.

"Do you really think you can hide this forever?" Grace asked Katherine. Monica's mother hesitated, teetering in the doorway.

"It's okay, Mom," Monica said. "I'll stay with Aunt Grace; you get her the water."

"I'm not going anywhere," Katherine said. "I need to speak with Grace alone." With surprising speed and strength, Aunt Grace stood up.

"Let's go," she said, tugging on Monica.

"Where?" Monica asked.

"To the woods," Aunt Grace answered. "Before it's too late."

"The woods?"

"That's where you need to go. Maybe you'll remember."

"Remember what?" Monica asked. Aunt Grace didn't answer. She headed out of the room. Katherine stepped in front of the doorway, blocking her exit.

"We're going to eat soon," her mother said. Monica looked helplessly from her mother to Aunt Grace. She hated to admit it, but it looked like her parents were right this time. Aunt Grace looked almost—crazed. Her face was flushed, her nostrils flared, and her eyes were definitely darting from place to place. Furthermore, she'd never showed an interest in the woods before; on the few family trips they'd taken into the woods, Aunt Grace was always the first to turn back with a "That's enough of the great outdoors for me!"

"Mom's right," Monica said. "It'll be dark soon." Aunt Grace stepped up to Katherine and squared her shoulders.

"Lacey," she said, looking Katherine directly in the eyes. "Lacey, Lacey, Lacey."

Katherine cried out; her hands flew to her mouth.

"Mom?" Monica said. "Are you all right?"

"I can't handle the secrets anymore," Aunt Grace said. "Do you hear me? I can't handle them." Her voice was ragged and growing in pitch and volume. Monica looked from Aunt Grace to her mother. Her chest tightened. Gibberish suddenly filled her head, insistent and nonsensical. It was so loud it was drowning out Aunt Grace, who was shouting something. What was she saying? Why couldn't Monica hear? What was this noise in her head? Monica slapped her hands over her ears and bent over.

"Monica?" It was her mother. She put her hands on her back. "Now look what you've done," she said to Aunt Grace. Monica wanted to yell at her mother not to talk to Aunt Grace like that, not on her birthday, but she couldn't speak. She pushed past her mother and Aunt Grace and almost ran to the living room. She just needed to get some air—maybe go out on the porch.

She almost rammed into Mike and Tina, who were standing in the middle of the living room, looking lost.

"Lacey, Lacey, Lacey," Aunt Grace said, following her. Katherine stumbled behind with her hands still covering her mouth. Mike caught Monica's eyes and held them. *Save me*, Monica thought. His eyes didn't leave hers for a second.

"Hey there," Tina said.

"Are you listening to me, Monica?" Aunt Grace said. "Are you listening to me?" Monica looked at her mother and mouthed, *Get Dad*.

"Lacey, Lacey, Lacey," Aunt Grace said. The crowd in the living room began to part, and quiet, as they tuned into what was sure to be a family fight.

"Who is Lacey?" Monica said. It was barely a whisper, but the name burned in her throat. She saw her mother's jaw start to quiver.

"Grace!" At the sharp sound of the Colonel's voice, everyone turned. Even Aunt Grace fell silent.

"Thank God," Monica heard her mother whisper.

"That's enough nonsense," the Colonel said. "It's time to cut the cake."

The blazing birthday cake stole everyone's attention. Monica tried to catch her mother's or father's eyes but they didn't glance her way once. Neither did Aunt Grace. She was staring at the flames on her cake as if she was considering diving into them. Joe put his arms around Monica's waist, nuzzled her neck. Her father must have been semi-nice to him. Then, everyone started to sing. Everyone but Monica, who moved her lips but couldn't find her voice. Someone yelled, "Make a wish!" and finally, Aunt Grace looked at Monica.

"I wish," she said.

"Aunt Grace," Katherine interrupted in a high, tight voice. "Don't say it out loud or it won't come true." Aunt Grace closed her eyes and clasped her small hands below her chin. She took a breath, bent down, and blew on the candles with thin, quivering lips. The effort made her cough. The crowd applauded. All but two candles stuck in the middle were extinguished. Aunt Grace looked at them and once again raised her gaze to Monica.

"Why, look," she said, pointing at the two candles. "My wish will come true." She smiled at Monica. The Colonel stepped up and extinguished the last two flames with his thick fingers. Aunt Grace snatched them up and held them to her lips.

"I'll get the plates," Katherine said. She disappeared into the kitchen. Monica extracted herself from Joe and followed. Her mother was hunched over the kitchen sink.

"Mom," Monica said. "Who's Lacey?" Katherine turned. Her eyes were red, her makeup smeared. She inhaled, wiped her nose with the back of her hand. "Mom," Monica said softly. She went up and put her arms around her. After a moment her mother put her hand on Monica's back and gave it a pat.

"You had a sister," Katherine said.

"What?"

"Her name was Lacey."

"What?"

"She died at birth."

"Oh my God."

"I don't ever want to speak of this again."

"Mom, I'm so sorry."

"I can't listen to that woman say her name anymore!"

"Shh, Mom, it's okay." Katherine opened the cupboard and began taking down little plates. Duty comes first, always. Monica stepped in to help. The door swung open and the Colonel stepped in.

"They're waiting," he said. "Monica, what have you done to your mother?"

"It's okay, Richard," Katherine said. "I told her about Lacey." Monica had never seen her father stand so still. "How she died as a baby," Katherine said. Monica hated the pained look on her mother's face. The plates were shaking in her mother's hand. Monica had so many questions, but it wasn't the time or the place. A sister? Who died as a baby? It was so sad. Why hadn't they ever told her? Monica always wanted a sibling, especially a sister to share her life. Once she'd even yelled at her mother for not having more children, a memory that now filled her with shame. She was constantly letting her parents down. Had the wrong child survived?

"Monica, would you take the plates to the table?" The Colonel took the plates out of Katherine's hands and handed them to her. When she left the kitchen, her parents were standing by the kitchen sink, and her father looked concerned. Good. Hopefully he'd make her feel better. Monica couldn't imagine a parent losing a child. Sure, she'd lost a sister, but it wasn't the same. Had she been older or younger? Was it way before she was born? Monica would give it some time, wait until her mother was up for the conversation. Maybe she'd talk to her father instead. He handled things better, less emotionally. By the time the plates were passed out and everyone was eating cake, Monica found she couldn't even take a bite. She had the beginnings of a tummy ache. She needed to lie down. She put down her fork. She'd wait until people finished their cake, then get up as if to help clean up, and sneak out.

"Why aren't you eating?" Joe whispered in her ear.

"I don't feel well," she said.

"I don't like Tina's new boyfriend either," Joe said. Startled, Monica looked over at Mike. He'd been watching her, but when she looked up, he immediately looked elsewhere.

"Why?" Monica asked.

"He stares at you a lot," Joe said. Monica snuck another look at him. To her surprise, he was standing next to Aunt Grace, whispering in her ear.

"He certainly likes to charm the ladies," Joe said.

"At least Aunt Grace looks normal again," Monica said. It was true, whatever Mike was saying had done the trick. She looked relaxed and happy; she was even clasping his hands in hers. Monica noticed her father staring at them too, only instead of relieved, he looked concerned.

"Grace," he said. "It's time for your present." He handed Grace an envelope. She kept her eyes locked with the Colonel's as she opened it.

"Oh my," she said. She was holding a ticket.

"What is it?" Monica said.

"Italy," Aunt Grace said. "A trip to Italy."

"Oh my God," Monica said. "That's so great." As long as Monica could remember, Aunt Grace had talked about going to Italy.

"I don't know what to say, Dicky," she said.

"Say you'll go," the Colonel said. "Say you'll get some deserved rest. Say you'll just relax and let things be." Aunt Grace smiled.

"You're right," she said. "I don't need to control everything." What was she talking about now? Monica wondered. Her mood swings were so hard to follow. Maybe she shouldn't be traipsing off to Italy by herself.

"Is there anyone who could go with you?" Monica asked.

"It's a tour," the Colonel said. "She'll be with a whole group."

"Thank you, Dicky," Aunt Grace said. "Thank you, Katherine." To Monica's surprise, Grace reached out and grabbed Mike's hand. He'd been standing behind her the entire time.

"Your handsome friend would like to see the grounds," Grace said to Monica. "Would you like to join us?"

"We'd love to," Tina said.

They strolled the grounds, all seven of them. First Tina had insisted on joining in, then Joe, then her parents. And why shouldn't they? It wasn't like Monica wanted to be alone with Aunt Grace and Mike, did she? They gave Mike the grand tour: the target practice range, the vegetable garden, the maze of flowers and shrubs, stopping just short of the woods.

Let's go into the woods. Maybe you'll remember—

What had Aunt Grace meant by that? What did it have to do with her sister dying at birth? Was she buried in the woods?

"So, Mike," the Colonel said. "What is it that you do?"

"He's an artist," Tina piped in. "A sculptor."

"For a living?" the Colonel asked.

"Yes," Mike said. "I do all right."

"That's so rare," Aunt Grace said. "You're one of the lucky ones."

"I'd love to see your sculptures," Monica said. Her face flushed the minute it was out of her mouth. She didn't dare look at Joe.

"As it just so happens, I have an art show coming up," Mike said. "Ten days from now. Nothing fancy, but any and all are welcome to come." They stood in a semi-circle by the woods, smiling at Mike. Once again, Monica noticed he was mainly looking at her.

"Oh, you should go, Monica," Aunt Grace said. "Don't you just love art shows?"

"Sure," Monica said. "Is it in Philadelphia?"

"Philadelphia?" her mother said.

"You're an artist in Philadelphia?" the Colonel said. Was it her imagination or did her parents just exchange some kind of look? What did they have against artists in Philadelphia? She hated to admit it, but sometimes, her parents were snobs. "Enough standing around," the Colonel said, putting his arm around Mike. "Why don't you and I do a little target practice."

"Sounds great," Joe said.

"No, thanks," Mike said. "I'm not a gun person." It was all Monica could do not to cheer. He'd actually stood up to her father. Not an easy thing to do, especially given the look on the Colonel's face, but Mike didn't look frightened.

"Not a gun person," the Colonel repeated. "We're talking target practice, son. Shooting cans. But don't worry—when we're done, we'll recycle them." Mike looked at Monica and smiled.

"Now I see where you get it from," he said.

"What?" Monica said.

"Your stubborn streak."

"I have a stubborn streak?"

"Yes," Mike said. "You both do." Then, without another word, he followed her father.

"My father was a piece of work tonight." Monica was lying in bed, staring up at the moose. Joe lay beside her reading the newspaper. Who reads the newspaper before bed? Why was she being so critical? Why couldn't she get Mike out of her mind? Tina, it seemed, changed her mind about spending the night; she couldn't get Mike out of there fast enough. But not before Mike had a chance to hug her good-bye, and here she was, replaying every second of his touch over and over again in her mind. He'd slipped something into her hand. She immediately slipped it into her pocket to read later. Imagine. Like children passing notes in school. Just because hugging him felt so good, just because she'd wanted more, just because in that split second she forgot all about Tina, and her boyfriend, and her dead baby sister.

Please come, the note said. Followed by the time and address of the art show. Why was she so disappointed? What did she think the note said? I'm crazy about you? I can't stop thinking about you? Monica tried to remember when she fell in love with Joe. She wanted the feeling back.

I'm not a gun person, Mike told her father. She was dying to ask Joe how their target practice went, but she knew she wouldn't get the kind of detail she wanted. Why wasn't she telling Joe about her conversation with her mother in the kitchen? A sister who died at birth. Lacey.

"The world could use more men like your father," Joe said suddenly, putting the newspaper down. "It's a shame the army turned that man down."

"He has one leg slightly shorter than the other. He's walked with a limp his entire life."

"So? That wouldn't have stopped him."

"Say what you want—I'm happy my father never went to war."

"He would've been a great leader, that's all."

"And, I might have wound up an orphan." Joe reached over and took her hand.

"I didn't mean it like that. I just think he would've been something."

"He's done all right with air rifles."

"He sure has." Monica sat up. She wanted to throw open the shades and look at the night sky. It would start a fight; Joe always liked the room dark. He didn't even like Monica to play the radio. There was something about the combination of dark and silent that always put her on edge.

"What are you doing?" Joe whispered. He always whispered in her father's house. Even though they had an entire floor to themselves and there was no way anyone could hear them. Monica climbed on top of Joe. When he didn't protest, she started kissing his neck.

"Monica," he said.

"Shhh," she said. She took off her pajama top. Sat on him with her breasts exposed, wishing he would tell her he liked them, or at least show her. They weren't going to be this perky forever, didn't he know that? Didn't he want to savor her, sink his lips into her? Wasn't he attracted to her? Why was she the one always initiating sex? Why did he turn her down so much?

"It's a full house tonight," Joe said. He handed back her top. She tossed it to the ground.

"So be quiet," Monica said. She started kissing his neck.

"You're just doing this to annoy me," Joe said. Monica stopped. She rolled off him and leaned over to retrieve her top. She slid out of bed.

"Monica," Joe said.

"Shut up," Monica said. Joe sat up.

"Hey," he said. "I don't talk to you like that."

"Oh, you don't? So suggesting that I'm trying to have sex with you just to annoy you was supposed to be a compliment?" Joe ran his hand through his hair, then slapped his thighs.

"I didn't mean it," he said. "Come back to bed." Monica walked over to the window and yanked open the curtains. She could see stars. She wanted to wish on one. She wanted Joe to be a wild animal in bed. Hell, at this point she'd settle for a domestic pet. She wanted to write a second book. All by herself this time.

"Monica," Joe said. "Shut the curtain." Monica opened it a little wider.

"I had a sister named Lacey," she said.

"What?" Joe said.

"She died as a baby," Monica said.

"Oh my God," Joe said. "You never mentioned this."

"I never knew," Monica said. "Aunt Grace told me. Well, she tried to. Then Mother told me the rest."

"That's sad," Joe said. "But it was a long time ago."

"What does that mean?" Monica said. "I can't grieve? Just because I never knew her? Just because it was a long time ago?"

"Please don't start a fight," Joe said.

"I'm sorry. It's just—shocking, you know?"

"I can imagine."

"I can't believe they kept that from me."

"That was another generation," Joe said. "Personally, I think there's something to be said for privacy. Nowadays, everyone has to air their dirty laundry on national television. I respect the strong, silent types."

"Thanks, Joe."

"Come back to bed. I didn't mean to upset you."

"I know." Joe pulled her side of the covers down. Monica got back into bed. He turned off the light. Then, he leaned over and kissed her. She tried to keep him there, tried to hold his head to hers. He eventually pulled away.

"Good night," he said. "Sleep tight." Monica lay in the dark for several minutes without speaking.

"Joe?" she said.

"Yes?"

"I'm going to write a second book."

"I'm not sure I'm up for that anytime soon," Joe said. He reached over and held her hand.

"I didn't say you," Monica said. "I said me."

"So you're ditching me, huh?"

"It's not like that."

"It's not like I've asked for any of the credit. Quite the opposite, I've—"

"You've pretended it's all mine. But we both know it's all yours, Joe."

"I can't have this conversation again, Mon, not tonight." Monica fell silent again. Soon, Joe's breath slowed, and he turned away. Monica waited a few more minutes, until she was convinced he was asleep. Then, as quietly as she could, she made her escape.

She stood in the hall, stepping lightly to avoid splinters and creaks, wondering if she should go back into the bedroom and put on shoes. It was too late, she was out, there was nowhere to go but forward. She crept to the attic door. But when she opened it and flipped the light switch, the steps leading up remained bathed in darkness. She would need a flashlight. There were at least a dozen boxes up there, mostly seasonal decorations and pictures. Would any of them hold a clue to her baby sister? Pictures? A birth certificate? A death certificate? Sympathy cards?

There was no point searching in the dark. Besides, what if someone heard her? She would have to carry each box down the ladder and open them in the hallway. It wasn't practical. A better bet would be to come back to the cabin another time, by herself. Monica turned away from the attic and headed downstairs.

She went out onto the porch. She loved summer nights. She loved being able to stand outside in bare feet and no coat. The air smelled like the earth, and the scent of lilacs from the tree in the front yard. Lightning bugs pulsed in the darkness, a beacon of hope. She looked at the edge of the woods. Why had Aunt Grace wanted to take her there? There was no way she was going into the woods alone in the dark. This was all so ridiculous. She would simply ask her parents more questions in the morning. Where was the baby buried? That was all she needed. A picture. A grave. A sympathy card. They had to have buried her, right?

She would visit the grave, bring flowers. Why had her parents kept her a secret all these years? Tomorrow she would ask more questions, she would feel better. Monica stood a little longer in the porch, staring into the darkness. How different would her life have been with a sister? She would have had a playmate, a confidante. Monica closed her eyes and imagined holding her baby sister. Was it possible to love someone you'd never met? It must be possible. For this sister, the one she never knew, the imaginary one she was rocking in her arms beneath the earth-scented stars, she knew she loved with all her heart; and she mourned deeply for her. She kissed her dead sister gently on the head. "Good night, Lacey," Monica whispered into the darkness. "Sleep tight."

And then silently, guiltily, she imagined herself wrapped in Mike's arms, imagined he would have no problem appreciating her, savoring her, desiring her—and for a second she allowed herself to imagine what he would be like in bed, imagine his lips on her lips, and neck, and breasts. Her hands on his strong chest. She wanted to feel his skin against hers, she wanted to know what he smelled like. What was the matter with her? What if Joe was up there right now wondering what some other woman would smell like? It was nothing, just a fantasy. That's all. Women were allowed to have fantasies, of course they were. It didn't mean anything. Sexual fantasies, perfectly normal. It wasn't only men who had them; they just got all the spotlight.

Monica laughed. She never imagined herself as a "bra burner" but she could see herself now. *Come on, ladies! Share your sexual fantasies. Tell the group how you wanted to rip into the stock boy at your local grocery store.* She laughed. She was awful. But it was a good idea for a workshop. Much more jazz.

There was no need to share every little thought that flitted through her brain with Joe. It felt good to fantasize. And she had this feeling inside her, this lifting-off-the-ground sensation in her solar plexus. Was this actually joy? Was joy interrupting her life, making her spontaneously smile? *Practice what you preach, Monica. Tell the truth. You're in love.* From the moment she'd locked eyes with him across the little poolside table at another generic hotel, everything about her world ceased to be ordinary. She knew it. Just from looking in his eyes. The thought even went through her head when they shook hands: *I want to climb on top of this man.* That's what she was thinking. Her! She wanted to straddle a perfect stranger poolside at a Marriott Courtyard. Shame on her. Ridiculous, childish, impossible. In love with a man she'd barely met. It felt delicious, harboring a secret. Why hadn't she ever done it before? It was so wrong. It felt so good. But not good enough to stop her from shedding a few tears over her dead baby sister.

Chapter 12

Richard was dreaming about trigger valves and bullets one minute and Monica's Pink Pumpmaster the next. Instead of bullets, it was shooting jelly beans. He was aiming it at a line of cans when suddenly Grace was sitting on the fence. He tried to stop shooting, but the trigger was stuck. For a moment he forgot the gun was loaded with jelly beans; he was convinced he was going to kill her. He was going to kill his little sister. She was laughing, even as he shot at her. She opened her mouth and started catching jelly beans as fast as she could. She was going to choke! *Don't take such big bites,* he could hear his mother scream at her. *Don't take such big bites!*

He was awoken by a sound. Something moaning. No, creaking. He sat up in bed. His heart was pounding, his palms and forehead dappled with sweat. The clock on the side of the bed glowed 3:30. Katherine was the culprit. She was awake and standing in front of their closet. The door was wide open; she was staring into it.

"Katherine," Richard said. "What are you doing?" Katherine turned toward him. A dark shape dangled from her arm, barely visible in the room. It was a woman's suit jacket.

"Look what I found in her pockets," Katherine said.

"What?" Richard asked. How could he possibly see in the dark?

"It's a bottle of sleeping pills," Katherine said. Richard looked at the clock.

"They work better if you take them," he said.

"They're not mine," Katherine said. "They're Monica's." Richard sighed and flipped on the bedside light. He put his hand over his eyes until they adjusted to the glare. What had he been dreaming about? Katherine padded over, opened the bedside drawer, and handed him his glasses. She sat on the edge of the bed and thrust a bottle of pills into Richard's hand. He examined the bottle.

"She has a prescription," he said. Katherine grabbed the bottle and shook it near his ear.

"She hasn't taken any of them," she said.

"So?"

"If she needs a sleeping pill, she'd be taking one a night. She's not taking any. Why?"

"Maybe she doesn't really need them."

"Why is she carrying a whole bottle of them around in her pocket?"

"Why are you going through her pockets in the first place?"

"Richard, not now!"

"First you're upset she has them, now you're upset she hasn't taken them?"

"You're not listening to me. This is a cry for help." Katherine began to pace the floor. It was the reason Richard had had plush carpet installed. He preferred wood floors, but installing the carpet in their room had eased the annoyance.

"Just come back to bed," he said. Instead, Katherine stood by the window and opened the drapes.

"Your sister outdid herself today."

"You handled it," Richard said. "And did you see the look on her face when she opened the ticket?"

"So what? She's quiet for another month? Then what? Are you going to keep bribing her?"

"I'll handle Grace. Please come back to bed."

"I want to see her," Katherine said quietly.

"You'll see her in the morning," Richard said.

"Lacey," Katherine said. "I want to see Lacey."

"Katherine."

"Don't you? Don't you want to see her?"

Richard threw the covers off and sat with his feet dangling off the side of the bed. "This isn't about what I want," he said in a controlled voice. "This has never been about what we wanted. It was about what was best for the girls. Have you forgotten that?"

"It's too late. That man. That artist. He's from Philadelphia, Richard."

"I heard."

"Did you see his face? He knows her, Richard! He knows Lacey. He's going to tell Monica."

Richard slid off the bed and approached Katherine. "Give me those pills."

She handed him the bottle.

"I'll pay him a visit," Richard said.

Katherine lunged forward and grabbed Richard's arms. "I want to come with you."

"This is not about seeing her. This is about damage control."

"I have to go with you. You have to let me come."

"Come to bed."

"Please, Richard. Please."

"Just come to bed." They lay in the dark.

"What are you going to say to convince him?" Katherine whispered after a moment. "What are you going to say?"

"What can I say?" Richard said. "He's a feel-good type. A do-gooder. Insulting me in my own home—"

"I didn't hear him insult you—"

"'I'm not a gun person.' What do you think that was?"

"Oh. So what are you going to do?"

"The only thing you can with those liberal types."

"What, Richard? Finish your sentence."

"The truth. I'm going to tell him the truth."

"The truth," Katherine whispered. "As if we know what that is anymore. As if we ever did."

Chapter 13

An eternity passed under the shadow of five days. Five days in which Lacey and Alan did not speak or sign. Five days of Lacey sleeping on the couch. Alan hadn't asked her to do this; she'd simply swiped her pillow and blanket from the bedroom the night after they came back from the warehouse, plopped them on the couch, and that's where she'd stayed. Alan continued to go to work, walk and feed Rookie, and go to the gym. Lacey spent the first day on the couch staring at a blank television screen. The second day she sat at the kitchen table with a mug of coffee. It was still full when Alan got home, grown cold and curdled in the cup.

Alan let her be on the first day, but the evening of the second, he stood in the doorway of the kitchen and simply watched her. Lacey, he had surmised, had three basic modes. Daredevil and Dreaming Artist were the two he'd grown accustomed to, but this third one was utterly heart-wrenching. Catatonic. He'd never seen someone sit so still for such long periods of time. It was so not Lacey. Not the woman he knew and loved. The woman who drove him crazy with worry whenever she got it in her head to do something—buy a motorcycle, go skydiving, climb Everest—the one thing she hadn't (thank God) followed through with (yet).

The first day he'd blamed her behavior on guilt and a hangover; the second day it gave him pause. But soon anger settled back in like a flock of birds, perching on his mind, flashing images of Lacey with her legs spread open in front of Mike—

Then he'd turned away from her, let her sit like a slab of stone. He walked Rookie, fixed himself dinner, and shut himself in their room for the rest of the night.

Day three he found her sitting on their front porch in nothing but a nightshirt and panties. He'd been about to set off on a run when the sight of her stopped him. She was sitting on the floor of the porch, in between the deck chairs, knees up, head thrown back against the wall of the house, eyes staring vacantly into space. Had she been there all night? And just when he thought she was ignoring him, she turned her head and looked directly at him. It was dark, so it was possible she was actually looking beyond him, but he didn't think so. As they stared each other down, Alan knew she was eventually going to win this one. Finding out you were a twin, and your biological parents kept your twin and threw you away, trumped any pain Alan was feeling about her almost cheating on him.

He knew this, he was fully prepared to concede the fight and focus on helping her, but he'd been waiting for an apology first. Surely, some kind of apology was in order, wasn't it? Some kind of acknowledgment?

He wanted them to get past this, he knew it now. He wasn't so sure the first few days, too hurt, too raw, but now he just wanted it over and done with. He'd be happy never to speak of it again. Lacey would have to find a new work space, that was for sure, but other than that, he wouldn't make any demands. She wasn't used to drinking, and she never could deal with stress—the shock of finding out what she found out—

But could he trust her? What if she did it again? Chances were, the next time she came on to some random man—he would do something other than stand there and stare at her.

How could they get over this if she wasn't going to even discuss it?

And what about this twin sister? Who was this woman, Lacey's twin? Where was she? Did she know she had a sister, or had she been lied to her entire life as well? Alan wanted to meet her. And her parents. He'd have a few choice things to say to them. Up until now, he and Lacey had shared everything. How could they not talk about something so huge?

Alan walked over to Lacey, knelt down, and took her hand. She held it for a second and then pulled her hand away and deliberately turned her head. The Deaf equivalent of sticking your fingers in your ears. His mother used to do the same thing when she was angry or disappointed with him. Oh, how it used to drive him crazy. *Look at me, Mother,* he would yell. *Look at me.* Of course yelling never worked. And of course he exploited their deafness too. He used to play the radio at top volume, sneak in and out in the middle of the night, ignore the phone ringing, fail to mention that their cute new puppy howled all night long and their neighbors were complaining. . . .

He stared at Lacey for a minute, and then walked away. He hesitated at the edge of the porch. She wasn't budging. He pushed off and went on his run. When he returned, forty minutes later, she still refused to look at him. That was the end of day three. Day four, Alan woke up determined to get her to talk, but when he went downstairs she was gone. The sheet and blanket she'd usually spread on the couch were folded neatly on the cushions. Alan checked the garage and, sure enough, her motorcycle was gone. He didn't like this, he didn't like any of it. This place they were in, this hideous, dark place, was not something he was used to. Alan worked things out. Alan built things step-by-step. This was not fitting neatly into the schema of who they were. Day five, she was back, coming into the house as he was leaving with Rookie.

Alan wasted no time telling her how worried he was. Lacey apologized and allowed him to hug her. He held her longer than usual. She was stiff and unresponsive in his arms.

"I'm sorry," she said.

"That's all I wanted to hear. But right now we need to focus on you. On finding your sister." Lacey looked at him and shook her head.

"I don't have a sister," she said.

Lacey put pen to paper and started writing.

Hearing aids, plastic black spider ring from True Value hardware, jar with three live grasshoppers and two dead ones, pink Barbie toothbrush, panda bear with two blue eyes, TV privileges for a month, baby teeth, panda with one blue eye, strands of hair, skin cells, fingernails, toenails, my hearing, brain cells, Very Berry lip gloss, coin from Portugal, Spanish dancer doll, AA batteries, butter knife, television remote, blue pens, red pens, black pens, letter *L* from typewriter, eyelashes, pink-heart socks, red-heart socks, white socks, black socks, knees off jeans, patches off jeans, hair barrettes, hair bands, diary key, purple curly straw, watch, necklace with a tiny but real diamond, tiny but real diamond earrings, pearl necklace, Claddagh ring, my mind, my heart, my virginity, cell phone, brand-new set of oil paints, keys, keys, keys, keys, keys, keys, conch shell from Atlantic City (made in China), cashmere scarf, money, money, money, money, money, money, sock monkey. Eyeglasses, drinking glasses, looking glasses. Hair, hair, hair, hair, hair. Sense of humor, manners, timing, love, brand-new packet of 100 Glow in the Dark Stars. Sea horse. Paintbrushes, canisters, pencils, erasers, charcoal, tape, tape, tape, tape, tape, scissors, scissors, scissors, scissors, tape, tape, tape, tape, jade bracelet, here, kitty, kitty, kitty, old best friend, new best friend, new boyfriend. Phone message, strapless bra, childhood photos, umbrella, umbrella, umbrella, umbrella, umbrella, umbrella, umbrella. Sunglasses, sunglasses, sunglasses, sunglasses, sunglasses. Gloves, gloves, gloves, gloves, gloves. Acrylic nail tips from four fingers. 101 Sex Secrets That Will Knock His Socks Off!, dead butterfly, here, kitty, kitty, kitty. My way. Twenty-four cupcakes left on top of the car, bubbles, lighter, white cardigan with pearl buttons, jump rope, breath mints, reservation, wallet, driver's license, driver's license, driver's license, driver's license. LEGOs, crayons,

Monopoly shoe, playing cards, tarot cards, passport, lottery, raffles, references. Homework, dog, cigarettes, mascara, blush, eyeliner, Hula-hoop, dates, Wicked Queen coffee cup, baseball caps.

Lacey put her list down and started to walk away. Then, she turned, came back, and added three more items to: "Things I've Lost."

    Plastic horse
    Alan's trust
    Sister

It was gone. That's all she knew. It was on the coffee table, and now it was gone. It had been on the coffee table for the past five days, on the coffee table in the bowl. She bought the bowl at an artist festival last summer. It was made by some schmuck who took a pottery class. The red bowl with the yellow stripe running through it and a large crack that allowed her to buy it for three bucks. The horse was in the bowl. Bowl horse. Horse bowl. Bowl horse. Horse bowl.

Maria.

Maria was here yesterday. It was her. She knew it was her. Maria was their housekeeper, their maid, their cleaning *lady*. Maria was no lady. Alan loved her, had known her for fifteen years; she'd cleaned his very first apartment, blah, blah, blah. Maria annoyed Lacey. Maria shouted and flapped her hands at Lacey whenever she tried to talk to her. It was like talking to a Spanish pterodactyl. Her breast were humongous and she loved smashing them into Lacey's comparably tiny chest whenever she ambushed her with a hug. She would touch, touch, touch. Tug at Lacey's hair to tell her she needed it cut. Pat Lacey's ass if she thought she was wearing something too tight.

But worst of all were her cleaning methods. She moved things. She moved Lacey's things. Alan thought it was no big deal if the Mickey Mouse cookie jar was on the opposite counter with his head screwed on backward, or the remote control was under the TV instead of on top of it, or the pillows on the couch had been rearranged. Lacey knew Maria was doing it on purpose. But up until now, even if they weren't in their rightful places, their things were always still there. The horse was gone.

She started with the living room. Lifted couch cushions, opened drawers, pulled books off shelves. Opened Alan's guitar, the one he said he stopped playing because he felt bad she couldn't hear it, when it was really because he was too lazy to practice. She turned the guitar upside down and shook it. Logic wasn't guiding her, only anger and panic. It was gone. She wasn't going to find it in the guitar, or in the couch, or behind the books, or in the refrigerator underneath the butter.

She looked anyway. She shoved things around, turned things upside down, shook things. Four hours later, the house looked like someone had broken in, and there was no sign of her horse. What if Alan came home and saw her standing in the middle of this mess? She wasn't even looking anymore, she was just throwing things across the room and kicking the furniture. Would he have her shipped off to a psychiatric hospital? Or would he simply pack his things and leave? *Let's look for her,* he told her this morning. *Let me help you find her.* No way was Alan going anywhere near her "sister." Neither was she. She was going to go back to painting cocker spaniels and permed trophy wives. This never happened, there was no twin, no parents, no life before Hillcrest.

Horse where, horse where, horse where? She filleted their bedroom, bathroom, guest room. She stopped at the door to the attic. Maria had probably thrown the poor horse up there with the bats. She put her hand on the doorknob. She took it off. She kicked the door to the attic three times. She stomped down the steps, back to the living room, hating herself for being so out of control. Hated herself for just being, which was so unlike her, the novelty of being someone new almost cheered her up. Hated her parents. Her sister. And really hated the stupid, broken, plastic horse.

The garbage. Maybe it was in the garbage. She stood over the bin in the kitchen. She reached in, grabbed the bag, and dumped it into the kitchen sink. There wasn't much to sort through. Maria must have changed the bag.

Lacey ran out the back door and trudged up the drive to the garbage pails. She lifted the lid. They were empty. They had been full this morning. She probably just missed the garbage truck. If she were hearing, would she still be able to hear it? She looked up the street. No truck in sight.

She marched back inside, headed straight for the computer, and clicked on her link to the Video Relay Service. She was going to call Maria and let her have it. No more Mr. Nice Guy.

A few minutes later, a sign language interpreter appeared on her computer screen, introduced herself, and gave her employee number. A few minutes after that and Maria's phone was ringing. It went to voice mail. Lacey signed and watched as the interpreter voiced her message. "Where's my fucking horse?"

It looked so crude on someone else's lips. So mean. Lacey started crying. She changed her tactic. "Please," she said. "Please tell me where you put my horse. It was in the bowl on the coffee table." Lacey and the interpreter stared at each other for a moment. The interpreter looked as if she felt sorry for her, as if she wanted to leap out of the computer screen and hug her. It wasn't any of her business. She was supposed to be neutral! Lacey hung up. She put her head down on the table and sobbed. After just a few short minutes of feeling sorry for herself, she got back online and looked up the number for the city dump.

Chapter 14

Ally Jensen, or Al, as she liked to be called, loved her job at the Philadelphia City Dump. First of all, she didn't have to deal with all that crap that regular office-goers had to deal with. No business suits, no power lunches, no squabbling over drab cubicles pasted over with sickening cartoons that made fun of the office life, or cute little kittens with pink bows. She had real cats at her job, tough cats that roamed through garbage and didn't like to be touched.

Of course she heard her share of ribbing—your office is a dump—your life is garbage—you're "wasting" your day—

Hardy, ha, ha. She didn't care, she could take it.

It wasn't that she loved garbage or anything, that would be mental; she just had a healthy appreciation for one man's trash being another man's treasure. If you really wanted to learn about another culture, screw their customs; go through their garbage. But perhaps the main reason Ally Jensen could tolerate her job was because of her disability. She suffered from complete congenital anosmia. She was born without a sense of smell. The job was a perfect fit. She loved being privy to things

the average guy or gal wasn't. It was astounding the things people threw away. After her first few months on the job, she felt
she knew more about human nature than any psychotherapist
with a PhD and a healthy dose of neurotic clients.

People didn't throw away just garbage. People and compa-
nies alike dumped brand-new things, perfectly good items.
Stores off-loaded surpluses, and lost souls dumped slightly imperfect items they were too lazy or stupid to fix. In her modest
one-bedroom on South Street, Ally had a practically brand-new
television, a DVD player that was perfectly functional as long as
you didn't need to rewind, a Picasso print with just a hint of
mustard (and really, who can tell, it was from his Cubist years),
and a frame with the tiniest of cracks in the corner, which she'd
expertly concealed with a little roll of black electrical tape, also
courtesy of the dump.

She worked the morning shift from seven to three and besides the cats, she mostly worked alone. She'd seen her share of
desperate people coming to the dump in search of an "accidental throw." Diamond rings, car and house keys, wallets,
cash, papers, driver's license, green cards, birth certificates—
you name it, they came and looked for it. Over the past two
years, Ally had created categories of dumping:

Accidental throws
Regrettable throws
Revenge throws
Wasteful or lazy throws
Necessary throws
Shameful throws

Regrettable and revenge throws were usually by-products of
a soured relationship. Shameful throws were how she helped
her guy friends build up their porno collections, and wasteful
or lazy throws were what she lived for. Oh yes, Al knew the
things we threw away said a lot more about us than the things
we kept, which is why she always went through a potential
boyfriend's garbage before committing to the relationship. She

could learn more from one bag than it took her friends weeks, even months, to ascertain. And by then it was too late—they were attached and doomed for heartache.

Yes, all you needed to work at the dump was a deep appreciation for the complexity of human nature and loads and loads of rubber gloves. This morning she was filled to the brim with both. She sat up in her little shack overlooking the dump, very much like a lifeguard's house, big enough for her, two chairs, and her most recent possession—Tim Brady's garbage. Nobody was going to disturb her this morning. She didn't know who the motley crew working their way toward her shack-on-sticks were, or why they were all waving their hands about, but there was no way they were getting in. Ally Jensen had love garbage to go through. Visiting hours were closed.

"Up there," Lacey signed. All five members of the unhappy group tilted their heads back and looked at the little shack lording over garbage land.

"Up there how?" Robert asked. This was his one day a week off, and he'd made it clear all he wanted to do was get a Philly cheesesteak, sit in the park with binoculars, and try to lip-read gay hearing men. Garbage was not his thing.

Also along for the ride was Maria, who had been threatened with deportation if she didn't come; Kelly, who was the only one of them pretending that spending a Saturday digging through garbage was just what she had in mind (Lacey wanted to ask her why she didn't bring the children; this would have been the perfect family outing); and of course, Alan. She could always count on Alan. Even if things weren't quite back to normal for the two of them, he was still willing to wade through mounds of muck. Maybe she should marry him here, at the dump. 'Til we pass out do us part.

"There's someone in there," Lacey said. She pointed, and everyone turned to see the tip of a baseball cap bobbing in and out of view. There was no obvious way up to the elevated shack, no stairs visible. Lacey picked up a stone lying by her foot. Alan grabbed it from her just as she pulled her arm back for the throw.

"Really? That's your solution?" Alan said. He tossed the stone over the fence. An enormous orange cat flew out from beneath a pile of garbage where it landed. "Whoops," Alan said. "Sorry, kitty." The group started to circle the lookout, hoping to discover the way in.

"I'm climbing the fence," Lacey said.

"We don't know what section your garbage is in," Kelly said.

"Let's look where the garbage is freshest!" Maria said, donning a surgical mask and sticking a plastic bag over each foot. Robert walked behind Maria, holding his nose but imitating her walk to perfection. When she turned around to see what the commotion was, she actually blushed and laughed.

"I've changed my mind about cheesesteak," Robert said, wrinkling his nose. Maria started talking to one of the cats in Spanish. Lacey started to climb the fence. A few seconds later, Alan tapped her on the shoulder and pointed to the shack. A window was thrown open and the head belonging to the baseball cap was leaning out the window. All Lacey could see were a pair of eyes and a huge mouth moving.

"Hey," she yelled. "Get DOWN." Kelly interpreted. "HEY," she yelled again.

"She can't hear you," Alan said.

"GET DOWN!"

"She's Deaf."

"I don't care if—she's what?" The girl suddenly stopped screaming. A rope lowered from the window of the shack, and the girl in the baseball cap slid down. Lacey hopped off the fence and stood with her hands on her hips as the girl marched up to her and stared. Lacey slid her eyes to Alan. Alan shrugged.

"Tell her I can't smell," the young girl said. She held her nose and shook her head.

"Did she say I smell?" Lacey asked Alan.

"She said she can't smell," Alan said.

"She can't smell what?" Lacey said.

"Anything, I guess," Alan said.

"Does she have a cold?" Lacey said.

"No, I don't have a cold," the girl interrupted. "I'm smelling impaired."

"Her nose is Deaf!" Robert said. His joke was accompanied by a huge laugh, his own.

"He's hearing impaired too?" the girl asked.

"We're Deaf," Lacey said. "Not hearing impaired."

"What's the difference?" the girl asked.

"Perspective," Lacey said.

"Look," Alan said. "We lost something very important this morning."

"Tell her I'll let you in," the woman continued. "Us disabled people have to stick together." She winked at Lacey. Lacey frowned. "So," the girl said. "What did we lose today?"

"A diamond ring," Robert and Kelly answered. Alan gave Lacey a look. Lacey shrugged.

"There was a diamond in that little plastic horse?" Maria said.

"Plastic horse?" Kelly said. "She's kidding, right?" Lacey forged her way behind the girl in the baseball cap before Robert and Kelly had a chance to wring her neck.

Coffee grounds, newspapers dripping with egg yolks, a half-filled sudoku puzzle, a Styrofoam cup smeared with lipstick and dirt. Alan had already divided his section into fourths, Kelly dived in with both hands, Robert was directing her, and Maria, as far as Lacey could tell, was simply moving garbage from one place to another, the same method she employed in her housekeeping. Lacey could only imagine they were all dreaming up payback, the favor they could pick off her years from now, a request that undoubtedly would begin with: *Remember the day I dug through garbage at the dump?*

A stinky hour passed and they were no closer to finding the horse.

"I can't believe this," Maria said. "I put the horse in the coffee table drawer. I know I did."

"I looked," Lacey said. "It wasn't there."

"Here's our garbage," Alan said, holding up a half-ripped bag. "Why did you throw out your Visa bill?" he added, holding up the envelope.

"Did I?" Lacey shrugged. Everyone rushed over. They all went through the bag, piece by piece.

"Do you want to shower first?" Alan asked. Four hours of digging through garbage and nada.

"Go ahead," Lacey said. Alan disappeared up the stairs. Lacey stared at the coffee table. She did look in the drawer, she did. Several times. She opened the drawer. There, in the back corner, peeking out from underneath another ignored Visa bill, was her horse. She snatched it up and put it in her pocket. There was no need to mention it to anyone; that would just be cruel.

"I think we should move," Lacey said. Alan looked up from his newspaper. He was sitting in the Adirondack chairs without her. There was only one beer on the table next to him.

"What?" Alan said. Lacey perched herself on her chair.

"We have to move," she said. "We have to move now." Alan took off his glasses and pinched his nose as if he were in pain. He shook his head but didn't open his eyes. She tapped him on the shoulder until he opened them again.

"What about Boston?" she said.

"Boston," Alan said. "Isn't that where your sister lives?" Lacey shot out of her chair.

"This has nothing to do with her." It was time for a change. She wanted to start a new life. She was sick of painting people and their pets. She didn't want any more tension between them. She was sorry she got drunk and almost slept with Mike. Couldn't he just forgive her? She missed sex. Why weren't they having sex? They could have sex right now, celebrate their move to Boston.

"I have a job starting tomorrow," Alan said. "In Rochester."

"Rochester?" Alan nodded. He was born and raised in Rochester, New York. There was a large Deaf population in Rochester because of NTID, the National Technical Institute for the Deaf. His father had been a professor at the college; his mother had worked for Eastman Kodak. Lacey and Alan had

toyed with the idea of living in either Washington, D.C., or
Rochester because of the Deaf communities, but in the end,
Rochester's weather was too cold and gray, and D.C. was too big.

"It's a huge shopping complex. It's going to last a couple of
months."

"How are you going to commute back and forth to Rochester?"
After his parents died, he'd sold the house. He always said they'd
use the money to build their dream house. Or, if Lacey had her
way, the lighthouse.

"I'm not. I took a room."

"When were you going to tell me this?"

"When you took your head out of the sand."

"That's not fair."

"It will give you the time you need to find your sister."

"I don't have a sister."

Alan finally got up from his chair. He threw the newspaper
across the porch. "We spent four hours digging through
garbage," he said. "Why did we do that if you don't have a sister?" Lacey didn't answer. She couldn't. "That's what I thought,"
Alan said. "That's what I thought."

Chapter 15

With Alan gone, all Lacey could do was throw herself into work, and Rookie. She'd been taking him to the studio with her every day. So far, there had been no sign of Mike. But this morning, his jeep was parked at the curb. She was dying to hear about his interview with Ms. Bowman. He'd texted her right away to let her know they'd met, and she was indeed Lacey's identical twin. He also swore he didn't tell Monica about her. It had been a spur-of-the-moment impulse, sending Mike after Monica. All good battles were won with a little reconnaissance, and she wasn't ready to face Monica herself. She needed time. She wasn't going in blind; she was going to arm herself with info. Hopefully, Mike had learned a thing or two. But her discovery would have to wait a little longer; she had to walk Rookie first. She jingled his leash and he twirled in circles at her feet before she finally got him calmed down enough to attach it.

Lacey loved this part of town, the brick sidewalks, the old lanterns, the wide array of coffee shops, wine bars, and restaurants. The air was warm and smelled like cinnamon buns. The streets were packed once again, youth was in the air, mothers pushed babies in strollers too wide for the narrow sidewalks. Lacey was so busy people-watching, she almost missed the blur racing toward Rookie, a charging three-foot Tasmanian devil in pigtails. Hands outstretched, mouth open and drooling, the toddler was on a mission. Rookie jerked his head up to Lacey. *Save me!* Lacey scooped Rookie into her arms, but knelt down. Seconds later the little girl rammed into Lacey's knees. She couldn't have been more than three years old. Lacey smiled at the little girl, then scanned above her head in search of her mother. Instead, she saw another toddler barreling toward her, identical to the sticky-fingered one mauling the top of Rookie's head. Twins.

They were dressed alike: jean skirts and white shoes, pink T-shirts with a big smiley face. The second little girl plowed into the first and knocked them both to the ground. Rookie pawed at Lacey and attempted to climb up her body like a cat. Lacey helped the little girls stand up, and that's when a woman sprinted at them with a look of pure horror on her face. Lacey glanced at the girls; other than a few specks of dirt and fresh tears, they seemed to be okay. The twin who had come in second lunged forward, pitched forward slightly as if she were going to topple, then straightened her arm out to her sister. But just as Lacey thought she was going to hit her sister, her tiny little hands wiped away the tears on her sister's cheek instead. The gesture was so spontaneous, so loving, Lacey's heart felt as if someone had twisted it with a wrench.

The mother was standing over them, talking a mile a minute. She scooped a girl into each arm as she jabbered. Lacey didn't understand a single word. She studied the woman's facial expressions and body language, trying to ascertain if the woman was thanking her or scolding her, just like she studied the faces of employees at banks, and restaurants, and grocery stores, to see who looked the friendliest. Those were the lines she stood in, regardless of how long.

The woman looked about Lacey's age or even a little younger. Women her age were having babies. It was so surreal. Lacey

couldn't imagine it. How old were her parents when they had
her and Monica? She pushed the thought away; she didn't want
to think of them.

The woman's expression turned from puzzled to slightly annoyed. She wondered why Lacey wasn't saying anything. Lacey
smiled and pointed to her ear.

"I'm Deaf." Then she extracted Rookie from her chest and set
him on the ground. She pointed between the girls and Rookie.
The mother broke into an exasperated smile and shook her
head.

"I'm sorry," she said.

"No, no," Lacey said. "They're so cute." Lacey didn't know if
the mother could understand her voice, but "your children are
so cute" was universal. The mother beamed with pride and
then shook her head again, indicating the amount of energy
required to look after them. Lacey strolled slightly behind the
mother, who, with a girl on each hip, ferried the kids back to a
small outdoor table in front of a café. Lacey stopped for a moment next to the table, enthralled with all the "equipment" that
littered it. There were two bottles, two pacifiers, two bibs, and
ten thousand wipes. Behind the table a double stroller awaited.
Back in their high chairs, the girls were banging the trays with
spoons and laughing as they tried to outdo each other. People
passing by smiled at the girls, who, oblivious to the attention,
only had eyes for each other. As Lacey stood watching the girls,
the mother watched her. Lacey didn't want the mother to think
she was strange, some kind of freak, staring at her children. So
she reached into her bag and pulled out the thick file she'd
been dragging around the past few days. She handed it to the
mother, noting the stricken look that crossed the woman's face,
as if she feared Lacey was about to peddle cheap items with a
card reading I AM DEAF.

Lacey pointed at Monica's picture in the file, then back at
herself. Finally, it dawned on her.

"You're a twin!" the mother exclaimed. Lacey smiled and
nodded. The woman gestured to an empty chair at the table.
Lacey sat down, feeling like a phony but enjoying the attention.
She took out her pad and pencil.

Do you always dress them alike?

I said I wouldn't, but everyone gives them the same clothes. Did your mom dress you and Monica alike? Lacey hesitated, pen poised over the paper. She was going to write *No, never,* but was it even true? After all, they were together until they were three. She must have dressed them alike at least once in those three years. *Sometimes,* Lacey wrote, not wanting to lie. She glanced at the girls again.

How old are they?

Two and a half. And they were so close. Babbling with each other, banging spoons together like musicians in the same band, chasing after each other down the street, racing to be the first to grab a strange dog. *Sometimes,* the woman wrote, *it's as if I don't exist.* Lacey took her file on Monica back, shoved it in her bag, and stood. She looked at her watch. "I have to go." The woman smiled and held out her hand. They shook. Lacey picked up the notepad and pen. She was about to put it in her purse when she jotted down one more thing.

Would you ever give one of them up? Not surprisingly, the woman looked alarmed. She emphatically shook her head no.

What if one of them was Deaf?

I would love her, no matter what.

You would never *give one of them up for any reason?*

That would be criminal.

Lacey nodded, and quickly stashed the notepad. She'd better leave before the woman thought she was creepy. She put on a big smile, picked up Rookie and made him wave his little paw, laughed as the twins laughed and reached for the dog with sticky fingers, and smiled at the mother again as she hurried away. *Criminal,* she thought as she walked on. *That would be criminal.*

By the time Lacey made it back to the studio, Mike was standing outside with an older couple. Lacey wondered if they were his parents. She hung back, not in the mood for introductions, explanations, scribbling. Had he told anyone about her drunken come-on? Hopefully not. He was the one who'd been willing to stake out Monica, he was the one who took a punch for doing absolutely nothing but standing there, staring at her, and really, who could blame him for that? Would she have told Alan if he hadn't walked in? Doubtful. She missed Alan something awful, but so far her BlackBerry had been silent. It had been only a few days, but it was the longest they had ever gone without talking to each other. Although she definitely had enough to distract her. The couple was leaving, getting into a black Mercedes parked at the curb. If they were his parents, it wasn't fair. Good-looking and rich. When Mike turned and went back inside, Lacey followed. He was standing in the front entrance to the studio, pacing back and forth, talking on his cell phone. He froze when he saw her, and she could have sworn she caught "She's here" on his lips before he clicked off. He attempted a smile and waved weakly. She waved back. They stood and contemplated each other like teenagers at the spring dance.

Lacey held up her index finger, walked over to the easel, and picked up a marker. *Tell me about her.* Mike took a folded piece of paper out of his pocket and handed it to her. It was her list of interview questions. She skimmed it. Barely any had been answered. It told her nothing she hadn't already ascertained from her Web site.

She didn't answer them all?!

Birthmark question freaked her out. She thought I was a stalker / pervert.

You didn't tell her?

Mike shook his head no. He removed his cell phone from his jeans, scrolled through it, and handed it to her. It was a picture of Monica. She was sitting near a swimming pool, smiling, wearing a dusty-rose sundress.

What are you going to do? Mike wrote. Lacey shrugged, looked away. *She's very nice,* he wrote. *Invite her to the show?*

Lacey stared at the question. Should she? Wouldn't that be something? After all, she'd seen Monica's work—if you could call that crappy book "work." No, that wasn't how it was going to go down. Lacey was going for the sneak attack, not the invitation. Besides, the art show was about her, her work. If Monica showed up, it would turn into some kind of Jerry Springer reunion. That wouldn't be good for business. Lacey tried to ignore the niggling jealousy she felt chewing on her at the thought of her famous hearing sister triumphing over her at her own art show. "No," Lacey said. His question reminded her of the couple she had just seen leaving the art studio.

Were those your parents?

Who?

Outside. Older couple.

When?

He was acting strange. Almost as if he was suspicious of her. Lacey threw open her arms and pointed to her watch, then jabbed her finger in the direction of the street.

"Just now," she voiced. There it was again, that expression.

No, he wrote. *Not my parents.* Lacey waited for more. Art lovers? Lost tourists? Jehovah's Witnesses? Mike put down the marker. He gestured with his thumb to his area. *Work,* he mouthed. Lacey smiled; for some reason she felt sick. She pointed at herself and nodded, à la "me too."

She walked toward her paintings, unsure of her balance. But instead of going to the portraits she should have been working on for the art show, she headed straight for the tarp against the back wall.

Chapter 16

Lacey worked for a few hours on a new horse painting. This one was purple with blue hooves, the hills behind his floating head, green. It was the last thing she should be doing; she should have been choosing which portraits she was going to put in the show, but she couldn't help herself. She knew this compulsion to paint the horse wasn't normal, but desire beat logic. After a few hours she stopped and stretched. She wandered into the kitchen. Mike was standing by the door. A pixieish woman with spiky blond hair was standing next to him. If she had been with Robert instead of Mike, Lacey would have pegged her as an actress and assumed they were putting on *Peter Pan*. She was definitely a Tinker Bell.

Was this his girlfriend? The woman caught Lacey's eye and gave her a smile and a wave. Obviously, Mike hadn't told her about Lacey's wanton behavior. Lacey waved back, making sure not to look at Mike. At least her curiosity was satisfied. She'd always wondered what kind of woman Mike would date. The girl was cute—not beautiful by any means, but cute. She looked wired too, as if she were about to burst into a spontaneous cheer à la

"Go, team!" Lacey turned away from them and had just started to put on a pot of coffee when the lights flashed. Mike looked over as if to ask her if she were expecting anyone. She shook her head no. Mike opened the door, and to Lacey's surprise, in walked Alan.

Lacey's first reaction was to hug him. Did he want her to hug him? She hung back, and her hesitation reminded her of where they were: stuck, stranded.

"What are you doing here?" Lacey asked before she could stop herself. His expression told her she'd hurt him even more. But she couldn't be too soft. After all, days had gone by and not even a text. Not even an RSVP to the show. He knew how much it meant to her.

"I'm here for the weekend," Alan said. "I came to see the show." Lacey stepped back and allowed Alan to step inside.

"Coffee?" she asked.

"Why not." They headed for the kitchen.

"Lacey," Mike said, following them. "I'd like you to meet a friend of mine."

"Hi," the woman said. She waved again.

"This is—" Mike started to say.

"Wait," the woman said. She turned to Lacey, beaming. She held up her hand and began to slowly finger-spell her name. "T-I-N-A." Lacey smiled. Thank God the woman had a short name; her finger spelling was painfully slow.

"Lacey," Lacey voiced.

"Nice to meet you," Tina said.

"You too." Lacey turned to Alan. "This is—" Lacey said. Then she stopped. Hurt welled up in her. Normally, she would introduce him as her boyfriend.

"Alan," Alan said, stepping forward and holding his hand out. Mike crossed his arms against his chest but said nothing. Tina held up the postcard advertising the show.

"Ready for the big show?" she asked. Lacey gave Tina a thumbs-up. Tina grinned and mirrored her. Then she pointed to Lacey's paintings. "Can I look?" Mike put his hand on Tina's shoulder.

"You should wait," he said. "It's only a couple days."

"I don't mind," Lacey said. "Go ahead." Tina giggled and headed for Lacey's paintings. "Do you want coffee?" Lacey asked Mike.

"No," he said. "I have work to do." Without another glance at Alan, he headed back to his space. Alan followed Lacey over to the pot of coffee and leaned against the counter as she prepared their cups. Then she threw herself into Alan's arms. He was stiff at first, and then she felt his arms wrap around her. He smelled good. She reached up and stroked his hair. Their lips found each other, and soon they were kissing. Lacey forgot all about their visitors. Alan, however, did not. He pulled back.

"Is that his girlfriend?" Alan answered, glancing over at Tina, who was examining Lacey's portraits so closely she wondered if the girl was extremely nearsighted.

"Yes," Lacey said.

"She obviously doesn't know," Alan said. And then, their romantic mood was gone. Lacey shrugged. She handed Alan's coffee to him black and put cream and sugar in hers.

"Have you talked to your sister?" Alan said.

"Are you using your voice?" Lacey said, glancing again at Tina.

"She can't hear me," Alan said.

"I told you," Lacey said. "I don't have a sister." Alan slammed his mug down on the counter.

"Lacey," he said. "Don't do this."

"Don't do what?"

"You're hiding your head in the sand like an ostrich." Alan started his little "act" of an ostrich.

"Stop it," Lacey said. "I don't need your stupid idioms. And I don't need you to tell me what to do."

"So you plan on just ignoring her? Ignoring us?"

"Ignoring us? You're the one who hasn't spoken to me for several days!"

"I was giving you time."

"I didn't ask for time." Lacey noticed Mike was back in the vicinity and he was glancing over. "You are using your voice," she said.

"I don't like that he's here," Alan said. "I don't like it a bit."

"We share the same space. That's all."

"Look what it's done to us. And he's still running around with his girlfriend as if nothing ever happened!" A few seconds later, Alan turned his head sharply. Lacey followed his gaze. Tina stood just behind them, hands on hips, mouth slightly open.

"What did she say?" Lacey asked, although Alan's face had already given it away.

"She said—'What did happen?'" Lacey glared at Alan. She'd told him to stop using his voice!

"Nothing," Lacey said. She noticed Mike was making his way over. "He's just—"

"They almost slept together," Alan said. Lacey stared at Alan. He wasn't usually vindictive. She'd underestimated how much she'd hurt him, how much he was still hurting. She wanted to tell him again how sorry she was. She wanted to punch him for causing more trouble for Mike. But there wasn't any time to deal with Alan—Tina stole the focus.

"Almost slept together?" Tina said. "You almost slept with her?"

"Nothing happened," Mike said. "Lacey was drunk and—" He glanced at Lacey and signed: "I'm sorry."

"It's okay," Lacey said.

"What was that?" Tina asked. "What did she say? What did you say?"

"I just told her I was sorry," Mike said.

"Is that why you were drooling all over Monica?" Tina said. "Are you hot for her too? You have some kind of 'twin' fantasy going on here?" Alan interpreted for Lacey. Lacey shot Mike a look.

"Did she just say Monica?" Lacey asked, turning first to Mike, then to Alan. "I saw 'Monica' on her lips." Alan nodded. Lacey turned once again to Mike. This time the expression on her face would've broken anyone. Mike looked stricken.

"She works with Monica," Mike said. "She's her assistant." Lacey glared at Tina, who seemed to shrink even more, even though she kept a fake grin plastered to her pointy face.

"You told her about me?" Lacey said. "You told her?"

"No," Mike said. He looked from Tina to Lacey. "She Googled me," he said at last. "She saw your picture on our Web site." *Another stalker,* Lacey thought. Just like Kelly. The world was apparently full of them. Lacey walked up to Tina and gazed directly in her eyes. Then she pointed at her with her index finger. Lacey knew pointing in hearing culture was rude. Pointing in Deaf Culture was normally a linguistic reference. But this point was the hearing-culture variety, for in this situation, "rude" was just fine with Lacey.

"Did you tell her?" Lacey asked. Tina met Lacey's stare without blinking, but she didn't answer right away. "Did you tell Monica about me?"

"No," Tina said. Her eyes slid over to Mike. "He asked me not to."

"You can't tell her," Lacey said. "It's none of your business."

"So it was a fake interview?" Tina said. Mike nodded. A look of glee passed over Tina's face, and this time her smile was genuine.

"Did he tell you all about your parents?" Tina asked Lacey. "Their cabin?"

"No," Lacey said. "He didn't." Her parents? Their cabin? She wanted to wring his neck. What was he keeping from her? He met her parents? He went to their cabin?

"I was going to tell you," Mike said.

"When?" Lacey said. "We just talked ten minutes ago. You didn't say a word about my parents. Or their cabin."

"Tina," Mike said. "We have a lot to talk about here. Can I catch you another time?" It was impossible to miss the look on Tina's face. Her eyes slid over to the front door, where a little red suitcase was propped up, waiting like a patient dog to be taken for a walk. Mike followed her gaze over to it.

"I can wait for you," Tina said. "I was hoping I could maybe crash on your couch for the night?" The look on Mike's face was just as easy to read. Lacey smiled at Tina. "Alan—keep her company—I need to talk to Mike." No one was playing poker; Alan looked like he would rather eat glass. "Please," Lacey

added. To his credit, Alan guided Tina away. Lacey almost forgot Alan had been interpreting; she was back to writing. Instead of using the easel, Lacey took out a pad of paper and pen.

You have to let her stay with you.

No, I don't.

She looks crazy. Don't piss her off.

I'm not interested in her.

Tina was right, Lacey thought. Mike was interested in Monica. Lacey wasn't happy about this either, but it was the least of
her worries at the moment.

I don't care. I need to keep her quiet. Lacey knew what Mike
wanted to say—she could see it in his face. He'd already taken a
punch, now she was pimping him out. *It's one night!*

"Tina," Mike said. She and Alan were standing just a few feet
away.

"Yes?"

"You're welcome to crash with me—but I still have things to
finish up here."

"No problem," Tina said. "I'll go explore. But I won't eat, because I am taking you out to dinner. What time should I come
back?" *Stalkers,* Lacey thought again. *There's one born every
minute.*

Through a reluctant-to-interpret Alan, Mike told Lacey all
about Tina inviting him to the cabin. He explained he was just
trying to learn as much as he could for Lacey, and she let it
slide for now, even though she knew it was a lie. He was totally
smitten with Monica. Was it because he couldn't have *her?*
Lacey couldn't help but wonder. Maybe she *had* turned him on
the other night, and Monica was the next best thing. Or maybe
he was intimidated because she was Deaf. Maybe Monica was
the Golden Goose with the Golden Voice.

He told her about Aunt Grace. Lacey was floored. She hadn't
even begun to deal with parents and a twin; now not only was
there an "Aunt Grace," she was yet another person threatening
to reveal Lacey's identity to Monica. If Lacey was going to confront her twin, she was going to have to do it soon, before

someone else got to her first. It wasn't fair. This was her twin, she had dibs. *Shotgun,* Lacey screamed inside her head. *I call shotgun!* Lacey pressed Mike for more information about Aunt Grace.

"She's got spunk," Mike said. He looked at Alan. "Is that word hard to interpret?" Alan interpreted the question to Lacey without answering it.

"He's interpreting the concept, not necessarily word for word," Lacey said.

"Oh. So there's no sign for 'spunk'?"

"Just like English, ASL has several options for almost any word you want to use, or it could just be spelled out. 'Spunk' sounds very dirty, so if that's what you're getting at—I'll show you." Lacey asked Alan to turn off his voice and after a few seconds of extremely graphic signing about "spunk," Mike shut up, even turned slightly red. "You were saying?" Lacey said.

"Aunt Grace walked up to Monica in front of everybody—and there was a huge crowd—and said, 'Lacey, Lacey, Lacey.' " Lacey and Alan exchanged a look. Lacey didn't want to think about this too much with two men staring at her, but a jab of pride, and even love, for this Aunt Grace stabbed at her. She existed! Someone was acknowledging that she existed!

"So Monica does know about me," Lacey said.

"No. Your father stepped in. Later, Monica followed her parents into the kitchen—and I don't know what was said—but I know she doesn't know."

"You don't know for sure—"

"Remember the couple you saw me talking to this morning?" Lacey furrowed her eyebrows, nodded for him to continue. "They're her parents. Your parents." Lacey took a step back. Alan bridged the distance and stood next to her.

"My parents?" Lacey said. "They came here? To see me?" Mike shook his head. He glanced at Alan. "Look at me," Lacey demanded.

"They came to see me," Mike said. "To buy my silence. Just like they bought Aunt Grace off with a trip to Italy."

"You took money from them?" Her head was spinning. She didn't care what the consequences were; if Mike took money from her parents, she was going to go berserk.

"No, no," Mike said. "Of course not. But when I wouldn't take their 'donation,' they begged. They begged me not to tell Monica about you." A cry escaped from Lacey. She slapped her hands over her mouth. She didn't want to break down in front of Mike, but the tears had already started.

"Why?" she said. "Why do they hate me so much?" Alan wrapped his arms around her from behind. She pulled away and doubled over. Then she stood, wiped her tears with the back of her hand. She scanned the room. She spotted the coffeepot and ran over.

"Maybe a cup of tea would be better?" Alan said. Lacey pulled the coffeepot out, held it up, and stared at it as if it were a curious thing, a thing that could exist without gravity. She raised it above her head and let go. It smashed on the ground. Glass shattered and bounced everywhere, and a brown river leaked over, and under, and through the jagged pieces like a polluted river. It was a strong visual. She didn't need to hear it shatter, she could feel it. The pungent smell of stale coffee snaked into the air. Alan gestured for Mike to stay back.

"Milk and sugar?" Alan said. Lacey gave him a look as he retrieved the broom and dustpan from the corner.

"Leave it," Lacey said. "I like how it looks." Alan leaned the broom against the counter and set the dustpan next to it.

"He said there's more," Alan said, gesturing at Mike. "Do you want to hear it or not?"

Lacey lifted her head to Mike. She nodded. They made their way to the couch. Mike continued to stand, but Lacey allowed Alan to sit her down.

"Your parents said if the two of you ever got together—it could be dangerous," Mike said after a long pause.

"Dangerous?" The word lifted Lacey off the couch. "Dangerous?"

"That's ridiculous," Alan said.

"That doesn't make sense," Lacey said.

"They said something about psychological damage."

"How dare they! How dare they call me damaged." Lacey started pacing. After a few minutes, she walked up to Mike and held her hand out.

"What?" Mike said.

"My parents' phone number and address," she said. "Give it to me. Now."

"What are you going to do?" Mike asked.

Lacey held up three fingers. "One. Get through this damn art show. Two. Meet my twin."

"And three?" Alan asked when she didn't offer it. Lacey smiled. She held up the number "three" in sign language with her left hand, her thumb-index-middle-finger, and tapped her middle finger with the index finger of her right hand, indicating she was speaking of the third item on her agenda.

"Three," Lacey said. "Make my parents wish they were never born."

Chapter 17

Lacey couldn't sleep, and she should be sleeping. She needed sleep or she'd be strung out at her own art show; she'd fit the definition of tortured artist, and Lacey hated the thought of fulfilling a stereotype. At the very least, if she was going to lie awake, she should be focused on her work, excited about showing it to the world.

Showing it to her clients was more like it. Weren't they the only ones interested in looking at portraits of themselves and their pets? Still, it was her livelihood, and the exposure was sure to generate new clients. But she couldn't focus on anything but her parents. She was trying to recall what they looked like, an impossible task given that she'd only seen the backs of their heads. They looked tall. Her father kept his hair military short, salt and pepper. Her mother's hair? It was dark, like hers. Wavier? Why hadn't she paid more attention? If only she'd seen their faces. Faces of parents who didn't come to see her, their long-lost daughter, but instead came to see Mike. The fact burned into her brain, along with the business card Mike finally turned over.

Richard Bowman. Bowman Air Rifles. BAR. Portland, Maine. Was this where Lacey's dream of living in a lighthouse came from? Was it part of her genes? It was insane, thinking like this, as if every scrap of her life—tastes, likes, dislikes, decisions— now had to be reexamined genetically. Who the hell was she if nothing about her was truly her own?

Maybe she would buy a lighthouse, sit in the top with a rifle aimed out the window, and, like a siren on the rocks, lure her parents to shore.

Pow! Bang! Dead!

Her father. Air-gun manufacturer. Oh God. Was he a member of the NRA? A Republican? Were they filthy rich? Should she take them for everything they had? She probably could too. Too bad blood money wasn't her thing.

Criminal, the mother of the twins had said. *It would be criminal.* Monica was the key. Their daughter, her sister. Criminal. Air guns. Twins. *They Shoot Deaf Daughters, Don't They?*

She would enlist Monica; together they would turn against their parents. A reverse parent-trap. Instead of getting them together, they would rip them apart—

Lacey got out of bed and went to the window. She hated the mean thoughts in her gut, hated confronting what she might be capable of doing. She should just leave them all alone, let them stay in their little fantasy life.

Dangerous? It would be dangerous if the two of them were together? What kind of people were they? She'd be doing Monica a favor by getting her away from them. Surely, once she found out what they were doing, what they'd already done to them, she wouldn't want anything to do with them. Or would Little Miss Architect of Her Soul forgive and forget? Lacey parted the curtains and held up an imaginary rifle. Sniper. Not a bad career move. Ready, aim, fire. She walked back to the bed, wishing Alan were here. Instead of spending the night with her, he'd taken a hotel room. As if they were going to tiptoe around each other, go back to formal dating, courting. She missed his body, she missed his lips, she missed his eyes, and his smile.

What had she done? Why was she so willing to drive him away, sacrifice their relationship? This sister thing was too much. She didn't need it in her life. She wished she'd never opened that envelope, never seen the poster in the bookstore. Never heard the name Monica Bowman. All Lacey had was a sea of questions, and the open bed, like a field, all to herself. Too bad it wasn't a field of poppies. At this rate, she was never going to sleep. She called to Rookie. She would go to the art studio. Anywhere had to be better than here. Air guns. Go figure.

There was a brick propping open the door leading to the studio. Lacey froze. Was Mike here? Maybe he had propped open the door, maybe he was bringing in another piece for the show. Logic told Lacey this wasn't the case. His jeep was nowhere in sight. Rookie wiggled furiously to get out of her arms, and she could feel a low growl coming from his belly. She looked up the long set of stairs leading to the entrance, but from where she stood, she couldn't see anything out of the norm. Rookie finally broke loose and tore up the stairs, most likely yapping his head off. Lacey hesitated, wondering if she should leave the door propped open or close it behind her. If she left it open, then someone could follow her inside. If she closed it and someone was already inside—

Rookie raced back down. His tail was wagging; he was no longer barking or growling. Once Lacey shut the door, she would be in pitch-black. The bulb at the top of the stairs had burned out long ago. Mike had promised to replace it before the show. Lacey dug a small flashlight out of her purse, turned it on, and kicked the brick out from underneath the door. She held on to the banister and took the steps one at a time, her heart pounding harder the higher she rose. At the top, nothing looked out of place. Still, who propped the door open with a brick, and why? It was ungodly early on a Saturday morning. What if a vagrant had slipped inside? Or a rapist—

Lacey glanced at Rookie. He was bouncing up and down trying to reach the doorknob with his tongue. If there was an intruder, some help he would be. News at 11:00. The suspect was licked to death by a puggle. . . . Lacey pointed at Rookie. "I wish you were a German shepherd," she signed. He licked her ankle. She examined the door. The panes of glass were all intact. She unlocked the bottom lock and tried to open the door. It didn't budge. The top lock was engaged. Lacey couldn't believe it. Mike never locked the top lock, which is why she didn't have the key. It was way too early to call him. She'd have to wait until at least eight A.M. Knowing it was futile, Lacey kicked the door anyway. Then she sank to the top step and let Rookie curl up in her lap. She fell asleep with her head against the banister and her hand on top of Rookie's little head.

A few restless dreams later, she felt heavy footsteps coming toward her. Rookie bounded off her lap and leapt down the stairs. Lacey fumbled until she found the flashlight, then shone it down the steps. It was Mike. He grimaced, threw his hands in front of his blinded eyes. Lacey aimed the flashlight away from him. Mike was unsteady on his feet, and as he drew closer, it was obvious he'd had a few to drink. He lifted his hand in a tipsy wave. Some pair they were going to make for the show, sleep deprived and hungover. And now that Alan was gone, Lacey and Mike were limited to simple words and gestures. Neither of them looked in any shape to write back and forth. Mike pointed at Lacey and then threw open his hands. *What are you doing here?*

Lacey stood and pointed to the top lock. She jiggled it to show him it was locked. Mike shook his head. He didn't lock it. She wanted to tell him about the brick, but she knew he'd never understand her. He motioned for her to get away from the door. Fueled by either confidence or Corona, he took the rest of the steps two at a time. As Lacey had done before him, he examined the door. Then, he dug for his keys, motioned for her to keep back, and disappeared inside. Lacey followed. This was her studio too. If someone had broken in, she was quite capable of helping Mike kick ass. Besides, Rookie had already disappeared inside, leaving her looking like a fool standing all alone in a dark stairwell.

Lacey stepped in, and hesitated. Mike hadn't turned on the lights. Apparently, he was going for the element of surprise.

Lacey didn't want to ruin the storming of the castle by turning on her flashlight either. Where was Rookie, the traitor? Finally she saw Mike heading out of his space. He was carrying a baseball bat. Lacey couldn't take it anymore; she flipped the switch and flooded the studio with light.

Once their eyes adjusted to the light, Lacey and Mike headed to the far wall, where Lacey had hung her portraits for the show. There were fifteen in all and it had taken two men several hours to hang them exactly where she wanted them, not to mention positioning the spotlights above them to illuminate them just right. The spotlights were off. That had to be why they looked funny to Lacey. She flipped on the overhead bank of lights, then stared in disbelief. Her portraits were gone. Instead, hanging in their place, looking as if they'd just burst out of the starting gate for the Triple Crown, were her horse paintings. And not just fifteen to replace the portraits. Fifteen were hung in portrait position, five dangled above them from chains attached to the ceiling, twirling as if galloping, and the last five were propped below the hanging fifteen, perfectly set to satisfy both the casual and artistic eye. If you came in close to them, you felt as if they were surrounding you. If you stood back, you were watching them gallop in the wild. Seeing them all together like this, Lacey momentarily forgot they were all cut in half. A giant blue mare, painted against a swirling red and orange sky. A green and pink swirl, nostrils flared, hooves coming off the canvas. A profile of a black beauty, framed in red, as if he were backlit by a raging fire. She'd used every color of the rainbow for their bodies (always with a tinge of blue), but the soulful big eyes on all of them made them so real, and their strong necks and heads gleamed in the way the paintings were lit, as if their manes were on fire, as if they were hot to the touch. A sign was hung in the center of the exhibit. It said:

PLEASE TOUCH.

It was the same type font used for the mysterious letter. She wanted to be furious, but she couldn't. She loved the idea. She was a tactile person, and she painted that way. She hated rules and stuffy museum environments where a slap on the hand was the reaction she got for wanting to explore the world through touch. Lacey reached out to one of the dangling paintings and touched the golden mare. It was as if she could really feel the bristles of her mane, and the silk of her belly, beneath her fingertips. She couldn't have come up with a better idea herself, couldn't have positioned them any better if she tried.

Mike tapped her on the shoulder, startling her. She'd forgotten all about him. "Wow," his lips said. He looked at her as if seeing her for the first time. "You did these?" Lacey nodded. "These are amazing." Lacey didn't have time for praise. She ran over to the tarp and lifted it up, even though she could see it covered nothing; it was just lying in a convoluted heap. Her pet-and-owner portraits were not beneath it. They were gone. Sheila Sherman was going to freak. She'd had Fran fasting all week, she'd told her, just so Fran could look good at the opening. Lacey told her no dogs were invited to the opening, leaving out the fact that Rookie of course would be there. Sheila was furious; she said Fran had finally lost enough weight to look like the thinner dog she'd asked Lacey to paint in the portrait. Lacey could only hope Sheila wouldn't throw a fit when she saw Lacey had painted Fran as she saw her, roly-poly.

Lacey had almost turned away from the tarp when she caught a flash of white out of the corner of her eye. There sat a familiar-looking white envelope. She didn't even hesitate; she grabbed it and tore it open.

> If wishes were horses, how Lacey would ride.

She stared at it. Read it again. And again. *If wishes were horses*—

What the hell? Who the hell? Was this some kind of a joke? Lacey glanced at her horses again, and this time it was as if she were seeing them for the first time. Twenty-five wishes. She'd been separated from her twin for twenty-five years. *If wishes were horses.* No. It couldn't possibly mean that. It was just a coincidence. Wasn't it? *How Lacey would ride.* Lacey felt tears threaten to overtake her. Not again. She was not going to cry again. Not over some person she didn't even know, didn't even know if she wanted to know. No. That wasn't why she dreamed of living in a lighthouse or painted twenty-five damn horses. That wasn't why, that wasn't why, that wasn't why. This was a break-in. A criminal act. Her portraits—her bread and butter—had been stolen.

If wishes were horses . . .

Mike was behind her again. If she weren't so furious with everything else, she would have lectured him about sneaking up on her. Instead, she handed him the letter. He shook his head, held his hands out in bewilderment. Then he pointed to her horse paintings again and mouthed either "unbelievable" or "under-the-weeble." Lacey darted to the easel, picked up their trusty marker.

There was a brick, Lacey wrote. *Propping open the front door. My portraits are gone.* Her clients. They were all coming to the show this evening, expecting to see themselves and their dog-children, cat-children, and in one odd case, iguana-child. They were going to freak. All that work down the drain. She was going to have to give them their money back. She didn't have it. They'd been paid in advance. They had all agreed to let her showcase the paintings; they were all expecting to take them home tonight. She was screwed. So why was there part of her soaring with joy? Wanting to cry out, yes, yes, yes! Her horse paintings were right where they belonged. On display. In the open. Exposed.

Oh God. All those eyes, looking at them, seeing inside her. Who was doing this to her? Torturing her like this? Could she really go on with the show? *The show must go on,* she could see Robert saying. The show must go on. She tried to pretend it wasn't intense joy she was feeling, looking at her paintings. Whatever her motives for painting them, they were good. She was proud of them. She just couldn't figure out who was behind the scenes pulling the strings. And she couldn't help but wonder what else they had in store.

Chapter 18

Maybe she shouldn't be here. After all, he hadn't reminded her about the show since giving her the flyer, hadn't called to see if she was coming. Even Tina wasn't coming, and she was the one trying to date him. Speaking of which, what was Tina going to think if she found out Monica was here? Dressed in a sexy little black, low-cut dress? Monica stood outside the art studio and watched as people made their way up the narrow staircase. Lights and jazz poured out of the space above. It looked like fun. There was nothing wrong with popping in, saying hello. *I was in town for business.*

But she wasn't. She was here to see him. To support another artist. That was all this was, artistic support. The fact that she wasn't frequenting art shows in Boston, or New York, or anywhere else was beside the point. She had a personal connection; he'd interviewed her—if you could call it that—and now she was supporting him. Besides, she still had to find out how he knew about her birthmark. She had several reasons for coming, and none of them were cause for concern. She didn't bother to invite Joe simply because she knew he was swamped with work. And she didn't tell him she was coming to Mike's show because he'd been jealous of him at the cabin. She was standing outside with the smokers. It was time to either light up or go up.

Within seconds of entering the space, Monica was glad she came. She was offered a glass of wine right away by a nice-looking woman, also in black, and soon after offered a tray of cheese and crackers. She was standing in the center of the space, facing a section with a leather sofa and chairs, and behind it, a kitchen. There were people clustered in the middle, then another cluster to her right, where she could barely see sculptures over the heads of those standing close to them, and paintings were hung to her left. Monica was about to turn to the sculptures first, when she got a good look at one of the paintings dangling from a chain on the ceiling. Taking her glass of wine with her, she moved closer. And then, even closer still. As if pulled by a magnetic force, Monica moved through people to get as close as possible. Then, she stood surrounded by paintings of horses, dumbstruck.

They were the most beautiful things she had ever seen in her entire life. She felt giddy, and yet grounded, as if she were rearing up like many of the horses in front of her. People were talking all around her; much of it didn't make sense. One woman was saying, "Where is my little Fran?" over and over, and another was on about a missing iguana. How could these people yak about nonsense in front of these masterpieces? She stepped even closer.

PLEASE TOUCH

Who was this artist? Monica held her hand out to a white horse rising out of an ocean's dark wave. The wave looked like a fist lifting him out. Even with the sign permitting her, she held back. Please touch. Monica made herself do it. For a second she swore she could feel the damp ocean, feel the roar. The horse was like silk, except his wet mane was coarse and slick. She looked to the corner of the painting to see the name of the artist.

"Monica?" At the sound of her name, Monica whipped around.

"Tina." What was she doing here? More important, what was she going to say she was doing here? Monica made up for her angst with a huge smile. "Hey," she said. "You're here."

"Yes," Tina said. "What are you doing here?"

"He gave me a flyer. Remember?"

"We talked about this. You said you weren't coming."

"Well, so did you." What was going on here? She and Tina never fought. Here they were squabbling like siblings. Tina looked around. She grabbed Monica by the elbow and pulled her in close to the wall.

"Has anybody seen you?"

"What do you mean?"

"Does Mike know you're here?"

"Not yet."

"Thank God." Tina slumped against the wall as if she were a blow-up doll and someone had let out the air. Then she took Monica's wineglass right out of her hand and drained it in one go. "Come on," she said. "Let's get you out of here." Monica yanked her arm out of Tina's grip.

"Tina," she said. "You're being ridiculous." She wasn't going anywhere; she was going to get another glass of wine and find the artist who painted these horses. "I'm not here for Mike, if that's what you're worried about," Monica said.

"Then why are you here?"

"To support the arts."

"Yeah, right." Tina looked over Monica's shoulder, scanned the crowd. "Where's Joe?"

"He couldn't make it."

"So you came all the way to Philly to support the arts?"

"Tina. Let's not fight like jealous schoolgirls. I just needed a night out, some time away from work. I'm happy to see you. Please don't be upset with me."

"Look," Tina said. "You're my boss. It's just too weird if we start spending all our free time together." Monica felt as if she'd been slapped. She and Tina had done plenty of things together; they'd always acted like friends. Was Tina this upset over a guy? Did she think Monica was going to try and steal him away? Even worse, the niggling fear that kept Monica thrumming with overblown defensive anger—was it true? Wasn't Monica here to see Mike? Hadn't she been thinking of him every single second since they'd met? They were two independent, strong, beautiful women. Were they really going to let a man come between them?

"Pretend I'm not here if you'd like," Monica said. "But I'm not leaving. In fact, I'm thinking of buying a painting." She turned back to the horses. "I wish I could afford them all," she said. "Do you know anything about the artist?" Tina stared at Monica. The corners of her mouth lifted in a tiny smile.

"I've met her," Tina said. "She reminds me of you."

"She does?" Monica said. "In what way?" Suddenly, someone stepped in front of Monica and started waving his arms about. At first she thought it was some kind of joke, but when another person came up and did the same thing, she felt like a complete fool. Waved their arms about. They were deaf, they were using sign language. But why on earth did they think she would understand them? Suddenly, another woman, an attractive brunette, was standing in front of her as well.

"Oh my God," she said, staring at Monica. Then she turned and signed to the deaf people who had been trying to talk to Monica. Whatever the woman signed to them had quite an effect. Their faces took on strange expressions; they looked from the woman to Monica, shook their heads. "Wow." Did she hear one of them say, "Wow?"

"I'm Kelly," the woman said. "I'm sorry. They mistook you for someone they know."

"No problem," Monica said. "How do you say 'hello'?" Kelly just laughed and waved hello. Monica felt like an idiot again. She waved hello. They waved back, then continued to stand there staring at her, as if they were microscopes and she were the specimen on a slide. Kelly waved them away. Then, just as Tina had done, she took Monica by the arm and started guiding her. To the front door. Monica stopped.

"Are you trying to throw me out?" she said. She'd only had a few sips of wine, what the hell was going on here?

"No, no," Kelly said. "I just thought we could go outside and talk. Get some fresh air."

"I don't want to go outside and talk," Monica said. She wasn't usually that rude to people, but she'd had enough aggravation with Tina, and really, who did this woman think she was?

"I'm sorry," Kelly said, pulling up her pant leg. "I need to move it around sometimes." Monica stared at the prosthetic leg. What a jerk she'd been! The woman probably needed help down the stairs. Was there no elevator? But couldn't she find someone else to help her? Monica wanted to see Mike's sculptures, and she wanted to talk to somebody about buying one of the horse paintings. She didn't care how much they cost; in fact, the more expensive, the better. She hadn't splurged much since the book came out; she and Joe, sensible Joe, were saving for their future. What better way to spend money than supporting the arts? On a painting she loved. The hard part was going to be choosing just one.

"I'll help you down the stairs," Monica said. "But if you don't mind, I'm going to come right back up. I have to find the artist of those paintings."

Monica is here, the text said. *Outside with me.*
Noooooooooooo!
She came to see Mike. Wants to meet you. Wants to buy a painting.
Nooooooooooooooooooo.
She has no clue. Panic-stricken, Lacey made her way out of the crowd surrounding her. She was about to find Alan or Mike when she ran into Robert.

"What's wrong?" he asked the minute he saw her face.

"Help me," Lacey said. "You have to help me."

"Wow," Kelly said, looking at her phone. "She just texted and said to bring you on up."

"Great," Monica said. "I can't wait to meet her." It turned out Kelly didn't need help on the stairs after all. She must have just been lonely, wanted Monica's company. Maybe Monica should give her a copy of her book. Then again, maybe the woman would think Monica was trying to tell her she needed help. Or she might think she was just self-promoting. This evening wasn't about her. It was about the art.

"I should probably find Mike first," Monica said when they reached the top of the stairs. "Say hello and see his work."

"Okay," Kelly said, gesturing to the sofa. "Meet me back here when you're done."

Monica barely had time to look at Mike's sculptures. They were as impressive as she'd imagined them, and even though Tina was hovering around him as if she were magnetically drawn, he was thrilled to see Monica. She could see it in his eyes. But like Tina, she read shock in his face, and if she didn't think it was crazy for thinking it, she would have said: fear. Seriously, everybody had crazy eyes and a nervous energy, as if they were expecting something to happen.

Why would they be afraid of her? Had he and Tina already slept together, was that what she was picking up?

"Monica," Mike said. "Why don't we get you out of here?" That was one too many. Everyone wanted to get her the hell out of there, as if she were wired to blow.

"What is going on?" she demanded. "Why doesn't anyone want me here?"

"She hates your book," Tina blurted out.

"What?"

"The other artist, the one whose painting you want to buy? She thinks you're a phony."

"Tina," Mike said. "That's not quite fair."

"She read your interview with Mike," Tina continued. "Thinks you're full of crap."

"Oh my God," Monica said.

"It's not as bad as that," Mike said, taking her arm. He gently led her away from Tina.

"She doesn't hate your book," Mike said. "In fact, I think she's really going to like you."

"I was just about to meet her," Monica said. "The woman with one leg—Kelly—she's taking me to her. I was going to buy a painting."

"I think I'd better talk to her first," Mike said.

"It's like I'm a leper or something."

"I didn't mean it like that."

"So she doesn't like my book. I don't care. Why should I care?"

"Tina shouldn't have said that."

"I shouldn't have come."

"I'm glad you're here." His voice was low, and soft. He didn't want anyone to hear it but her. She looked into his eyes. Oh God, she was after him. She was a horrible person. A horrible girlfriend, a horrible friend. No wonder nobody wanted her. Her pores were oozing "horrible" and she didn't even know it.

"I have to go," Monica said. "Congratulations. I like your work." She meant it, he was very talented. She just couldn't stay. Because no matter what, no matter what she said, she didn't want to face this woman who hated her book. Wasn't this what she feared all along? Hadn't she waited for someone to come up to her and tell her she was a phony? Full of it? Then why did it hurt so much? Especially coming from someone whose work she loved, wanted to buy. It made it all that more humiliating.

"Why don't you stay with me tonight," Mike said. Monica was about to answer when she spotted Tina over her shoulder, eyes flashing.

"Thank you," she said. "But I have to get back home." Everyone was right. She didn't belong here. She didn't belong here at all.

Mike found Lacey standing in the middle of the room, waiting. She was wearing a black mask with peacock feathers.

"You can take that off now," Mike said. "She's gone."

Chapter 19

"Please, stop packing." But Tina kept at it as if she couldn't hear a word Monica said. She sealed the last box. Movers had just pulled up to the curb. "Please," Monica said. "Don't do this."

"I'm doing it," Tina said. "I should have done it a long time ago."

"But we have workshops to do. You committed to me—"

"I'm not an East Coast girl. I'm a West Coast girl." Tina was from San Diego. She was moving to LA. Worse, she was blaming it on Monica—on the "Build Your House Where the Foundation Suits You." But Monica knew better. This was about Mike. He must have turned her down flat. Was it true? Was it Monica's fault? It had been three days since his art show and she hadn't tried to contact him. He hadn't contacted her either.

"Things change. 'If your house is crumbling down around you—at least you save on the demolition costs,' " Tina said. She glanced at her copy of *The Architect of Your Soul*. It was the only thing she hadn't packed in a box. Looked like it was staying behind.

"Don't quote the book. Please talk to me."

"Are you deaf?" Tina said with a strange laugh. "I'm moving back to California."

"But I need you."

"You'll find someone else."

"I don't want to find someone else—"

"I'm doing you a favor. You've no idea how big."

"What is that supposed to mean?"

"Never mind. Just forget it. I'm leaving. I'm sorry." The doorbell buzzed. "The movers are here. I'm sorry, Monica—but you're kind of in the way here."

"I'll help you bring down boxes." Monica lifted the nearest box. Tina lunged for it.

"No," she said, grabbing it back.

"I'm just trying to help."

"You want to help? Then leave. Don't you get it? I can't talk to you, I can't think about you, and I certainly don't want to look at your face."

"My face?" Monica touched her cheeks with her hands. Then she threw her hands down and grabbed the duffel bag Tina heaved over her shoulder. "What is wrong with you?"

"Poor Monica. I'm sorry. I just can't take your advice anymore. You two deserve each other."

"I told you I'm not after Mike—"

"Don't lie to me. It doesn't matter. I wasn't even talking about him—"

"Who were you talking about?"

"You know," Tina said as she opened the door, "everyone is going to feel sorry for her. But not me. I care about you, Monica, I really do. And you're right, I'm jealous. But it's still time for me to go. Just don't let anyone walk all over you, okay? You can't help it. It's not your fault."

"I can't help what? What's not my fault?"

"I'll just be a phone call away," Tina said. "I'm sorry." She hugged Monica, kissed her on the cheek, and then showed her the door.

*   *   *

"Mr. Paris will see you now." Monica followed the petite woman down the hallway. Josh Paris sat behind a desk that was covered in stacks of paper, barricaded behind an ordering-form moat. That's what it was all about. Sell, sell, sell. Buy more books, attend more workshops, listen to more crap. She thought of the sign her father used to hang next to the front door: SOLICITORS WILL BE SHOT.

"Monica." Josh stood as she entered but didn't come out from behind his fortified wall. He held out his hand, and after a quick shake, he gestured to the chair in front of him. Monica sat, and crossed her legs. "What can I do for you?" he said.

"It's about my remaining workshops," Monica said. She was dreading this, but it had to be done. "I'm afraid we're going to have to cancel them." Josh Paris laughed.

"Funny," he said. "You had me there for a minute."

"I'm serious. My assistant just quit—"

"You can hire another one." He pushed the buzzer on his desk. "Shirley, can you send me a pile of résumés? We have a sales assistant position available." Sales assistant. Just like she wasn't a writer, or even a speaker, she was a motivational sales agent. Why had she ever agreed to do this in the first place? Because 150,000 books come out every single year and hardly any of them stayed afloat?

"Mr. Paris—"

"Josh." He was all teeth. He'd had them whitened, lasered, she was sure of it.

"Josh. I have to be completely honest. My heart isn't in this anymore." There, she said it. It felt good. It was honest. Josh opened a drawer in his desk. He flipped through a row of hanging files. He pulled out a bundle of papers and handed them to Monica. Her contract. Monica took it, but didn't look at it. She already knew where he was going with it.

"As you can see on page thirteen," he said as if she were expected to turn to page 13. "If you cancel the remaining workshops, you will owe us not only the weekend registration fee of one hundred fifty dollars per person, but the potential loss of sales that each participant is projected to generate—" Monica stood. She slid the contract back across the table. He knew she couldn't afford any of that.

"Look," he said. "It's a demanding job. I understand that. If you'd like, I can recommend some great tapes on recharging your battery—"

"No."

He held out his arms as if to say *Look how unreasonable you are.* "Shake it up, then. You mentioned you didn't like 'Celebrate Good Times.' Why don't you pick out some other songs and I'll have a listen."

Monica stood.

"That a girl. Chin up. Let me know if you change your mind about those tapes."

Joe sat in the front row. Since Tina left her high and dry, and Monica refused to hire a new assistant, he'd been very supportive. She hated being back in Philadelphia, hated that Mike lived here and wasn't sitting in the front row instead of Joe. She burned with shame at the thought of the artist—the one with the haunting horse paintings—finding out she was in town and telling everyone, "That phony woman with the crap book is doing a workshop at the downtown Marriott."

"I am the architect of my soul," Monica said to the crowd. "And so are you. Remember that castle in the sky? Well, you can have it. And I'm going to spend the rest of the weekend showing you how."

Suddenly the interpreter standing to the left of Monica started talking. This was the first time Monica had ever had a hearing-impaired person attend her seminar. There were two sign language interpreters on stage with her, and they were switching back and forth every twenty minutes. It was totally distracting. Not that she didn't fully support the idea, but it was weird to have someone standing so close; she kept catching their hand movements out of the corner of her eye. It was one of those strange phenomena, like learning a word for the first time, then hearing it everywhere. First she'd seen hearing-impaired people at the art opening; now they were at her workshop. Which was totally great. Monica welcomed the handicapped. She just wasn't sure how to behave. And the hearing impaired, she was starting to realize, liked to ask a lot of questions.

"I don't understand," the interpreter interrupted. "What do you mean by 'castle in the sky'?" Monica looked at the interpreter. Was she joking? The interpreter slightly nodded her head out toward the audience. Right. She wasn't asking the question herself, she was simply relaying the information. Where was the hearing-impaired person?

"This is a question from the hearing-impaired attendee?" Monica asked. As soon as the interpreter signed her question, a woman in the second row shot out of her seat. She was dressed strangely, wearing a long trench coat and hat, and sunglasses. She had curly blond hair falling down past her shoulders.

" 'Hearing impaired' is not a term I accept," the interpreter voiced as the woman signed. Her hands were flying so fast, Monica was worried she was going to hit one of the attendees next to her. She didn't accept the term "hearing impaired"? Wasn't that the polite way to say it?

"I'm sorry," Monica stammered. "What would you like to be called?"

"I am Deaf. Not impaired. Impaired implies something is broken and needs to be fixed. I am not broken. I do not need to be fixed."

"I'm so sorry," Monica said. "Did you have a question?"

"I don't understand you," the woman said. "Castle in the sky. Architect of your soul. What does any of it really mean?" Monica froze. It was finally here, the moment she'd be "outed" as phony, a fraud. But she never pictured it happening with a hearing-impaired—deaf—woman with sign language interpreters, and Joe staring at her from the front row.

"It means there are no limits to what you can achieve. The sky is the limit." *That's it*, Monica told herself. *Keep talking*. She believed in some of what she had to say, she really did. "This weekend is about creating a vision," Monica continued. "Planning out step-by-step the life you want to lead—"

Instead of just falling into it, crashing into it, following the pack—

"I will be leading you through specific exercises to help you get started. By the time you leave here this weekend—" The deaf woman waved her arms again.

"I want to confront my family," she said. "Can you help me with that?" Joe stood up. *No,* Monica shouted inside her head. *Don't.* He turned toward the hearing-impaired woman.

"Maybe you're in the wrong seminar," Joe said. "This isn't family therapy." *He did not just say that.* "This workshop cultivates visionaries." *Oh, but he did.*

"Please," Monica said. "I'd like to answer her question—"

"Who the hell are you?" the deaf woman said, staring at Joe. *I like this girl,* Monica thought. The air was thick with anticipation, as if everyone could feel a good fight coming on. They were probably all wondering who Joe was, wondering why Monica was letting him take over like that, as if Monica couldn't handle a heckler.

"This is my fiancé, Joe," Monica said. "He helped me write the book—"

"Oh," the woman said after a smattering of applause. "No wonder it doesn't sound like you."

"Excuse me," Joe said. "I'm sorry you're hearing im—deaf—but it doesn't give you the right to—"

How does she know? Monica thought. *How does she know it doesn't sound like me?*

"Whoa, whoa, whoa," the interpreter translated. Her voice rose in volume. "You're sorry I'm Deaf? You're sorry I'm Deaf?" *Oh God, Joe, you didn't just say that, did you? You didn't mean that. Tell her you didn't mean that.* "That's a disgusting thing to say. That's like saying 'I'm sorry you're black,' 'I'm sorry you're Latino,' 'I'm sorry you're a woman.' "

Joe threw up his arms. He looked at Monica and shook his head. *She can see you,* Monica wanted to say. *She's not blind.* So why was she wearing those huge sunglasses? She looked like a deaf terrorist. Monica took a step forward.

"You want to confront your family?" The woman crossed her

arms against her chest and nodded her head. "I can definitely help you construct a blueprint to guide you through the—conversation—"

"Confrontation—"

"Confrontation you want to have with your family." Monica paused. "Although," she said, "if you're already thinking of it as a confrontation rather than a conversation, I think you'll be setting yourself up for failure." There. She did it. She took back control. Now move on before the woman picks up her hands again. Monica was suddenly grateful she wouldn't be the recipient of this confrontation; the woman was terrifying. Monica could almost see waves of light pulsing from her. "So," Monica said, addressing the entire crowd again, "please look at the number on the scraps of paper I passed out. This is your group number. Please meet your group in the sections of the room marked with your number. Then we'll get started with our first group exercise."

The deaf woman picked up her things and moved through the aisle as if she were leaving. Monica didn't know why, but she couldn't let her go.

"Wait," she called after her. "Don't leave." She looked at the interpreter, who just shrugged. Monica walked down the steps off the stage and started after the woman.

"Monica," Joe called. "Let her go." Monica ignored him.

"Stop," Monica yelled, even though she knew it was foolish and futile to yell at the back of a deaf woman. "Please, stop." Nobody was gathering in their groups; they were all standing and gaping back and forth between her and the woman. Monica felt her hair start to come out of its bun; her underarms were suddenly soaked. She picked up speed. The woman maintained a quick pace, but Monica broke into an out-and-out run. When she finally caught up with her, Monica didn't know the proper way to get her attention. She didn't want to scare her, but she couldn't let her go, and didn't the woman see the entire room full of people staring? Didn't she know someone was behind her?

Monica reached out, caught the edge of the woman's coat

sleeve and tugged. The woman stopped, then finally turned around. Monica stared at the oversized sunglasses and long blond wig. Both were too big for the woman's face. She reminded Monica of a little girl playing dress-up in her mother's shoes.

"Don't go," Monica said. Could the woman understand her, read her lips? "Interpreter," Monica yelled. It wasn't necessary, there was one right behind her. Joe was also following. She wanted to yell at him to go away. She wanted everyone in the room, everyone but this woman, to disappear.

"Tell her to wait," Monica said to the interpreter.

"You don't have to say 'tell her,' " the deaf woman said. "Talk to me directly."

"You were right," Monica said. "The book isn't my voice." She pointed to Joe. "I'm a fake. It's his. All his." The microphone Monica wore on stage was still attached to her, and she was aware that her voice was being carried throughout the seminar hall. The participants were clinging to every word, and after her declaration, the murmurs turned into steadily growing chatter. Monica didn't care. Strangely, as long as the woman in front of her didn't go anywhere, she felt as if she could say or do anything. Maybe it was true. Maybe the truth did set you free. Monica started to laugh.

"Monica," Joe said. "We can hear you." He touched her shoulder. She brushed him off.

"Who are you?" she said to the woman.

"I work with Mike," she answered. "I believe you wanted to buy one of my paintings?"

"The artist," Monica said. "The one who hates me."

"What?" the woman said.

"Mike?" Joe said. "Tina's boyfriend?"

"I was told you think my book is 'total crap,' " Monica said.

"Should I call security?" Joe said.

"Shut up," Monica told Joe. A hundred thoughts crashed the gates of her mind. Meeting Mike for the first time. How he stared at her. His interview. How he knew about her birthmark. Tina's last words to her. "Everyone is going to feel sorry for her." Aunt Grace. "Lacey." Her mother—you had a sister—

Monica stepped forward, reached for the wig, and tore it off.
"Monica!" Joe said. She ignored him and snatched off the
sunglasses.

"Holy shit," Joe said from somewhere far, far away. "Holy
shit." Monica kept staring. She couldn't make sense of what she
was seeing. The participants suddenly burst into applause, as if
they'd just witnessed a performance.

"Twins," Monica heard someone say. "They're twins." Monica heard the words echo her own thoughts. *She looks like me.
Her hair is longer. She has a freckle by her chin, she's dressed way casual, but she looks just like me. I'm not crazy, someone just said twins.
I'm not seeing things. Joe just said "holy shit." Joe never ever swears.*

"Lacey," Monica whispered, touching her own freckle-less
chin. "Lacey."

"Hello, Monica," Lacey said.

"I don't believe this," Monica said. It was true, she didn't. It
was a dream. She felt light, as if gravity itself had been snatched
away from her, lighter than a helium balloon soaring to the sky.
Her head was going to come right off and float to the ceiling.
Maybe it was a dream, or she'd been drugged. Either way, she
didn't care. She couldn't stop staring. She stopped short of
feeling her face like a blind woman.

"Believe it," Lacey said. "Believe it."

"I understood you. I understand your voice—"

"Good for you," Lacey said, switching back to sign language.
Everything Monica wanted to say, an onslaught of words, fun-
neled through her mind and hardened to a stop like a puddle
of congealed grease. *She's deaf,* Monica thought. *I'll just use my
hands.*

Monica lifted her hands and then didn't know what to do
with them. They hovered mid-hip, then sank to her side like
kites without enough wind to soar.

"Joe," Monica said. "Take over the workshop."

"You got it," Joe said. Monica took Lacey's hand. "Come with
me," she said, pulling her out of the conference room. Lacey
signaled for one of the interpreters to follow. Both trotted after
them; apparently, neither of them wanted to miss this. Monica
stopped.

"Can you read my lips?" she asked.

"A little," Lacey said.

"Do we need them?" she said, pointing to the interpreters, a little embarrassed that one of them had to interpret her asking that question.

"You're paying them anyway," Lacey said.

"You're so pretty," Monica said. They were out in the courtyard of the hotel, sitting at a little table.

"You too," Lacey said. Monica laughed. After a few seconds, Lacey joined in. Monica's laughter was feminine and lilting, Lacey's was guttural and hollow. Monica started to cry. Lacey held out her hand. Monica grabbed on to it. She had such soft hands. Were they just like hers?

"I don't understand," Monica said. "How can I have a twin? How?"

"I didn't know until I saw your book," Lacey said.

"Oh my God," Monica said. "I'm adopted."

"What?"

"This means I'm adopted," Monica said. "I have to be adopted." She stood up suddenly and looked at the surrounding fauna and plants as if waiting for them to rally to her side. "No wonder I'm such a bad shot," she said. "And the cabin, maybe that's why I hate the cabin. It's not in my blood." Monica patted herself down. Where was her cell phone?

"Hey," Lacey said, standing. "You're not adopted."

"I have to be. Because if I'm not adopted, then—"

"Your parents are my parents."

"But that's impossible. My parents wouldn't have—they couldn't—" She slapped her hand over her mouth. "That's why there's lace all over the house. Every surface of the house— lace." Aunt Grace. Her mother in the kitchen. *You had a sister. You had a sister.*

"You didn't die at birth," Monica said. "Oh my God." She went to the wall and put her head against it. She had an urge to bang it against the bricks. She actually wanted to feel the pain in her head. It scared her, this sudden urge. She felt a hand on her back, rubbing her. She turned around and threw herself into Lacey's arms. She hugged her as if she'd known her all her life; she sobbed into her shoulder. When she was done she lifted her head.

"Let's go somewhere," Monica said. Lacey turned to the interpreters. They were both in tears. Lacey hugged them goodbye. Then she held out her hand. Monica took it, and without even discussing where they were going, they headed out of the courtyard and started walking, hand in hand, down the street.

Chapter 20

They sat across from each other at a small wooden table in a café they'd never recall the name of, and soaked each other up like shipwreck survivors who'd just been told their deserted island was actually inhabited, always had been. There was a bittersweet feel to it, as if Tom Hanks in *Cast Away* found out at the end of the movie that he had formed an unhealthy attachment to a volleyball for nothing.

She cries more than I do, Lacey thought. *Do I look like that when I cry?* She vowed never to do it again. A pile of napkins sat in front of Monica. *Is she always this messy?* Lacey thought. *I can't be the neat one.* Monica swiped the last napkin from the dispenser, blew her nose, and added it to the germ-filled heap.

"These are happy tears," Monica said. *Happy tears,* she wrote on the pad of paper sitting between them. Lacey took the pen out of her hands before she could draw a happy face with fat tears dripping out of it. "I have so many questions," Monica said. Lacey held up her hand. *Rules,* she wrote at the top of the paper and underlined it three times. Monica became a bobble-head, nodding her agreement.

I would've always gotten my way, Lacey thought. *Mother,* Lacey wrote under *Rules. Father.* Then she slashed a diagonal line through them. Will not discuss. A pained look passed across Monica's face. Then she shifted, smiled, and it was gone. *Tell no one,* Lacey wrote. Monica opened her mouth. Closed it. She dug in her purse and pulled out her own pen. *Interpreters. Joe. Two hundred participants, Mike, Tina, Aunt Grace, parents,* Monica wrote.

Lacey laughed. *That's it for now.*

"For now," Monica repeated. "Just for now." Monica's cell phone buzzed. She looked at Lacey and mouthed, *It's Joe.* She turned off her phone and stowed it in her purse. The waitress came over, flipped open her pad, and waited. Lacey pointed at a sandwich on the menu. The waitress pointed back at it. Lacey nodded. Still not convinced, the waitress looked to Monica.

"Would she like anything to drink?" the waitress asked Monica. Lacey pounded on the table. The waitress continued to stare at Monica. Monica pointed to Lacey.

"She's capable of ordering for herself," Monica said.

"Pepsi," Lacey said.

"I'll have the same exact thing," Monica said. "My God," she said when the waitress left. "It was like you were invisible—or a child. Does that happen often?"

All the time. I once had a doctor try and hand my prescription to the interpreter. Why did you copy my order?

"It's exactly what I was going to order. I swear. I love curry chicken salad and Pepsi." Monica tore off a sheet of paper for each of them. "Write down your top ten favorite foods," she said.

"Including dessert?"

"Anything—your favorites. Go."

They hovered over their papers and began writing. When they were done, they exchanged papers. They had pepperoni pizza, curry chicken, and cheesecake in common.

"We both work in creative fields," Monica said. She wrote *Writer* and *Artist* on the paper. Lacey scrolled through her BlackBerry until she found what she was looking for. Then she held a picture of Rookie up to Monica.

"My puggle, Rookie," she said.

"No way!" Several heads turned as Monica shouted it out. Her enthusiasm was undeterred by the gawkers. "I have a puggle named Snookie!"

"I know," Lacey said.

"How did you—" Lacey held up Monica's book. "My bio." Lacey pulled the cover of the book out of her bag and slid it over to Monica. Monica looked at the mustache and horns and laughed. Then, she stopped suddenly.

"The bookstore," she said.

"I'm sorry," Lacey said, doing the sign for "sorry." Monica repeated the sign. She laughed again. "I thought you were a face thief," Lacey said. Monica laughed even louder. Lacey mimed her reaction when she had seen the poster in the window of the bookstore. Monica scribbled on the pad.

Where did you grow up?

Just outside Philly. Hillside Children's Center. Monica's face registered surprise. Then it flamed red and she examined her fingernails before picking up the pen and putting it to paper again.

Why, why, why, why, why, why????????????

Lacey tapped the first rule. Then, she wrote. *You never knew?*

Of course not. But they . . . Monica looked at the words *Mother, Father.*

"We have to go to them. We have to confront them."

"No."

"We deserve answers. There has to be an explanation."

"No, no, no, no." Their curry chicken sandwiches and Pepsis arrived. Lacey put the pad of paper away and concentrated on her food. Monica played with her straw and watched Lacey.

"Sorry," Monica signed. "Just us," she added. "For now." Lacey smiled. "I just . . ." Monica continued. "This is the most incredible. I want to tell people. I don't want to hide." Lacey, her hand clenched in a soft fist, brought the nail of her thumb up to her lips and drew it down twice, teaching Monica her second sign for the day.

"Patience," she signed. "Patience." Monica repeated the sign, but there was no patience in her eyes, only wild desperation. The waitress caught Monica's eye as they were walking out the door.

"A ton of people order the curry chicken salad and Pepsi," she said. "It's not that special." Monica gave her a huge fake smile, and the finger.

It was Monica's idea to rent a canoe. Float. Escape. Along the way, they noticed people staring. "Double takes," Monica told Lacey. Lacey laughed. They went to Boathouse Row; Monica insisted on paying. They floated out onto the Schuylkill River, gently paddled to nowhere, and simply looked at each other across the boat. Monica was wearing her skirt and jacket, Lacey jeans and a T-shirt. Monica slipped off her pumps and pointed to Lacey's feet. Lacey peeled off her tennis shoes. They put their feet together, Monica in stockings, Lacey in black socks, making a little bridge over the canoe.

"Same feet," Monica said. Lacey whipped off a sock and showed Monica her toenails. Each nail was painted a different color: green, orange, blue, red, violet. Monica laughed. She stuck her hands up her skirt and peeled off her pantyhose. She showed Monica her foot. French manicure. Lacey whipped off her other sock. Then Lacey reached forward, grabbed Monica's hose and chucked them into the water. Monica laughed, lifted them with her oar, and threw them even farther. Then she grabbed Lacey's socks and flung them overboard as well. Lacey reached under her shirt with both hands and wrestled until she had removed her bra. She dangled it in front of Monica. Monica looked at the tag.

"Me too." She winked. Then she too removed her bra. They each set theirs on their oar and Monica counted. One, two, three. The bras went flying, in two directions. A couple of kayakers stopped to gawk. Lacey and Monica broke into laughter. They couldn't have explained to anyone else what they were doing or why. They just knew they were having fun. It wasn't every day you found out you were a twin. They could strip if they wanted, they could skinny-dip, they could bend over and moon the cars whizzing past on the Schuylkill Expressway.

It hurt a little, walking in their shoes without hose and socks, and they couldn't quite jog without bras, but after the canoe ride they still managed to walk downtown. They found a little store and bought matching pink flip-flops. Then they set off down the street, taking in the little dog park next to the church, talking about their puggles.

"So weird," Monica said, pointing to the picture of Snookie on her phone. "Snookie and Rookie. I mean, that's just strange!"

"Pepsi and curry chicken," Lacey said. She pulled a business card out of her pocket. It said ALAN FISHER, GENERAL CONTRACTOR. She wrote on the back of the card. *My boyfriend.*

"My God," Monica said. "Joe is an architect." Lacey nodded; she knew this. Monica pointed to her ring finger and then at Lacey. Lacey shook her head no. Monica pointed at herself, shook her head no. She rocked an imaginary baby. Lacey shook her head no again and pointed at Monica, who did the same. No husbands or babies, just boyfriends and dogs. Suddenly someone grabbed Monica around the waist and yanked her off the ground, swinging her around like a child. Just as suddenly, she was dropped. When Monica turned around, a huge man in a jester's outfit was staring at her like she was the weird one. Then he signed furiously to Lacey, who was laughing so hard, tears were coming out of her eyes. As the two signed rapidly back and forth, Monica looked helplessly from one to the other.

"Monica, meet Robert," Lacey said. "Robert, this is Monica. My twin." Robert's expression couldn't have been clearer. He was truly shocked. He mimicked coming up and picking up Monica and then doing a double take when he spotted Lacey. The three of them laughed. Then Robert hugged Lacey, waved at Monica, and headed off. As he walked away, the little bells adorning his costume jingled with every step he took.

"You have a lot of friends," Monica said, remembering all the deaf people at the art opening. "I'm so glad."

"The Deaf Community is my family," Lacey said. "The only one I've ever had."

This time, Monica moved through Lacey's studio as if she herself planned on painting it later from memory. She took in her worktable, her brushes, her pads of paper. She was so creative, so beautiful, so confident. Was that why Monica was so insecure? Had Lacey been given her dose of confidence? Monica was the one who had been given everything, yet Lacey was the one who walked with her chin up. Along the side wall, Monica saw new paintings. Fifteen portraits of people with their pets were propped against the wall. They weren't captivating like her horse paintings, but they were well done, with a whimsical touch. "Cute," Monica said. She would have to get Lacey to paint her with Snookie.

They were stolen, Lacey wrote. *Right before the art show.*

Monica frowned. *How did you get them back?*

Someone mailed them all back.

Weird!

You don't know the half of it.

Monica waited politely, but Lacey didn't offer any more information. A picture! She had to have a picture of the two of them. Monica mimed snapping a camera. Lacey shook her head no. Monica took out her cell phone. She stood by Lacey and held the phone toward them, ready to snap. Lacey pushed her hand away.

"What's wrong?" Lacey shook her head no. They moved over to the horse paintings still hanging where they were for the art show.

"You're so talented," Monica said. "I'm mesmerized. Really, I've been thinking of them nonstop, I can't get them out of my mind—" Monica stopped babbling; she was talking way too fast.

Lacey ran to a large easel with a huge sketch pad set up and picked up a marker. *Do you like horses?* she wrote.

Monica followed, picked up the marker. *I love yours.*

Do you ride?

No.

Did you have toy horses as a kid?

No. Monica didn't know what she said wrong, but Lacey was definitely upset with her answer. It was as if she thought she was lying to her. Was it because she was disappointed she obviously didn't share the same passion for horses? Monica pointed to the paintings again. *Really AMAZING!!!*

Lacey dropped the marker with a shrug. She went to the kitchen, grabbed a bottle of red wine and held it up.

They sat on the couch, laughing at everything after only one glass of wine each. They continued to communicate through a series of gestures and lipreading and writing. Monica indicated she got drunk easily, after only one glass; Lacey confirmed she was the same. Monica asked her how old she was when she first got drunk. Lacey leaned her head back on the couch as she tried to remember. Then she held up nine fingers.

"Nine?!" Monica shrieked. "Nine?" Lacey laughed.

Orphans, she wrote. *House mother had a whole cabinet of liquor.* Monica wished she knew sign. Whereas earlier she had wished them away, now she wished there were an interpreter here. Suddenly writing and gesturing weren't enough. She wanted detailed stories. She wanted to tell Lacey a searing pain went through her side when Lacey wrote the word "orphan." She wanted to know everything she'd missed about her twin's life. She wanted to tell Lacey all about hers. She wanted to call her parents. She wanted to bring Lacey home right now and demand an answer. True to her promise, she hadn't brought them up again, but surely they couldn't ignore it forever? How could they have done this to her? To them? Lacey offered Monica another glass of wine. She glanced at Lacey's empty glass and raised her eyebrow. Lacey shook her head. *None for me.* Monica copied her. Lacey stuck the cork back in the bottle and stood up. She looked at her watch. She pointed to Monica.

"Time you go," Lacey said. Monica stood, unsteady and confused. It felt like someone had just shut off the television midmovie.

"Okay." She flipped open her phone. "Your phone, text, e-mail, the works," she said.

"Why?" Lacey asked. Monica laughed, searched her sister's face for signs of humor. She stopped laughing when she saw none. Lacey was completely serious.

"When am I going to see you again?"

"You're not."

"Excuse me?"

"I wanted to meet. We've met. The end." Lacey moved to the front door of the studio, opened it, and waited for Monica to leave. Monica ran to the pad of paper and ripped off the old sheet.

YOU CAN'T BE SERIOUS.

Lacey walked over to the pad of paper.

I am.

WHY???????

What did you think? Best friends?

Sisters. Twins.

You're a stranger.

I don't have to be.

I'm sorry.

You can't do this.

Lacey put the pen in her pocket and walked back to the door. She didn't respond to Monica's pleas. Tears in her eyes, Monica followed.

"Please? Please?" Lacey turned her head away. "I don't care if you can't hear me. Can't understand me. This isn't the end. You're just upset. I forgive you. You're my twin. I'm not losing you. Do you hear me? I will be back." Monica lunged forward and kissed Lacey on the cheek. Lacey pulled away and wiped her cheek dry.

"Your parents dumped me like garbage and kept you," Lacey said. Her speech wasn't perfect, but Monica understood every word.

"No," Monica said. "I know they must love you. We have to go to them. They'll explain everything."

Lacey marched back to the pad of paper. *They've already been here,* Lacey wrote.

"No," Monica said. "No."

They came to see Mike. To ask him to keep quiet about ME. To keep you away from ME.

"I don't care. I don't care. I want you. I want you." Lacey shook her head no and gestured for Monica to leave. "Please," Monica said. "What will it take?"

Lacey went over to the pad of paper again and wrote down

her answer. Before Monica could read it, she ripped it off, folded it in half, and thrust it at Monica. Then, she pointed to the door again; she didn't want Monica to read it in front of her. Mustering every ounce of courage she had, Monica lifted her head and walked out the door. Once outside, she leaned against the brick wall and took a deep breath. Her heart was pounding. She opened the poster-sized paper.

Dump them. Dump your parents like they dumped me.

Chapter 21

Monica stood on the sidewalk, stunned and disoriented, like a loyal patron tossed from her favorite bar eons before closing time. She was clueless about what to do next. Go back to the hotel, back to Joe, start the workshop Saturday, home to Boston Sunday as if nothing had ever happened, as if she were the same old person living the same old life? It wasn't possible.

She placed her fingertips against her forehead and pressed. She tapped her fingers on her head, tap, tap, tap, like a woodpecker, tap, tap, tap; it didn't help, too light, not enough pressure, not enough to beat out the noise inside her head, the pain.

She had a twin, a twin, a twin, a twin, an identical twin. This should be a day of celebration. It started that way. Curry chicken salad and Pepsi and writing notes across the table like schoolgirls. Floating in a canoe, peeling off their shoes, and hose, and socks, and bras. Drinking wine in the middle of the day in Lacey's art studio. Like best friends, like sisters.

Monica didn't have very many female friends. She was one of

those who always felt more comfortable around men. Tina was a friend, up until she dumped her—

Because of her, because of Mike. But where did it go wrong with Lacey? What did she do, what did she say, what didn't she do, what didn't she say? What if she called a taxi, waited out here for Lacey no matter how long it took, grabbed her the minute she came out, shoved her into the cab, and yelled, "Drive!" Would that be considered kidnapping?

"Monica?" She removed her hands from her forehead and turned around.

"Mike," she said. That was all she could manage to say, but a lot more was going on in her head. *Tina's a bitch. Now I understand why you looked at me as if you saw a ghost. How did you know it was me out here and not Lacey; is it the suit? It has to be the suit.*

"Nice flip-flops," Mike said. "Very pink."

"It's a girl," Monica said with a laugh. "My pumps are in the river," she added. Mike followed her gaze down the street, as if they could see the river from where they stood. God, he was really, really attractive. Like really sexually attractive. No wonder Tina went around the bend. Was he looking at her feet again? They were normally very cute, but right now they were dirty. Maybe he liked dirty feet. God, she hoped not. That would make him weird and she really, really didn't want him to be weird. Didn't Lacey say she tried to sleep with him? Even weirder. Why didn't he? Did he not find her attractive? That was ridiculous, they were beautiful—

"You should've told me," Monica said. "At the cabin."

"I know," Mike said. "I tried. There were so many people around and Tina thought—"

"Tina knew? She knew back then?" Monica had never considered this. Probably because there were way too many things to consider. The shock of meeting her twin had knocked all logic straight out of Monica's head. She just couldn't trace all the little footprints—

"Monica, I'm so sorry. I can't imagine everything you're trying to process."

"How about after my parents paid you a visit, huh? How

about telling me then?" Mike sighed, jammed his hands in his pockets, kicked the sidewalk with the tip of his tennis shoe. She realized it sounded as if they were having a lovers' quarrel, and even more surreal than that, he was engaging in it too. Was she crazy? Was some kind of mental infection invading her body through the soles of her feet?

"They were very insistent," Mike said quietly.

"My father got to you too," Monica said.

"What's that, now?"

"You stood up to him at the cabin. I noticed that about you." *It made me think of you doing things to me, very dirty things. Women have sexual fantasies too, you know.* If he only knew the number of times and ways she'd imagined him taking her. They locked eyes. She completely forgot what they'd been talking about. Sexual fantasies were the murderers of intellect.

"Remember, I'm the one who gave you the invitation to the art show," Mike said. "I *wanted* you to meet Lacey." How quickly it all came back.

"What exactly did my father say to you?"

"Monica, I can't—"

"You have to. Please. I have to know."

"They didn't say much, okay? Look, you really need to talk to them."

Monica glanced up at the studio. "She doesn't want me to say anything just yet," she said. *She just wants me to abandon them without a word.*

"There seems to be a lot of that going around," Mike said. He gave her a soft smile.

"Tina left," Monica said. "She went back to California."

"I'm sorry," Mike said. "I never led her on."

"No, I know," Monica said. The moment hung between them; they maintained eye contact. Mike looked away first.

"So how was it?" he asked.

"It?"

"Meeting your twin."

"Oh. I love her. I love her." Monica stopped. She sounded way too fierce. It probably wasn't normal to love her. Even though she did. She might never be able to explain it to anyone, but she did.

"That's great," Mike said.

"She hates me," Monica said.

"Oh," Mike said, looking away. He knew her sister better than she did. He probably knew exactly how Lacey felt about her. "I'm sorry about everything," he said.

"It's okay."

"It's not. The fake interview, the birthmark. I hated freaking you out. I hated you thinking I was some kind of pervert—"

Monica laughed. "It's okay," she said. "Lucky for you you're a very talented artist. Because interviewing is definitely not your thing."

"Thanks a lot," he said. "So are you in town for—"

"I have to go," Monica said. She couldn't stay. There wasn't room in her head for everyone. Mike or Joe? Her parents or Lacey? She couldn't handle any of it right now.

"I might have some shoes, or—"

"I'll be fine," Monica said. She stuck out her hand for a shake. He laughed, then took her hand. She pulled him toward her, rolled up on her toes, and kissed him full on the mouth. She pulled back first, not because he wasn't kissing her back, he certainly was, but because she couldn't stand the thought that he might push away first, ask her what the hell she thought she was doing, for she had nothing, no explanation to offer. She pulled back as abruptly as she'd gone in, and found herself once again looking up at the studio. Only this time, instead of feeling foolish for being so paranoid, she thought she saw Lacey looking out the window. Without another word to Mike, just a pat on the chest, near the heart, she walked away.

The flip-flops were sticky, the thong digging into her toes. She was dying to take them off but she might step on broken glass, or a discarded needle, or one of many disgusting things she wished she were not thinking about. She kept walking. Kissing Mike had given her some kind of strange adrenaline kick, helped mitigate the pain of Lacey kicking her to the curb. She'd never been dismissed so thoroughly by anyone. She found herself back at the little dog park by the church. If only she had Snookie with her. He was in doggy day care in Boston.

She sat on a bench, not caring about the view or the company as long as she could rest her feet. She zoned out, tried to think of nothing but her dirty toes and the cracked sidewalk above which they hovered. Joe had called so many times her voice mail was full. The workshop was over by now. If they could see her now. Practically barefoot, braless, and aimless. That should be the title of her new book. *B.B.A.* When a hand slid over, holding half a tuna sandwich, it took her a moment to figure out what was happening. The owner of the sandwich, an old black man, sat next to her. He wasn't wearing any shoes, not even cheap flip-flops. A large shopping cart, filled to the brim with what looked like junk, was parked next to him. He had one hand resting protectively across the cart, the other was stretched out, offering Monica the sandwich.

"Oh, no, thank you," she said. He looked at her feet. He jabbed the sandwich at her again.

"Take it," he said. "You never know when the next one's a-comin'."

"Thank you," Monica said. "But I'm not homeless, just hopeless." She didn't know why she said that; the absurdity of blurting out something like that made her laugh. She glanced at the old man again. "Not that there's anything wrong with being homeless," she said. He withdrew the sandwich, unwrapped a tiny corner of it, and began to nibble.

"Mmm, mmm," he said. "Sure is good."

"Seriously," Monica said, pointing in the direction of her hotel. "I'm staying at the Marriott." He looked at her feet again.

"So why you hopeless? Lost your boyfriend? Dog? Job?" Monica shook her head. No, no, no. "You gotta boyfriend, dog, job?" Monica nodded. Yes, yes, yes. "Then why you so hopeless?"

"I lost my sister," Monica said. "Yesterday I didn't even know I had her and I've already lost her." Saying it out loud shook loose the sadness Monica could feel clinging to her. She started to cry. A second later, the sandwich was back in her face. She tried to stop crying, but still refused the sandwich. The old man put the sandwich on the bench in the space between them and whipped out a napkin from his pocket. Just when Monica thought he was going to offer it to her, he began twisting it with his thick, calloused fingers. A few seconds later, he'd transformed it into a rose. He held it up. Monica wiped her eyes, laughed, and took the flower.

"Now that's hope, darlin'," he said.

"Thank you."

"I'm Henry," he said. "But most folks call me Doc."

"Nice to meet you, Doc," Monica said. "I'm Monica."

"So what's your job?" Doc asked.

"I'm a motivational speaker," Monica said. She burst into tears again. Doc just nodded.

"You want to know a secret?" he said. Monica sniffed, nodded. "Ain't nobody got nothin' figured out. Nobody."

"That's oddly comforting," Monica said.

"Don't I know it," Doc said. "Don't I know it." He offered her the sandwich again. This time, she took it.

"So how'd you lose a sistah?" Doc asked.

"I don't know," Monica said. "She's mad at me in a way, I guess."

"Well, now, everybody gets mad. I get mad all the time. Don't worry, I ain't mad right now. But I get mad. I sure get mad."

"Me too."

"Don't worry, she'll get glad again."

"I hope so."

"You know so. You bettah know so. Whatever you gotta do, you do it."

"You're right," Monica said, pulling the folded easel paper closer. "I think you're right."

"I is," Doc said. "I sure is. Except when I'm wrong. Problem is, I don't always know the difference."

"Me neither," Monica said, handing him back the rest of the sandwich. "Me neither."

Chapter 22

When she first found out they were going to have the twins, Katherine Bowman vowed never to dress them alike. But soon the gifts poured in. Matching booties, onesies, bibs, and caps. It was a losing battle; she just couldn't let them go to waste. Sometimes, late at night when the world fell dark and Katherine tortured herself with decisions of the past, she wondered if it could have been that simple. If she'd just refused to dress them alike, would they have been healthy and independent? She knew logically that was foolish, but she visited questions like rosary beads, turning them over and over again in her mind as she said a little prayer. But one thing she knew for sure. The real trouble started with the blue shoes.

They were going out, and they couldn't find Monica's right blue shoe. Instead, Katherine slipped brown ones on her little feet. Monica looked over at Lacey's feet. She was wearing the little blue shoes. Monica lasered Katherine with a look of pure hatred, then became a shrieking, wailing ball on the floor. She didn't stop until Katherine removed one shoe on each girl and traded. Monica stopped crying long enough to look at her feet. One brown shoe, one blue. She looked at Lacey's feet. One brown shoe, one blue. She squealed and she and Lacey raced out of the room and down the hall.

I can't take this, Katherine thought as she hurried after them. *I'm going to lose my mind.* She'd had these thoughts often lately, but told no one. The twins were a blessing, a miracle. She couldn't let anyone know she was feeling ungrateful and exhausted, wishing in fleeting moments that she didn't have them, that she could go back to a life with just her and Richard.

One day Katherine laid out a blanket near the edge of the woods where the front line of trees could provide protection and shade. Soon the girls crawled off the blanket to explore a small patch of dirt behind them. If Richard had been there, he would have immediately scooped them up and scolded them. But Katherine wanted the girls to get dirty, touch the pungent grass, feel the grain and soot beneath their fingers. The dirtier the bath water was at the end of the day, the better the day.

They sat on the ground, heads bowed so close together it was hard to tell where one began and the other ended. The game had been going on for a week now. Katherine tried to figure out the rules as she watched them, but it was impossible. Who dug the deepest, the fastest? Whose nails and cheeks were caked with the most dirt? *They're so adorable,* Katherine heard all the time. *They're so close, aren't they?*

Yes, they were very close. Too close. Whenever Katherine tried to tell Richard there was something wrong with the twins' behavior, he dismissed her as a worrywart. He just didn't want to face it, she knew that now. What did either of them know about twins? Maybe all twins wrapped themselves in a cocoon and shunned the outside world, became members of a club nobody else could enter. Whenever Katherine tried separating them, Lacey would play happily and bond with her caretaker, but not Monica. Monica would get so upset she would become physically ill. She'd claw, and cling, and scream. One day, when her wailing failed to immediately summon her sister, Monica crawled over to the nearest wall and began to bang her head against it. Soon, she was wearing a helmet on the days when

Lacey would go with the neighbors. It was then Katherine insisted on bringing Monica to see Dianne.

She came highly recommended, a child psychiatrist specializing in toddlers. Most of the children she saw were victims of abuse. Things you could hardly believe. Four-year-olds threatening to kill younger siblings. Covering their brothers' or sisters' mouths with pillows while they slept. One child, a boy, dropped a hair dryer in the bathtub where his brother was happily playing. They used foul language, hit, bit, kicked, screamed. Katherine knew she was a failure as a mother. But there was no abuse in their home. Richard was a strict disciplinarian, but he never raised a hand to the twins.

And they were good girls, they really were. As rambunctious as boys, but Katherine didn't mind. But when Richard came home and saw two-year-old Monica wearing a helmet, banging her head against the wall, he finally agreed. Dianne Wells, head psychiatrist at the children's psychiatric unit at Boston University School of Medicine, agreed to see them. They were told to bring the twins together for the first visit. Later she would work with Monica alone.

The first visit, Katherine sat in the waiting room while Dianne observed the girls at play. She didn't realize how stressed she'd been until that moment when someone else, a professional, was there to help. After thirty minutes, Dianne called Katherine into the room. It was a large, comfortable space, like a living room with a desk in the corner. The girls were playing with a red ball in the middle of the floor.

"They're so adorable," Dianne said. Katherine's heart thumped. Was she going to be snowed like everyone else? "Their play is slightly advanced for their age," Dianne continued. "Two and a half years old, correct?" she said as she flipped through a legal pad. Katherine nodded, afraid that if she opened her mouth to speak, she was going to have a breakdown. Dianne motioned for Katherine to sit. If the twins noticed she had entered the room, they gave no sign of it. "They certainly seem capable of sharing," Dianne said, sitting on the arm of a chair a few feet from the girls. "Monica mirrors everything Lacey does," Dianne noted. Katherine scooted to the edge of the couch.

"Yes," she told Dianne. "She can't make a single move without Lacey." Lacey dropped the red ball and picked up a yellow one. Monica dropped her red ball and found a yellow one.

"That's actually very normal," Dianne said.

"Give Lacey the red ball," Katherine whispered. "But take away all the other red balls so Monica can't get one." Dianne glanced at Katherine. Terror clutched Katherine as Dianne hesitated; they couldn't leave the session without her seeing what she was going through every single day, what the girls were going through. They had to get help. "Please," Katherine said. "Please."

Dianne leaned forward, picked up a red ball, and handed it to Lacey. Lacey happily dropped her yellow ball for the red. Monica's head snapped up. Dianne quickly picked up the other red balls. Monica dropped her yellow ball and crawled to Lacey. She held her hand out for the red ball. Lacey put it in her mouth. Monica opened her mouth in a soundless scream, and swiveled her head around to glare at Katherine, as if she knew this was all her fault. Katherine put her hand over her mouth; did Dianne see that? Did she see the anger and hatred in Monica? Monica wasn't wearing her helmet. Katherine reached to the side of the couch, where Dianne insisted she hide it. Monica began to wail. Katherine held the helmet to Dianne. Dianne waved it away. Monica began to shriek.

"She's going to bang her head any minute," Katherine said.

"Put it away," Dianne said, grabbing the helmet and hiding it behind her back. "You may have created a trigger," she said.

"What do you mean?" Katherine said as Monica headed for the nearest wall. Katherine knew she'd reached a cutoff point. It didn't matter which ball you gave her now, she was going to start banging her head.

"The helmet could be a trigger, a stimulus to start the head-banging," Dianne explained. Seconds later, Monica reached the wall. She put both hands in front of her and pulled back her head. Both women leapt to their feet, but Katherine got to her first. When Monica's head made impact, it was with Katherine's soft palm instead of the hard wall. She continued to pound her head into Katherine's palm.

"See?" Katherine said, tears filling her eyes. "See?" Lacey dropped the red ball, toddled over to her sister, and hugged her around the waist, swaying with her like a drunken dancer until she stopped.

Chapter 23

"What do you mean, you quit?" Joe followed Monica into the bedroom. She wished he would go away. She needed to concentrate, needed to figure out exactly what she was going to do. She'd finally treated Joe to every single detail of her day with Lacey, and he just didn't get it. Oh, he politely listened at first, murmured "oh really" or "that's nice" a couple of times, but then didn't flinch when Monica told him Lacey ended the relationship just like that. He said he should give her time, they were adults now, with their own lives. That's when Monica knew for sure. It was over with Joe; he wasn't the guy for her, he never had been. She didn't need him, she didn't need the book, she didn't need to make another stupid blueprint to know what she wanted. She wanted Lacey. She wanted her twin.

It had been seventy-two hours since she was thrown out of her sister's art studio. Seventy-two excruciating hours. Joe was the least of her worries. If not for the promise she'd made to her sister, the one and only promise she'd ever made to her sister, she would have been at her parents' doorstep in an absolute rampage. She wanted answers and she wanted them yesterday. But for now, she would keep her promise. She and Lacey would confront them together, side by side. But first she had to get her sister to agree to see her again, and for that she needed time to think. She wandered their condo, looking at it with new eyes. It was so generic. So plain. So un-artistic. Joe had this theory that clutter "cluttered the mind," but after seeing Lacey's studio, Monica now hated her sterile environment. Lacey was so expressive, so colorful, so alive!

"What are you looking at?" Joe said.

"I hate those pillows," Monica said. She walked over, grabbed a drab, gray pillow, and hurled it to the floor.

"You picked them out," Joe said.

"And now I'm throwing them out," Monica said. She examined the walls. Decorator's white. Cream. Taupe. Whatever. "I'm going to paint," she said. "We need color in here."

"Monica," Joe said. "What are we going to do about next weekend?" Next weekend. The big San Francisco workshop. She couldn't go to San Francisco. Not now.

"You do it," Monica said. "Call it quitting. Call it a break. I don't care. I need some time off."

"We've been over this," Joe said. "I have a job. I can't take time off my job to do your job!"

" 'When things are crumbling down around you, don't duck, get out of the way.' "

"Don't do that," Joe said. "Don't quote me."

"Aha!" Monica said. "Don't quote you. Admit it. You wrote the book. Not me."

"I helped—"

"I helped," Monica said. "You wrote it."

"So what? You're the face of it. You're the one people come to see. You didn't even ask me how the rest of the workshop went."

"How did it go?" Monica began to strip the bed. What was she thinking, shades of gray?

"It was a total disaster. I stumbled over my words. I forgot huge chunks. I sounded like a total idiot. People walked out, okay? They didn't like me. They like you."

"I can't go to San Francisco," Monica said. "I need to be here." What if something happened to Lacey while she was gone? She couldn't lose her now, she couldn't let anything happen to her.

"Bring her with you," Joe said.

"What?" It was the first thing he'd said in a long time that didn't make her want to hit him.

"She could be your new assistant." Monica stepped over the pile of bedding on the floor and walked over to the painting on the wall. It was a reproduction. A generic rendering of a girl standing on the beach.

"Where did I get this piece of shit?" Monica said.

"How do I know?" Joe asked. "Bed Bath and Beyond?"

"Exactly," Monica said. "Some generic superstore." She took it off the wall.

"Monica," Joe said. "What are you doing?"

"Giving the bedroom a makeover," Monica said. She let the painting drop to the floor.

"So what about it?" Joe said, picking the sheets and comforter off the floor and tossing them back on the bed. "Take her with you."

"She doesn't want to see me," Monica said.

"So give her some space, then," Joe said. "Send her a postcard of the Golden Gate Bridge." That was the dumbest thing Monica had heard in her whole life. She wanted to push him off the Golden Gate Bridge. He didn't understand, she was different now. He didn't feel the same rage and betrayal. He defended her parents. Maybe they'd done the best they could for Lacey by sending her to a "special school."

There's a difference, Monica told him, between sending someone to a special school and abandoning them. Burying them. Erasing them. Tearing them apart. My twin, my twin, my twin. Why, why, why? Joe, of course, couldn't answer her.

There was nothing else she could do with the bedroom right now. She opened the closet, took out her suitcase.

"Oh, thank God," Joe said. "But aren't you packing a little early?"

"I'm going to Philadelphia," Monica said. "And I'm going to stay there until I have my sister back." She hadn't planned on doing this. But it made so much sense. Lacey had been abandoned; of course she was scared. Monica needed to prove she would never abandon her again. If that meant making some sacrifices, so be it. She would take sign language classes too, private lessons if she had to. She would take Snookie. That was it. Lacey couldn't say no to Snookie. She clapped her hands.

"Snookie!"

"You can't be serious," Joe said. "Monica, you can't be serious." Snookie came racing in, jumped on the bed, slid off the pile of sheets, and landed belly up at her feet. Monica laughed and picked him up.

"Can you believe it, Joe? Rookie, Snookie? Both puggles?"

"It is weird," Joe said. "It would make a good book."

"Is that all you ever think about?"

"At least I think," Joe said. "You're just reacting. You know that's not the best approach."

"I'm going to Philadelphia. I'm taking Snookie. And I'm not putting him in a stupid crate either."

"I'm going to call your parents," Joe said. He pulled out his cell phone.

"Don't you dare," Monica said. "Or you and I are over."

"Excuse me?"

"I mean it, Joe. I've never been more serious in my entire life. If you so much as dial the first number, you and I are through." Joe snapped the phone shut. She'd never seen such a pained look on his face. She was surprised how little it moved her. He was plain too—the serious professor type. It wasn't his fault, it was hers. He was the boyfriend version of her Bed Bath and Beyond painting. Nice-looking, but generic. No originality whatsoever.

"You've had a shock," Joe said. "I get that. I really do. And I'm so proud of you for wanting to reach out to her—"

"Proud of me? Why? Because she's deaf?"

"No—because she's being a bitch—" Monica put Snookie down, walked over to Joe, and slapped him across the face. The sound of it made her cry out, as if she were the one being hit. His cheek was red. Joe didn't move, or yell, or even put his hand up to his face. Monica stared at her hand as if it had done it without her.

"Joe," she said. "I'm sorry. I'm really, really sorry."

"I don't even know you," Joe said.

"I know," Monica said. "I've been having sexual fantasies about another man. A lot of them. Several a day."

"Jesus, Monica."

"I'm sorry, but I can't help what I fantasize about." Joe moved closer.

"Is this all about sex? You want it, fine." He pulled her to him and started unbuttoning her shirt. Monica pulled away.

"Stop it," she said.

"I thought it's what you wanted."

"Not like this. Not anymore."

"Who is he, huh? Who is this guy? Oh—wait—let me guess. This wouldn't have anything to do with Mike 'I'd like to see your sculptures' Dawson, would it?"

"No," Monica said. "It's no one."

"Bullshit."

"Joe." It was funny; this was what she wanted from him just a short while ago, a little passion, a little flare. Only it was too late. She knew that as she watched this man before her: It was too little too late.

"It's not important. It's just a fantasy. But my sister isn't. My sister is real."

"She's a total stranger, Mon. A total stranger."

"No," Monica said. "She's my flesh and blood."

"You don't even know her," Joe said. "And she asked you to leave her alone."

"Because she was abandoned as a child! By my parents. Her own family—"

"She's a grown woman now." Monica walked out of the bedroom and headed downstairs. Joe was right at her heels.

"You're not well, Monica. Cancel San Fran if you have to, but stay here and calm down." Snookie was hiding behind the couch. Monica knelt down and called his name. He came over, slowly, eyeing her as if he too might get slapped.

"I'm sorry," Monica said. She picked up Snookie and walked out the door. She'd pack later, when Joe was gone. It was amazing how much a person could change in just seventy-two little hours. She'd stood up to Joe. She'd quit her job. She'd slapped Joe, for God's sake, not something she approved of but something that fascinated her, as if she had not only discovered she had a twin, but inside she'd found she was a completely different person too. Triplets. Something inside Monica had opened up, and the gap between the life she wanted to live and the one she was actually living widened. It was no longer a crack she had to step over, it was a chasm. Lacey was what had been missing from her life. And now that she knew, she was going to do something about it, she was going to fix it; she wasn't going to live another day like a broken bookend.

Lacey stood outside the burgeoning shopping complex, awed at how quickly things had progressed. Alan showed her the original pictures; a short while ago, the site was nothing more than an overgrown field where teenagers went to toss their beer cans and cigarette butts. Now it was paved and sprouting a foundation and skeletal structure. Scaffolding rose high into the air, workmen wove in and out of the Genie cranes, shouting orders Lacey couldn't lip-read from the edge of the fence. Lacey had often fantasized about working in construction, and here she remembered why. The excitement was palpable. And even though Lacey thought America needed another mall like she needed a second head, she still admired the scope of work, the coordination involved, the attention to details and safety and quality—the daily sweat required to make it happen. And Alan was running the show.

She'd been on a roller coaster since Monica left, but no matter what else it was going to do to her, she now knew one thing for certain. Alan was family. Alan had never hurt her, never abandoned her, never really left her. She was the one who had been holding back, the one turning down his marriage proposal, pushing him away. Maybe Monica came into her life for one reason: Wake Lacey up to who her real family was before it was too late.

Lacey pulled out her BlackBerry. Should she warn Alan she was here or just walk inside, throw her arms around him, and tell him she loved him? Maybe she should have waited in his hotel room, her naked body wrapped in cellophane. She'd actually rushed into the store before she left, but all she could find was tinfoil. Instead of sex-on-a-stick, she'd end up looking like a burrito. She'd pull out the kinky stops later; for now she just had to find Alan and tell him she was different now, she was ready for a commitment.

In fact, she should prove it. She should ask him to marry her, right now, in front of all these people. He'd been humiliated when he saw what she'd written about marriage on the flip chart; this was her chance to make it up to him. She needed a ring. Too bad the mall wouldn't be finished for another six months. She had to have something. Maybe she could make one out of scrap metal—just for now. Then, she would get down on her knees, beg his forgiveness, and ask him to marry her.

First she followed the fence to the nearest opening, then she followed the clouds of dust billowing out of the center of the structure. She walked ahead until she came to what appeared to be an entrance onto the ground floor. She was soon walking past outlines of offices. At the first partition she saw a man standing by a steel work desk. He was a tall, bald man with a long auburn beard. Lacey had met him before. She didn't know his name; she'd always called him Red Beard.

He was the only one in the office, and he was standing with his hands on his hips, staring at the phone. Only when his lips started moving, and his head remained rooted to the phone, did Lacey realize he must have it on speaker. If hearing people only knew how silly they looked, mouths moving up and down all the time. He noticed her then, standing in the doorway, and how could he not? Between her suitcase and Rookie, she definitely stood out. The high heels, low-cut blouse, and miniskirt probably didn't hurt either. His eyes lingered on her as he held up his finger, asking her to wait. She set Rookie down and walked closer. She grabbed her pad of paper out of her purse. He pushed a button on the phone and said something to her. She pointed at her ears and shook her head.

She caught "Alan's girlfriend" on his lips. She nodded. *I'm looking for scraps of steel and a welding gun,* she wrote. He frowned as he read the letter, then looked at her with raised eyebrows. Lacey smiled and pointed to her ring finger. He pointed back at her.

"You want a ring?" he asked. She shook her head no. She grabbed the pad of paper back.

For Alan, she wrote. *I'm going to propose.* The man broke into a grin. He clapped his hands together and rubbed them.

Can I tell the guys? he asked.

As long as they don't tell Alan, Lacey wrote back. He pounded her on the back, headed out of the office, and motioned for her to follow. Rookie jumped into the chair by the desk and curled into a ball of bliss. Lacey tapped the man on the shoulder and pointed at Rookie. He gave her another grin and a thumbs-up. Lacey hurried after him as he strode down the hall.

In the next room, workmen were suspended from makeshift decks, unfazed by the sparks flying out of the ends of their soldering irons. Red Beard picked up a couple of scraps of metal off the floor. He turned and showed her his hands. Alan's were a little bit smaller, and Lacey pinched together her index finger and thumb to show him this. Suddenly the man whistled and yelled, and before she knew it, three other men were standing around them. He pointed at her and as he talked to them, she caught "Alan's girlfriend" and "propose." The men clapped. He then asked them each to hold out their hands so Lacey could pick whose fingers were closest to Alan's in size. She laughed as she examined their dirty hands; it was like a reverse Cinderella. When she found the one that was the closest, Red Beard measured his finger with a piece of string and then dismissed the men.

He motioned for her to follow him again, and soon he was

wrestling a soldering iron out of another man's hands. The man shut the sparking tool off and lifted his goggles. Red Beard went into charade mode, indicating what Lacey planned on doing, and what he wanted. The man grinned, took the scrap of metal from Red Beard and went to work on it. Within minutes, Lacey had a makeshift ring.

She and Red Beard walked down the hall like two Pied Pipers, for at least ten workmen were following them. She could see Alan at the end of the hall, bent over a table, a pencil sticking out over his ear. He'd never looked sexier. And not only was he a good-looking man, he was a good man. He was her family. She would never need anybody else. Feeling eyes upon him, Alan looked up, and spotted her immediately. She saw confusion in his face, but she also saw exactly what she needed: He was happy to see her. It was her Alan, the one who loved her. He asked her what she was doing there, with a smile on his face. He frowned at the men gathered behind her. "What's going on?"

Lacey walked right up to him, then got on her knees. She knew her skirt was probably showing a little too much action to the men in back, but she didn't care. Alan did. He tried to pull her up.

"Floor, dirty."

"I don't care." Lacey held out the ring. "Will you marry me?" Alan reached out and pulled her up. This time, she let him. He was looking behind her. Lacey followed his gaze. The men were whistling and clapping. When she turned around, there were more thumbs-up. Lacey took Alan's hand and slipped the ring on.

"I was supposed to ask you," he said.

"Yes or no?" Lacey asked.

"I love you," Alan said.

"Yes or no?"

"Why did you change your mind?"

"Last chance. Yes or no."

"Yes," Alan said. He picked her up and twirled her around. Then he kissed her. Lacey had never been happier in her life. But suddenly, Alan wasn't looking at her. He was looking over her shoulder.

"Oh my God," he said. Lacey didn't have to turn around; the look on his face told her he was seeing double. But of course, she turned around anyway. There, standing in the center of the workmen, tears in her eyes as if she too had just gotten engaged, was Monica. A stab of jealousy hit Lacey so sharp, so unexpectedly, it almost knocked her over. Alan took a step away from her, toward Monica. "Oh my God," he said again. And it was no wonder. Monica too was wearing high heels, a low-cut blouse, and a miniskirt. Her glasses were off, her hair was feathered like Lacey's. And under her arm was a wriggling puggle Lacey could only assume was Snookie. *My evil twin,* Lacey thought as she stared at Monica. *And her little dog too.*

Chapter 24

Lacey's first instinct was to attack, but there were way too many people around. Monica's little fan club. The men looked as if they had abandoned all thoughts of going back to work. They were chatting Monica up and taking unsolicited pictures with their cell phones. Only Rookie was equally horrified; he growled and shook his head at Snookie, as if warning him to either stay back or become his newest squeaky toy. Alan stayed by Lacey's side, but from the way he kept shifting his gaze from Monica to Lacey, she knew he too was fascinated. She was losing control of the situation. She needed to get Alan out of here. But Alan was already gone, chatting with Monica, head-to-head, mouths moving a mile a minute. She wasn't used to watching Alan talk without signing; it was like an out-of-body experience. What did their voices sound like? Was Monica's pretty? With any luck she sounded like a truck driver. Lacey marched over and put her arm around Alan's waist.

"Let's go back to your hotel," she said. "Celebrate. Romantic. Just the two of us."

"I'm taking you two out to dinner," Alan said.

"Alan knows of a great Italian restaurant," Monica said. Lacey understood her surprisingly well, but she looked at Alan as if she didn't. Alan interpreted.

"What about the dogs?" Lacey said. "We can't just leave them in the car."

"We can drop them off at the hotel," Alan said. "Along with your suitcases." Suitcases? Lacey only brought one. She looked at Monica. There it was, hiding behind her, an overstuffed bag on wheels.

"Is she going on a trip?" Lacey asked Alan. He laughed, as if she had made a joke.

"She said she's staying with you," Alan said. He had a big grin on his face. "It's perfect," he said. "I don't like being away from you; it's nice to know you'll have company." Lacey stared at Monica, and waited for her to set him straight. But Monica just stared back at Lacey with a smile bearing equal portions of guilt and hope. It was surreal, looking at someone with such a familiar face. *Mirror, mirror, on the wall,* Lacey thought. *Who's the—.* She dropped in mid-silent-sentence. What did it matter? She knew nothing about this was, or would ever be, fair.

Back at the motel, Lacey stood on the balcony and gazed down at the kidney-shaped pool. She neither knew nor cared what Alan and Monica were chatting about inside. She found herself imagining Monica leaning over the balcony with her, clearly saw herself give Monica a little shove. Would she hit the water and drown, or splatter all over the concrete?

I'm not evil, Lacey told herself. *I'm not.* Don't siblings always want to kill each other? Did this actually mean she loved her sister? No. She didn't know that woman in there, let alone love her. She didn't invite her into her life, and she couldn't believe anyone would have the nerve to pack a suitcase and invade a total stranger's life. Why was everyone else so thrilled? She was being stalked, her life was being invaded. For all she knew, Alan was in there calling the *Today* show. Maybe it would just be easier if Lacey threw herself off the balcony. Monica could comfort him, she could fall in love with him, she could marry him.

Over her dead body. Monica might have won this round, but she was definitely going to come out the loser. Even if it killed her.

She's stalking me, Lacey texted Kelly Thayler from the restaurant. *She brought a suitcase.*
Where are you? Can I come?!!!!!
Lacey shoved her BlackBerry into her purse. That's all she needed, her other stalker. They sat at the table like normal people, tearing into bread that was going to fill them up before dinner, sipping wine, pretending everything was normal. It wasn't. Lacey purposefully let Monica order first, resenting the obvious glee Monica showed as if she were relishing the thought that they would order the exact same thing again, regaling Alan with the story of their luncheon, as if a double order of curry chicken salad were some kind of miracle. Whatever Monica ordered, Lacey was going to get the exact opposite. She prayed Monica would order anything but the penne à la vodka. Lacey really, really wanted the penne à la vodka.

"I'll have the penne à la vodka," Monica said when Lacey gestured for her to go first. Lacey didn't dare look at Alan; he knew that's what she always ordered. She was going to kick him under the table if he said anything. He didn't, but he did treat her to a look and a big grin. When the waitress looked at Lacey, she pointed to her least favorite item on the menu, a seafood medley with mussels, scallops, and clams. Disgusting, but necessary.

"Mussels, scallops, and clams," she saw the waitress repeat slowly and clearly, as if repeating the order back to a child.

"Really?" Alan said. "You hate seafood." It was true, she did, but she hated Monica more.

"I can't eat anything that won't come out of its shell," Monica said. Alan roared with laughter and slapped the table.

"That's just like her," he said pointing at Lacey. The waitress, now thoroughly confused, looked at Lacey again. Lacey pointed to the seafood medley again, nodded yes in an exaggerated manner, and waved her away.

"Thank you," Monica called after the waitress.

"Why were you thanking her?" Lacey asked, using Alan as the interpreter. After all, it was his fault they were here; the least he could do was interpret.

"I was just being polite," Monica said. "Waiting tables is such a hard job." She gave Lacey a little smile. Lacey realized with a start that she'd just embarrassed Monica. Is this how it would have been growing up? Would Lacey have been the Black Sheep Twin? The evil doppelganger? An embarrassment to the entire family? She could picture Monica trailing after her, demurely apologizing for her after every outburst. As if she could feel Lacey was thinking bad thoughts about her, Monica excused herself and went to the restroom. *I have to pee too,* Lacey thought with a surge of resentment. *Are we really that much alike? Identical taste buds, identical bladders?* She hated the constant comparisons but she couldn't help it. Why did she have to go by Benjamin Books that day? She wanted to go back in time, back when there was only one of her.

Alan leaned forward. "What is going on with you?"

"What?" Lacey asked.

"You hate seafood, especially anything in a shell, and don't tell me you don't."

"She followed me here. How did she even know I was coming to see you?"

"You didn't tell her?"

"No, I didn't tell her." *Mike.* She should have known. *The traitor.* "I told her I never wanted to see her again."

"Why? She told me about your afternoon together. Lunch. Canoeing. It sounds like a lot of fun."

"And then I told her to get lost." Alan pushed back from the table.

"Here we are again," he said. "You didn't tell me any of this."

"I don't want to talk about her. This is supposed to be a romantic dinner for two. We're getting married, remember?"

Alan pointed to the restroom.

"Is she the reason you asked me to marry you?"

"What?"

"Don't play games with me. I know you."

"I don't want her here. I didn't ask her here. You invited her to move in with me! A stranger. Without even asking me." The look on Alan's face shifted back to neutral. She was coming back.

"Just give her a chance," Alan said. "She really wants to get to know you." Monica smiled as she took her seat, but Lacey knew she felt the tension between them. Or was Lacey just assuming Monica felt everything she did? It had taken a month to get back in a good place with Alan. Now Monica was poised to ruin it, make Lacey look like the bad guy, the twin who wouldn't "play nice." So that's what she would do. For now. When they were away from Alan, it would be a whole different ball game. When the waitress set the mound of clams, mussels, and scallops in front of her, Lacey looked at her with her best helpless and confused expression. She held out her hands.

"I can't eat this," she said. She pointed at Monica's dish. "I'll have that." The waitress whisked her seafood away with a pitying nod. Lacey picked up her fork, leaned in, and stabbed it into Monica's plate. Alan gave her a dirty look, but Monica looked as happy as a rejected clam.

Back at the hotel, Rookie and Snookie were standing at opposite sides of the bed, snarling at one another. A shredded pillow lay between them. Monica scooped up Snookie, who continued to snap and growl from her arms.

"I'm so sorry," she said. Lacey shrugged and then snuck Rookie a treat. At least someone was on her side. Lacey glanced at Monica's suitcase.

"Did you break up with your boyfriend?" she asked.

"We're just taking a break," Monica said.

"Why?" Lacey asked.

"This sounds like a private conversation," Alan said.

"But you have to interpret," Lacey said.

"I won't be there when you two are back in Philly," Alan said.

"We're fine," Monica said. "We spent the whole day without an interpreter, didn't we, Lacey?" Lacey understood every word she said. She turned to Alan.

"What did she say?"

"She said you spent the whole day without an interpreter."

"We wrote back and forth, we used gestures, we took off our clothes," Monica said. Alan, who was about to leave the room, stopped.

"You did what?" he said. Monica giggled.

"Just our bras and panties," she said, winking at Lacey.

"We should go," Lacey said. "Alan has an early day tomorrow."

"I'll pay for the cab," Alan said, taking out his cell phone. Monica picked up her suitcase.

"I'll wait outside," she said. "Give you some privacy." The minute she left, Alan wrapped Lacey into a hug.

"I'm glad you gave her a chance," he said. "I think this is a good thing."

"We'll see," Lacey said. "I just don't want to lose you." He took her in his arms and held her. Then he let her go, kissed her, and signed: "Never." She reached for his zipper.

"What are you doing?" Alan said. "She's waiting."

"Let her," Lacey said.

Monica went through Lacey's house like a prospective buyer, touching everything in sight, making constant comparisons. She had this or that book, she liked this or that magazine, her clock was almost exactly the same except it told time in Swahili. Lacey didn't know what she was saying half the time and she didn't care the other half. She was too busy figuring out how to get rid of her. Her options, thus far, were:

(a) Drop in on Monica's boyfriend, make him take her back.
(b) Drop in on Monica's parents, tell them their daughter was stalking her.
(c) Use reverse psychology: Crawl into Monica's skin like she was trying to crawl into hers.
(d) Take her to a Deaf event.

Monica didn't know sign language. One on one, she was handling herself pretty well, but if she was surrounded by Deaf-

ies, she might just crack. For many hearing people, it was a bewildering and isolating experience. That was it. If Monica
wanted a taste of her world, Lacey would give her a whole meal.
With any luck, Monica would choke on it, or at least eat and
run.

"I want to introduce you to some of my friends," Lacey said.
She picked up her BlackBerry and texted Robert.

"Really?" Monica said. "You're not mad I'm here?"

"You should have called first," Lacey said.

"I couldn't take the chance that you would say no," Monica
said. "I had to see you again. I had to."

"You don't mind hanging out with a few Deafies, do you?"
Lacey asked. Monica smiled at Lacey.

"I want to meet your friends," she said. It was crude and imperfect. Nevertheless, Lacey was completely horrified. Monica
had said it in sign language.

Monica had the best night ever. There were so many Deaf
people packed into the little downtown bar, and the room had
a palpable excitement, an energy you could feel all around the
room. Deaf people were funny, and talkative, and smart, and nice.
They were nothing like her sister. Much, much nicer. And American Sign Language was so beautiful. And she noticed she liked
some people's signing better than others; she could see Deaf
people had individual signing styles, like hearing people had
accents and intonations. She loved her sister's signing the best,
she was pretty sure, and she wasn't just saying that because they
were sisters. People's expressions varied too, in intensity and
style. It was a whole new, cool world.

She was hugged a lot too, genuine hugs from people she didn't
even know. And they were so patient with her, for signing so slow,
for asking for so much repetition. She couldn't understand everything, they were so fast. Signs started to blur together, and she
nodded her head as others were talking to her, but a few times
she was nodding to nothing, just praying they wouldn't ask her
a question and catch on that she was clueless. How could she
suddenly forget everything she learned in class? But she had, it

was gone, she was simply watching movement in the air. She couldn't wait until her sign language improved and she would know what these vivacious people were talking about. They seemed so happy to be together, and why wouldn't they? Most of their time was spent where hearing people were the majority; here they could just be themselves. She noticed saying good-bye was a process that often took hours, folks standing by the door, hugs and kisses over with an hour ago, still chatting away. She was exhilarated but drained, and suddenly felt tired, as if she needed to sleep. Did Lacey notice? Is that why she took her home so soon?

"That was so much fun," Monica said. They trudged up the steps and plopped on the porch chairs. Monica noticed they both had only two drinks apiece. Again, Monica thought about the evening. She learned a lot. And looking back on it, it was definitely not a "silent" experience. It was loud. And Deaf people were so cool. She learned it was okay to ask a Deaf person how they became Deaf. They would just tell you straight out.

"It's genetic."

"My mom had the measles."

"I had a fever when I was two." The origins and stories varied; the willingness to talk about it applied to everyone Monica met that evening. And it was starting to make sense to Monica. People only hid things they were ashamed of. Deafness was not something the folks she met tonight were ashamed of. So why not tell anyone who asked how they became Deaf? After the tight-lipped culture she grew up in, it was refreshing to be around people who shot from the hip. Robert and his actor friends were there, and she met so many new people. She met a Deaf doctor, a Deaf lawyer, students, artists, teachers. And even though she didn't understand much of the sign language, she was able to glean a lot from facial expressions and body language. They were completely shocked to learn that Lacey had a twin—that required no interpretation whatsoever. Especially from the actors who kept doing double takes at the pair of them just to make everyone laugh.

Monica knew the evening had been some kind of test. And from the sour look on Lacey's face, she figured she'd passed. Monica leaned her head back on the chair and listened to the sounds her sister couldn't hear. Crickets. An occasional car passing, a dog barking. She picked up the pad of paper she'd carried to the bar.

How did you become deaf?

Don't know. Ask your parents.

There it was again, the resentment. Monica dropped it. After a moment, Lacey picked up the pad and pencil again.

The doctor says it's a congenital loss in my left ear (maybe from birth) but sensorineural loss in my right ear—due to accident or infection or an illness.

We have to confront them (parents), please!

It's my fight.

Not fair. I lost you too.

Remember the rules.

I haven't spoken to them since we met.

Lacey waved at Monica until she was sure she had her full attention. Then she picked up the pen again.

You have to keep talking to them. Act normal. You have to give me time.

Time for what?

I don't know yet.

I thought you wanted me to DUMP THEM.

Eventually. Not now.

Okay.

Promise?

Cross my heart and hope to die.

Chapter 25

Lacey grudgingly had to admit that Monica was fun to have around. And she provided Lacey the perfect excuse to take time off of work. She needed a little break. Who wouldn't approve of Lacey taking time off to get to know her long-lost twin?

They took the dogs for walks in all her favorite neighborhoods, grocery shopped at open markets, and scribbled notes on the porch in their pajamas, filling in the cracks of their lives.

How old were you when you got your period? Both age twelve, around Halloween for Lacey, Christmas for Monica. Monica's aunt Grace took her out to dinner to celebrate. Margaret gestured tampon insertion instructions in a crowded bus depot bathroom.

Margaret: "Stick it up the hole!"
Lacey: "Which one?"

Biggest fear?
Bats, for Lacey.
The woods, for Monica.

Favorite holiday? Monica asked.

Hate them. All of them.

Why?

Group home. We'd be paraded around the community, given gifts by people we'd never met, baked dry cookies by old ladies, dragged to church, reminded we didn't have real families.

Monica was crying again. So Lacey told her about her one bright spot, Miss Lee. She could've been a Mrs. Lee; Lacey didn't know for sure, or really care. She knew enough. Miss Lee was tall, and funny, and beautiful. She always made an effort to encourage Lacey, made her feel special. Every holiday Lacey got some little gift from her. That was something, it wasn't all bad.

Halloween, Lacey wrote. *I also like Halloween.*

Our birthday! It was true, the twins were born under a full moon, in a night filled with witches and broomsticks, and buckets of candy. What their life might have been. Two little girls in disguise. Trick or treat. Monica felt bad for bringing up birthdays. After all, she had celebrated every single one with her parents.

Don't forget she collects lace, Monica wrote. *She keeps it all over the house. Lace, lace, lace.*

Who?

Mother.

Lacey was asleep on the sofa. Lying on her side, arms hugging a green silk pillow, mouth slightly open, a stray dark hair snaked across her upper lip. Rookie was curled up in the space between her stomach and the sofa's edge. Snookie was nestled at her feet. *They both like Lacey better,* Monica thought as she watched her sister sleep. It was now or never. Even though she knew Lacey couldn't hear her, she still crept up the stairs. It wouldn't take long; there were only two rooms and a bathroom on the second floor. She was staying in the guest-room-slash-office to the left; the room on the right was Alan and Lacey's. The closet in her room offered nothing but Alan's suits and a few high heels that Monica could only hope belonged to Lacey, as she'd already tried those on. She slipped into the bathroom.

She'd start with the medicine cabinet first; that was hardly a crime.

Toothpaste, dental floss, Q-tips, tampons, shaving cream, deodorant, men's cologne, perfume. No prescription pills, not even a bottle of pain reliever. Monica's pills were in her suitcase. She hadn't carried them in her pocket lately. When was the last time she'd even thought about them? A pair of jeans were slung over the towel rack. She loved how Lacey dressed: casual, artistic, confident. Before she could talk herself out of it, Monica slipped off her tan dress pants and slipped on the jeans. A perfect fit. She took her socks off and looked at her feet. Just plain old pink polish. How mundane, how utterly ubiquitous. She opened the cabinet underneath the sink.

There it was, a basket filled with polishes, every shade under the rainbow. Monica closed her eyes and tried to remember which colors her sister had on her feet. She picked the colors out of the basket, sat on the toilet, and propped her foot up on the edge of the tub. Red, she was sure, for the big toe. Red, green, yellow, blue, purple. Right foot, then left. She put the polishes back in the basket and was about to close the cabinet when she noticed the makeup bag next to it. She slipped it out and stood in front of the mirror. The glasses had to go. She'd taken them off when she visited Lacey and Alan at his job site, but soon the need to see won out over vanity. Now, though, she hated them again. Did Lacey wear contacts? Or did she get deafness while Monica got the poorer vision?

Monica took her glasses off, shook out her hair. Lacey's hair was longer; there was nothing Monica could do but let it grow. Lacey wore a dusky eye shadow, a trace of brown eyeliner, black mascara, and at times a shiny copper color on her lips. Monica did the same. Then she added a freckle near her chin with brown eyeliner. Except for the hair, and the way-too-conservative blouse, she dared anyone to tell them apart now.

She tossed her dress pants and socks over the towel rack and padded into the bedroom, careful not to mess up her toes. She headed straight for the closet. It was a shame she didn't have time to try everything on. She took off her blouse, threw it on the bed. She picked a billowy cream-colored blouse with color-ful flowers. It was low-cut, with strings that could be tied in a bow. She left them hanging down, as she imagined Lacey would. She found a pair of brown flip-flops, perfect for show-ing off her new toes. She found a group of perfumes gathered on the dresser, sniffed each one until she found one she liked the best, a soft vanilla fragrance, and sprayed. She opened the dresser drawer. She avoided Lacey's rings but put on a pair of gold hoop earrings and a small gold bracelet. The transforma-tion was complete.

It's amazing how easy it was, how suddenly she wasn't herself anymore. She was sexier, way more confident. What would Joe think? Would he throw her down on the bed, take her right here, right now? But it wasn't Joe she imagined ripping off her clothes, it was Mike. Michael Dawson, sculptor. She could feel his lips on hers, his arms holding her, crushing her, as if he couldn't get close enough, couldn't take her clothes off fast enough; then, he's on top of her, inside her, all about her. Could she do it? Could she go to the studio and surprise Mike over the weekend? No. Because no matter how she looked on the outside, inside she was still the same old boring, conserva-tive Monica.

She crept back downstairs, stood next to the couch, and lis-tened to her sister breathe. She was very loud. Just like she chewed loudly, and tapped pencils to a beat she couldn't hear, and sometimes shuffled her feet noisily along the sidewalk be-cause she couldn't hear herself walk. Would Monica have told her these things about the hearing world if they'd grown up to-gether? Would Lacey have wanted her to, or would she have hated her for it? Just like she might hate her for going against her plan to dump her parents. Because nothing was going to get resolved until they all met face-to-face. Monica would do it; somehow she would get them all in a room together. They were a family. Whether they liked it or not.

"Okay," Lacey said. "Tell me about our parents until I say stop." Monica glanced at Kelly Thayler, who was perched across from Lacey, ready to interpret and offer comfort as if she were the sister here. Why did she even have to be here? They were doing fine on their own. And it was just rude of Kelly to always sign back and forth with Lacey without telling her what she was saying. Weren't there already enough barriers between them without adding her to the mix? Just because they spent a couple of years together as children, years that should have belonged to Monica—that didn't give her the right to storm in and take over. Although she did like hearing stories from when Lacey was a girl, stories that should have never happened, stories that should have been both their memories.

Lacey was a hellion at school, she learned. Always playing practical jokes, always breaking the rules. Once, at Lacey's insistence, she and Kelly tied their bedsheets together and slid out the window.

"We were only on the second floor," Kelly laughed.

"Where did you go?" Monica asked. Wishing it had been her and Lacey sliding down the sheets together.

"We collected lightning bugs," Lacey said. Monica loved watching her sister sign. She could see the lightning bugs brought to life before her very eyes, flying and blinking, then being trapped in a jar. Lacey even bugged her eyes out as if she were the one who'd been captured.

"That's right!" Kelly said. "You snuck into the kitchen and poured an entire jar of spaghetti sauce down the drain just to get the jar to put them in."

"Ragu," Lacey said. "Margaret was furious. She didn't let me eat spaghetti sauce for an entire year."

"Bitch," Monica said. "Total bitch." How could her parents have done this to her?

"It was no big deal," Lacey said. "It was worth it."

"It's so easy to picture," Monica said. "And of course I know exactly what you looked like as a little girl. Exactly like me."

"You two don't look exactly alike," Kelly said. "I can easily tell you apart."

"Care to put that to a test?" Monica said. Monica had been practicing "changing into Lacey" every day she could get away with it. She was getting good at it. She doubted Little Miss Interpreter could tell them apart.

"We're not trying to look alike," Lacey said. "I don't want to look like anybody but me." *It's too late,* Monica wanted to shout. *You do look like me, I look like you, and there's nothing you can do about it.* Lacey was, of course, a different person. Monica was shocked her sister rode a motorcycle, jumped out of airplanes, and didn't seem to care what anyone thought of her. Monica wished she were more like her.

"Back to the subject," Lacey said. "Tell me about our parents until I tell you to stop."

Monica started with the Colonel. He was very tall, dark hair, blue eyes. They definitely had more of his genes than their mother's. He grew up in Savannah, Georgia, with his sister, Grace. They came from money. He learned to fly airplanes when he was just sixteen—

"That's where you get your sense of adventure from," Monica said, interrupting herself. "From our father."

"No," Lacey said. "I got it from being abandoned. Alone. Having to fight my way through the world." Lacey stared Monica down, daring her to say otherwise. Monica felt as if she'd been punched in the stomach, but she didn't argue the point.

"When Dad and Grace were little, their mother, our grandmother—"

"Stop," Lacey said. "Grandparents. I never thought about grandparents. Aunts, uncles, cousins. I never thought about any of that." She leapt off the couch and began pacing. This time it was Kelly's turn to give Monica a dirty look. It was true. A whole world had been taken from Lacey. Gifts, and kisses, and hugs. Birthdays and Christmas and—

It wasn't just her parents who'd kept this secret, it was an entire family structure. Everyone lied. Why? How could they have possibly convinced them to keep quiet? Was that why they hardly ever visited their relatives? Had her father set some kind of condition, complete with punishment if anyone ever opened their mouths? He probably had.

Grandma and Grandpa Bowman were very old. They died

when Monica was seven. She supposed it wasn't their place to tell a seven-year-old what her parents had done. Her mother's parents lived in California. And although she'd begged many times, Monica was never allowed to stay with them alone. At the time they said it was too far, she was too young. But was it really because they were afraid if she were alone with her maternal grandparents, they would tell her about Lacey? They should have. Somebody should have.

Aunt Grace. Monica's favorite. She'd finally done it—but look at all the years that had gone by. Could she even look at Aunt Grace the same again? Her parents were first on the list, but Aunt Grace wasn't off the hook either. Monica was going to confront her too, hopefully with Lacey at her side.

"What's your first memory?" Lacey asked. Monica thought about it. She closed her eyes, hoping, praying a memory involving Lacey would come to her. But there was nothing. Nothing.

"Playing on a blanket on the grass. At the cabin," Monica said. "I think it had Peter Rabbit on it."

"Cabin?" Lacey asked.

"Our summer home," Monica said. "Moosehead Lake. An hour from Portland. We went there every summer. Mom and Dad are there now." She stopped, as if venturing any further would set off a land mine. But Lacey seemed calm, taking it all in. "We should go there," Monica said. "We should go there right now."

"Moosehead Lake," Lacey repeated. She headed for the stairs. "Come on," she said. Monica and Kelly followed without even asking why. Soon they were standing in front of the computer in the guest bedroom. Lacey brought up Google Earth. "Show me," she said. Monica entered the address for the cabin. Soon they were hovered over it, zooming in close. "Wow," Lacey said. "It's huge."

"It's more like a hunting lodge than a cabin," Monica said.

"Her father makes guns," Lacey told Kelly. *He's your father too,* Monica thought.

"Air guns," Monica said out loud. "For target practice. For fun." Soon the screen filled with the faraway image of the cabin, then zoomed closer and closer until it loomed so large they felt as if they could have put one foot through the screen and they'd be standing on the wraparound porch.

"See the woods," Monica said, pointing it out on the screen. "I used to play on a blanket at the edge of them."

"In that first memory," Lacey said. "How old were you?"

"Four?"

"No memories before the age of four?"

"No. You?" Lacey shook her head no. "No memories before Hillcrest," she added.

"We should get hypnotized," Monica said. They fell silent. Parents. Grandparents. Aunts. Uncles. Cousins. Lies.

"Hey," Kelly said. "Let's get out of the house. Go shopping. See a movie. There's a new foreign film playing at the mall."

"Ugh, I hate foreign films," Monica said. "Always so dramatic. Let's see a comedy instead."

"Foreign films are captioned," Kelly said. "Just-released movies at the theatre are not." Monica felt awful. Kelly did know her sister better than she did. Monica knew nothing.

"I didn't know," Monica said. "I'm sorry."

"It's all right," Lacey said. "There are a few theatres that have special nights where you can get a captioning device. And if it's an action film, I can enjoy it without all the dialogue."

"We could rent a movie," Monica said.

"You two need to get out of the house," Kelly said. "From the looks of it, you're trying to barricade yourself in here." Kelly stared at Monica. "What about your job?" she asked. "Don't you have seminars to give?"

"My sister is more important," Monica said. "Nothing is ever going to come between us again." She didn't like the look Kelly and Lacey exchanged after that. Monica might have a million questions for her family, her entire life had been a lie, and she no longer knew up from down. All of it, she could handle. Kelly Thayler, on the other hand, was definitely in the way.

Chapter 26

It wasn't a cabin, or even a lodge. It was a freaking mansion. This was the summer home? So much for the parents not being able to afford both girls. Lacey's heart was pounding out of her chest. It had been a whirlwind—first the flight to Portland, then renting a motorcycle and riding all the way out here. The grass looked greener than any grass she'd ever seen. It was so crisp she could smell it down to its original seed. Competing scents hung in the air: grass, apples, hay, lilacs, and the pungent earth beneath her feet; and the humidity clung to even the little hairs on her arms, or was it sweat? She could feel everything vibrating around her. She should have come at night; she was overexposed in the daylight, like a piece of film snatched out of the darkroom and paraded into the sun. There was an apple tree standing guard to her left, heavy with fruit. She wanted to crawl underneath it, unseen, and sleep until evening.

If anyone spotted her, they would think she was Monica. At least from a distance. So, for now, she could hide in plain sight. But what would happen if someone called out to her and she didn't respond? People may have "eyes in the back of their

head" but they certainly couldn't lip-read through the back of
their head.

It's the other one, someone might say behind her back. *What
does she want?*

What did she want? She wanted to look them in the eye, she
wanted to let them know that she knew. She knew what they
had done. And now, Monica knew what they had done. She
wanted them to know that they knew. She knew she should've
had a better plan than "I want them to know that we know," but
what did she know about stalking and plotting revenge? She
was an artist, not a fighter. And her plan was pretty good for an
amateur, if she did say so herself. Monica would hate them. The
only problem was, now Monica would cling to her, and Lacey
didn't want to have to deal with that either. Who started this
mess? Who left that letter in her mailbox? It was too late, it had
been done. Now she had to see it through.

I'm back, she wanted to say. *I'm back.* Lacey looked at the
woods, a dark canopy stretching into the distance. And that's
when it hit her. She'd been here before.

Lacey flattened herself against the side of the cabin, hoping
the logs would be enough to hide her. The lodge was located at
the end of a winding dirt road, hugged along the front and the
back by long stretches of manicured grass and ending in the
woods behind her. The motorcycle Lacey rented was parked in
the woods at the entrance to the road, underneath a tall pine
tree.

Someone was definitely home; a Range Rover was parked in
the driveway. Lacey wasn't sure what she was going to do if and
when she got into the house, but she had to see if Monica was
telling the truth about their mother collecting lace. She didn't
turn it around any further in her mind, she let it sit, untouched,
like ambiguously dipping a toe in a swimming pool you were
afraid to dive into. No matter what else, she just had to see a little
piece of lace.

But it wasn't until she was flattened in broad daylight against
the side of their summer cabin, that she remembered Monica

said "the Colonel" was a gun collector. The Colonel. What kind of ridiculous name was that? Every time she thought of it, a bucket of fried chicken and a heavily mustached man floated in front of her. Monica said he'd never even been in the armed forces because of a bum leg. Hey, maybe he'd get along with Kelly Thayler. Her father, "the Colonel," air-gun manufacturer. Lacey had never shot a gun, but it was something she could picture herself doing. Especially now.

She edged along the side of the house, opposite the driveway. She should have asked Monica about dogs. Or an alarm system. But that would have raised suspicion. If Monica could see her now. She thought Lacey was visiting Alan at his worksite, and even then she was texting her twelve times a day. Lacey wasn't texting back; she needed a break.

She reached the back of the house by scooting over like a suicidal maniac on the ledge of a twenty-story building. There she encountered an enclosed porch. Lacey reached for the door before she could talk herself out of it, reasoning that breaking and entering, from the force of the word "breaking" alone, should be quick and decisive.

The door opened. If any kind of alarm went off, Lacey couldn't hear it. Maybe her deafness made her braver; sound, it seemed, went a long way in scaring people. The porch was adorned with wicker furniture, yellow-flowered cushions, and potted trees. Not plants, trees. They looked like palm trees, but it wasn't warm enough for palm trees, was it? If they put a large sandbox back here and the Hollywood sign, they'd be in LA.

A broom and a dustpan were propped up beside the outside door. Directly across from it was the door leading to the inside. The three windows behind the wicker couch were sealed with shades. So much for peeking in. Other than the wicker couch, settee, and chairs, there were three end tables. They were all wiped clean except for the smallest one next to the couch; on it lay *The Architect of Your Soul*. Lacey wished she had a Sharpie marker with her. At least she knew she had the right house.

Now what? This was not a well-thought-out plan. Did *The Architect of Your Soul* have any advice? Don't hesitate!? She didn't have a lot of time; she didn't want to leave the motorcycle there for long. What if a teenage cow from a nearby field got bored, wandered in, and tipped it over?

Someone could come out of or into the porch at any moment, from either door. She'd actually be safer in the house. Most likely the door to the inside would be locked anyway, and she had no intention of actually breaking the window, nor did she have any credit-card or bobby-pin tricks up her sleeve. It would be locked and she would go home. Or into the woods. Something about them felt so familiar. She remembered Monica saying she was afraid of the woods, yet another thing they didn't have in common.

Again, fast, so she couldn't change her mind, Lacey snuck up on the door, turned the knob, and gently pushed. It opened. Stunned it was that easy, Lacey stepped inside with a sense of giddiness she hadn't felt since she was a little girl up to no good at Hillcrest. Lacey entered a small mudroom. It was crammed with coats, and shoes, and boots, and caps, yet there was a clear order to the chaos. A stacked washer and dryer combo sat to her left. The dryer was on; the flipping clothes looked like children jumping up and down in a bouncy hut. A sleeve waved at her, and she couldn't help but wave back. She started laughing, then slapped her hand over her mouth, remembering hearing people could actually hear.

Were dryers loud? Hopefully, loud enough to mask any noises Lacey was inadvertently going to make. But the flip side was that someone, most likely her mother, would be back soon to check on the laundry. They didn't seem like people who abandoned warm clothes. Just daughters. A single shelf ran along the entire wall close to the ceiling. It was neatly jammed with products: laundry detergent, softeners, mosquito repellent (no long-lost-daughter repellent, a purchase they were going to soon wish they had made?), WD-40, dish washing liquid, paper towels, toothpicks, BBQ lighter—

Lacey, darling. Someday this will all be yours.

Lacey felt her stomach rumble. She hadn't eaten in over fifteen hours. She was suddenly starving. She didn't want to pass out. Hell, who didn't come to their parents' house to raid the fridge? There was nothing edible on the shelves, and Lacey had no inclination to swallow the lighter fluid. Now, where did that come from? She actually pictured herself uncapping the bottle and drinking. Hunger was turning her pea brain into mashed peas.

The expansive kitchen was right off the mudroom. Where did these people get off calling it a "summer home"? The entire kitchen was bigger than the home Lacey grew up in. Okay, not quite, but definitely nicer. It had granite countertops, slate floors, subdued orange walls interspersed with ornate taupe tiles. Obviously a "professional decorator" had been hired for the little summer cabin, or Snow White had learned a thing or two about sprucing up other people's places.

There was no food sitting on the counter, not even an obligatory bowl of fruit. She had to open either the double-decker stainless steel fridge or the cherry cabinets. There had to at least be a package of cookies or chips. Which would be quieter? Things from the fridge most likely had to be cooked. So even though she was in the mood for some big fat steak, she wasn't about to fire up the grill. She wished Alan were here to see this, but since he wasn't, she snapped some pictures with her Black-Berry. Lacey opened the fridge. It was jammed with Tupperware.

Lacey was standing in front of the refrigerator with her mouth full of the best potato salad she'd ever tasted, when a tall man with broad shoulders entered the room. But instead of a gun, her father was carrying a large shrub and a shovel. She turned toward him with a fork still sticking out of her mouth and the refrigerator door open.

"Monica," she was pretty sure he said. She waved. He waved back with his rake. He wasn't intimidating at all, this Colonel. She liked his energy. She looked like him around the mouth, and they had the same thin nose.

"Does your mother know you're here?" Lacey nodded. He nodded back and held up the shrub. She gave him a thumbs-up. He started across the floor, stopped, turned. "Why skeicd sleid iekd that?" She was pretty sure he was looking at her clothes. She looked down at her ripped jeans, and tank top. She shrugged, rolled her eyes. He squinted at her. Then he blabbed some more. She didn't catch a word of it. She winked. He laughed, shook his head, shook his finger at her. Then, he held up his shrub again and left.

Katherine and Richard Bowman pulled into their driveway and parked behind the Range Rover.

"John's here," Katherine said.

"I don't see why we need another bush," Richard said. "We're surrounded by woods."

"He gets them at a discount," Katherine replied.

"He always leaves our back porch unlocked," Richard said. They got out of the car and walked around to the back, each taking grocery bags out without saying any more. They headed into the house.

"I have to get the laundry out before it gets wrinkled," Katherine said, setting the bags on the counter. Richard didn't answer; he simply went about putting the groceries away. Katherine stopped short just before entering the mudroom. The clothes from the dryer were folded and sitting on top of her antique dry sink.

"Richard," Katherine said. "I think John folded our laundry." Richard was standing in front of the refrigerator, holding it open.

"He also wrote *HELLO* in the Jell-O," Richard said.

"What?"

"He wrote *HELLO* in the Jell-O."

"You're joking."

"Come see for yourself." Katherine stood beside Richard and stared into the fridge. Sure enough, *HELLO* was clearly visible in the red pan of Jell-O she'd made just the other night.

"Is everything okay with him and Barb?" Katherine wondered out loud.

"Hello, folks!" Richard and Katherine turned to see John, sprinkled in dirt, carrying a shovel.

"I planted the bush just outside the porch, Mrs. B.," he said.
"Thank you, John."
"It's going to grow like a weed."
"Are you hungry, John?"
"No, no. The Mrs. and I are going out for brunch. Whatever that is. Personally I prefer lunch or dinner. I think she just uses it as an excuse to have a cocktail in the middle of the day!"
"John," Richard said. "Did you fold our laundry?" John's smiling face morphed into a pool of confusion. He glanced behind him at the folded clothes.
"Nope," John said. "Must have been Monica."
"Monica?" Katherine said. "Monica's here?"
"She was. Found her standing in front of the fridge like you two are—"
"Oh, thank goodness," Katherine said.
"Stuffing her face with potato salad."
"She hates potato salad," Katherine said. John shrugged.
"She's a great woman," John said. "You know, I didn't think she really liked me. But today, we had a great little talk. I thought maybe all that fame would go to her head, but she's a real down-to-earth girl, isn't she?"
"She's our joy," Katherine said. "She wrote *hello* in the Jell-O."
"I'm going up to the office," Richard said.
"Where is Monica now?" Katherine said. "I didn't see her car in the driveway."
"You know," John said. "Neither did I. Last I saw her, she was standing right where you are."
"I hope she didn't leave," Katherine said. "I haven't seen her in weeks."
"I'm sure she's around," John said. "Otherwise wouldn't she have written *good-bye* in the Jell-O?"

"Where are you?" Monica looked down at Rookie and Snookie, as if they could answer her mother's question. Instead, they looked back up at her, whined, and then tugged on their leashes. She was walking around downtown Philadelphia. They'd already passed Lacey's art studio several times. If Mike was up there, he certainly wasn't popping out for lunch, or anything else. Why did she answer the phone? Her mother's voice sounded full of panic as always. Had Monica forgotten some kind of family gathering?

"I'm on the road," Monica said. "You know how it goes."

"Joe said you aren't working. He said you haven't been working for weeks." Traitor. Monica was going to have it out with Joe the next time she saw him.

"I needed a break, Mother."

"I know you're here," Katherine said. "Why did you sneak into the house and then take off?" Monica stopped in the middle of the sidewalk.

"You're saying you saw me at the cabin?" she said.

"John saw you, darling. And even though I appreciate you folding the laundry, I had to throw the Jell-O out."

"Why did you have to throw the Jell-O out, Mother?"

"Because I don't think sticking your fingers in it is very hygienic, do you?"

"I guess not."

"There are easier ways to say hello. Why don't you try—I don't know, sticking around until we get home and doing it in person?"

"I was just passing through, Mother. I had to use the bathroom."

"Passing through? You're behaving strangely, Monica. You haven't seen us or talked to us in weeks—now you're passing through to use the bathroom, borrow my lace coasters, and defile the Jell-O?"

"Borrow your—" Monica stopped herself, and laughed. What would her mother do if she just told her? *It wasn't me. It was Lacey. Lacey stole your lace. Remember her? She's wonderful. She's beautiful. And she's totally pissed. So am I, Mother, so am I.*

So much for Lacey's visit to Alan. Why didn't she tell her where she was going? Why was she still shutting her out?

"I have to go, Mom."

"Monica, you can't have gotten far. Why don't you just turn around and come home?"

"I have plans with Joe—I'm sorry. I'll stay longer next time. I promise." Monica shouted "I love you" and hung up.

Alan was sitting on the front porch when Monica returned with the dogs. He was dressed in running clothes and stretching. Monica sat down on one of the lounge chairs.

"She went to my parents'—our parents'—cabin," Monica said. Alan stopped stretching and turned to face her.

"Pardon?"

"Lacey. She went to my parents' cabin."

"How do you know?"

"My mother just called. Our friend John, who does odd jobs around the place, ran into her. She also folded the laundry and—apparently—did something vulgar to the Jell-O."

"Where is this cabin?"

"Moosehead Lake. Maine."

"Jesus," Alan said. He leaned against the porch rail. "How did she know where it was?"

"I showed her on Google Earth."

"How did she get in?"

"Dumb luck. Our friend John was over planting shrubs. He always leaves the back porch unlocked."

"She probably would have found a way in anyway," Alan said.

"She's braver than I am," Monica said. "Same DNA, but I'm a coward."

"She's her own woman, all right," Alan said. Monica got up and slowly approached Alan.

"I don't want you to betray any confidences," she said.

"But?"

"But what does Lacey think about me? What did she say to you when she found out about me?"

"She was in shock, of course." Alan looked pained himself, and his gaze remained anywhere but on Monica. There was definitely more to that story, but she wasn't going to push it.

"Still. You must have quite the life," Alan said. "Best-selling author. Workshop circuit."

Monica shrugged. *It's not my life,* she wanted to say.

"I lost my assistant," Monica said. "I haven't done a workshop since. And Joe, my ex-fiancé, is the mastermind behind the book." Monica moved away from Alan and fixed her gaze on the small backyard. "I've been searching for something my entire life," she said. "I always thought I was crazy. But I'm not. It's her. I've been searching for her."

"From what I've heard, you two were very close as toddlers."

"I wish I could remember. How can I not remember?"

"Do you have the horse?" Alan asked. Monica looked at him. "What horse?"

"Lacey has half a toy horse. Her house mother said she came to the orphanage with it. We assumed you had the other half. The head and the front legs." Monica shook her head.

"Where is it?" she said. "Can I see it?"

"Would you believe we spent an entire day digging through garbage looking for that horse?"

"You did what?"

"It's a long, stinky story," Alan said. Monica laughed. "Did you have horses growing up?" he asked.

"Lacey asked me the same question. No, we didn't have horses growing up. My mother wouldn't even let me get a dog; she was afraid my dad would accidentally shoot it. What? Does she think I was some spoiled little rich girl? That I had the perfect life? My father is a wannabe military colonel who doesn't know how to bond with you unless you're holding a rifle, and my mother is so nervous she's afraid of her own shadow. I love them, but it wasn't all angels on parade, if you know what I mean. If Lacey got to know my parents, she might be glad she grew up in an orphanage." Monica slapped her hand over her mouth. "Oh my God," she said. "I can't believe I just said that."

"It's okay," Alan said. "Nobody's family is perfect. Nobody's life is perfect."

"Was it that terrible? The group home?"

"Well, I don't think they beat them into submission or anything, but how great can growing up an orphan be? She definitely carries scars. And she doesn't attach to people easily. Besides some art teacher that visited once in a while, I don't think she formed any real bonds as a kid. Now she has me and her Deaf friends."

"What about your parents? Is she close to them?"

"My parents passed away a few years ago. They never got to meet her, but they would have been thrilled I was dating a Deaf girl. They would have treated her like a daughter."

"Your parents were deaf?"

"I see she has been talking to you. Yes, my parents were Deaf."

"My parents aren't evil people, you know. They wouldn't have given Lacey away because she was deaf. Send her to a special school—a private school—of course—"

"Maybe you're adopted. Did you ever consider that?"

"I'm not. I'm not adopted."

"How do you know? It makes sense. You and Lacey lost your real parents at a young age, then along come your parents—they don't want to take on a deaf child—so they adopt you."

"I look like them. We look like them."

"People see what they want to see. Do you have baby pictures?"

"Of course. Not ones as an infant. Those were—"

"Lost in a flood?"

"A fire," Monica said. "Oh my God." She stumbled back to her chair. "There's another explanation for that," Monica said. "They've hidden those pictures because Lacey is in them."

"True."

"Do you think it would make things easier?" Monica asked. "If they aren't really our parents?"

Alan shrugged. "I don't know. Maybe."

"Then she wouldn't feel so rejected. Unwanted."

"I didn't mean to make you cry."

"I've been crying for the past two weeks." Monica wiped her eyes and stood. "I want to see that horse."

"I think I'd better let Lacey—"

"Please. It's just a blue plastic horse, for God's sake!" Alan nodded and headed into the house. He stopped when he reached the door.

"How did you know that?"

"What?"

"You said, 'It's just a blue plastic horse.' I never told you that. How did you know?"

"Oh my God," Monica said. "I don't know. I didn't even think about it. It just slipped out." Alan smiled, but it was a sad smile nonetheless.

"Wait here," he said. "She might have taken it with her. If not, I'll get it."

"I'm sorry," Alan said, coming into the dining room, where Monica was having a cup of tea.

"You can't find it?"

"No. But that's not what I was talking about." Alan sighed, held up his cell phone. "Lacey just texted me."

"Is she on her way home?"

"Yes."

"That's great. Did she say—"

"She wants you to leave."

"Excuse me?"

"She asked me to tell you—she just wants some time alone with me." Monica smiled, drank her tea.

"I see," she said. The cup shook in her hand. Alan took a seat across from her.

"You just have to give her some time." Monica wished he'd go away. She didn't want to cry in front of him. She wanted to throw the coffee cup across the room too, watch it break, an urge that surprised her.

"She didn't text me," Monica said.

"In her own way, I think she's trying not to hurt your feelings," Alan said. Monica stood, knocking into the table as she did. Jostling the tea.

"I'm going to tell my parents," Monica said.

"Didn't Lacey ask you not to do that?"

"She snuck over to their house. She broke in. She obviously wants to meet them."

"Because nothing says 'I love you' like breaking and entering?"

"I never would have been attracted to you."

"Excuse me?"

"I can't help comparing our lives. Our tastes, our mannerisms, our experiences. You aren't my type." Alan studied her for a moment with eyes that were wise and kind.

"It was good to see you again, Monica," he said before leaving the room.

Monica hated herself; she was acting like a child. Alan was good to Lacey, just like Kelly Thayler was good to Lacey. The problem, Monica realized, was that she wanted Lacey all to herself. She also wanted to yell out an apology to Alan, but the words were stuck in her throat.

Chapter 27

"I don't like what you're suggesting," Katherine said. She sat across from the psychiatrist, whom she still couldn't call Dianne, despite the many encouragements to do so.

"Monica is extremely dependent on Lacey—"

"They're twins—"

"We've been over this. It's not a healthy bond. She has severe separation anxiety when they're apart."

"Which is why it would be cruel to separate them."

"Cruel to whom, Mrs. Bowman? You've seen it yourself. Lacey wants independence from her sister. She's desperate for autonomy. I've been working with them for several months and—"

"And I've been working with them for two and a half years—"

"Then you know I speak the truth. Your daughters must be free to form other bonds. With you. With their father."

Katherine stood. "I'm afraid this has all been a waste of time," she said. "They're just babies."

Dianne remained seated. "Violence and aggression in toddlers isn't a topic people like to talk about. But it does happen, Mrs. Bowman."

"I don't understand why you're telling me this."

"Monica's aggression has multiplied since starting therapy. You've said it yourself. She's withdrawn from everyone except Lacey."

"What am I supposed to do? Just ship her off somewhere? What in the world are you thinking?"

"Maybe there's an aunt she can stay with a few days a week? I'm just suggesting fostering time apart, a little at a time. I'm not suggesting anything permanent. To make a comparison, this is like an operation to separate Siamese twins. Just because they're close, connected, doesn't mean it's healthy. Doesn't mean it's best for both girls."

"Thank you for your time. But they're just babies. This is just a phase." Katherine walked to the door.

Dianne finally stood up. "I strongly disagree, Mrs. Bowman. I'd like to talk to your husband."

"How dare you."

"Monica needs help."

"She's two years old."

"Under stress your daughter acts out physically. She bites, she hits, she throws things. If something isn't done about this now, I'm afraid one of them could get seriously hurt."

"All siblings squabble."

"I don't think you grasp the seriousness of this situation. You came to me for help, remember?"

"Thank you for your time. But we won't be coming back."

"Mrs. Bowman, please. Just take some time and consider what I'm telling you. Talk to your husband."

"Good-bye, Dianne."

"My door is always open. And for the record, I hope I'm wrong. I hope to God I'm wrong."

She is wrong, Katherine thought hours later as she watched the girls play in the sandbox. They were so happy. All they needed was each other and a bucket. They had their own language between them, and more than that, they could speak to each other with just a look. Lacey started to crawl out of the sandbox. She held her arms out for her mother. Katherine smiled and reached for Lacey. But the moment Katherine grasped Lacey, she felt a whack on the top of her head, and sand fell over her eyes like a sheet of ice. She tried to keep a grip on Lacey, but the sand blinded her. As gently as she could, she set Lacey down. Lacey immediately began to cry and scream for her mother. Katherine clamped her hands to her eyes and tried to claw out the sand. She needed to rinse them out with water before any real damage was done. But the third nanny this year had quit just last week. *It's just a phase,* she told herself again as she stumbled across the lawn toward the garden hose. *It's just a phase.*

Chapter 28

"**M**onica?" Joe said, stepping into the house. "What's all this?" The dining room table was set with their best china. She even ironed the tablecloth, one she bought years ago but never took out of its packaging. Candles were lit, a Wynton Marsalis CD was playing softly in the background. Monica wore a black silk nightgown that barely kissed the top of her knees. Her hair was piled on top of her head, with the exception of a few soft tendrils hanging long and loose. She wanted to scream, "What the hell does it look like, you idiot," but she was worried it might ruin her romantic mood.

She hadn't seen Joe in weeks; Lacey had actually sparked the idea. It had been so sweet, watching her propose to Alan. So romantic. That's when she realized she could do the same thing. It was time to stop fantasizing about a certain sculptor whom she didn't even know and who hadn't even called her, and start paying attention to the one who loved her. The simple gold band she bought at the mall was sitting in a little box in the middle of the table, next to the vase of roses. She had bought a new nightgown and made his favorite meal: wild salmon with a lemon caper sauce, rice, and broccoli steamed on the side. They would eat, hopefully get a little drunk, and she would ask him to marry her before clearing the table and throwing herself down on it. She wanted, more than anything, to seal the deal by having sex on the dining room table. If he said yes, she wasn't going to take no for an answer.

And this new approach to life wasn't going to stop with Joe. She was going to go back to the workshop circuit, but this time things were going to be different. Enough with blueprints and visions and planning out every little step. She was going to urge people—no, inspire people—to be impulsive, take chances, grab life by the reins. Or horns. Or whatever they can grab. Because her new motivational mantra was simple: *Someday, we're all going to die.*

So we all deserved what we wanted out of life. Love. Laughter. Connection. Sex on the dining room table. She'd been too timid to ask for any of it, too shy. No more. And instead of waiting around for Joe to make an extraordinary move like a kidnapped victim waiting to be rescued from the trunk, she was going to take matters into her own hands.

Monica walked over to Joe, conscious of the wiggle in her hips, her slow smile. She threw her arms around him, kissed his neck.

"Did you miss me?" she whispered.

"Of course," Joe said in a normal tone of voice. He pulled back and gave her a quick peck on the cheek. "Why are you dressed for bed?"

"You don't like?" Monica twirled around. "Well, I can rectify that." She started pulling the nightgown over her head.

"What are you doing?" Joe sounded truly alarmed. He came to her side and pulled the nightgown back down. Monica brushed her hair out of her eyes and stared at him.

"Most men would be helping me take it off," she said.

"I thought we were going to eat."

"I can't wait. I want sex. So drop your pants and let's do it right here, right now."

"Or what?"

"I don't know. There's not supposed to be an 'or what.' " Joe pulled out a chair, sat down, folded his arms.

"I thought we were going to have a nice dinner," he said. Monica nodded and left the room. She took the stairs to their bedroom two at a time. Her suitcase was still on the bed. She rummaged around in it until she found the jeans and shirts she'd taken from Lacey's closet. She took off her nightgown and put them on. She went back downstairs, took the salmon out of the oven. She stirred the rice, steamed the broccoli, and started plating. They ate in silence.

If she stayed with Joe, this would be her life. Nothing daring or spontaneous. A short while ago, she wouldn't have seen anything wrong with it. A solid man, who'd basically earned her parents' stamp of approval, a man who'd helped her launch a successful career. A short while ago, that would've been worth more to her than a boring sex life. Didn't that eventually go downhill anyway? So what if they practiced the same missionary position, with few exceptions? So what if they never talked about sex, or flirted with each other, or ripped off articles of clothing in the heat of passion? So what if he always came and she rarely did?

"I know you've been through a shock," Joe said, putting down his fork for a moment. "I can't imagine what it's like finding out you're a twin."

"Don't forget finding out your parents have been lying to you your entire life," Monica said. "Lied to us, I should say," she added.

"Us?" Joe asked, the familiar line materializing on his forehead. "When have they lied to me?"

"Not you," Monica said. "Lacey. Lacey and me. Me and Lacey. My sister. My twin. I can't believe you found a way to make this about you."

"That's not fair, Mon. It's just—I'm not used to this—suddenly everything is you and Lacey. What about the rest of your life? What about a little balance?"

"My mother told me Lacey was stillborn," Monica said. "Do you call that balanced?"

"Look, you don't know their reasons—"

"Excuse me?" Monica slammed down her fork and pushed her plate away. "Whose side are you on, Joe?"

"Let's not get dramatic. Please?"

"I quit," she said. She threw down her napkin.

"You quit what?"

"Us. I quit us." Joe continued to eat.

" I don't need this tonight," he muttered. "I have drawings to pore over, I have a site meeting in the morning."

"I'm not happy, Joe. I no longer want to be in this relationship." Monica hiccupped. Then she started to laugh. She couldn't help it, it was just such a relief to finally say it.

"You think this is funny? You really think this is funny?"

"I was going to propose to you tonight," Monica said. "I think that's kind of funny." The look on Joe's face made her laugh even harder. He finally put his fork down.

"You are really worrying me now," Joe said. "I think we need to look into professional help." Monica pushed away from the table and stood.

"I don't know the protocol," she said. "Should you move out or should I?"

"Are you drunk?" Joe asked.

"Not yet," Monica said. She picked up the bottle of wine from the table and drank straight out of it. Then she slammed it down. "I should have stayed in Philly," she said. "I'm going back." She stared defiantly at Joe, waiting for him to challenge her.

"You need professional help," Joe said. "I'm sorry to say it but you do." Monica giggled. Then curtsied. She just didn't care anymore. She took the wedding ring box from the middle of the table.

"Things might have been different if you'd fucked me on the dining room table," she said.

If she had examined all the reasons she went straight to Lacey's art studio, she might have stopped herself. Lacey didn't want her here. Lacey had kicked her out again. She didn't want Lacey to know she had moved here, at least not yet. She was so relieved when she heard the sound of welding coming through the door, she could have wept. She pushed the button for the flashing door lights and waited. Minutes later the welding stopped and she heard heavy footsteps approach. Mike pushed up his goggles and smiled.

"Hello, Monica." He looked at her suitcase. She started to cry.

"Please don't tell her I'm here," she said.

"You look so lost," he said. His voice was soft and comforting. "Come in. I think I have just the thing."

It was screaming loud and a little hard to hold the wand in her hand, but it was exhilarating. Sparks flew in every direction as she aimed the blast at the large piece of steel in front of her. She didn't really know what she was doing, but Mike said it didn't matter, it was just scrap material anyway. *Like me,* she couldn't help but think. *I'm scrap material too.* Lacey probably would have challenged her on that thought. From now on, no matter how close they got, Lacey would always have the orphan card to play. It wasn't fair.

"Thank you," she said. "That was so cool." The smile was back.

"Anytime," he said.

"I should go," Monica said. "I need to find a place to live."

"This might be weird," Mike said. "But—"

"I'll take it," Monica said. Mike laughed, and the deep richness of it filled Monica with an inexplicable, childlike joy.

"I have a spare room," he said. "I'd been thinking about taking on a roommate. But it's nothing fancy. I'm sure with your book money—"

"Nothing fancy is perfect," Monica said. It was true. She needed time to think, to plan. Living with Mike would be perfect, as long as she could keep her hands off him. Mike scribbled down his address.

"I still have work to do," he said. "I can give you the keys, or you can leave your suitcase here, run around town for a bit, and meet me back here this evening."

"The latter," Monica said. "I want to go check out some things in the city."

"Great," Mike said. "So meet me back here at seven?"

"Is Lacey coming in today?"

"I don't know."

"Can we meet around the corner or—I just—she's not really ready for this," Monica admitted. "She's not ready for me."

"I don't want to get in the middle of anything," he said.

"And I don't want to put you there," Monica said. "I promise."

"I wouldn't be doing this if I didn't like you," Mike said. "If I didn't think you had Lacey's best interests at heart." Monica nodded, afraid that if she spoke, she'd burst into tears. "I'll call you closer to seven. If Lacey's here, we'll meet at the pub around the corner."

"Thank you," Monica said. Then she threw her arms around him and kissed him. It was another long kiss, one he, once again, returned. Monica felt everything inside her pressing, as if she couldn't get close enough. She couldn't remember the last time she'd felt such need. It wasn't romantic; she was like an animal. He felt so good against her, she could feel the muscles in his arms and back; soldering steel did wonders for the man. She pulled back first, her lips felt raw and abused. They stared at each other, as if knowing one more kiss like that and they'd be naked and on the floor. It was tempting. But it would be a mistake. Monica couldn't afford the distraction; she had a sister to win over.

"Later," she said as if it had been nothing more than a casual peck on the cheek.

"Later," he said with a smile that almost made her wish her sister would disappear.

Chapter 29

Big news. Let's meet! Robert texted Lacey. She glanced away from her BlackBerry, pondering what to answer as she stared at the half-finished portrait in front of her. A golden retriever with a petite Asian woman, proving all pets and owners didn't look alike. She did need a break. Getting back to work was exhausting. Besides, it had been a while since she'd really talked to Robert. He didn't know about her engagement, breaking into her parents' house, or thinking a gardener she met at the house was her father. Monica had been all too happy to give Alan the scoop. It was kind of funny, she supposed. But also a letdown. Here she thought she'd finally met one of the breeders and came out unscathed. The gardener. Who has a gardener?

Seven, Lacey said. *Dillions?* She named the little English pub around the corner, where they both liked to sit and secretly mock all the drunk hearing people at the bar.

C U there!!! Robert replied. Lacey smiled to herself as she clicked off. Then she frowned as she glanced at her BlackBerry again. No messages from Monica. It had been at least a week without contact. In a way, Lacey kind of missed her persistence. In another way, it was a huge relief that she was gone. Monica was too clingy. Lacey had the feeling all she had to do was say the word and Monica would be at her doorstep in an instant. She could ask Robert his advice on this matter too. She picked up her brush and finished highlighting the retriever's golden ears.

Lacey had to ask Robert to repeat his news several times. It didn't click the first time or the second, and she wasn't having any easier a time with the third.

"She's what?" Lacey asked again. Robert smiled, not minding the repetition, seemingly enjoying every second of the shock he had delivered to his friend.

"She's taking ASL level one!"

"Here? In Philadelphia?"

"Down the street. At the community center!"

"Are you sure?"

"I heard from Tony who heard from Gary who talked with Marjorie who's friends with Remy—know Remy? Remember? The woman with the curly hair shaved in the back, moved from Cali? She's teaching the class on Saturday and she ran into Barry at his birthday party—how come you didn't go to that party?—tell me in a minute—he teaches the class on Wednesday. Tony texted me and said—he said—'Did you know that Lacey is pretending to be hearing and she's taking sign language classes with Remy? ASL level one?' I died," Robert said, slamming his fist on the bar and laughing. "I told them I was the same when I saw you two—except I saw you together—I was like, I'm seeing double! So I told Tony you had a twin, and I think half of them know that now and the other half are totally confused about why you're pretending to be hearing and taking beginning ASL from Remy. They think you might be a lesbian, because Remy is hot for a gay woman."

Lacey let her head drop onto the bar. Robert started tapping her on the shoulder. Tap, tap, tap. Lacey finally lifted her head.

"What's wrong?" he asked. "Don't worry. I told them you're straight."

"I don't care," Lacey said. "She's stalking me!"

"Who?" Robert looked around the bar. "Kelly?" he asked.

"No. Monica."

"You didn't know she was here?"

"No."

"My God."

Lacey finished her beer in one long drink. She signaled the bartender. When he looked at her, she pointed at the tequila bottle and mimicked doing a shot. Then she put up two fingers. He winked at her and poured the shot.

"Lime?" She nodded. He put one of the shot glasses in front of Robert. Lacey moved it back over to her.

"You're drinking both of them?" Robert said.

"I'm not responsible for getting anyone drunk but myself," Lacey said.

"I hate tequila," Robert said, eyeing her over his cosmopolitan.

"Good," Lacey said before drinking the second shot. "I'm engaged. Did I tell you that?" Robert choked on his cosmopolitan, then slammed it on the table as he reached over and practically lifted Lacey off her stool in his approximation of a seated bear hug. Then he grabbed her hand and searched for a ring.

"We're going to have them made," Lacey said.

"This is great news! Great news!"

"It would be," Lacey said, sliding off the stool. "If she weren't ruining everything. Seriously, Robert—she's totally crazy! She's stalking me."

Robert shrugged. "If I had a twin stalking me," he said, "I'd make him do my laundry. And make him interpret for me. And send him on blind dates. And make him be my stand-in when I'm bored with a play."

"You can have mine, then," Lacey said. "Because I don't want anything from her. Where is she even staying?"

"I'll ask around," Robert said, taking out his Sidekick.

"I broke into my parents' house," Lacey said. "I thought I met my father." Robert stopped texting. "But he was really just a gardener."

"You suck," he said. "I had a hot date to tell you about. And

look at you. My twin is stalking me. I'm engaged. I broke into
my parents' home. I met a gardener. Spill. And then I don't
care if you screwed the gardener in the middle of the tomato
plants. Actually I do. If you did, I definitely want to hear about
that. But, even if you found a dead body in the bathtub, it's my
turn after that." Lacey laughed and started to sign her story.
Anyone watching who didn't know sign language would have
no idea that the movements she was making in the air were de-
scribing a large man holding a rake and a bush, a summer
cabin that was really a mansion, and an innocent bowl of Jell-O
in a refrigerator that Lacey just had to molest. When she was
done, Robert asked her to tell it again.

"Do you have Remy's e-mail?" Lacey asked.

Robert nodded and started scrolling through his phone.
"Why?"

"Oh, I just haven't talked to her in a while," she said.

"Lacey."

"And you never know when she might need a substitute
teacher for that beginning ASL class." Robert's eyes widened
and he broke into a big smile.

"You are bad," he said. "Very, very bad."

"I know," Lacey said.

"Got it right here," he said.

"Every country has its own sign language," Monica said. "But
American Sign Language originates from France because in
the 1800s a man named Gallaudet went to Paris and learned
their system of signing for the Deaf, then brought it back to the
United States. And even though it's evolved into its own language since then, French Sign Language still has similarities to
ASL."

"They taught you all that in your first few classes?" Mike
asked. They were walking through Rittenhouse Square park
with Snookie. The park was teeming with other dog walkers,
students, and lovers. It was the perfect blend of nature,
plopped in the middle of an urban environment. Still, it was
hard for Monica to pay attention to her surroundings; she

couldn't stop talking about her classes. Mike was probably bored to death, and would have probably been pointing out all the sculptures and other commissioned artworks in the park; instead he was patiently listening to her ramble on.

"No, but they recommended some books on Deaf Culture and I've been reading everything I could get my hands on."

"Impressive," Mike said.

"Have you ever heard of Gallaudet University?" Mike shook his head no. "It's in Washington, D.C. It's the only liberal arts college for the Deaf. I wonder why Lacey didn't go there."

"I don't understand why they call it Deaf Culture," Mike said. "I mean—I've never heard of a blind person talk about blind culture or a person in a wheelchair talk about wheelchair culture."

"It's because culture is intrinsically linked to language," Monica said. "Language, history, and a shared experience."

"So there's Deaf history too?"

"Absolutely. From a history of oppression such as—did you know back in the day, some Deaf people were put in mental institutions?" Mike shook his head. "Some had their hands tied behind their back so they couldn't sign. Called them Deaf and Dumb, the works. There was a Deaf population on Martha's Vineyard—the history of the education of Deaf people—sign language first, then came the oral method. Did you know a lot of Deaf people hate Alexander Graham Bell?"

"Because they can't talk on the phone?" Mike said.

"No," Monica said. "Because he was totally against sign language—even though his wife was deaf. He thought Deaf people should be forced to speak and read lips. That's when what's called the "oral" method was brought about and sign language was forbidden in schools."

"Wow," Mike said again. Monica stopped talking, and they stopped walking. She had been living with him for over a week now, and although they took walks together every single night, they hadn't kissed again or mentioned the other kisses. Still, it was a constant presence, a slight giddy pressure every time she looked at him. And the way he was looking at her now, Monica wondered if they were about to do it again, and her body was gearing up to give its approval. "Tell me about your book," he said instead.

"Did you know that ninety percent of deaf children are born to hearing parents?" Monica said.

"Nope," Mike said.

"And sometimes it takes years before the parents know their child is deaf. By then, they've missed out on years of language. They haven't been able to learn by hearing their parents talk, listening to the television or radio—so then they're put into a school where, if they're lucky, the teacher is fluent in sign language. But often they're not. You have to have a firm basis in one language before you can learn another—"

Mike put his hand on Monica's shoulder. "Monica," he said. They looked at each other again. Monica felt a little thrill run down her spine.

"Am I talking too much?" she said. Mike laughed and held up his fingers in a pinch.

"It's fascinating," he said. "It really is. But to be totally honest, I'd rather hear about you."

"I'm sorry," Monica said. "I feel like everything I learn brings me closer to knowing Lacey."

"Fair enough," Mike said. "But I'm trying to get to know you. Do you not want to talk about your book?" He gestured to a nearby bench. Monica scooped Snookie into her arms and they sat.

Mike stroked Snookie's head while Monica talked.

"I didn't write that freakin' book," Monica said. "Not really. Most of it was Joe's idea."

"I can't tell you how glad I am to hear that," Mike said. Monica's first instinct was to be defensive, but when she saw the look on Mike's face, she just laughed.

"Did you totally hate the book?" she asked.

"I totally hated it," he said. Monica leaned back on the bench and closed her eyes. *I could totally fall in love with you,* she thought.

"You look lost again," Mike said.

"My parents," Monica said. "They've been lying to me my entire life. And I've spent years promoting a book I didn't really believe in for a man I didn't really love. I'm a total mess. And I don't know what to do next. And I don't want to even imagine what I'm going to do if Lacey doesn't want to be a part of my life. That's me in a nutshell. I'm a motivational mess." Mike reached over and held her hand.

"Or," he said, "you have the soul of an artist. You have to make a mess before you're finished. It's just part of the process."

"Tina would kill me if she knew I was here with you," Monica said. "And Joe. Maybe even Lacey." She hadn't planned on saying it, especially not directly to Mike, but it was true. And she felt guilty.

"We've certainly had a strange beginning," Mike said. "But if someone is going to kill us, let me do this one more time before we die." Leaving Snookie curled up under the bench, he rose up and brought her with him. He grabbed her and kissed her. He walked as his lips pressed down on her, moving her backward. She didn't know where they were going, he simply let him guide her. Soon she felt the rough bark of a tree behind her back, and his body was full on hers as they kissed beneath it. When he finally pulled away, she felt as if all the air had been sucked out of her body. "I've been dying to do that all day," he said, gently moving a strand of her hair off her mouth. "You are so beautiful."

"Let's do it right here," Monica said.

"What?" Mike said. It was a hesitation, but it wasn't the judgmental way Joe would've said it. It was "What?" as in "Tell me more."

"I want you to take me right here, right now."

"There's a grandmother on the bench behind us."

"I don't think her eyesight is very good."

Mike laughed. His hand caressed her leg. "I know of a little spot, it's a ways on, but it's a lot more private."

"Take me there."

"Do you mean—show you the spot. Or do you mean—take you there?"

"Both."

It was private. But she was still in the great outdoors. They tied Snookie to a tree several feet away. The sky of Philadelphia above them, tall trees with green stretching branches, the quickest quickie she'd ever had, urged on by the fear of someone coming around the corner at any minute. Clothes barely taken off, just pushed down or up, Mike took control, shielding her body with his, so that if anyone did come up on them, it would be his poor backside taking the shock. Luckily, they were unseen. Monica laughed as Mike hurried to pull up his jeans, and she adjusted her skirt and her bra. Snookie glanced their way, thoroughly disgusted. But Monica didn't feel guilty, she felt great. If someone had told her she'd meet a guy who could give her an orgasm in a public park, she would have called them crazy. Life was truly surprising.

The air rushed back into Monica's body, most of it going to her head. She was sure she looked stupid with the huge grin on her face, but she couldn't stop smiling. Mike stepped away from the tree and took Monica's hand. Then pulled Monica closer, and she leaned her head on his shoulder. "There's nothing to feel bad about," Mike said. "And despite what just happened—God, that was great, wasn't it? Despite that, Ms. Daredevil, we are going to take this slow. Very, very slow." As if wanting to be included, Snookie ran over and made circles around Monica, wrapping the leash around her legs, like securing a victim for a plank walk.

"We gotcha," Mike said, pulling her toward him. "We gotcha."

Chapter 30

He slapped her square on the forehead. Lacey hadn't been expecting this, and she jerked back more from shock than from actual pain. His large lips were moving; she could tell he was shouting from the spit flying out of his mouth. She wanted to wipe it off her face, but she was afraid he was going to hit her again. He pushed her away, and she stumbled as the next person was offered up to him. This time it was an old woman in a wheelchair. Two assistants helped her stand. Lacey watched with her mouth open; he hit her too, and he flicked water in her face. Lacey whipped her head around to Margaret.

"He hit me," she signed. Margaret shook her head no. Lacey stomped her foot on the floor and pointed at the man dressed in a long, white robe. Then she started toward the man, her fist curled and poised to punch. Margaret grabbed her and pulled her back to the front bench. Lacey knew who was responsible for this. It was the new woman. The one who came on Wednesday nights. She'd seen her whispering with Margaret, the two of them constantly glancing over at Lacey. The next thing she knew, she was in church.

"He's a healer," Kelly Thayler told her that night. Lacey finger-spelled the word back to Kelly; she didn't understand what it meant. "He was supposed to make you hearing," she said. "Are you sure you can't hear anything? Not even a little bit?" Lacey stretched her neck until her ears were sticking out. She tried hard to hear something. Finally she brought her neck back in and shook her head no.

"Why are you crying?" Lacey asked.

"Because I was going to be next," Kelly said. "If he made you hearing, he could've made me a leg."

"I hate him," Lacey said. "I don't want to hear."

"Well, I want a new leg," Kelly said. "Like a starfish. If a starfish loses a leg, it grows one back. Did you know that?" Lacey did not know that. But now that she did, she intended to rip the leg off the next starfish she saw to see if it was true.

"It's her fault," Lacey said. She imitated the woman with the frizzy hair and big nose who'd been coming on Wednesday nights. Then she got up, stuck her chest out, and waddled across the room in imitation of the woman. Kelly laughed and laughed.

"I have an idea," Lacey said, giving Kelly the look. Lacey always had an idea. Kelly didn't look happy about it, but Lacey knew she'd go along with it. She always did.

The next Wednesday, Lacey begged Margaret to take her to church again. Margaret narrowed her eyes at Lacey.

"No," she said. Lacey knew this was what Margaret would say. Luckily, she waited until the woman with frizzy hair was back, listening to every word.

"I want to be healed," Lacey signed. As promised, Kelly interpreted for her. Lacey knew Kelly had said the right words, for the woman clasped her hands in front of her face and smiled. Lacey felt a pinch on the soft part of her underarm, Margaret's signal that she was going to let her have it later, but Lacey didn't care. This time it was going to be worth it.

Kelly sat in the front row where Lacey could see her. This time when the man hit her, Lacey was ready. She stumbled back from the blow. This time when his mouth moved, she knew he was shouting—"Be healed!" Lacey took a deep breath and hoped everyone would understand her voice. She'd never used it in public before.

"I can hear," she said. "I can hear!" Although she couldn't hear the gasps, she could see their faces. Oh, to see their faces! All of them had their mouths open to one degree or the other, and some were starting to moan and cry. Lacey glanced at Kelly.

"Car," Kelly signed. Lacey pointed to the front door of the church.

"I hear a car!" Lacey said. People leapt to their feet! The man who hit her suddenly grabbed her and hugged her. She hated having her face smashed into his thick white robe. She struggled. She pulled back and looked at Kelly again.

"I hear a woman's scream!" she said. The entire room was applauding, leaping to their feet. Those in line who could walk started to sway, or dance with each other. Lacey looked at Kelly again. Lacey didn't even question what Kelly signed next, what did she know about hearing?

"I hear a fart!" Lacey said even louder than before. She'd never seen faces fall so quiet so fast. She looked to Kelly again, but Margaret had reached her first and was dragging her out of the church. The man in the robe was shouting at her again, his spit flying farther than ever before. Margaret tightened her grip on Lacey's arm. There would be bruises. Lacey looked at the ceiling, where everyone looked when they talked about God, and treated the crowd to a parting shot. "Thanks for nothing," she said.

"No," Kelly said. "I'm too old to go along with your schemes." Lacey answered her with nothing but a smile and the look. "Just out of curiosity. What are you planning on doing?"

"Teaching her a lesson," Lacey said. "Like old times."

"I don't understand you," Kelly said. "We kidnapped a cat and dug through garbage to find your sister. Now that you have her, you want to get rid of her. Why?"

"I wanted to meet her. I didn't want her to crawl into my skin and stay there."

"She quit her job and moved to Philadelphia just to be close to you."

"And you think that's a good thing? It's insane! She's stalking me."

"So what's the plan?"

"Remember when you were studying to become an interpreter, they did that exercise with you where you wore earplugs and had to see what it felt like to be Deaf?"

"Yes," Kelly said. "We had to go to a restaurant and shopping mall like that. When people realized we couldn't hear them, they either started yelling at us like we were eighty years old, or treated us like we were retarded—sorry."

"I think it's time Monica got a little taste of it," Lacey said.

"And then what? It's going to make her even more sympathetic—I don't get it."

"You'll see."

It was strange being with her group of four other students, sitting in a diner with earplugs, unable to speak to each other except for the little signs they knew, plus gestures. Monica had already had a glimpse of how Lacey was treated in the hearing world, so the awkwardness of the waiter didn't throw her. One of the other girls kept trying to ask Monica something but the only sign she understood her using was "sister." Finally, the girl ripped out a piece of paper, something they were told not to do, and wrote: *You grew up with a Deaf twin. Why didn't you learn sign language?*

What was she supposed to say? She'd promised Lacey she wouldn't tell anyone about their past. She shouldn't have even told her she had a Deaf twin, but it just slipped out one day.

We had our own language, Monica wrote. As she wrote it, she had the strangest feeling it was true. Was this a memory, or was she extrapolating? After all, it was a common myth that identical twins made up their own language. She'd since read that twins often picked up each other's mispronunciation of words, so what sounded like a foreign language to outside ears was actually English, just slightly mispronounced in a way only the two of them understood. But since Lacey was Deaf, it wouldn't have worked out that way for the two of them. Had they made up their own signs? Monica wished she knew; she wished she could remember. Remembering might be the breakthrough she needed to get close to Lacey.

One of the Deaf volunteers suddenly came up to their table. She signed clearly and slowly so the students could understand.

"Time for part two of our game," she said. "Everyone will have an individual task to perform as a "Deaf" person. Some of you will have to run to the grocery store, some of you will have to ask a stranger for directions, and so on. I'm going to pass out these slips of paper with your assignments. At our next class you'll have to talk about your experience. Good luck!"

Monica looked at her assignment. *Meet with Susan, a puppy breeder. Pick up two puppies and take them to their new homes.* That should be easy. The breeder lived in a part of Philly that Monica had never been to, but thanks to her GPS she was at the house in no time.

It was weird not listening to the radio on the way there, but other than that, so far, Monica wouldn't have much to share with the class about her experience. Susan lived in a modest Victorian, on the outskirts of the city. Monica could hear dogs barking in the background, even through her earplugs. She rang the doorbell, and waited. A petite woman with slicked-back gray hair answered the door. She waved at Monica. Monica waved back. It was obvious Susan thought Monica was really Deaf. She was being overly friendly, lots of smiling and several "pats" on the shoulder. She led Monica down a hall that smelled like dog and into a back room where puppies ran amuck in a small bedroom cordoned off by a baby gate.

The woman clapped her hands and most of the puppies came running. One stayed in the corner chewing on a stuffed cat. The woman scooped one of the puppies up, the sweetest little chocolate Lab Monica had ever seen. Monica kissed the

puppy and placed it in a carrier box she'd been told to bring.
Then the woman walked over to the lonesome puppy in the
corner, still chewing away on the stuffed cat. When she touched
him, the puppy jumped a little. This was also a Lab, smaller
than the other, with a reddish tint to its little coat. She picked
this puppy up and brought it to Monica. Then the woman said
something. Monica couldn't read her lips. Monica shook her
head to indicate she didn't understand. The woman kept
pointing to the puppy's ears and then back at Monica. Monica
finally brought out her pad and pen. The woman set the second puppy in a carrier and took the pen.

Did they tell you this puppy is deaf?

No.

The family is only going to take one puppy, the woman wrote.
*Here's the address. You will have to bring back the puppy they don't
choose.*

It was a setup. Monica knew that. The question, she thought
to herself as she sat in the car with the pair of puppies, was what
to do about it. She wanted to quit on the spot, but that was exactly what Lacey wanted her to do. Well, Lacey had misjudged
her. Somehow she'd found out that Monica was taking the
class. It must be that Deaf Grapevine that Monica heard so
much about—news apparently traveled fast in Deaf Culture.
Still, why rub this in her face? It wasn't Monica who put Lacey
up for adoption; didn't she get that?

Then there would be the added humiliation of standing up
in front of the class and telling her experience. She could hear
herself now. The loving, wealthy family picked the hearing
puppy so I had to take the deaf puppy back. What kind of
twisted canine Sophie's choice was this? The puppies whined in
agreement from the backseat. Monica yanked the earplugs out
of her ears and cranked the radio. Then, she started the car
and drove them home.

"I'm sorry," Monica said for the fourth or fifth time. The
puppies were going on the second straight hour of whining.

"Just let them out," Mike said. "At this point I'll take peace and quiet over pissing and chewing."

"I'll take them outside first," Monica said. "And give them access to my things to chew." She threw a coat over her pajamas and slipped on her shoes. "I'll look for my own place in the morning," she said. Snookie growled from underneath the couch.

"Are you sure you really want three dogs?" Mike said.

"She's testing me," Monica said. "And I don't intend to fail."

"It wasn't your fault, Monica."

"It doesn't feel that way. I grew up with everything. She grew up—"

"Don't start. She has a perfectly good life." The puppies wriggled so hard in her arms, Monica almost dropped them.

"It's like trying to hold a goldfish," Monica said. "I'd better get them outside." Mike grabbed a jacket from the hook near the door. "You don't have to," she said.

"Come on, Snookie," Mike called. Snookie poked his head out from underneath the couch. "Snookie want a cookie?" he said. Monica laughed. Snookie raced out and led the way outside.

Chapter 31

The girls were in a good mood, on the kind of day that made all the other days seem worth it. They were jabbering away, singing some sort of song they'd heard on the radio that morning. Lacey, especially, loved music. She would immediately start dancing and humming whenever a tune came on that struck her fancy. In the middle of the breakfast table sat a blue plastic horse for Lacey and a blue plastic cow for Monica, birthday presents from Aunt Grace. The girls were turning three. It was hard for Katherine to believe. Why in the world would Aunt Grace give them different presents when Katherine had made it clear it would cause trouble?

She was doing it, Katherine knew, to spite her. So far, Monica had been eyeing the horse, but she had yet to make a fuss. Maybe, just maybe, Monica was outgrowing her obsession that everything be absolutely equal when it came to her twin. Maybe it was just as Katherine thought, it was a phase. Maybe she was right to stop therapy, ignore Dianne's warning—

Very unhealthy, possibly dangerous—

A three-year-old—dangerous. And yes, Dianne chronicled

stories of toddlers who had become physically violent with their siblings, but those children were abused or mentally ill. Her children were perfectly normal. And unless you were a twin yourself, how could you judge the closeness?

Separate the twins. That was the actual suggestion. A trial separation. Monica might get violent. It was ridiculous. Watching them now, on a day like today, Katherine knew she'd made the right decision. The girls had finished their breakfast and were getting antsy.

"Down," Lacey said, kicking her feet. "Down."

"Down," Monica said, kicking her feet. "Down."

"Outside," Lacey said.

"Outside," Monica said. Katherine lifted the girls out of their chairs and set them down. Lacey reached for her toy horse. Monica lunged for it. Lacey held it to her chest. Monica cried. Katherine handed Monica her cow. Monica threw it across the room. Lacey handed her the horse. Monica's tears stopped immediately. Katherine walked across the room and handed Lacey the cow. Lacey took it with a smile on her face; Monica scowled from across the room.

"Outside," Lacey said.

"Outside," Monica said.

Someone was pounding on the front door. Snookie was barking, the puppies whining. Monica opened one eye and stared at the clock. It was six A.M. She rolled out of bed, put on her robe, and tried to hush Snookie, who was by now completely out of his mind. Monica threw open the front door to find Lacey standing there with Susan, the puppy breeder.

"I can hear them," the woman said the minute Monica opened the door. She was yelling loudly and pointing at her ear. "I want my puppies back," the woman said to Monica. "It was just a class assignment. You weren't supposed to keep them!"

Monica shrugged. She didn't bother speaking clearly or gesturing. Lacey glared at her. It surprised even herself that she didn't care if Lacey was angry with her. She almost welcomed it.

"Come in," she said to the woman. "They're all yours." The woman ran in and scooped up the puppies. Monica stood staring at Lacey.

"That was a lousy trick," Monica said. She spoke the words clearly, but made no attempt to gesture or sign. Lacey crossed her arms and glared. Monica was sure Lacey had a million things to say to her. Was she angry Monica was living with Mike? She was suddenly weary with the weight of how difficult it was to communicate. The few sign language classes she had taken made it all the harder. She could produce a few signs for sure, but whenever anyone signed back to her, she was lost. Susan barreled past them with the puppies, got into her car, and drove away. Lacey continued to stand and stare.

"Go home," Lacey signed. Monica understood.

Mike came up behind Monica. "Hey," he said rubbing his eyes. "What's up?"

Lacey put her arm around Monica and pointed at Mike.

"Want to do us both?" she clearly voiced.

"Lacey," Monica said.

Lacey jerked away from Monica.

"Go home," she said again.

Mike stepped in. He pointed at Monica and then himself.

"Roommates," he said slowly and clearly.

"It's none of her business," Monica said.

"What?" Lacey said.

Monica pointed at Mike, then at herself.

"None of your business," she enunciated as clearly as she could.

"Monica," Mike said. "Please don't drag me into this."

"Can you give us some privacy, Mike?" Monica said. Mike shook his head, but left.

"You're my sister," Monica signed. "We're twins." Like that, the cloak of anger Monica wore evaporated. She didn't know what to say or do anymore. But she knew she couldn't imagine life without Lacey. This was the person she was supposed to be closest to in the world. How could Lacey not know that? How could she treat her like a total stranger, or even worse, an enemy?

"Please," Monica signed. "Please." Lacey signed something back. It took several tries, but Monica finally got it.

"What do you want from me?" Lacey had said.

Monica had too many words. She had the words but not the signs. *I want a sister. I want you to love me. I want to know everything I've missed in your life. I want to go on vacations with you. I want pictures with you to put on my fridge. I want to be the maid of honor at your wedding. I want to be Aunt Monica to your children. I want to hang one of your paintings in my apartment. I want to talk every day. I want to make up for lost time. I want to go back to when we were kids. I want never to be separated from you. I want you to forgive me. I want you to forgive our mom and dad. I want you to meet them. I want you there to make putting up with them easier. I want you to have to shoot cans in the woods with the Colonel. I want you to receive a million e-mails from our mother and put up with her constant worrying. I want to talk to you about sex, love, religion, and politics. I want a real life with you. I just want a real life.*

But Monica didn't say any of that. She only knew how to sign: "I want."

"Go home," Lacey said.

But she didn't have a home, not anymore. Mike made it clear he didn't want to get in the middle. Maybe he wanted a break from her and Snookie. *What would Lacey do if she were me?* Monica thought. She took Snookie to doggy day care and got on an Amtrak train headed for New York City. It was less than two hours away and the ticket was affordable. She walked around Times Square, taking in the crowds and the lights, wondering if she should move here, really could lose herself in the city. She saw a man playing a guitar in his underwear. Good for him, he was living his life. Monica wondered what it would feel like to be him as she watched him, wondered what all those eyes would feel like on her. She thought about her canoe trip with Lacey, how they took off their bras and flung them into the water. But this man was playing the guitar. She didn't have a guitar.

Maybe she should join him anyway. Strip down to her panties, stand next to him, and play the harmonica. She didn't know how to play the harmonica, but she figured she could fake it. Wouldn't that be something. It would certainly be daring. It would certainly be taking a chance. Is it something her twin would do? Probably not; she couldn't hear music. Monica kept forgetting her sister was Deaf. Lacey told her to go home. Lacey didn't want anything to do with her.

Was she wearing clean underwear? Clean enough to be stared at by strangers? It probably didn't matter she didn't even have a harmonica. She thought of Joe reading about her standing naked in the middle of Times Square. She could imagine her mother's face too. How would they know it was her and not Lacey? She could strip naked, get photographed, and give her name as Lacey Gears. She could commit a crime and tell them she was her sister. She'd read about this, twins once, was it in the nineteen-forties? One of them committed a crime, a murder, Monica thought, but she couldn't remember exactly. They arrested one twin, who then accused the other. They had the same exact fingerprints, identical DNA, and they couldn't figure out which one was the guilty party, so they had to let them both go—

Lacey and Monica aka Bonnie and Clyde! But her sister didn't even want to be with her, let alone break the law with her, did she? Or would that have been appealing to her daredevil sister? If Monica got arrested, who would be her one phone call? If she called Lacey, would she come?

Stealing wasn't for her. Exhibitionism out too. She could go to a club and pick up a strange man. Pretend to be her sister. Pretend to be Deaf so she wouldn't have to talk to him. She wondered if Mike would miss her. She probably should have left him a note. Monica started walking, wondering what little caper she would pull off as Lacey. Maybe there was an art contest she could enter. Maybe she could apply to grad school.

Maybe she had a painting talent she wasn't aware of. She could test it out. Conduct an experiment. Twin discovers identical hidden talent. There had to be an art store nearby. She started investigating the crowd, looking out for anyone whom she considered "artistic" to ask where she could find paint. She was in luck. He was a very nice young man, a boy, but he showed her the way. Minutes later she stood in front of oils, and acrylics, and watercolors. It was too much. She felt dizzy.

That's where she saw it. A can of spray paint. It was the right thing to buy, she knew it. Graffiti artist, that was her, could be her, she knew it. And one color would not do; she needed a rainbow at her fingertips. First she picked up a can of black. Then gold and silver. Purple, pink, blue, yellow, red. She felt so happy. She was alive, she was almost swooning. Lacey Gears, graffiti artist—

Where did she get the last name Gears? Yet another mystery, another question, another family lie. Her arms were stuffed with paint cans. She liked the clinking sound they made as she wrestled them to the counter. She tried to imagine what she would paint. Maybe something simple. Maybe just: *Lacey was here.*

Whoever she was, she thought as she watched the clerk punch in number after number, the bill doubling, then tripling, she wasn't Monica. Monica didn't spray paint anything. Should she climb up a bridge? Spray paint a trestle. The side of a building? Should she practice first? Yes, otherwise how would she find out if she was any good? Practice made perfect.

Lacey stopped mid-brush. *Monica needs you.* It was clear as day, and it was a voice. Lacey could hear a voice. She tried to ignore it and focus on the eyes of the Siamese cat, but she couldn't get rid of the voice. What was this? Guilt? What had she done that was so bad? *Go home,* she'd said. *Go home.*

There were worse things she could have said. She was probably doing Monica a favor. Encouraging her to get back to her life, her fiancé, her book tour. But Monica hadn't gone home; Lacey could feel that too. What the hell was this? Some kind of psychic link with her twin? She didn't want that. She didn't believe in that.

Go home. Lacey saw it in color. Big, splashy, billboard color. *Go home.* She took out her BlackBerry. She texted Monica. *Are you okay?*

* * *

That should do. Monica dropped her cans of paint at her feet. She didn't care what the building was. It was enough that it had a smooth, gray surface area in which to spray. Now that she was here, however, she saw the flaw in her plan. She was too close to the building. She would need to be about twenty feet in the air and farther away. How was she going to work under these conditions? If she tried to back up, she'd be standing in the middle of the street. There were too many people about. They were stopping and staring at the pile of cans at her feet, whispering. They were wondering who she was, what she was going to paint. Nobody suspected the pretty woman of potential vandalism. She was obviously an artist for hire. Besides, who in their right mind would spray paint a building in broad daylight unless they had permission to do so?

But just like her experience with the Naked Cowboy, she was choking. When it came right down to it, she couldn't do it. She picked up her paint cans one by one, stopping, dropping, squatting, scooping the cans back up until she had them all safely in her arms. This wasn't the right building; she would walk on, find something a little more private, out of the way. Perhaps she needed to wait until dark. She could hear her phone ringing, but her hands were too full to fish in her purse. She started walking.

The Hotel Chelsea. 222 West Twenty-third Street. It was a sign. Monica had seen a fascinating documentary on the Hotel Chelsea, and it was on her list of places to visit. Elegant old bricks standing since the late 1800s. A colorful history to boot. Bob Dylan composed songs here and Allen Ginsberg waxed philosophical with other poets within her walls. Dylan Thomas is said to have died of alcohol poisoning here, and Sid Vicious of the Sex Pistols stabbed and killed Nancy Spungen in room 100. Monica's little plan paled in comparison. It was the perfect place for a budding artist to make a statement. She walked into the hotel with the cans still in her arms.

A spiral staircase rose from floor to ceiling, drawing Monica's eye to the artwork depicting the hotel, staged up and down the wall behind the turning steps. *Perfect,* Monica thought, *I'm spiraling out of control.* She approached the front desk.

She pointed to her ears and shook her head. She gestured, wanting a pen. The man behind the counter eyed her paint cans, but gave her a notepad and pens.

My carrying case broke, Monica wrote. *I paint theatrical backgrounds. I need a nap before I go back to the theatre. Single room, please.* With lots of wall space, she thought. His face remained still, only his protruding eyes flicking from her to the computer screen in front of him. He slid her a form and she filled out Lacey's name and e-mail. He showed her the total on the computer screen. She paid in cash. He handed her the key and pointed up the spiral stairs. The entire transaction was completed without uttering a word.

The room was simple but beautiful: a white four-poster bed, a fireplace with an ornate mantel, salmon-colored walls. Modern touches as well: a round glass coffee table, a plasma TV mounted to the wall. She couldn't do it to this beautiful room, could she?

Go home, go home, go home. . . .

First she sprayed it on the far wall in black. Then she sprayed it above the bed in red. She sprayed it underneath the window in silver. The fumes were suffocating, but she'd been unable to open the windows. Did they keep them locked so people couldn't leap to their death? She stepped into the bathtub (what a nice pedestal tub; she should come back sometime and enjoy it) and tried to pry open the little window behind the shower. She was in luck; after considerable effort it opened a crack. She leaned forward and tried to suck in the outdoor air. It was only slightly better than the paint fumes. She looked around the bathroom. It too could use some spray paint.

She brought in the can of blue. Repetition was the mother of invention? Or master of invention? What did it even mean? Repetition leads to new inventions? So far she wasn't learning anything new, wasn't convincing herself of anything, she just couldn't stop writing it. Maybe soon she'd feel it, get under her sister's skin, really know how she felt when she said it. She'd never know if she had any artistic talent or not. This was hardly painting. It was just writing with paint. She surveyed the walls. Everywhere was written on.

She was so dizzy. She could barely read the label on her bottle of pills. Monica Bowman. She would just take three. Three would let her sleep. The ceiling was spinning. Her eyelids were heavy. Suddenly, the shadows above her looked like trees. They were the woods behind her house. She could hear two little girls singing. She smiled as she watched them hold hands, identical raven-haired girls singing. *Sweet,* Monica thought. *They're so sweet.* One of the girls was gripping the other's hand very tight. The farther they got into the woods, the little girl singing the loudest pulled her hand away.

"No!" Monica heard herself say out loud. Or did she? Maybe she shouldn't have taken three pills. Or was it six? Three for herself, three for Lacey? The little girl who pulled her hand away was skipping ahead. She had something else to occupy her, a plastic toy horse. The other little girl started to cry. She ran after the girl with the blue plastic horse, hands outstretched.

"Mine," Monica heard one of the girls say. "Mine." They were playing tug-of-war. It wasn't so sweet now. Back and forth they tugged, tears and screams from both girls now. Where was their mother?

"No," Monica cried. She felt her big hand join the hand of the little girl who had managed to yank the horse away from the other. The other was reaching for it, she was going to take it back. Monica felt her hand raise in sync with the little girl's, the front leg of the blue plastic horse tilted back as if rearing up. Then it went black.

What happened? What's with the screaming? There she is, the mother. Oh, that look on her face. Her mouth open in horror, her hands clasped over her own ears, two little girls on the ground, one with a blue plastic horse sticking out of her ear. The mother grabbed the little girl on the ground. Blood pooled around the toy horse and spilled down the little girl's cheek.

Monica woke in a sweat. It was just a dream, it was just a dream. Wasn't it? Oh God. She felt like she was going to be sick. It couldn't have been real. In the dream, Lacey was singing and babbling and—

Lacey was singing and babbling. Lacey could hear. Until Monica stabbed her in the ear with the horse.

Monica tried to scream again, for real this time. She couldn't find her voice. *I'm the reason Lacey is deaf. I'm the reason they separated us.* It was just a dream. Just a bad dream. It couldn't be true. It couldn't, it couldn't, it couldn't.

Monica sat straight up and reached for the bottle of pills.

Chapter 32

Lacey checked her BlackBerry again. An hour had gone by and Monica still hadn't answered the text. Lacey's feeling that something was wrong was stronger than ever. She opened her e-mail to send Alan a quick message, when another message caught her eye. It was from the Hotel Chelsea in New York City.

Welcome to the Hotel Chelsea. We hope you are enjoying your stay. Do you have a few minutes to complete our quick customer satisfaction survey? . . .

Lacey had never stayed at the Hotel Chelsea in New York City. She hovered the mouse over the message to delete it. Something made her stop. That feeling again, that something was wrong with Monica, came back full force.

Lacey got up from her easels and walked into the living area to find Mike. He was leaning against the kitchen counter, staring at his phone.

"Would Monica ever hurt herself?" he asked when he saw Lacey.

"What's going on?" Lacey asked. He showed her his phone.

First text: *It's all my fault. Tell her it's my fault.*
Second text: *I'm so sorry.*
Third text: *I'm so sleepy.*

Lacey motioned for Mike to follow and they ran over to her computer. She showed him the e-mail from the Hotel Chelsea. He held his hand out in confusion.

"Not me," Lacey said.

"You tried texting her?" Mike asked. Lacey held up her BlackBerry.

"She won't answer."

"Something's definitely wrong, then," Mike said. "She worships you. She would answer." Mike took out his phone. Lacey watched him dial 4-1-1 and ask for the number to the Hotel Chelsea. Lacey waited as he made the call. Lacey shook her head when Mike asked for Monica Bowman.

"Lacey Gears," Mike corrected himself. "She's Deaf?" he said. "Actually, she's not. Please, just ring her room. Just do it!" Mike counted as the phone rang. When he reached six, Lacey tapped him.

"Tell front desk 9-1-1," Lacey said. "Hurry."

The phone was ringing. She counted them, there were six. Someone should really answer that. She was so heavy, but not quite asleep. Funny, because she'd taken enough to put her to sleep, hadn't she? Her head was pounding, or was it the door? She couldn't move.

"Open up," a man's voice yelled. "I was told I needed to call 9-1-1. Either answer the door or I'm coming in." *The nice man sounds nice, man,* Monica thought. *I wonder who he's mad at. He shouldn't get mad at the little things.* Getting mad at the little things wasn't good for your health. Getting mad at the little things wasn't recommended in *The Architect of Your Soul.* Still, Monica understood how the poor man felt. She was upset about something earlier too. Only now she couldn't remember why. What was it about?

"Jesus Christ," she heard the man say. He sounded closer now. "She spray painted the freakin' walls," the man said.

"She's swallowed a whole bottle of pills! Jesus. Call it in." *Who spray painted the walls? Who swallowed a bottle of pills? Why were they in her room? They should be taking care of the poor person.* Monica didn't hear anymore. Everything went black.

"She spray painted the walls," Mike said.

"Why?"

"I don't know. They said she wrote *Go Home* all over the place." Lacey slapped her hand over her mouth. "Let's go," Mike said. "She's at Beth Israel hospital. They say she'll be okay, but I want to be there—I don't know about you—"

"I'm coming," Lacey said.

"What about her parents? Her—boyfriend?" Mike seemed to have a hard time getting the words out of his mouth.

"She broke up with Joe," Lacey said.

"Okay," Mike said. "We'll wait and call whoever Monica wants us to." Lacey sent Alan a text on her way to Mike's car. She prayed he wasn't going to be mad she was going with Mike. But he offered to drive, and even though she could probably make it there faster on her motorcycle, she was too upset to be speeding. After all, this was all her fault. None of this would have ever happened if it hadn't been for her. And there was now no denying what deep down she'd known all along. There must be a bond between twins. Because Lacey's heart was breaking as if it weren't her own.

"I'm sorry," the nurse behind the counter said. "She's resting. Unless you're family—" Lacey stuck her face in front of the woman and pointed to herself.

"Oh my," the nurse said. "You're twins."

Lacey's eyes filled with tears.

"Yes," Lacey said. "Twins." The nurse said Lacey could see her. Lacey took out her pad and pen. *Gift shop?* The nurse drew a little map on the piece of paper and pointed down the corridor.

Lacey stood irresolute in the middle of the gift shop. She didn't know what to buy. Flowers? A teddy bear? With each item she picked up, she was at a bigger loss. None of them said "I'm sorry." None of them said "This wasn't your fault." The responsibility for what happened to them as children lay squarely on their parents' shoulders. Lacey could buy every present in the store and it wouldn't give them what they really deserved: twenty-five years of their lives back. She settled on a bouquet of flowers and a mug. It said: YOU CAN KID THE WORLD. BUT NOT YOUR SISTER.

Lying in the hospital bed, with the covers snug against her, eyes closed to the world, Monica looked so helpless, so frail. Lacey pulled up a chair and simply watched her. Her eyes were moving behind shut lids, she was dreaming. Did they have similar dreams?

"You're beautiful," Lacey signed. "I'm sorry." Lacey snuck her hand underneath the covers and took her sister's hand in hers. They said she hadn't taken the entire bottle of pills, that it may not have been a true suicide attempt. The paint fumes had led to dizziness that may have made her confused about how many she had taken. Still, Lacey knew it wasn't completely accidental, just like writing *Go Home* all over the walls wasn't by accident. This was a new and bewildering experience, having someone need you, but there was no doubt about it, Monica needed her. Her BlackBerry buzzed. It was Alan.

Lacey. Where are you? Are you okay? Is Monica okay?
I'm at the hospital. She's sleeping. They pumped her stomach.
Are you okay?
Yes. I love you.
I love you too.

Someone touched her on the shoulder, and Lacey jumped, almost dropping her BlackBerry in the process. A nurse, a doctor, and a woman dressed in black stood behind her.

"This is Dr. Barns," the nurse said. The woman in black interpreted. "He's the psychiatrist. He wonders if he can speak with you?"

"Of course," Lacey said.

"This way," Dr. Barns said.

On the short walk to the doctor's office, the interpreter introduced herself to Lacey and they chatted briefly. Her name was Melanie, she was one of the interpreters on staff in the hospital. Soon they were sitting in a small office covered in plants.

"I'm sorry for the circumstances which bring us here today," Dr. Barns said. Lacey kept quiet. "I'm preparing your sister for admission to our psychiatric unit," he added. "And I was hoping you could tell me a little bit about her history. Has she attempted suicide before?"

"I thought they said the paint fumes made her dizzy," Lacey said. "This may not have been a suicide attempt at all."

"Has your sister spray painted hotel walls before? Is this a pattern of acting out with her?"

"I think that was the first," Lacey said. She didn't like the doctor. And he certainly wasn't locking Monica up here. "I'd like to take her home instead," Lacey said. "I can take care of her."

"Are you two very close?" the doctor asked.

"We're twins," Lacey said.

"Yes, identical twins, I can see that. But that doesn't really answer my question now, does it?"

"You can't imagine how close we are," Lacey said. She sat back and smiled at the doctor. There. She wasn't sure exactly how the interpreter phrased it, but word for word she wasn't exactly lying.

"It's standard procedure to admit any patients who have attempted to harm themselves into the psychiatric unit for evaluation. If this proves to be an isolated incident and a case of vandalism and—dizziness—as you say, then she will be released in twenty-four hours. I'm not here to debate where she goes next, Ms. Bowman—"

"Gears."

"Mrs. Gears—"

"Ms. Gears."

The psychiatrist stopped, looked at her. "I'm simply trying to get an idea of her history from you."

"It's our parents' fault," Lacey said. "They suck."

"I see." He scribbled something on a piece of paper. "Have you contacted them?"

"Did I not just say they sucked? That they were to blame?"

"Is that a no?" the doctor asked. He took off his glasses, rubbed his nose, and stared at the interpreter. Lacey slammed her hands on the desk and stood.

"Are you an idiot?"

"Ms. Gears, I will not tolerate name-calling."

"I just said our parents are the reason my sister is lying in a hospital bed and you ask if I'd called them."

The doctor turned to the interpreter.

"Is this normal behavior for a Deaf person or is she over-animated?" he asked her.

"Excuse me?" Lacey said.

"You weren't supposed to interpret that," the doctor said to the interpreter. "Stop signing. I'm talking to you, Melanie, I'm not talking to her." Lacey crossed her arms and glared as Dr. Barns continued his futile attempt to persuade the interpreter to have a nonsigned conversation about Lacey right in front of her face. Lacey didn't care how she was going to do it, but Monica was getting out of this hospital.

"When will she be admitted?"

"We should have a bed ready in a few hours," Dr. Barns said.

"Fine," Lacey said. "And where do I file a complaint?"

Dr. Barns stood.

"A complaint?"

"Yes. I find your behavior despicable," Lacey said. "And discriminatory."

"I'm sorry you feel that way. You can speak to someone in the visitors' lobby, I suppose."

"Thank you," Lacey said.

Lacey tried not to run all the way back to the room. Monica was still sleeping. According to the nurse, she could wake at any time and other than feeling tired and pangs from her stomach being pumped, she shouldn't be in any physical danger. She found Mike sitting next to her bed.

"I lied," Mike said. "I said I was your brother."

Lacey winked.

"Welcome to the family," she said. "Now help me wake her up."

* * *

An hour later, Lacey and Mike walked out of the hospital. On their way past the nurses' desk, the nurse called out to them.

"How is your sister?" the nurse asked, half yelling, half over-enunciating. Mike pretended to sign the question to Lacey, who responded.

"She's still resting," Mike interpreted. "We'll be back after a bite to eat."

"They'll be checking her into the psychiatric unit while you're gone," the nurse said. "So when you come back, you should go to the ninth floor." Mike interpreted again; Lacey smiled at the nurse and gave a thumbs-up.

"Thank you," Mike said. "We'll do that."

A few minutes later, Lacey walked past the nurses' station again. This time she was alone. The nurse said something to her. Lacey pointed to her ears and shrugged. She walked on, but as she neared a pair of glass double doors, she could see the reflection of the nurse behind her, frantically waving her arms. Lacey stopped and waited as the nurse ran over with a piece of paper. She shoved it at Lacey.

You just left. You just walked out the door with your brother.

You must be mistaken. I don't have a brother.

Lacey smiled but walked on, leaving the nurse frustrated and alone.

Lacey met Monica and Mike three blocks away at a diner. "We did it," Monica said as Lacey walked in. Lacey smiled. Monica looked cute in her clothes. She had the mug Lacey bought her on the table in front of her. Monica slid down the booth to make room for Lacey. Lacey slipped in and put her arm around her twin. They stayed that way until the waitress came back to take their order.

"Curry chicken salad sandwich and Pepsi for two," Lacey said. Monica smiled and clutched Lacey's hand as two fat tears dripped down her cheeks. Lacey's BlackBerry buzzed. It was Alan again, making sure they were okay.

We're fine, Lacey texted. *We're coming home.*

Chapter 33

Lacey knelt in the grass, patting dirt around the recently planted rosebush. It was gorgeous. Monica would love it.

"What are you planning on doing?" Alan asked. "Are you just going to keep her?"

"She's not a puppy. Of course I'm keeping her." Lacey and Monica had been back from the hospital for over a week. Monica had practically moved in, and Alan was no longer needed every day at the shopping mall site, so he was spending more and more time at home. Only he was the one on the couch, and Monica was sleeping in the bed with Lacey.

"Can't she sleep on the couch now?" Alan asked.

"Hand me the watering can," Lacey said. Alan picked up the watering can.

"I'll do it," he said. He watered the rosebush, set the can down, folded his arms across his chest, and waited.

"It's just temporary," Lacey said. The truth was, she was terrified to let Monica out of her sight. What if the doctor had been right, and she needed psychiatric help? It was hard enough dealing with the hotel, trying to come to a payment they'd accept instead of pressing charges. Lacey knew "the parents" had plenty of money, but Monica refused to call them. Lacey couldn't very well argue; she was the one who forbade Monica to tell them about her, and Monica had kept the promise. Still, Lacey wasn't going to let Monica go to jail; she would do whatever it took.

"She needs more than you can give her right now," Alan said.

"She needs to get laid," Lacey said. She moved over to the next project, a tray of various flowers she needed to put in a large porch pot. She started filling it with dirt, wishing Alan would either help out or leave her alone. She knew he had a right to talk about this, but she was exhausted, and she wanted to get the flowers done before Monica woke up.

"Laid?" Alan said. "Are you kidding me?"

"It might cheer her up."

"I think that's a really bad idea," Alan said. He knelt down beside her and started scooping dirt into the pot. Their hands touched in the bag. Lacey kissed Alan on the cheek. He gave her a proper kiss, neither able to take it too far with their hands stuck in the dirt. He brought his dirty hands out first. "I miss you," he said touching the tip of her nose with his finger. " I want to get laid."

Lacey laughed.

"I miss you too." She touched the tip of his nose with her finger, then laughed at the brown spot. He swiped dirt across her cheek next. She marked his forehead. They kissed again.

"You know we haven't," Alan said. "Since she moved in."

"That's why I need to get her laid first," Lacey explained. "So I won't feel guilty."

"Guilty? Why would you feel guilty?" It was a legitimate question. But how could Lacey explain something she didn't quite understand herself? Kelly told Lacey she could sometimes feel her left leg, years after it was gone. That was the only way she could describe how she felt about Monica now, as if she were a part of her that, despite being severed, Lacey could still feel. Suddenly everything Monica felt, Lacey did too. And vice versa. Lacey assumed if she was hungry, Monica must be hungry. They slept the same hours. Lacey checked Monica's pockets constantly for pills. To her relief, she had yet to find any, but instead of calming her down, Lacey's anxiety ratcheted up. More than anything, Monica was now Lacey's responsibility.

"When are you going to call your parents?" Alan asked. The flirtatious mood was gone; now they were just two dirty faces sitting near a pot.

"Monica doesn't want to talk to them," Lacey said. Lacey didn't know what to make of Alan's about-face. First he'd wanted her to forge a relationship with her sister, now he wanted her gone.

"She doesn't want to talk to them," Alan said. "Or you don't?"

"What?" Lacey asked.

"Haven't you noticed? Monica doesn't seem to think or feel anything for herself when you two are together. It's like she's trying to be you."

"She needs to relax," Lacey said. "Don't be so hard on her."

"Just be careful."

"Of what?"

"She tried to kill herself. She needs professional help."

Lacey shoved her hands back into the bag of dirt and threw it into the pot. Alan jerked back.

"Watch my eyes," he said.

"She doesn't need professional help," Lacey said. She gave up on the hand-scoop method, picked up the bag of dirt, and poured it straight into the pot. "She needs me, she needs flowers, and she needs to get laid," Lacey said.

"I have to take a shower and hit the road," Alan said.

"I'm sorry," Lacey said. Alan was back in a jiffy. He grabbed Lacey and pulled her down to the grassy floor. He kissed her hard; she gave in and wrapped her hands around him.

"No more 'sorry,' " Alan said, pulling away just enough to sign. "I'm proud of you."

"I just want her to be okay," Lacey said.

"I know," Alan said. "I do too. But she's a grown woman. It's not your fault. It's not your responsibility."

"She spray painted *go home* on the walls. What I told her. Then she tried to kill herself. It is my fault."

"No. She's responsible for herself," Alan said. "You were

right, I was wrong. She is kind of stalking you. She moved in
with us. Who does that?"

"Stop it."

"I'm not using my voice. She can't hear me."

"She might be able to feel you."

"Feel me?"

"I can feel her. I can feel her thoughts."

"I think you're the one who needs to get laid," Alan said. He
moved his hand down to her zipper. Lacey pushed him away.

"Next time," she said. *When my sister is okay,* she added
silently. *Only when my sister is okay.*

Lacey and Monica strolled through the Philadelphia Museum of Art and imitated the poses of nearby statues, exagger-
ating the shapes and faces to make each other laugh. It had been
Monica's idea to dress alike, then Lacey came up with the idea
of one walking slightly behind the other at a delay, just to make
people think the same woman had passed them twice—watch
them scratch their heads and try to figure out how this was possible. Despite Alan's warnings, Lacey had never had so much
fun with someone in her entire life. She knew anything she said
or did would be immediately accepted by Monica, and it wasn't
just because Monica was desperate to keep her attention, was
it? It wasn't unhealthy like Alan suggested; it couldn't be, they
were sisters, they were twins. Yes, she'd resisted her in the past,
but now, now there was no turning back. Separate, they were
missing part of themselves, but together they were a force to be
reckoned with. And sure, Lacey noticed how Monica was growing her hair out, how she was always wearing Lacey's clothes,
how she was now wearing contacts instead of her glasses—but
that was normal bonding, nothing more. Once Monica felt
confident Lacey always planned on having a relationship with
her, she would probably go back to Boston, back to her old
haircut and glasses, back to being her.

Lacey knew she could ask Monica to rob a bank with her
right now and Monica would do it; luckily, Lacey had no such
desire. She wouldn't even let Monica ride her motorcycle, even

though Monica had been out-and-out begging her. Everything would get better, they just needed some time. The past few nights, Lacey had woken up in a cold sweat, heavy with dreams. In one she was all grown up but Monica was a child and she'd lost her. In the next she was standing at her parents' cabin, about to meet them for the first time, wondering how she was going to break it to them that she had lost Monica.

In another dream she'd forgotten who she was. It was as if someone had burrowed inside her, snatched her soul—

She didn't share any of her dreams with Monica. In the first place, even though Monica's ability to read and express sign language was improving, she wasn't quite at the stage where they could have in-depth talks about their dreams. For another, she didn't want to worry or frighten her sister. They were doing so well together.

Often, strangers wanted to take their picture. And they didn't even know their dramatic story! They'd be a media sensation if anyone ever got wind of the details, but neither of them wanted that. It was too public, they wanted to bond in public. But that didn't stop them from posing for pictures. It was as if they were trying to make up for lost time, for all the childhood pictures that should have been. Sometimes, Monica pretended that she was Deaf too, other times she did her best to interpret.

"Your paintings should be in here," Monica said, gesturing toward the walls. "Your horses." Lacey shook her head.

"I mean it," Monica said. "You're very good."

"You're a good writer."

"I hated that book."

"Me too. I'm not talking about the book. I'm talking about the writing. When you go home, you should write something you want to write."

"When I go home?" Monica looked stricken. Lacey grabbed Monica's hand and held it.

"I'm not telling you to go home. I just meant—"

"It's okay."

"I want you to stay."

"Okay."

"I mean it. I don't want you to leave."

"I won't. Don't cry. Lacey, Lacey, Lacey, don't cry."

Was she crying? What was this? When she was with her sister, she thought of Alan and felt guilty for wanting to be with him; when she was with him, she felt guilty for wanting to be with her sister. Maybe she was the one who needed professional help, the one who was about to crack up. Or maybe, like she'd been saying all along, she just needed to get her sister laid.

"Are you going to see Mike?" Lacey asked. Monica shrugged and looked away. Lacey tapped her on the shoulder.

"You don't fool me," she said. "I know you like him."

"I'm sorry. I know you two—"

"Please," Lacey said. "I love Alan. I'd be really happy if the two of you were dating."

"Really?"

"Absolutely. We should invite him over, do something just the four of us."

"Wouldn't that—I don't mean—but—Wouldn't that be weird for Alan?" Monica asked.

"Sometimes I think you can read my mind," Lacey said. Monica beamed. "We'll figure it out later," Lacey added. They moved away from the statues and over to abstract paintings. Lacey hesitated at the entrance, waiting to see which way Monica would turn. But Monica held back and didn't budge until Lacey picked a direction. Then, she followed. *It's normal,* Lacey told herself as she tried to concentrate on the paintings. *She's just a little insecure right now. But she'll get better. In no time she'll get better.*

"I have a brilliant idea," Lacey said an hour later, when they'd had enough culture for one day.

"I can't wait," Monica said.

"Let's go mess with the guy at Benjamin Books," Lacey said.

"The one who thinks I'm rude?"

"That's the one."

"Oh my God," Monica said. "That's the best idea I've heard all day."

As soon as they walked into Benjamin Books, Lacey spotted the manager who hated her, and she waved. At first he put his hand up to wave back. And then recognition dawned. He shook his head. He whipped around to walk the other way and plowed right into Monica. He gave a half scream, took a few steps back, and plunged into Lacey. His head swiveled back and forth between the girls. They broke into raucous laughter. It was too much, even for him. He laughed along with them.

"You got me," he said. "You got me."

"You have no idea," Monica said.

"We could write a book," Lacey said.

Chapter 34

It wasn't a well-thought-out plan. It wasn't a plan at all, it just happened. Monica's phone buzzed and when Lacey swiped it up, it flipped open. She hadn't intended on reading the text, it just happened.

You're not answering your phone. Lunch? Please? I'm coming to Boston. Mother.

Great, Lacey texted back. *When? Where?*

Wed? Harry's Grill. One p.m.

It was Monday. There was plenty of time to get to Boston. Lacey had always wanted to go. How would she dress, wear her hair? What if she got it cut like Monica's? What if she wore one of Monica's skirts and blouses? Monica certainly wasn't using them. What if she brought the green glasses Monica had all but abandoned?

The switch wouldn't last long, just as long as it took for their mother to realize this daughter was the spare. But it didn't matter. The surprise, the shock, would be worth it. Lacey confirmed the details, then quickly pocketed the cell phone. Monica could do without it for a few days. Who didn't lose their cell phone from time to time? Monica had been ignoring all her calls anyway; she probably wouldn't even notice it was gone.

Lacey was going to meet her mother. Would there be tears? Screaming? Excuses? Maybe she would be aloof, make polite conversation, pay for lunch, and leave with her head held high. *Despite you, I've grown into a mature adult. I did it all on my own.*

Maybe she would make a scene. Maybe she would tell her Monica never wanted to see her again. Maybe she would tell her Monica tried to kill herself and it was all her fault.

"You're leaving for a couple of days?" Monica asked.

"My client lives a little too far out," Lacey said. "So it's just easier to spend the night. I'll finish the portrait faster that way."

"Why don't I come with you?" Monica said. "We can get a hotel room."

"You promised Robert you'd go to the Deaf picnic," Lacey said. "You need the practice."

"You're right," Monica said. "I just hate the thought of being separated again."

"Text me anytime," Lacey said. Then she picked up her duffel bag and hustled out before Monica could search for her phone.

From her stool at the bar, Lacey watched Katherine Bowman enter the restaurant. She was right on time, and just as Monica described her. Tall with dark hair, like them. Lacey waited until Katherine was seated. She watched her adjust herself. She tucked her purse into the empty chair beside her, fiddled with her hair, which was swept into a bun. She spoke to the waiter using her index finger as punctuation as she talked. He nodded and hurried off. She smoothed the tablecloth in front of her and took a sip of her water. She smoothed her hair again, looked around the restaurant. Lacey slid off the stool and walked over, trying not to wobble in Monica's straight skirt and heels.

Katherine looked up and met her eyes. Then she smiled, and stood as Lacey neared. Her napkin fell to the floor. She opened her arms, and then Lacey was allowing herself to be wrapped in a hug. Lacey pulled away as soon as she could and picked up the napkin. Her mother was talking a mile a minute. As soon as Lacey sat down, Katherine thrust a newspaper article at her. Lacey glanced at it; it was something about working women molested by food vendors in big cities, trading free fruit for a free feel. *I'll give you a free banana if I can touch your melons,* Lacey imagined the vendor saying. She tried not to laugh. Instead, she held the article up with a studious nod of her head, then tucked it into her purse. She sipped her own water, smiled, and nodded as Katherine spoke. The transition happened rather quickly. Katherine stopped talking mid-sentence. She frowned.

"You haven't said a word," she said. Lacey could read her lips perfectly.

"Hello, Mother," she said. Katherine's eyes widened and she grabbed on to the table like it was a life raft. She must have let out a cry, for the waiter hurried over.

"Are you all right?" he asked with a glance at Lacey. Lacey's eyes never wavered from her mother's face. *I'll never remember you young,* she thought.

"No, no, no, no," Katherine Bowman said. With each "no" her head dropped lower, until she was sobbing on the table. The waiter was visibly upset. Lacey was not.

"What's wrong?" he asked. "What can I do?"

"Go away, go away," Katherine said. The waiter threw another bewildered look to Lacey before hurrying off. Lacey shrugged and did the gesture for "crazy" that hearing people liked to use, index finger twirling in circles near the head. Katherine Bowman wiped her eyes, then took a deep breath, like a scuba diver preparing to descend into the murky depths. Only her quivering lips and shaking hands gave away her earlier collapse.

"Lacey," she said. She reached across the table, hands and eyes pleading. Lacey stuck up her middle finger. "You don't understand," she said. "You don't understand."

If there was anything Lacey Gears understood, it was the phrase "You don't understand." That and "I'll tell you later" she'd heard often. Conversations around dinner tables that she tried to grasp, only to be told, "I'll tell you later." *It's not important.* Decisions made for her, around her, about her. It was Katherine Bowman who didn't understand. A long list of misunderstandings, years of bad decisions, an endless well of wrong.

Lacey reached into her purse and pulled out the first note card. All of her questions were written in black marker, thick, tall letters asking the unanswerable. She held it up like a game show host.

Was it because I was Deaf?

"No, no, no." Katherine was moaning, Lacey knew by the drop of her head as she spoke, the shake of her head. Katherine reached into her purse and pulled out her cell phone. Lacey snatched it away, removing her mother's safety net like a burglar cutting the phone wires. Lacey slammed the first card facedown on the table and held up the second question.

Did you pay for my school?

Katherine nodded.

My private speech lessons? Another nod.

My art teacher? Katherine frowned, shook her head. Lacey thought for sure the answer to that would be yes. She was glad. She loved Miss Lee; thank God she didn't owe that one to the parents who abandoned her.

My college tuition? Another nod.

Margaret knew? You paid her off too? Lacey was pleased to note the shame that crossed over her mother's face like a rain shadow as she nodded yes to that one.

"You can't tell Monica," Katherine said. Lacey reached into her purse again and pulled out a Polaroid picture. She slid it across the table. It was one of Lacey and Monica taken at Benjamin Books by their new best friend, Benjamin. The girls were smiling, their arms thrown around each other, their mouths open in identical smiles. Katherine let a sob break loose.

"My girls, my girls, my girls."

A man in a suit hurried over, trailed by the waiter. "Ma'am," he said. "Is everything all right?"

"They said it was for the best," Katherine said to Lacey. Then she dove into her purse. Lacey suspected her mother was looking for a piece of paper and a pen. Her own were tucked in her purse; she didn't offer them. Her mother came up with a tube of lipstick. She uncapped it and tipped it toward the tablecloth.

"Ma'am?" the manager said again.

Katherine tipped the lipstick down and wrote on the tablecloth. *I love you*. Lacey crossed her arms and shook her head. She took her fingers and smeared the lipstick message until it was nothing more than a blur. Perhaps sensing a second act, the manager reached for the lipstick tube. Her mother pushed his hand away, then slid the bread basket out of the way. She stood up, leaned over the table, and wrote: *THE DOCTOR!!!* As quick as she could, Lacey snatched a bottle of ketchup from a nearby table, opened it, and upended it all over the table, trying to obscure the messages. Both the waiter and manager ran away, no doubt preparing to call the police.

Katherine scraped the ketchup away with a knife and wrote *I'm sorry* in the remainder of the sweet, sticky red. Lacey stuck her finger in the spicy mustard, found a clean, white spot. *Too late*. A few lookie loos were leaning over in their seats to see what was going on; others were eyeing their own condiments with renewed interest.

Giant cards, ketchup, lipstick, spicy mustard—who knew communication could be so hard, so messy?

"Lacey, Lacey, Lacey," Katherine said. Lacey knew just the thing to shut her up. She reached into her purse and pulled out her half of the severed blue horse. All color drained from her mother's face.

"You were wrong," Lacey said using her voice, drawing upon every speech lesson she'd ever taken to be heard. "Not the doctor. You." Lacey pointed at her mother. "You were wrong."

Then, Lacey threw down the bill from the Hotel Chelsea, the three-thousand-dollar agreement they'd come to for the damage Lacey Gears had done to room 812, and made her exit. She knew her mother was still causing a scene behind her: She could see it in the faces of those she passed by, she could feel it in the back of her head. She picked up speed, as if she could outrun the pounding of her heart, her clenched stomach, and the tears, the damn uninvited tears that were pouring down both cheeks. She burst out of the restaurant and there was Monica, standing, waiting. The shock of it dried Lacey's tears instantly. Monica smiled, opened her arms, and without hesitation Lacey fell into them. It felt good. For the first time in her life, she really knew what it felt like to have a sister.

Chapter 35

"It's good to see you," Mike said. All Monica's fears about seeing him again evaporated the minute he opened the door.

"You too," Monica said.

"If you're looking for Lacey—"

"I'm not." Monica moved in on Mike before she could change or mind or clue him in on what she was about to do. She wrapped her hands around the back of his neck, pulled him close, and kissed him. His arms circled her waist and he kissed her back. It was a long time before Monica pulled away.

"We have a workshop coming up," Monica said. "And we'd love it if you come."

"We?" Mike asked.

"I'll explain everything," Monica said. "But first there's something I'm dying to do. And I know it's going to sound a little strange—"

"Try me," Mike said. Monica talked. Mike listened to every word. Then, a smile came over him.

"Well," he said. "There's no dining room here, but there's always the kitchen counter." He grinned again and held out his hand. Monica took it, and he led the way.

Lacey and Alan were lying in bed, relaxed and happy after a long-overdue lovemaking session.

"This Saturday?" Alan said. "We have a big site meeting—"

"Cancel it," Lacey said. "Please?"

"What are you two up to?" Alan asked. Lacey straddled him, kissed his neck.

"No more questions," she said. "Just come."

"Okay," Alan said pulling her into him. "Anything for you."

"Good morning," Monica said. "Welcome." The room was packed. Monica made sure not to look at anyone in the front row, the one usually reserved for friends and family. "My name is Monica Bowman," she continued. "And I am not the architect of my soul." A few people clapped, some because they misunderstood, others because they were terminally polite. "I hate this job," Monica continued. She held up her book. "Every time I quote from this bullshit, I want to gag." A few people laughed nervously, the others waited to get the joke. "The idea to write the book wasn't mine. It was my ex-boyfriend's. He should be up here telling you how to Construct a Blueprint, Build a Foundation, and How and When to Remodel. Those aren't my words, and I certainly don't practice what I've been preaching." Monica caught her new assistants, the ones assigned to her by Help Yourself! Inc., whispering in the back of the room. One of them clutched a cell phone, and the other looked around, no doubt scanning the room to find the large hook with which to drag her off.

"I do want you to lead better lives," Monica said. "Because as far as I can work it out, this is it, the only life we get. Don't waste it on Time Management crap. Don't waste it on Thin Thighs in Thirty Days. How to Catch a Man When You're Out of Bait. This workshop isn't going to take two days. It may not even take twenty minutes. And don't worry, if you're not fully satisfied, I'm sure Help Yourself! Inc. will be more than happy to refund your money. Right, girls?" Monica gestured to the two assistants. They slunk as far as they could in their seats.

"If you prefer the flashing lights and eighties music, get an iPod and a disco ball. If you're expecting words like 'up sales' and 'down sales' with smiling presenters dripping in bling, bragging about another new idea or product to shove down the throats of the gullible American public, then just go across the hall. I'm sure there's one of those over there. Scream yourself silly and convince yourself you can only be happy if you have more things. A new house, a new car, diamonds dripping from your wrists.

"But that's not what I want for you. Or me. I'm going to tell you a few simple things that I think could be stopping you from leading your best lives. They've certainly kept me from leading mine." Monica reached into her pocket and pulled out the bottle of sleeping pills that had been her constant companion the past year.

"These are sleeping pills," she said. "I've been carrying them around like a security blanket for the past year. And not because I was having trouble sleeping. In fact, I was pretty sure if I ever broke the seal on them, I would swallow every single one. Luckily, when it finally happened, I only took about half. I really thought I'd only taken three, but I was kind of dizzy from all the paint fumes. That's another story. I vandalized a hotel room." There was a small eruption of noise from the audience, gasps, and at least one "Oh my God." A few people looked around, as if wondering if it were their hotel room she'd "vandalized." Knowing a heart-to-heart when they heard one, the audience quieted down, afraid to miss a single word.

"At the same time that I was contemplating taking my life, I was standing up here, pretending I could help people like you live better lives. I, myself, was given everything growing up. I had two parents who loved me. Two nice homes. Money. Privilege. But something was missing. A sadness lived inside me. I couldn't get rid of it, and I certainly couldn't outrun it." Monica stopped and took a deep breath.

"I've recently been lucky enough to hang out with some

artists," she said. "I asked my friend the painter what drove her to paint. I asked my friend the sculptor what drove him to sculpt. An actor what drove him to act. The essence of their answers was exactly the same. The pursuit of two things. Truth and beauty." Monica stepped forward.

"I wondered how I too could apply truth and beauty to my life. Because carrying a bottle of sleeping pills around because I wasn't sure I wanted to live wasn't beautiful. And pretending to be the author of a book I didn't really write was not the truth. And then I wanted to get to the root of every ugly lie that's been weighing down my life." For the first time since she began, Monica looked at the front row. "My mother and father are here today," she said. "I'm sure it's been very difficult for them to listen to this, my truth. It's so hard to look at the people you love and tell them the truth. Isn't it, Mom? Isn't it, Dad?" Her parents stared back. At least they were still there, they hadn't walked out. It gave Monica the courage to continue.

She gazed out at the audience. "I wonder how many of you are keeping secrets, both large and small, from the people you love. I know they're weighing you down. Forcing you to build a false self in front of the true you." Monica took off her jacket; her armpits were soaked. She took a sip of water, then looked at the four empty seats on the stage.

"Mom, Dad," she said. "Please join me on stage." This was it. From here on out, she would not be able to control what her parents did. They could walk out. They could deny everything. But she was willing to take that chance. Then, no matter what they did, she was going to live the rest of her life out in the open. She caught Mike's eye in the second row. He smiled and gave a slight nod.

Her mother stood first, then the Colonel. Monica could tell his left leg was stiff from sitting, and his jaw was locked with tension. He gave her a look she knew well, the look that said she was humiliating him in public and he would not forget it. Strangely, she took this in without the usual dose of guilt or shame. She wasn't here to humiliate them, she was simply facing the truth. She also knew with a sudden and sure clarity that they were her parents and she would love them no matter what. Her mother had tears in her eyes. She looked at Monica, then headed for the stage.

"Katherine," Richard said as quietly as possible. "Katherine." She looked back at her husband, and they stared at each other. An understanding must have passed between them, for a minute later, Richard Bowman gave one curt nod and then followed his wife on stage. They settled into the chairs, and the audience burst into applause.

"Thank you, Mom, thank you, Dad," Monica said. "Six months ago something happened to me that changed my life as I knew it." Monica's voice faltered, but she forged on. "I have a sister," she said. "Her name is Lacey." The audience waited. "She's my identical twin. And I didn't know she even existed until six months ago." This time, the audience went tilt. They broke out in loud murmurs; Monica heard the same woman say "Oh my God" again.

"Monica," Richard said. "This isn't an appropriate discussion for a public forum."

"It's the way she wanted it," Monica said. "It's the only way she would meet with you." Monica found the interpreter in the audience, sitting slightly in the middle and to the side of the chair Lacey occupied.

"Lacey," Monica said. "Would you please join us on stage?" Richard stood.

"Monica!" he said. Katherine pulled him back down. She'd started to cry, but to her credit she stayed in her seat. Heads turned as Lacey and the interpreter made their way on stage. There were more gasps and murmurs as the twins stood side by side and a few more "Oh my God"s floated along with the flashes of cameras. Monica and Lacey exchanged a look; this would be the end of privacy as they knew it.

"This is my sister, Lacey," Monica said. "And these," she gestured to Richard and Katherine, "are our biological parents. I was not adopted." The audience made the loudest ruckus yet. Richard and Katherine leapt to their feet.

"I'm taking you home," Richard said. He took Katherine by the elbow; she jerked away.

"You don't understand," she said to the girls. "Lacey. We've never stopped loving you." Katherine turned to Richard. "Tell her," she said.

Richard cleared his throat, nodded.

"We've always loved you sweetheart," he said. "We knew where you were, we knew you were happy, we paid for your school, your college—"

"You threw me away like a piece of garbage," Lacey said.

"No," Katherine said. "They said it was for the best."

"They?" Monica asked. "Who are they?"

"We will not discuss this here," Richard said. "We will not." He took Katherine by the arm and began guiding her off the stage.

"Phase one," Monica said as they watched them leave.

"On to phase two," Lacey said. The girls quickly followed their parents offstage. Monica's new assistants tried to stop her at the door.

"What do we do with them?" they said, gesturing to the audience, who looked as if they were going to pounce if everyone didn't come back on stage soon.

"Celebrate good times," Monica said. "Just celebrate good times."

As promised, Alan and Mike were waiting in Alan's car at the curb. Lacey and Monica hurried into the backseat.

"Have they left yet?" Monica asked. Alan pointed to the black Mercedes pulling out.

"Let's go," Lacey said. "But not too close." Alan started the car and pulled out.

"I know the way to the cabin," Monica said. "It's okay if you lose them."

"Why are you so sure they're going to the cabin?" Mike asked.

"The Colonel is mortified," Monica said. "He's going to need to shoot something." Lacey waited until the others had settled into their own, hunkering down for the long drive. Mike and Alan were talking up front. Monica was resting her eyes, mouth moving to a song on the radio, Lacey assumed. She snuck the latest note out of her pocket, and her stomach clenched with anticipation as she read it again.

> Parents. Cabin. Lock them in the cellar
> until they talk. There's rope and duct
> tape in a silver garbage pail under the
> shelf of canned peaches if you need
> them.

Chapter 36

Kelly Thayler stood at the exact spot Lacey told her to stand. Maria and Robert were up closer to the cabin, probably breaking the cellar window and throwing Kelly's prosthetic leg into it at that very moment. Next they would help Kelly lure Mr. and Mrs. Bowman down to the cellar, then shut and lock the door behind them. After that, all they had to do was wait until Lacey gave the word, then let them all out.

Kelly hoped she'd get the chance to follow them down to the cellar. She didn't care if Lacey got mad, she wanted part of the action. They'd been staying at a motel down the road, and she was ready to get this over with, get her leg back. Most of the time she leaned against a tree, but when Lacey texted her and said they were almost there, and she saw the black Mercedes coming down the road, she hopped on one leg out to the middle of the street. She was just going to have to trust Monica's assurance that the Colonel had terrific reflexes. He did. He braked several inches away. Dirt from the country road flew into Kelly's eyes. She wiped it away as she gave an exaggerated hop toward the car. A woman Kelly believed was Katherine Bowman was the first out of the car.

"My dear," she said. "Are you all right?"

"No," Kelly cried. "I'm not all right." At this very moment, Alan was taking a second road to the cabin, a route that took slightly longer, but if Kelly delayed them long enough, they should beat them there.

"What in the devil are you doing in the middle of the road?" Richard Bowman yelled.

"Richard," Katherine said.

"I could've killed you," Richard said.

"I don't care," Kelly said. "I want my leg back! I want my leg back!" Richard and Katherine exchanged a look.

"I'm sure you do, dear," Katherine said. "I'm sure you do."

"It's in your cellar," Kelly said.

"I beg your pardon?" Richard said. "It's what?"

"There were these two boys. They said they just wanted to see how I took it on and off. I believed them. But the minute I got it off—they took off." Kelly pointed in the direction of the cabin.

"Oh my God," Katherine said. "I've read about this kind of thing."

Richard gave her a look.

"How do you know it's in our cellar?" he asked.

"Because I followed them," Kelly said. "I can hop, you know."

"Of course you can, dear," Katherine said.

"I saw them break a little window on the ground of your cabin and chuck it in—I assume it's your cellar," Kelly said.

"How did you know this is our property?" Richard asked.

"Everybody knows you, Mr. Bowman," Kelly said. "Everyone with an air gun, that is."

"You shoot?"

"Yes, sir. I may only have one leg, but I have two good arms."

"That you do, dear," Katherine said. "That you do."

"Well, let's stop standing around. Hop in the back," Richard said, holding open the car door.

It was dark and smelled like damp peaches. When Monica located the chain and filled the small space with light, Lacey could see why. Canned peaches lined the walls, and the stone floor was slightly wet beneath their feet. Lacey pointed to the silver trash can. Monica opened it, leaned down, and when she came back up, she was holding duct tape and rope.

"Nice to know it's there," Lacey said. "But I don't think we'll need it."

"Are you sure?" Monica said.

"Locking them in will be enough," Lacey said.

"The Colonel might shoot his way out," Monica said.

"We have the only gun down here," Lacey said. Otherwise there were only spiderwebs, and peaches, and mold. "Can you hear anything?" she asked for the millionth time. Alan glanced at the broken window, their only link to fresh air.

"Not yet," he said.

"Kelly's doing a good job of distracting them," Monica said.

"Are you sure you don't want us to wait upstairs?" Mike asked.

"I want you here," Monica said.

"Just keep quiet," Lacey said. "Mon and I will do all the talking." Alan suddenly put his finger up to his lips. Shhh. He heard a car. It was time.

Lacey could feel the Colonel clomping down the steps.

"The light is on," he said. Monica and Lacey exchanged a look. Lacey saw a second pair of feet, small black flats, following him down the rickety wooden steps. Lacey could also feel the door at the top slam shut. The Colonel stopped moving. She watched his feet race back up the stairs. Monica slapped a hand over her mouth. *Nervous laughter,* Lacey thought as she watched her sister's shoulders shake. At least she was holding it together somewhat.

"What the hell?" Alan interpreted. She could tell by his facial expression it was the Colonel. He pounded on the door. "Hey. Hey." The pounding and screaming stopped. He stomped back down the stairs. As soon as he reached the landing, Monica stepped out, holding Kelly Thayler's leg. Katherine screamed.

"Looking for this, Dad?" Monica said. Lacey stepped up beside her.

"Welcome home," she said, using her voice. Alan would interpret for them when she signaled him to.

"How did you get here before us?" the Colonel said.

"You stopped at that diner," Monica said. "We went hungry." She gestured to two folding chairs they'd brought down from upstairs. "Please," Monica said. "Have a seat." Katherine obeyed. Richard stood with his hands on his hips.

"I will not," he said. "Now let's go back upstairs and discuss this around the dining room table like civil human beings."

"We're in charge here," Lacey signed. At the sound of Alan's voice, the Colonel's head snapped around. He was truly startled; neither of them had noticed the men in the corner.

"I'm Lacey's fiancé," Alan said. "I'm interpreting for her. Everything you hear me say will be her words." The Colonel finally took his eyes away from Alan and looked at Lacey.

"Please," she said gesturing to the chair. "Sit."

"We loved you," Katherine said, leaping out of her chair. "We loved you both. Our girls. Our girls."

"Then why?" Monica asked. "Why, Mom?"

"Enough," the Colonel said. Lacey looked at Monica, who raised her eyebrows and held the duct tape up where only she could see it. Lacey flipped another light on the wall, one she'd already staked out. It illuminated a shelf behind her. On it sat the huge head of a buck. Its wide antlers and glassy eyes stared at the Colonel. According to Monica, the Colonel shot it when he was twelve. It had sat on the upstairs fireplace mantel as long as Monica could remember. Bucky. Nothing gave the Colonel more pride than Bucky.

"What the hell," the Colonel said. He stepped toward the shelf. Mike suddenly stood in front of him, holding a paint gun.

"One more step and he gets a paint job," Lacey said. The Colonel backed up. But he didn't sit down. Instead he stomped back up the stairs.

"Mom?" Monica said. "Finish what you were going to say."

"You had an unhealthy attachment to your sister," Katherine said. "You couldn't stand it if Lacey was out of your sight."

"Katherine," Richard warned from the top of the steps.

"We took you to a psychiatrist," Katherine said. "She watched you two play for months. She said it wasn't healthy."

"We were twins," Monica said. "We were close."

"She said you might get violent," Katherine said, maintaining eye contact with Monica.

"That's ridiculous," Lacey said. "Don't blame her."

"We were afraid she was going to kill you," Katherine blurted out. Then, before either girl could respond, Katherine doubled over.

"Mom," Monica said running toward her.

"I didn't want to believe her," Katherine moaned. "I didn't want to listen."

"It's okay, Mom, it's okay," Monica said. Lacey didn't move. She stared at Katherine.

"I should have never let you go to that stupid birthday party! That toy horse. That Goddamn toy horse!" Monica had never heard her mother swear before. Richard pounded back down the steps and got in Lacey's face.

"Are you happy?" he said. "Is this what you wanted?"

"I just turned away for a minute," Katherine said. "You two always played in the woods."

"The horse," Lacey said. "The blue plastic horse." Katherine nodded.

"She's been painting horses for years," Monica said. It was almost a whisper.

"You had a cow," Katherine said.

"You mean I was upset?" Monica said.

"No. I mean you had a toy cow. You fought for that horse all morning."

"I don't remember," Monica said.

"You were just a baby. I thought it was just a phase. But then—"

"Then?" Monica said. Katherine glanced at Richard. He opened his arms, then sat down. He folded them across his chest, glanced at Bucky, and nodded.

"I heard a scream," Katherine said. "Lacey's scream. I'll never forget that sound as long as I live. I ran as fast as I could. But it was too late. You'd already done it."

"Done what?" Monica said. Perspiration clung to Monica's lips. She looked terrified. Lacey wanted to tell everyone to stop, wanted to assure her it was okay.

"You pierced her eardrum with the leg of the horse," Katherine said. She looked at Lacey. "There was blood everywhere. We didn't take it out, they told us not to. We rushed you to the hospital. But they couldn't repair the eardrum. A few days later, you got an infection, spiked a fever. You survived, but you lost your hearing in your other ear too."

"It wasn't a dream," Monica said. "Oh God." She looked as if she were going to fall. She reached out and grabbed the shelf nearest to where she stood. The board tilted, and canned peaches rolled down and smashed to the floor. Lacey went to her.

"It's okay," Lacey said turning her sister around and signing to her.

"How can you say that?" Monica said. "You're Deaf because of me! We were separated because of me!"

"First—I say thank you," Lacey said. "I'm happy being a Deaf woman, remember? It's who I was supposed to be."

"It was only going to be temporary," Katherine said. "We weren't giving you up. We were just waiting for Monica to calm down."

"The horse," Lacey said. "I have half of it."

"After the accident, it was all you asked for," Richard said. "For some reason you still wanted the damn thing."

"So you gave me half?" Lacey said.

"Yes," Richard said. "It sounds ridiculous, but parents will do anything to make their children happy. I couldn't let you have the half that had taken away your hearing."

"I visited you every weekend for the first year," Katherine said. "Monica was inconsolable. But you. You were happy, Lacey. It got so that you would cry when you saw me coming because you thought I was going to make you come home. I'd never seen a child blossom so fast. And gradually, Monica stopped screaming and banging her head—"

"Banging her head?" Lacey said.

"We had to have a helmet on her whenever you two were separated," Katherine said. "Monica would bang her head against whatever surface she could until you came back."

"It's my fault," Monica moaned. "It's all my fault."

Lacey sat next to Monica and put her arms around her.

"I don't blame you," she said. "I've already told you. I'm happy to be a Deaf woman. I love my life. I love my culture, my language, my people. I'm happy. And we're going to do everything we can to get you happy too. Truth and beauty, remember? I love you." Lacey stood and faced her parents.

"You two have a lot more sucking up to do," she said.

"Fair enough," Richard said. "I've got just the way to start."

"How?" Lacey asked. "Group therapy?"

"Hell no. The shooting range," Richard said.

"Are you kidding me?" Lacey said. "I'm not a killer."

"They're just cans," Richard said. "But don't worry. After we shoot them, we'll recycle them."

Chapter 37

"It's pink," Lacey said, staring at the gun.

"It matches mine," Monica said.

"Do you have a black one?" Lacey said. Richard took the pink gun out of Lacey's hand and handed her a black one. They were standing outside the shooting range at the cabin. It was a full house: Richard and Katherine. Lacey and Monica. Mike and Alan. And of course Lacey's accomplices: Kelly, Robert, and Maria.

"After you're all done shooting, come in for lunch," Katherine said. She glanced at Lacey. "I made Jell-O," she said with a wink.

"Pick a can and line up behind it," Richard said. Everyone took their air gun and lined up behind a can on the posts twenty feet away. Lacey shot first. It hit the can square in the middle with a zing. It exploded like a carbonated geyser. It felt so good. It wasn't enough; the others were too slow. In broad strokes from right to left, Lacey swept her air gun back and forth, shooting up everyone else's cans as well, until they were all exploding, water bursting forth and up, like a Las Vegas water and light show. Lacey jumped up and let out a celebratory yelp.

"You are my daughter," Richard said. Kelly, who should have been interpreting, was too busy lamenting her usurped can, so Monica relayed Richard's comment to her. Lacey shrugged and waited as new cans popped into place. Everyone shot as fast as they could, in hopes of preventing Lacey from attacking theirs again. Can after can, they shot. The time flew by, with Lacey the clear winner. It was almost time for dinner. Kelly said she was going to take a nap. Mike and Alan were going with Richard into the woods. Monica wanted to show Lacey family pictures.

"I'm never going to remember all these people," Lacey said as they walked down a hallway littered with photographs.

"You'll see them all at the family reunion," Monica said. Lacey smiled. Monica had come up with the idea for a family reunion and Lacey reluctantly agreed.

"You and Mike seem very happy," Lacey said. "I see the looks you're giving each other."

Monica smiled, her face flushed.

"It's so new," she said. "But exciting."

"Maybe we should do a double wedding," Lacey said.

"Uh—no," Monica said. "Way too early to talk like that." Lacey stopped at a picture at the end of the hall and stared. She took it off the wall.

"What are you doing?" Monica said.

"Why do you have this?" Lacey asked.

"You know her?" Monica asked. "It's Aunt Grace," she said. "My father's sister."

"Oh," Lacey said.

"What is it?" Monica asked.

"I just noticed the family resemblance," Lacey said.

Monica took the picture out of her hands and hung it back on the wall.

"I'll get you copies of all of these if you'd like," she said. "But we'd better leave them up for now." They started to walk away. Monica stopped and tapped Lacey on the shoulder. Then she snatched Aunt Grace's picture off the wall and handed it to Lacey. Lacey smiled, took the picture, and stuck it down her pants.

Kelly Thayler was the last one to the dinner table. She had to come in a wheelchair. Her leg was in the middle of the dining room table. Flowers from the backyard were sticking out the top.

"That is so not funny," Kelly said.

"I agree," Katherine said. "I couldn't stop them." Everyone looked at Monica and Lacey. They emitted guilty laughs in unison.

"I'm sorry," Lacey said. She took the leg off the table and handed it to Kelly. Kelly took the leg and shook it at Lacey.

"Just for that," she said, "you're my free babysitter for the year!"

They gathered at the table, Richard and Katherine at the ends, Lacey and Alan on one side, Mike and Monica and Kelly on the other. Apparently, Robert and Maria wanted to eat in front of the television. Everyone at the table stared at the mounds of food, including two large trays of Jell-O, with *WELCOME HOME* written in them. Lacey had to smile.

"Who wants to say grace?" Katherine asked. Lacey and Monica exchanged a look, and then a laugh.

"What's so funny?" Kelly demanded.

"Sorry," Monica said. "It's a twin thing."

"I can't believe this day has come," Aunt Grace said. "My beautiful niece. Come, sit by me."

Lacey remained standing. Aunt Grace glanced at Kelly, who was there to interpret. Then, she patted the empty space next to her on the couch. They were gathered in the back den, away from the crowd. What a day; Lacey had met so many people her head was swimming. Aunts, uncles, cousins. Finally, Aunt Grace. Everyone seemed thrilled to see her, and they were doing pretty well with her Deaf friends too. Robert and his gang were once again keeping everyone entertained. And the Deafies were all great shots, Lacey noticed. They were certainly giving Richard a run for his money. It must be true that when you lost one sense, you made up for it with the others.

"Lacey?" Aunt Grace said. "Aren't you going to sit?"

"Do you really think I wouldn't remember you?" Lacey said.

"What are you talking about, dear?" Aunt Grace said.

"I thought you were Miss Lee," Lacey said. "But I was wrong. It was Miss G, wasn't it?" Aunt Grace didn't move or blink. "You visited me every Wednesday. My beautiful art teacher. My surrogate mother. Your encouragement stuck with me my entire life."

"Oh, honey," Grace said. "You must have me mixed up with someone else."

"Cut the crap," Lacey said. Aunt Grace's hands absentmindedly went to her cheek. They were shaking.

"You're the one who's been leaving me notes. You took my portraits and set up the horse paintings. How did you do it? How did you get in?"

Grace smiled. Lacey could see herself in the mischief of it.

"Some little pixie stole the key for me," Aunt Grace said.

"Tina," Lacey said. "Monica's assistant."

"And mine," Aunt Grace said.

"I thought you were all for clearing the air," Lacey said. "No more secrets. Or did that change when Richard threatened to pull your money? He does control all of your money, doesn't he?"

"But not this time," Grace said. "I didn't get on that plane to Italy. I didn't get on the plane." She started to cry.

Lacey finally sat beside her.

"You were young, weren't you? When you had us?"

Aunt Grace looked at Lacey.

"Yes," she signed.

"You learned sign language to talk to me, didn't you?"

"Yes," Aunt Grace signed. "I couldn't believe it when they put you in that school. I wanted to take you back. But they wouldn't hear of it."

"How old were you, when you had us?" Lacey asked again.

"I was sixteen," Aunt Grace said.

"And they convinced you you couldn't raise two babies on your own."

"It was very shameful in those days," Aunt Grace said. "And my father was furious." She reached her hand out to Lacey. She took it.

"So your big brother stepped in," Lacey said.

"Katherine always wanted children," Aunt Grace said. "She wasn't able to conceive."

"Who was our father?" Lacey said.

"His name was Thomas," Aunt Grace said. "Thomas Gears. He was fifteen years older than me. I told him I was in the family way and I never saw him again."

"This is a lot to take in," Lacey said. "A lot to take in."

"Please," Aunt Grace said. "Don't tell Monica."

"What did she say?" Monica asked. She and Lacey were walking through the woods. "Did she admit it?"

"Yes," Lacey said. "She had us when she was sixteen. Our father's name was Thomas. He was fifteen years older. When Grace told him she was in the family way, he ran off."

"Oh boy," Monica said. "This explains a lot."

"She told me not to tell you," Lacey said.

"Of course she did," Monica said.

"Are you going to tell your parents we know?" Lacey said.

"You mean our aunt and uncle?"

"Come on. They're still your parents."

"I don't know," Monica said.

"It's a lot to take in."

"Yeah."

"This family sure likes to keep secrets," Lacey said. She made the sign for "secret," similar to the sign for "patience," but instead of moving down the lips, the thumb stayed put, locked against the lips, representing the thing you promised never to tell. Monica plopped down underneath a tree. Lacey sat next to her. Monica leaned her head against the trunk.

"At least we're not keeping anything secret from each other," Lacey said. Monica stared at Lacey. "What?" Lacey said. "What is it?"

"It's not a secret," Monica said. "I just hadn't gotten around to telling you yet."

"What?"

"The *Today* show called. They want to book us as guests."

"Oh," Lacey said.

"And I've talked to a literary agent. They want to know if we're interested in writing a book."

"A book," Lacey said. "You're the writer."

"I want us to write it together."

"I'll do as much as I can," Lacey said.

"Absolutely," Monica said. "I mean you've got the wedding coming up, and portraits to paint, two mothers and a father to get to know—and that's without mentioning the baby. I wonder if you'll have twins?"

Lacey stared at her sister in surprise.

"How did you know?" she said.

"I'm your sister, remember?" Monica said. "You can't fool me." She put her hand on Lacey's tiny bump. Lacey put her hand on top of Monica's.

"Do you want a boy or a girl?"

"I don't care," Lacey said. "But we hope he or she is Deaf."

"That's hard for me to understand," Monica said.

"It's okay," Lacey said. "Hearing people really don't understand. It still comes down to the fact that we're really happy being Deaf and would celebrate having a Deaf child, but hearing people think deep down we still want to be fixed, we want to be like them."

"I'm sorry," Monica said. "I have a lot to learn."

"We've got time," Lacey said. "And we will love this child, Deaf or hearing, boy or girl, twin or solo. Because whoever they are, one thing is for sure. He or she or they are always going to know who their parents are. And they are going to have one kick-ass aunt."

"I'm going to spoil him or her or them rotten," Monica said.

"When they're mad at me, I'm going to pretend I'm you," Lacey said.

"They'll know the difference," Monica said. "They'll know." Monica slid her hand over to Lacey's and held it. "Are you going to tell them I'm in therapy?" Lacey rubbed her stomach. She signed on top of her tummy.

"There," she said. "I told 'em. They don't care. They just want you to get better."

"Who are you going to let be the grandparents?" Monica said.

"I was thinking of holding auditions," Lacey said. Monica laughed "But no air guns," Lacey said. "Not until they're four."

"I hope it's twin girls," Monica said. "And I hope they look like you." Lacey laughed. Her tiny belly moved up and down as she did.

"And I hope they look like you," she said.

MY SISTER'S VOICE

Mary Carter

ABOUT THIS GUIDE

The suggested questions are included to enhance
your group's reading of Mary Carter's
My Sister's Voice!

DISCUSSION QUESTIONS

1. How are Monica and Lacey alike? How are they different?

2. How does Lacey feel about being Deaf? What kind of discrimination or misconceptions about deafness does she face?

3. Do you think Lacey would have reacted differently to Monica if they were biological sisters but not identical twins? If yes, how so, and why?

4. What do the professions chosen by Lacey and Monica say about their personalities? In what ways is each successful in her career, and in what ways has each been holding back?

5. Who do you think had the worse childhood? Why?

6. Was one twin betrayed more than the other by their parents? If yes, which twin?

7. What role do secrets play in the book? Which twin is more likely to keep secrets?

8. If Monica had been sent away and Lacey raised by Richard and Katherine, do you believe Monica would have had the same reaction to being given up that Lacey had?

9. Which twin is the happiest?

10. Would Lacey have the same personality if she were hearing?

11. Would Monica have the same personality if she were Deaf?

12. Do you understand Katherine's decision to give Lacey up? Why or why not? Was Richard a passive voice in the decision, or an active participant? Does it make him more or less responsible?

13. Would Monica have stayed with Joe if she had never met Lacey?

14. Would Lacey and Alan have parted ways if Lacey had never met Monica?

15. What influence did Aunt Grace have on Monica's life? On Lacey's?

16. Besides speaking and signing, what methods does Lacey employ to communicate with hearing people?

17. Which twin is more jealous of the other?

18. If they had been raised together, would one twin have overshadowed the other? If yes, which twin and why?

19. Will Monica and Lacey ever confront all the family secrets, or will they perpetuate the cycle?

20. Is it normal for Lacey to want a Deaf child?

21. Which has had more influence on the twins: nature or nurture? Which commonalities prove or disprove either side of the debate?

22. Which twin changes the most by the end of the book?

**Please turn the page for a very special
Q&A with Mary Carter!**

Is it true that you are a certified sign language interpreter?

Yes. I am nationally certified through the Registry of Interpreters for the Deaf (RID) and have worked as a freelance American Sign Language interpreter for the past thirteen years.

Where did you get your training?

I took American Sign Language classes at the American Sign Language Institute (ASLI) in New York City. After several years of conversational classes, I studied interpreting at the National Technical Institute for the Deaf (NTID) at the Rochester Institute of Technology, in Rochester, New York.

What made you interested in becoming a sign language interpreter?

My sister and I learned a few signs when we were children because our cousin and his wife were Deaf, and we had a few Deaf children at our school. The signs we learned were very rudimentary, and I did not understand most Deaf people I met, nor did they understand me. Most of the time when they signed to me, I would smile, nod my head, and pray they wouldn't ask me any questions. Later in life while I was studying acting, I went through a period of time where I just seemed to meet Deaf people everywhere I went, and I was frustrated that the little sign language I had learned as a child wasn't sufficient to carry on a conversation. I decided to take classes for the fun of it, and it eventually led into a career!

What and where do you interpret?

Freelance interpreters go pretty much everywhere. They interpret business meetings, employee trainings, conferences, college classes, religious ceremonies, medical procedures, concerts, plays, speeches—you name it!

What is the best way to learn sign language?

Hands down, from Deaf people. Take a class taught by a Deaf person, then hang out in the Deaf community. Plenty of colleges offer sign language courses or majors now; and / or check out classes in your community.

Is sign language universal?

No. Every country has its own sign language. In America, it's ASL—American Sign Language.

I noticed that in the book sometimes the word Deaf is with a capital *D* and sometimes it is with a lowercase *d*. Can you please explain?

When the word *Deaf* is used to refer to a person's identity— meaning the Deaf person considers him- or herself part of the Deaf Community, uses American Sign Language, and takes pride in his or her Deafness, regardless of the degree of hearing loss—this cultural identification is signified with a capital *D*. When a hearing person is using the term *deaf* to describe a person with a hearing loss without any understanding of Deaf Culture, then the small *d* is used. There were times I debated which one to use, so to all the ASL linguists out there, forgive me if there were times that I erred!

Why didn't you write the dialogue of the Deaf folks in American Sign Language word order instead of in English word order?

American Sign Language is a visual language, with no written form. Had I attempted to put the dialogue into American Sign Language, it would have sounded as if the characters were speaking in broken or "bad" English. American Sign Language is a rich, complex, and legitimate language; it should not be construed as a "coded system" for English.

Are all Deaf people like the character Lacey in the book?

I'm glad you asked. No! No, no, no! Deaf people are as individual as you and me, and so are their outlooks, beliefs, and actions. Although as a writer I always draw upon my experiences to help shape characters, this book is a work of fiction and so is Lacey. She is not based on any real person, nor does she speak for the Deaf Community. If you want to know what anyone thinks, feels, or believes, Deaf or hearing, there is a simple and foolproof way to find out: Ask them!